ACCUSATIONS

Colleen Snyder

Acknowledgments

My Editor: Joan Alley, who I work to death, but she makes me a better writer.

My Sensitivity Editor: Dr. Katherine Hayes, who I have just begun to know.

My Publisher: Cynthia Hickey, who thinks I'm a "hoot," but she lets me write for her.

My Advance Readers: Who suffer through my rough drafts and make my stories make sense.

My Sister, Sue: Who gives me a place to write, to live, to create all these stories for the
Glory of the Lord I love and serve.

You, My Readers: who give me a reason to keep writing. Thank you!

A Brief History of Names

Collin Walker = Caitlin Winger = Cane

Born Caitlin Winger, at fourteen, she was abandoned to the streets. Posing as a boy for safety's sake, she took the name "Walker." She added the name "Collin" "because I got tired of people 'calling' me Walker." At eighteen, she had her name legally changed to Collin Walker.

Cane is the nickname **only** her twin brother calls her. It started with his inability to pronounce "Caitlin," which sounded more like "Ca-yun." From that came "Cane."

Erin Winger = A-One

His name was to be "Aaron" at birth. His father was so incensed at his being born second that he declared, "If he can't beat a girl out of the womb, he doesn't deserve a man's name." Robert Winger changed the spelling from Aaron to Erin.

Erin thought about changing his name but learned the name can be for either a male or a female. In Ireland, "Erin" means "the one of Ireland." In the end, he decided to keep his birth name, considering it a badge of honor that Robert Winger could not take from him.

A-One is the nickname **only** his twin sister calls him. It started with her inability to pronounce "Erin," which sounded more like "A-won." From that came "A-One."

.

FRIDAY

In the dark, Erin strained to hear. Hearing was the only sense they left him. Bound in a fetal position with his knees buried to his chest, his arms wrapped around his knees, he lay on his side on a hard, unyielding surface. Mouth and eyes taped shut.

Where am I? What happened? The woman by the side of the road...two small children beside her. A car with the hood up. I stopped. The battery, maybe? Infant in the backseat. I looked under the hood.

That's it. That's all I remember.

Erin's world jolted. He felt the sensation of falling, of being dropped. The sudden stop at the bottom jarred his bones. Voices. He heard muffled voices. Near him? Above him?

"You can't leave that here. Hook it back up and tow it out of here."

"My boss wants it crushed. Now."

"Can't happen. No pink slip. No registration. I can't crush a car without something to prove who it belonged to."

Crush? Car? Erin's eyes would have widened in fear if he could have opened them at all.

"I got five Benjamins says I own this car, and I want it smashed."

"I don't care if you've got ten Benjamins. I can't crush a car without the proper paperwork. Not while the boss is here."

Silence.

"What time does your boss leave?"

"Come back around six with the Benjamins. Ten of them. I'll crush your car. You can leave it where it is for now. I'll tell the big man you went to get the title."

"You got a deal."

"What's so important about this car? It's a sweet roadster. I'd almost pay to take it off your hands."

"I have instructions to stay and watch this car be crushed. Then I load it on a flatbed and drive it to Oakton. Supposed to leave it at some house. My boss wants pictures. I wouldn't sell it to you for any price. It's not worth crossing my boss."

"Suit yourself. See you tonight."

Silence. A diesel motor came to life. Drove away. Someone banged the trunk of the car serving as Erin's prison. "Shame. She is a sweet ride. Wonder who he made mad?"

Silence again.

Crushed?

* * *

Collin Farrell stared at her steak, sizzling on the grill plate, the red juices pooling on the sides. Piping hot butter spat little geysers on top of the medium-rare boneless New York strip. A side order of portabella mushrooms stuffed with minced crab meat and topped with crispy browned Panko breadcrumbs sat beside the meat. Everything exactly the way she loved it.

Collin folded her napkin, placed it on the table, and with deliberate movements, stood. She forced a smile at her husband, her lips tight. "I'll be right back." She turned from the table, walked to the back of the restaurant, into the restroom, and closed the door behind her.

She sank to the floor, holding her stomach. Waves of nausea swept over her again and again. She felt clammy and hot and sweaty and sick. Collin bowed her head on her knees and whispered, "Not now. Not here. It's my birthday. Please?"

How long she sat, she didn't know. But the nausea faded, the sweating stopped, and her mouth quit salivating. She let out a deep breath, stood, and returned to the table.

Jeff glanced up from eating. "Are you okay? This nausea stuff has been going on for what, a couple months now?"

"Four or five. And it'll pass. I saw the doctor today." Collin sat and nibbled at the vegetables. "How did your day go?"

Jeff shrugged and again attacked his steak. Between bites, he said, "Same as every other day. Too much work, not enough me. It'll get done, but only if I keep pushing. Taking tonight off will set one job back…" He smiled at her, touched her hand. "But it's worth it. You're worth it."

Collin touched his hand in return. "Thank you, kind sir. I didn't mean to pull you from your labors." Her lips tensed to a forced smile. "But thanks for celebrating with me."

Jeff turned around. "I thought Erin would make an appearance. He's usually around when food's involved."

Collin swallowed the retort she wanted to make. *1 Peter 3, remember? 'Won without a word.' Smile and say nothing. He knows my brother is out of town. He sent him to survey the farm Grandfather Fenton owned. He heard us when Erin borrowed my car. He knows all about it.*

Collin breathed through her nose, keeping her mouth shut from the words she wanted to say. She gathered herself. "Is there an end in sight? The rec center projects should be finished this month. And the new housing complex has been opened to residents. That should free some of your time, right?"

Jeff chewed his steak. "Mom called this morning and asked if I could take over the Billings project. She's trying to work Dad out of the business. Since his heart attack scare last fall, she's been after him to cut back."

Collin placed her hands in her lap. "You promised you weren't going to take on any new projects."

"It's Mom. You want me to say no to Mom? After all she's done for us?"

Collin chose her words carefully. "We agreed you were carrying too much of a load. We talked it out, and you weren't going to take on anything else. If you take the Billings project, you need to give one of your other projects up. We agreed." *Otherwise, you'll never come back to church. Or me. Especially when I'm going to need you most.*

Jeff scowled. "I knew you would get cranky about it. It's not like I have a choice, Collin. I can't tell Mom no."

Collin breathed in and out. Carefully. "I didn't say tell Mom Lacey no. I would never turn down anything she asked." *Unlike you, who's been dodging every invite, every family dinner, every family gathering...* "I said we agreed you would need to give up one of the other projects. The rec center on the west side can be put off for a few months."

"And lose all the workers I have lined up? Those people need the jobs. You want to take food out of their families' mouths?"

Collin put her fork down. "I have no intention of taking food out of anyone's mouths, Jeff Farrell. But there are ways to get the jobs done without you working yourself into an early grave." *And making me a widow long before you ever die.* "The rec centers are my dream, my projects. I know two good men who could handle the job. They know the areas, the regulations, and what we want to accomplish. Don Jacobs and Tim Weiskopf. You know them. We can hire them to take over the project. It gets completed on time, no one misses any meals, and the kids get their rec center."

"Why would I hire someone to do what I can do myself? Collin, you're being unreasonable again. Are you saying I can't manage your project as well as Jacobs and Weiskopf? Excuse me for not living up to your standards."

Collin breathed in slowly and counted to fifty. She took a sip of water. "I never said you couldn't manage my project. I never asked you to live to any standard you might think I hold. I don't know why we can't have a discussion without it turning into a fight. I'm sorry you feel the way you do. You are under no obligation to take on the west side project. As you said, it is mine to begin with. I am taking it off your hands. I will oversee it myself."

Jeff laughed. "Right. What do you know about buildings and contractors? You'll be fleeced out of millions within the first two weeks. I'm not going to lose money because you don't trust me."

Collin stood. "We're done. I'm done. I'm going home and see if the man I married is hidden anywhere in the house."

Jeff caught her hand. "No, Collin, I'm sorry. Sit. Finish your dinner, please. I don't mean it the way it sounded."

Collin sat. She picked up her fork, stilled the trembling of her hand, swallowed hard. "I'm sorry, too. I need you to cut back on your hours. I'm going to need help at home, and I really, really need you to be there."

Jeff's eyes narrowed slightly. "For what?"

"For changing diapers. And helping with laundry. And playing games on the floor with your children."

She couldn't hide the smile any longer. "I'm pregnant, Jeff. We're pregnant. We're going to have a baby. Two babies, in fact." Jeff's eyes widened in shock. Collin continued, "Right. Shock to me, too. My cycles aren't regular anyhow, so I didn't know I'd missed anything." Collin put down the fork. "I thought I might be putting on a little weight but figured diet and exercise would take care of it. We'll know better next week after the ultrasound, but the doctor guesses I'm maybe six, six and a half months along."

Jeff's face continued to reflect disbelief, which turned to anger, and disbelief again. He found his voice. "You're what? You can't be. There's no way."

Collin stared at him. Not the reaction she'd anticipated. "Why can't I be? I don't understand."

Jeff pushed away from the table. His face turned dark, his eyes wild. "No. You weren't supposed to get pregnant. He told me you'd never… He promised… I've got to call…" Who he wanted to call remained a mystery as he plowed his way through the tables, out the front door of the restaurant and out of sight.

Well, okay. That went worse than I expected. Collin stared after her husband for several moments. When he did not return, she sighed. She searched for their server, motioned for him. "Sean, thanks. It looks like Jeff has an emergency he needs to take care of. Can you box all this to go?" She smiled. "It's not going to taste nearly as good heated over, but that's the life of a fireman."

Sean nodded. "Sorry he had to interrupt your birthday dinner. I'll have these out in a minute."

Collin waited until the food had been boxed and the bill paid for, then stepped outside to look for her husband. His truck was gone. Collin's eyes widened in disbelief. Now what? They'd come together. Collin had no way to get home without calling a taxi or an app service. *Unbelievable.* She dialed Rideshare, waited fifteen minutes, caught the ride, and went home.

The darkened windows were proof Jeff had not made it there ahead of her. Not that it would make it any better, but at least she'd have someone to yell at. She sighed. "I know, I know. No yelling. Quiet, calm demeanor. Controlled. You're trying to win him back, right?" *After tonight, I'm not sure I want him back.*

Collin sank into the couch in the family room. She did not turn on the lights and curled around a throw pillow. She dropped her head to rest on the cushion. Tears born of hormones dribbled from her eyes. Her voice trembled. "Where did you go, Jeff? My Jeff, the one I married three years ago? When did I lose the man I loved?"

She cast her mind back six months to when Jeff stopped coming to church. *"It's only for a month, Collin. One month. The Lord knows my heart. This housing tract matters to a lot of people. It'll be done before you know it. All it needs is a little supervision before the rest of the crew can take over. I promise."*

One month became two, became four, became six. And no end in sight. But it went back further. A year before? Jeff had stopped going to Men's study, a group he'd organized before they were married. She'd found out by accident.

"Jeff, Giball asked me if you were ever coming back to Men's group. He said you'd been missing for three weeks. He said they were worried about you."

"Oh, yeah. I stopped going. I thought I told those guys I wasn't going to come anymore. I need the time to review the financials. We've got year-end coming and the tax audit. I need to get the figures in order. God knows my heart, Collin. I'm good. And it's just for the next two months. Once the audit is over, I can go back to the study. Don't worry, milady. I'm not running out on anyone."

Collin let her mind drift back further. *Our wedding. The week before. We'd planned to have communion with everyone present. You came home from playing round ball and said you'd pulled a muscle in your thigh. Then you told me we shouldn't have communion. "It might make some people feel bad, being left out. We shouldn't have it."*

"Can the wedding party take it? I know everyone in it knows the Lord and has accepted Him."

"No. It would look weird."

"No, it won't. It will be fine. Lots of wedding groups do it."

"I still feel like we shouldn't do it."

"You and me?"

"No. I don't think we should make a public display of something so private."

"But you were all for it when we planned it. You said it would make a clear statement of our faith, of what we believed, and would provide a clear Gospel message to everyone present."

"I've had time to think it over. I don't think it's a good idea. I don't want to do it. I want to cancel that part of the service. Our faith will still be on display. Anyone who knows us knows where we stand. God knows. And that's what matters in the end. Let's not do it."

"So we didn't, did we?" Collin sighed. "You quit taking communion at all, didn't you, Jeff? What is it between you and the Lord you can't confess and be done with?"

Keys unlocked the door from the garage. Collin strangled the pillow. She held her breath as Jeff walked past the family room without stopping, went to the living room, and sank in his recliner. He turned the TV on, flipped channels, finally settling on a college hoops game between teams she knew he didn't know and could care less about.

Collin prayed hard, waited for the next commercial break, then walked in quietly. *Meekness. Submission. Call him "Lord" like Sarah did Abraham…*

Sarah also laid him out for Hagar's being insolent to her. She hadn't hesitated to tell him, "This is your fault." Maybe you should get a backbone again.

Unable to properly discern between the voices, Collin ignored both suggestions. She stood beside his chair. "I brought home the leftovers. Do you want me to reheat them?"

"No. Not tonight."

"Did you talk with whoever you needed to speak to?"

Jeff avoided her gaze. His eyes were guarded, his face drawn. "Yes, I did."

"You want to tell me about it?"

"Not tonight. It's late, and we agreed never to argue after eight p.m."

We agreed to a lot of things, and it hasn't stopped you from breaking those covenants. What makes this any different? "In the morning? Over coffee? Jeff, I hurt. This is killing me." Her tears choked in her throat. "Please? Can we talk it out like we used to?"

Jeff shrugged and turned back to the TV. "Yeah, I guess. I'm going to sleep out here tonight."

Collin didn't bother to argue. She walked to the back bedroom, slipped out of her clothes and into her nightgown. She hit her knees. "God, please. Show me what's wrong. Show me what I did to bring this on. I don't understand any of it. I don't. Please, please, show me."

What came was the warm assurance she wasn't alone. It was enough. She crawled into bed, turned off the light, and fell asleep.

SATURDAY

Collin slipped out of the bedroom at five a.m. and went to the kitchen to make coffee. She kept the noise to a minimum as she started the drip maker. Maybe the aroma of the brew would wake Jeff, put him in a better mood, and they could get to the bottom of what ailed him lately. While the coffee worked its magic, Collin dressed for the day. Blue jeans and a pullover t-shirt.

She lowered her head and prayed, *My best behavior, Lord. If there is any of it left. I want to do this Your way, not mine. It's the only way there's any chance of finding out what's going on in Jeff's heart. We were so much in love. He did everything for me during my recovery from the aneurysm. We walked in such sweet communion with You. Both of us. Together in You. We started our companies, made our plans for the future, always with You as the center. We got married, and he changed. Three years now, and he hasn't been the man I knew. I miss him. I know You do, too. Bring him back, please. Amen.*

She went and poured two cups. Jeff liked to get a jump on activities, even on a Saturday. That hadn't changed. Collin expected him by six.

By eight, she'd had three cups of decaf coffee, shut off the coffee maker, and eaten breakfast of toast and a tangerine. Remembering who she needed to be eating for, she'd added an egg for protein's sake and went outside to work in the garden.

At nine, she heard Jeff's phone ring. She listened to see if he would pick it up or sleep through it. The ringing stopped after the second go-through. *Oh, sure. You'll get up to talk to someone else, but not me. Figures. Just like…*

Not the way. Not the attitude. Keep it even.

Yeah, yeah, yeah. Just once, I'd like to tell him what I'm really thinking.

Jeff stepped outside, still talking on the phone. "Yeah, we'll be over as soon as we can. It'll be about forty-five minutes. No, we can't make it any sooner. We'll take care of it when we get there. I promise I'll talk to him about it when I see him. Right. Good-bye, Tom."

Collin cocked her head. "Which Tom?"

"Erin's neighbor, Tom. The one who watches the place for him when he's gone."

And everyone else's when they're not. "What does he need?"

"He said some unknown person or persons backed a flatbed trailer in front of Erin's house and dumped off a pile of junk car. Tom felt he should remind Erin the HOA rules prohibit all car maintenance except changing light bulbs and batteries. Anything else has to be done in a commercial garage."

Collin frowned. "Erin isn't the mechanical type. Not when it comes to cars. He borrowed mine for the weekend."

Jeff laughed. "Yeah, give Erin a wrench, and he thinks he's supposed to hurt himself with it."

Collin smiled but said nothing. Defending Erin against Jeff would be the surest way to a fight. Almost as if Jeff had become jealous of her twin brother. Yet Jeff brought them together again after twelve years apart. And Erin continually thanked Jeff for bringing him to the Lord. *Jeff insisted my brother be part of the business and our lives.* Erin never gave Jeff cause to be jealous of time with Collin. *And I make sure I don't, either.*

Jeff stood in his skivvies and t-shirt. Collin suggested, "You want to get dressed while I make you a fresh cup of coffee?"

"I think I'll shower first. Tom can cool his heels the few minutes it'll take me to get in and out. Have you had your coffee already?"

"Yes, dear." *Don't say it. Do not say it. DO NOT SAY IT...*

I won't. I'll just think it in his direction. Of course, I've had my coffee! We were supposed to have it together! You promised!

Feel better now?

No.

Collin set about making a fresh pot of coffee and poured it in Jeff's travel cup for him. It took the man twenty minutes to get in and out of the water, dressed, and ready to leave.

He swallowed his first gulps of coffee. "I don't think we should talk about last night until we settle whatever Erin's problem is, okay? We need to focus on him. Like always."

Collin gritted her teeth. She nodded, compliant to the end. Whose end had yet to be determined. The couple climbed into Jeff's truck and drove the twenty miles to Erin's home in the Lakeside Community. As they rounded the curve to Erin's cul-de-sac, the "wreck" Tom had mentioned to Jeff came into view.

"Wreck" didn't describe it. The car had been totally crushed, as if by a compacting machine. All four tires were blown out, and the vehicle had been shortened by several feet. As Jeff pulled to the side of the driveway, Collin's eyes flared. "Jeff…that's my car. My less-than-a-year-old car. My doesn't-even-have-five-thousand-miles-on-it car. What happened to it?"

Jeff walked around the perimeter of the wreck, checking it from all angles. "I'd say it got crushed by a car compactor."

Collin's voice rose. "But why? Who does this to a new car?"

Jeff shrugged. "You'll have to ask your brother, I guess."

Tom ambled across the street to join Jeff. "You'll tell your brother-in-law he can't leave this here, right?"

"Of course, Tom. As soon as I see him."

"When will that be, you think? He told me he'd be going to Indiana on business but would be back Friday night. Never heard from him. Be nice if he told me he'd be late or something."

Jeff agreed. "I appreciate that you keep track of Erin for his own good."

Collin knew better but threw in, "I'm sure he would have told you if he could, Tom."

Tom ignored her. He continued speaking to Jeff as if Collin weren't even present. His face remained wooden, expressionless no matter what went on around him. "I don't think this is the sort of thing someone rebuilds, do you? Your brother-in-law never said anything to me about wanting to rebuild a car. He doesn't seem like the car-building type."

Jeff patted Tom on the shoulder. "No, he really isn't. But you're right. This isn't the kind of junk people generally rebuild." Jeff stroked his chin. "Tom, I don't suppose you got the license plate number off the truck, did you? Or maybe the name of the towing service?"

Tom shook his head. "Doors didn't have a name on them. Black truck, black windows. I wanted to tell him those weren't legal here in Ohio, but he left before I could tell him."

"Uh-huh. What about the license number?"

"The plate wasn't from here. Might have been from Indiana. I wrote the numbers. Have them in the house if you want me to get them."

"Would you? It might be helpful if we need to call him to take this back to whoever it belongs."

It belongs to me! It's mine! She wanted to shout, to scream, to throw a fit like the two men had never seen before, but she didn't. Collin walked over to the car and examined the pile of metal. She put a hand on the trunk, or what had been the trunk, and felt the slightest of *thumps.* Collin glanced at Jeff, then back at the wreck. She stood still.

Thump. Collin yelled, "Jeff, someone's in there."

Jeff turned from Tom. "What? No one…"

"I heard it. Twice. Someone is trapped in there."

Jeff rolled his eyes but walked over to the car. "Halloo? Anyone in there?"

Frantic thumping answered. Thumping that faded in intensity. As if whoever or whatever had expended all the energy they had.

Jeff went into rescue mode. He yelled to Collin, "Get the crowbar out of the toolbox. Bring the whole thing here."

Collin jumped to get the box. Jeff pulled out his phone. "Trevor? Yeah, Jeff. Listen, I need a squad and the jaws as quick as you can get to this location." Jeff gave Erin's address. "Roll an ambulance, too. Yeah, I don't know. Someone's trapped in a car that's been crushed. I mean compacted. Yeah. Fast as you can."

Jeff took the crowbar from Collin and began trying to wedge the trunk open. The metal had fused to itself and wouldn't budge. Jeff tried several other points of entry and got nowhere.

Tom never changed his expression. "You know what you need is a chop saw."

Jeff spun around. "Do you have one?"

"No. But it's what you need."

Jeff returned to trying to wedge the metal apart. The crowbar sank an inch, two inches, into a crevice along the top of the trunk. Jeff grunted and pulled for all he was worth. The metal moved. Barely.

Collin joined the effort. Maybe she wouldn't add much, but at least she would be doing something other than watching. Together she and Jeff pushed, pulled, yanked. The metal separated. Half an inch.

Sirens sounded, coming close. Collin and Jeff continued battling the unyielding steel. Collin muttered, "Hang in there, please. Please. Don't die. Oh, Lord, help him." The thought it could be Erin chilled her heart.

The rescue squad from Station Nine pulled around the corner, braked, and two men jumped out. Fire Engine Nine followed close behind. Suddenly there were people and cutting and welding tools and an organized rescue. Collin moved aside. She continued to pray. *God, please. Keep whoever it is in there alive. Lord, You understand. You know. Don't let it be Erin. Please. But if it is, save him. Your will is all that counts, but if there is room in it, please, keep him alive. In Your Son's Name. Amen.*

Collin couldn't see the trunk for the mass of muscle working around it. But the words she heard were terse. "Here."

"Here's a better spot."

"Over here."

"Careful with the saw."

"Not too deep. We don't know where this guy is."

Finally, the words she wanted to hear, "Got it."

"There. There he is."

Curse words followed. Someone yelled, "Get the gurney. We need help over here!"

Jeff directed, "Careful. Lift him out. Someone get the scissors and start cutting him loose. But careful. Don't move his limbs. His muscles may be frozen. Gently, gently."

The gurney cleared a path for Collin to finally see who the rescuers had rescued. *Oh, dear Lord...it's Erin. Oh, Lord, please, please keep him alive. Please let him be okay.*

Multiple voices began speaking at once.

"Erin, listen to me, brother. We're going to get this tape off you. But don't try to move. Not yet. Let me help you, okay? One inch at a time."

"Get an IV started as soon as you can, Tami."

"Call Sisters of Mercy. We're bringing in a car-crash victim, and he's in bad shape. Have them get a team ready."

Collin kept her eyes on her brother, wincing as they yanked the bindings from his mouth. Erin didn't move. Tearing the tape from his eyes brought the same non-response. Erin had been taught the same maxims she had. Never show pain. Never show weakness. Never show anything. *Lord, let it be why he's not moving, please. Please.*

With the remainder of his restraints cut or pulled away, the paramedics carefully strapped Erin to the gurney, still in the fetal position. Collin pushed her way through the bodies and kneeled beside him. She lay her hand on his cheek. "You're safe, A-One. We got you. Now you have to live. Got it? Hang in there and live."

She watched as his thumb moved, jerking into a "thumbs-up" signal to her. Collin sagged on the ground. *Thank You, Lord. Thank You.*

Jeff pulled her to her feet and hugged her. Hard. No smart remarks, no insults. Collin felt the first real hug from her husband in many months. She clung to him in return. After a few moments, they broke, and Jeff kissed her on the forehead. "Take the truck. Go to the hospital. Be with him. I'll get a ride with one of the guys."

Collin's voice trembled. "No. We'll go together." She forced a smile. "I don't want you walking home because someone forgot to wait for you."

Jeff smiled. "My guys? Forget me? Never. Well, maybe a few times. But in their defense, they're morons." He hugged Collin again. "We'll need to wait and answer questions from the police. It could be a while."

Collin sucked on her lower lip. "Hadn't thought about that."

Jeff squeezed her shoulder. "I'm sure Mom will be happy to meet the ambulance when it arrives and sit with your brother until you can make it. She loves him like another son. Like she needed four."

Collin let out a breath she didn't know she held. "He loves her like a mom, too."

Or he would if we'd had a mom.

Collin shelved the thought, not sure why it came up. Pregnancy hormones again. "Do you want to call her, or should I?" Jeff was avoiding his mom's calls. Collin didn't know why. So many unknown whys...

Jeff shrugged. "You call her. It's your brother."

Collin refused to add the "It's your mom" retort. She pulled out her phone. As soon as Lacey picked up, Collin began, "Mom Lacey, there's been an...accident with Erin. He's being taken to Sisters of Mercy, and he's not in good shape. I'm with Jeff, and we have to talk to the police, then we'll go to the hospital. Can you—"

"Sit with him until you get there? Of course, Collin. I'll head out right now."

"Are you sure? I'm not interrupting, am I?"

"Wouldn't matter if you were. I'd still go. We love both of you. Tell my son..." Lacey trailed off. "Oh, never mind. I can talk to my son myself. You don't need to be carrying messages between us. Love you, Collin."

"Love you, Mom Lacey." Collin smiled at Jeff. "Done."

"Good." Jeff motioned to the sedans, which pulled around the corner and parked next to the junked car. "Police are here."

Two men in plainclothes got out of the car and walked over to the remains of the sports car that had been Collin's ever so briefly. Both men looked around the area.

Jeff walked over to them. "I'm Jeff Farrell. It's my brother-in-law we pulled out of this can."

"Detective Troutman." The two men showed their City Police ID's and the taller of the men shook hands with Jeff. "Did you see the car being delivered?"

"No, sir--that would be Tom Upton." Jeff turned around, and Tom had disappeared. "He lives in the yellow house across the street. He called me to tell me about the car being left here. We came over." Jeff pointed to Collin and himself. "My wife, Collin, is sister to the victim."

Detective Troutman motioned to Collin. "Your brother's name?"

"Erin Winger."

"Age?"

"29."

"Occupation?"

"Erin is an independent contractor. He handles real estate." *Grandfather's mostly. Now ours. We keep finding all these plots of land we knew nothing about.*

"Any idea why someone would want to kill your brother?"

"No. None." *The ones who did are in prison. We do keep tabs on them.*

The detective pointed to Jeff. "You have any ideas?"

"No, sir. My wife and Erin are twins. If she doesn't know, no one does."

Troutman shrugged. "Not unheard of for people to keep secrets." He pointed to the house behind them. "Is this his residence?"

Collin nodded. "Yes. We have keys and permission to access."

Troutman raised an eyebrow. "In writing?"

"Yes, Detective. We're joint owners."

The man glanced at the neighborhood. "Couldn't qualify on his own, huh? We see it all the time. Two owners, someone gets upset, and we get called on a domestic dispute."

Collin smiled. "We'll be careful. Do you want to go inside?"

"Haven't got a warrant."

Collin moved up the walk. "I'm giving you permission to enter and to look, Detective."

Troutman eyed his partner. The man shrugged. "If she's giving the okay, no harm in looking."

All I want is for you guys to get anything you need, get out, and let me get to the hospital.

They'll be going through his stuff.

Erin has nothing to hide. I trust my brother with my life.

After he betrayed you with Robert Winger and his brothers.

Old news. Shut up.

The detectives inspected the interior of the house, spending precious minutes looking at Erin's office. Her brother's OCD meant everything was labeled and in order. Troutman's eyes flared. "I'm impressed. Very organized." He sifted through some papers. "Do you know where your brother went this weekend?"

Collin deferred to Jeff. Jeff sighed slightly. "He went to Fort Newton to check on a piece of property his grandfather held out in the country. We thought it might have the potential to be developed. The reports he sent back indicated the land would be more suited as a wildlife refuge, not a development. We're going to investigate the possibility."

"Fort Newton, huh? When did he leave to go out there?"

Collin answered for her husband. "He left Thursday evening after he came and borrowed my car."

Troutman glanced from a file he thumbed through. "Your car? You mean that is your car outside?"

"Yes, Detective Troutman. The car is mine. Registered and paid for. I have no idea why anyone would want to destroy my car with my brother in it."

Troutman called to his partner. "Ideas, Leon?"

The balding detective frowned. "No. But if someone wanted to make a statement, that would be as good a way as any."

Collin glanced from man to man. "Statement? About what?"

Leon pursed his lips for a moment. "Usually a drug deal gone bad. Someone trying to cheat someone else out of either money or goods."

Collin's face burned. "My brother does not run drugs. He does not sell drugs; he does not use drugs. He—"

Detective Troutman held up his hand. "No one says he does, ma'am. My partner merely speculated who might do something like what happened to your brother."

Leon eyed Troutman sideways. "Know who this reminds me of? Rudy the Red."

Troutman shook his head. "Been dead ten years."

"I know, but this is something his organization used to do when they wanted to make a point. I remember a couple of times finding people in their cars…and they didn't live to tell about it."

Detective Troutman repeated, "He's dead, Leon. Ten years."

Leon rolled his eyes. "His organization didn't get shut down. Someone could have picked up where he left off."

Collin spaced her words carefully. "My brother would not be involved in any deal that has to do with illegal drugs of any kind. Can we please move on to something that might be a reason?"

Jeff touched Collin's arm. "They're doing their job, Collin. Calm down."

She glared at Jeff but said nothing. Jeff turned to Leon. "Detective, uh…"

"Netherton. Leon Netherton."

"Detective Netherton, my brother-in-law inherited a large sum of money three years ago. He has no need of funds of any kind. If he got caught in a drug deal gone bad, I'm sure it's a case of mistaken identity. Wrong place at the wrong time."

Detective Netherton shrugged. "It happens. More often than we like, certainly." He picked up Erin's laptop. "May we have permission to exam his computer files?"

Collin held out her hand. "Give it to me, and I'll open it for you." Leon handed her the laptop. Collin set it on the table and typed the password. The two detectives turned their backs on Collin to look at other files Erin had earmarked. Collin pulled up the home page. As she prepared to give it to Detective Netherton, a folder caught her eye. The label said, "Veronica and friends." Collin opened the folder. There were individual files in it: *Barbara. Bethany. Celine. Dante.* The list went on.

Collin's eyes went wide. She wanted to open the individual files but stopped. She trusted Erin, or she didn't. He always told her he had nothing to hide on his computer or anywhere else. After he accepted the Lord, he cleaned it all out. Never again.

So what were these files? Dare she look? Did she want to know? Or be forever bothered by doubt?

Trust much? He's either true to his word, or he isn't. Which one are you going to believe?

Collin handed the computer to Detective Netherton. "Here. I don't think there are any files with passwords. It's all yours."

Netherton put the machine down and began scanning through the files. His first words were admiration. "Nice boat." He smiled at Collin. "He's got quite the shopping list here. Tell him Celine is overpowered for fishing but great for tubing."

Collin smirked at her inner accuser but smiled at Detective Netherton. "I'll be sure to tell him. I'm not sure what kind of boat he's looking for." *Didn't know he was looking. But glad it's boats and not brides.*

Netherton got serious. "He's got video from Friday." He motioned to the laptop. "You want to look at it?"

Troutman nodded. "Yeah, let's see what he has."

Jim queued it up and hit play. Landscape came into focus, followed immediately by an aerial view of the same spot. The scene widened out, panned around, then took off in flight.

Collin turned her eyes away. She did not need a case of vertigo to go with her nausea. She would let the detectives do the detecting on this one.

Jeff peered over Troutman's shoulder. Collin saw his face turn to puzzlement at the same time Troutman said, "Stop it right there."

Netherton said, "I saw it."

Collin wanted to look but didn't. Not taking any chances. But she did listen with renewed interest.

Troutman said, "There. You see that?"

Collin saw Jeff nod, though the question wasn't addressed to him. Whatever they saw, Jeff saw it, too.

Netherton snorted. "Dead ten years, huh? Maybe the guy's a zombie."

Collin gazed at Jeff sideways; Jeff frowned. Collin focused on Detective Troutman. "Who's a zombie? What are you talking about?"

The detective closed the case on the laptop. "We'd like to take this with us, if we may."

"But only if you tell me what you saw. Will it help find who tried to murder my brother?"

Troutman dipped his head a little. "I think your brother recorded something he shouldn't have seen. Something no one should have seen. I think that's why they stuffed him in your car and sent it home. We need to go over this footage very carefully. Have our video experts look at it. We'll know for sure." He handed Jeff a card but addressed Collin. "I hope your brother makes it. If he does, and if he can remember anything, have him give us a call. Otherwise, we'll come visit him and take his statement."

The two detectives left. Collin watched them go. "What did you see, Jeff?"

Jeff rolled his jaw around. "I saw a small building where there shouldn't be one. And a man standing in front of it. I don't know who it might have been, but the detectives seem to know."

Collin narrowed her eyes. "Rudy the Red? But who is he? Or was he?"

Jeff shrugged. "I don't know. I'll look him up. From a library with a public computer which can't be traced to any one user."

Collin's eyes flared of their own accord. She felt herself go still and silent in anticipation of danger from unknown forces. "You think it's bad?"

"I won't take chances. A guy who stuffs people in trunks and has the cars crushed? Not somebody I want to play with."

Collin chewed on the thought. "Um, yeah. Me neither. Can we go to the hospital now?"

"Of course. Call Mom and see if she got there and what's going on with him."

They walked to the truck, got in, and Collin dialed Lacey. After the third ring, she picked up. Collin bit her lip. "Mom Lacey, how is he doing?"

"Well, they're still shooting pictures inside and out, but it seems your brother has been the recipient of a rather wondrous miracle. He'll not only live but has no major injuries. I think the beating took more out of him than being squashed in the trunk. He's going to be fine, Collin."

All the tension collapsed in her body, melting into a puddle on the floorboard. "Thank you, Mom Lacey. Thank you."

"The nurse tells me he won't be in a room until later tonight. But family can always come and go. Just two at a time, you know."

"We're on our way. Be about half an hour or so. Tell him I love him when you see him."

Lacey laughed. "I think he knows by now, dear. But I'll remind him."

Collin put her phone away and let out a deep sigh. One crisis down. One to go. She sat back in her seat. "Can we talk about what happened last night?"

"No. Not now. I don't think this is the time or place for it."

"When will be?" Collin kept her tone gentle and even. *No accusations. No boxing him into a corner. Keep it light.*

Jeff snorted. "Never?" Collin couldn't read his mood. Jeff glanced at her. "We'll discuss it, Collin, yes. When we're not rushed and can both have a logical, rational conversation."

"Do you want to set the time and place? I can make sure not to have anything else going on."

Jeff drove several minutes without answering. "After you get home from visiting your brother. Visiting hours end at eight. We'll talk after."

Confusion tinged her voice. "You're not coming in to see him?"

"I've got extra work now that Erin is laid up. I'll drop you off and pick you up at eight."

"Make it six. Eight is beyond our agreement."

Jeff's voice reflected bitterness. "I think our agreement about talking times is the least of our worries."

"Tell me what our biggest worry is." Collin lost her patience. "I'm flailing here, Jeff. I don't know what you're thinking, and I don't like it. I tell you I'm pregnant, and you run out of the room like I told you I had the plague."

Jeff shrugged. "I had my reasons."

"Tell them to me because I need to know, too."

"Tonight. When you get home."

"Have it your way." Collin closed her eyes and went internal. *Lord, I don't understand. Make this make sense to me. Help me. What is happening?*

Three things will last. Faith, hope, and love. Hang onto all three. Especially faith and love.

They arrived at the hospital, and Jeff pulled to the visitor roundabout. "Tell Mom I'll see her later. Tell that brother of yours to get better soon. I'll pick you up at six."

Collin slid out of the truck, shut the door, and watched Jeff drive off. Tears came unbidden and unwelcome. She brushed them away, walked to the entrance of the hospital, and went inside. The elevator was empty.

Good thing, as a wave of nausea swept over her, leaving her doubled over. *Do not throw up. Do not throw up.*

She managed to avoid embarrassment and righted herself before she reached the third floor. She pasted a smile on her face as she exited the elevator. After Jeff's reaction to her news, she absolutely would not tell another soul until she and he settled this thing going on between them.

Collin peeked her head around the curtains in ER 22. Mom Lacey sat reading. Erin lay in the bed, his face a mass of cuts and bruises. His eyes were closed. Collin tip-toed in, kissed him lightly on the forehead, and whispered, "I love you, A-One."

Mom Lacey smiled. "You could set a bomb off in here, and he's not going to hear it. The doctors had to sedate him to do the MRIs. They told me he'd be out another hour or two."

Collin took the chair beside her mother-in-law. "Did you get to talk to him at all?"

"Some. He doesn't know anything about how he ended up in the car. Said he stopped along the road to help a woman with kids whose car broke down…went to look under the hood, and that's the last he remembers."

Collin snorted. "He wouldn't know what to look for."

Lacey laughed. "Neither would I, but it's still the thing you do… Look under the hood and say, 'Yep, there's an engine.' Even I know that."

Collin bumped Lacey with her shoulder. "You know more than that, Mom Lacey."

"Maybe."

Erin moved. Collin's head snapped around. Lacey patted her hand. "He's going to be fine, Collin. I promise."

Collin hung her head. "I know. I know."

Lacey pulled Collin over to her side, kissed her on the head. "I've got to go take care of Harmon and Leesa. I love you, Collin. Give Erin a kiss for me when he wakes up. Tell him to think about recuperating at our house instead of at home alone. And tell my son to get his act together." Lacey smiled. "Okay, leave out the last one. I love you, Collin."

Lacey stood and walked out the door. Collin twisted her hands in her lap, letting the older woman's advice settle over her.

A voice whispered, "Is she gone?"

Collin startled. Erin's eyes were open. She jumped to her feet and came to his side. "Yes, she's gone. Why were you hiding from her?"

"Because I want to do this." Erin let out a long, low groan of pain only Collin could hear. Her brother stretched his frame and whispered a groan again. Collin stood and watched as he rolled from one side to the other, finally settling flat on his back. He sighed. "I've been wanting to do that all afternoon, but every time I made a sound, someone stuck a needle in my arm."

"They were trying to help you."

"Their idea of help is screwed. I need to stretch." He acted on his words and stretched again. "Don't tell anyone you heard this."

Collin made the x-mark over her heart. "I promise."

Erin rolled and stretched and moved his arms and legs, letting out grunts and growls and words of despair and agony until he finally gave up. Or finished up. Collin couldn't be sure. In either event, he stopped. He settled on the bed. "How bad's the car messed up?"

"Bad? Well…let's say there is no car. There's a compressed and compacted block of metal and plastic."

"Uh-huh. They did put me in the crusher."

Collin's eyes flared. "You were conscious at the time?"

"I was until the thing started moving around. One of the moves knocked me out, I guess. I only came to in the ER." He stretched. A little. "Did you have to see the mess?"

"I'm the one who heard you thumping in the trunk."

"Thumping? I didn't thump anything."

"You did. That's why we pried the mess open. I heard you knocking, yelled at Jeff, he heard you, too, and we started the rescue."

Erin insisted. "I didn't make any noise. I thought the bad guys would find out they hadn't killed me. I didn't know I'd been taken anywhere."

Collin kissed Erin's forehead. "Little brother, there must have been an angel flapping its wings because that's how we knew there had to be something alive inside."

Erin closed his eyes. "Thank You, Lord, for saving my life. Do with it as You will. But thanks."

Collin added, "Amen." She dragged the chair beside the bed. "You don't remember anything?"

"Maybe. Maybe it means something, maybe not. I heard guys talking. Saying the car appeared clean…someone would be upset."

"Did you hear a name?"

Erin's face drew into a mask of concentration. After a moment, he shook his head. "I can't remember."

"Arnold? Parson? Benny? Rudy? Gene?"

"Rudy?" He stared at her a moment. "Rudy? Maybe."

Collin harrumphed. "Whatever. Then what?"

"I got tossed to the floor."

"Wait. You weren't in the car?"

Erin stared through her. "No. No. I might have been…sitting. My arms were fastened to something, but not in the car."

Collin breathed out silently. "Go on."

"That's all there is, Cane. I'm only getting spits and spurts of memory, and I don't know what order it's in or isn't. Of if it's even real or not."

She squeezed his hand. "It's okay. Give yourself some time. I'm not sure all the brain cells have settled yet."

"I'm not sure they're even still there. I do remember getting beaten soundly and repeatedly." He sighed. "Ah, Cane, what have we gotten into now?"

A figure blew past Collin and collapsed on the bed with Erin. A young female began hugging and kissing him, showering him with tears, moaning, "Erik! Erik! What happened? Why did you have to go and get hurt? What am I going to do without you? Erik, oh, Erik!"

Collin tapped the girl on the shoulder. "Excuse me, that's my brother you're mauling."

The girl—woman—might be in her early twenties. Long black hair spilled over her face and into Erin's. Slight build, complexion tanned. Not someone Collin had seen before. The girl spared a quick look at Collin, then focused her attention back to Erin. "Are you okay? Tell me you're going to be okay. I can't live if you're not okay."

Erin pushed her back firmly. "I'm fine, Franny. I'm fine. Give me a little air to breathe, okay?"

The girl sat but refused to budge from the bed. Collin held out her hand. "I'm Collin Farrell."

Franny laughed. "No, you're not. He's an actor, and he's famous. Why would you chose a name like that?"

Collin raised her eyebrows. "Bad planning, I guess. I'm Erin's sister."

She lifted her head. "Oh, you're the sister. I see." She glanced from Erin to Collin and back. "You don't look like twins. You don't look anything like Erik."

"Erin. His name is Erin."

"I like Erik better. It's more manly." The girl eyed Collin. "Erik says you have nicknames for each other. Why can't I have a nickname for him?"

Collin lifted a brow. *No wonder you hid this one from me. Oh, A-One, not another los…work in progress.*

Erin shrugged and tried again to move his friend off the bed. "Franny, please. I'm bruised everywhere, and you're not helping the situation."

"Oh, am I hurting you? I'm sorry!" She burst into tears. "Erik, I didn't mean to hurt you. I'd never hurt you. I love you." She threw herself back on top of him to hug and kiss him, sat, got up, and sat in the chair beside him.

Erin turned to Collin. "I'm sorry about your car, Cane. Maybe I can fix it. I bet those scratches will buff out."

The corner of her mouth twitched. "Uh, no. I don't think so. Not this time. I'm grateful the Lord protected you. There's no reason why you should even be here."

The girl glared at Collin. "Your car? What's your car got to do with anything? Why are we even talking about your car? We should be talking about poor Erik and what he's been through."

Collin pointed to her brother and waited for him to explain. Erin addressed Franny. "I borrowed Cane's car to go to Ft. Newton."

The girl came unglued. "You borrowed her car? Instead of taking your truck? Oh, Erik! I detailed it and everything. I had it all looking sharp and new. Why would you take her car?" She began to cry again and leaned on Erin's shoulder.

Erin pushed her away carefully. "Collin's car has a better suspension. Better shocks. It gives me a smoother ride."

Collin cocked her head. "Since when has suspension been an issue for you?"

"Since I started having back spasms. Like electric shocks running up one side and down the other. Put me on the ground a time or two. Rich says it's probably nerves regenerating. I'd as soon they didn't. I'd rather go back to my wheelchair than put up with that kind of pain."

Franny sat and eyeballed Erin, her mouth wide open. "Don't say that. Don't ever say that! You're not going to live in a wheelchair. How can I marry you if you're in a wheelchair? It would ruin our wedding! Promise me you'll keep walking."

Collin closed her eyes to roll them. Erin patted the girl's shoulder. "I'm not giving up on walking, Franny. But I wanted Collin to know about the nerve cramps. And talking about a wedding is way premature."

Franny wasn't pacified. "But you love me, right?"

"I think you're very special."

There would no private time with Erin. Collin leaned back in her chair and checked the time on her phone. Six o'clock, and Jeff hadn't come. Maybe he'd stayed waiting in the parking lot? She called his cell. No answer. She left a voicemail. "I'll be in the lobby. Flash your lights, and I'll come out. Love you, Jeff."

Collin rose, but Erin reached for her hand. "Don't go. Or…" He peeked at the woman clinging to him, then back to Collin. "Come tomorrow morning after church, and we can talk. The nurse said they'd be moving me to a room on the third floor, um, 352."

Franny glared at Erin. "Without me? Is that what you mean? You want to talk about me, don't you?" She turned her fury on Collin. "You want to poison our relationship, don't you? You know he loves me more than you, and you don't like it. You're jealous of me. Admit it."

Collin held out a hand to stop Erin's protest before he could voice it. She stared dead even at the woman. "One, my brother and I made an agreement long ago we wouldn't interfere in each other's love life. Two, I am not jealous of you or anyone else my brother spends time with. Three, Erin and I do not talk about people behind their backs. It's not something the Lord would do, so we don't do it, either."

She sneered at Collin. "You think you're better than everyone else, don't you?"

Collin didn't take the bait. "No, that's why I go to church. So I can be better than myself. Not better than anyone else. I'm sorry if you feel threatened by me."

The woman sniffed. "I'm not threatened by you. Erik loves me. We're going to have a baby."

Collin turned on Erin, eyes wide. Erin's eyes were as wide as Collin's. "Baby? What baby? We haven't even been—"

She laughed. "Oh, I don't mean now. I mean, you love me. We'll have a baby, get married, and have our life together."

Erin cleared his throat. "Uh, first, we aren't anywhere near talking about a future beyond today. And you get married before you have the baby."

She laughed again. "You're so old-fashioned, Erik. That's why I love you so much."

Collin stood. "I'll go wait in the lobby for Jeff." She tapped Erin's shoulder. "And we'll talk tomorrow." She leaned over and kissed Erin on the forehead. "I love you, Erin."

"Love you, Collin." Franny merely glared at Collin.

Collin walked out. *Oh, little brother. What kind of train wreck have you gotten involved with?*

Seven p.m. came and went. Eight p.m. came. Collin called Jeff's phone again, but still no answer. She shook her head in frustration and dialed a cab. Twice in two days. This would get old and expensive quick. *I'm going to have to break down and use Erin's truck, like it or not.*

Fifteen minutes later, her chariot arrived. Collin confirmed the address and sat back to decide how to play this. *Past eight or not, we will talk tonight. No more putting it off. If I have to get in Jeff's face, I will. I will not let him continue to ignore whatever it is that's shattered our "oneness."*

Collin paid the driver and walked the front path. There were no lights on in the house. She walked softly into the bedroom, and yep, Jeff was asleep in bed.

Love is patient. Love is kind.

I'll be kind. I won't throw a bucket of water on him to wake him.

Collin flipped the light on.

Jeff woke immediately. He sat and caught sight of Collin with a mixture of confusion and fear. "What? What's going on?"

"That's what you're going to tell me, Jeff. It's now nine o'clock. You were going to pick me up at the hospital at six, remember? We were going to talk, remember?"

Love is not rude, is not self-seeking.

I'm not being rude. I'm stating facts. And this isn't about me. It's about us.

Jeff rubbed his hand over his face. "I'm sorry, Collin. I didn't sleep well last night. I—"

"Save it. Get out of bed, and meet me in the kitchen. We're going to talk."

"It's after eight—"

"Fine. We won't talk. You'll talk, and I'll listen. You're the one with the explaining to do."

Jeff's eyes narrowed. "And you're not?"

Collin glared at him. "Which is one of the things you're going to explain about. What it is you are accusing me of doing. You have two choices: coffee or no coffee. But you are going to tell me where the man I married disappeared to."

Collin didn't give him time to think up any other responses but turned on her heels and walked to the kitchen. She poured out the remainder of the pot from the morning, reheated it, and waited for Jeff to join her.

He came in and sat at the coffee bar. Collin asked, "Coffee or no?"

"Coffee."

"I'll make you a fresh pot." *Since you didn't drink any of the pot we were supposed to share this morning. Like you promised.*

Scripture echoed in her mind. *Love keeps no record of wrongs.*

This is war. Because I love him and am fighting for my marriage.

Collin waited until the pot filled halfway, poured Jeff a cup, set it in front of him. "Talk. What happened last night that made you run out on me?"

Jeff swallowed some of the coffee. He ran his hand through his hair. "You told me you were pregnant."

"And…?"

"And that's it. That's why. You said you were pregnant."

"So because I'm pregnant, you get angry and declare I can't be, it wasn't supposed to happen, then you run out to call someone. Someone you won't identify."

"Those would be the facts."

Collin breathed out slowly. "Now, fill in the details. Why can't I be pregnant?"

Jeff stared into his coffee cup, swirled the dark amber brewaround, raised his head. "Because I can't have kids."

"Why not? You always wanted…" Collin trailed off. "What do you mean you can't have kids? Explain it to me."

Jeff tossed his head. "It's what you think. I can't have them."

"Since when? You never said anything to me about not being able to have them. We were excited about the possibility of children. You wanted four." She felt the emotions kicking in again, and tears swelled her eyes. "When did you find out you couldn't have them? Who told you?"

Jeff lifted his coffee cup to his lips. "The week before our wedding. I made sure I couldn't. To save your life."

The cold look in his eyes, the calmness of his demeanor, made Collin's stomach drop. She stared at him. And stared at him. And… "This is what you've been hiding. Why you and the Lord aren't—"

Jeff snapped at her. "Don't talk to me about the Lord. You're pregnant. What does that tell me?"

Collin drew in a sharp breath as the reality sunk in. "You think I cheated on you. You think I went behind your back, got pregnant, and now am trying to pass the babies off as yours. That's what you're saying, right?"

Jeff merely stared back at her.

Collin began to shake. She caught hold of the countertop to keep from going across the bar at him. "I see. Now it's me. Now you're off the hook because while you lied, I cheated. And that's so much worse than living a lie for three years, isn't it?"

She scanned around the room, her head spinning. She swallowed the million and one things she wanted to say, wanted to throw at him, wanted to slice and dice him with. She drew in another breath, lifted her head. "I see three different possibilities for why I'm pregnant, Jeff. One, the surgeon screwed up…" She stopped. "Did Rich do this? Ever since my aneurysm, he's been telling anyone who'd listen I shouldn't have kids. It would kill me. Like he's God and knows this for a fact…"

Collin trailed off. "But it couldn't be Rich. He's a neurologist. His operating on you would be malpractice. So someone else. And when you called him, he told you, 'I don't make mistakes.' Right?" Jeff shrugged.

Collin wouldn't keep the bitterness out. "So the first possibility, counselor, is totally invalid. Can't happen. Of course not. Next defense? Things grow back. The body repairs itself. Oh, but wait, that can't happen, either. Your surgeon friend would have made certain. Overruled. Anything else before I'm convicted?"

Collin breathed hard. "Except you've already passed judgment. But here's my last defense. Consider it well, Jeffrey Farrell. Maybe, just maybe, the Lord intervened. Maybe He decided to reverse your lie because He had a greater purpose." She closed her eyes against the tears and the pain. "But you can't conceive of that since you turned your back on Him so you could, 'save my life.' And play God yourself."

She moved from behind the counter and stomped to the bedroom. Jeff did not follow her. She pulled out a carry-on size shoulder bag, stuffed it with clothes, threw in a pair of extra shoes, and walked back into the kitchen area. She stared Jeff dead in the eyes. "When you come to your senses, call me. I have never loved anyone the way I loved you. I never will again. And I've never had my heart ripped open like you just did to me."

She walked out the door, climbed into Erin's oversized pick-up, and drove off. She turned corners without thought or reason. Muscle memory took her to the rec center downtown where she pulled the behemoth into the empty lot. Collin shifted the truck into park, lay her head on her arms on top of the steering wheel, and cried.

SUNDAY

The alarm went off at five a.m. Jeff buried his head under the pillow and waited for Collin to turn it off. It was her wake-up call, not his. She had to get to church early to start the coffee. All the important fellowship stuff, designed to create a welcoming atmosphere. Come as you are and meet the Lord of Life. *Sure.*

The buzzing continued. And continued. Jeff muttered, "Collin, your alarm is going off. Get up, wo…"

A cold realization swept through him. *Collin is gone. Drove…driven away.*

Jeff launched his pillow at the offending clock. "She cheated on me! She had an affair with someone else, and now she's pregnant!"

Jeff swung his feet to the floor and stumbled to the kitchen. No smell of coffee to greet him. Only emptiness. Jeff stared at the cups left from the night before, the cups he never emptied or put away. The coffee pot still had coffee in it, having warmed for two hours, then shut off automatically. Jeff grabbed his cup, threw out last night's remains, poured a cup from the carafe, and warmed it in the microwave. He sipped it.

Terrible. He'd drink it anyhow. What difference did it make? Collin was gone.

Jeff carried his cup to his office. Her picture sat on his desk. Taken at Camp Grace on their honeymoon. They both were smiling as big as could be. He remembered the day, the moment. So happy. He'd fixed things so she wouldn't have a child and die on him. Wouldn't leave him alone…

Like you are now?

Jeff ignored the taunt. He examined the invoices and blueprints which papered his office. Strategically placed to give the appearance of busyness, of utmost importance. Done, so Collin couldn't possibly ask him to do anything more. Like, accompany her to church? How could he? She could see his office. All of it needed his attention.

And I created the wall.

Jeff sunk into his chair. Tears made him madder. "I didn't expect her to have an affair!" But with who? Jeff cast his mind around his circle of friends, fishing for a likely suspect. No one came to mind. He cast wider. Anyone Collin may have mentioned? Suspicious letters she'd tried to hide? Lunch dates she hadn't wanted to tell him about? Was she such an accomplished liar?

Can anyone hide anything from the Lord?

Jeff flung an innocent book across the room into an unsuspecting floor lamp. It rocked, tipped, crashed…and Jeff ignored it. "She sure could, God! You didn't do anything to make her life miserable."

The "highpoints" of the past played in his mind. Collin's aneurysm. The ten longest days of his life, waiting to see if she would live or die, or live forever in a vegetative state. The miracle of her recovery. Their engagement. Rich's words. "She'll die. If she gets pregnant, she'll die. Period. No questions, no appeal. She'll die, and the baby with her." Better to tell a little lie…or not tell her the truth…and save her life. Right? The only loving thing to do. Right? Right.

Except the guilt ate at him. Ate at him, so he couldn't face God. No more communion. No more life group. No more church. No more praying together at home. And each time, Collin tried to bring him back…

Jeff yelled, "I get it! I get it! She tried, okay? I admit it. She tried to understand. But what did you want me to do? Tell her the truth? And what?" Jeff breathed out hard. "She'd have been furious." *But would she have left?* "Yes. No. I don't know."

Jeff threw his arms wide. "And what difference does it make? She's gone now!" Jeff mocked Collin's voice. "'Either the doctor made a mistake, or your body repaired itself, or God intervened.' Never mentioned her maybe having an affair, did she?" *But did she have an affair?*

Jeff left the thought unanswered. He went and got dressed, came back to his office, and shuffled around the projects on his desk. Collin had been right, of course. He could pass off the rec center project to Jacobs and Weiskopf. They were capable, honest men, and they would do an excellent job with the project. Better than Jeff if he would admit the truth. But truth wasn't a commodity he knew how to deal with. Or wanted to.

* * *

Collin walked into the hospital at seven in the morning, and she stopped first at the woman's room. She looked in the mirror. *Gads!* Her eyes were puffy and bleary. She splashed water on her face in hopes of improving the appearance. Make it look like she hadn't spent most the night crying. *Fat chance.* Collin combed her hair with her fingers, patted it, fluffed it, and generally tried to remove the night's trauma.

She straightened her clothes as best she could, smoothing out wrinkles from lying on the steering wheel all night. The fact she had on the same clothes as yesterday might be a give-away, but Erin wouldn't notice. She hoped.

Satisfied she'd done as much as she could, Collin took the elevator to the third floor. She walked past the nurse's station like she knew where she should be, and no one needed to stop her. No one did.

Collin slipped into Erin's room to find her brother lying with his eyes open, staring at the ceiling. Collin chuckled, kissed his forehead. "What are you doing?"

"Visualizing world peace." He sighed. "Trying to remember anything I can about what happened. Bits and pieces keep floating around, and I'm trying to get them in order."

"Having any luck?"

"Not much." Erin turned to look at Collin. He studied her a moment. "You look like something the cat wouldn't even drag in. What happened?"

Hormone-fueled emotions swept over Collin. Tears threatened to cascade down her face as Collin lifted her head to swallow the pain. "Jeff and I had a fight. I…uh…I walked out on him." She sighed, bit her lip. "I'm pregnant, Erin." Tears rained down. Collin bowed her head, unable to contain them any longer.

Erin reached out to take her hand. "Cane…" He gave her a half grin. "You're just now finding out? I've known for two months!"

Collin smiled despite the tears. "How did you know when I didn't?"

He chuckled. "I know you. Your face has been filling out. Along with other parts of you. I wondered if you were ever going to figure it out."

She gazed at the floor. "I went to the doctor this week. I kept having these strange pains in my stomach." She couldn't help it. She smiled. "It's twins. One of them may have a heart murmur. The doctor said he heard an echo. But he says the hearts sound strong."

Erin lowered his head to look Collin in the eyes. "Okay, that's all good news. What did you two fight about?"

Collin lifted her head. "Jeff told me he had himself 'fixed' the week before the wedding. He can't have kids." Collin covered her mouth with her hand.

Erin's eyes blazed with anger. "He did what? Without telling you?"

"Yeah. He did it to save my life, he said. But I'm pregnant. Which means I had to have an affair. No way these babies are his, according to him."

Erin sat straight in the bed. "He accused you of having an affair?"

Collin couldn't keep the bitterness out. "Had to have. It's the only option. No way the surgeon made a mistake. No way things could grow back. And God forbid, God might intervene. No, the only possible answer is I had an affair."

Erin squeezed Collin's hand. "No wonder you look so dragged out. Where did you spend the night?"

"Parked at the rec center downtown. I slept in your truck." She half-smiled. "Your suspension is terrible. The babies don't like it."

Erin smiled. "Well, by all means, we must keep the babies happy."

Collin breathed deep, lifted her chin. "I didn't come here to make you hate Jeff. You and I made the covenant. No taking sides. I needed someone to talk to, that's all."

Franny came singing in. "Good morning, my love! How are you this morning?" She ignored Collin, went straight to Erin, and kissed him full on the mouth.

Collin bit her lip and managed a smile. "I'll leave. Thanks."

Erin dodged around the intruder's embrace. "Go stay at my place. You've got your key."

Franny raised her head, and her eyes were as wide as her mouth. "She has a key? Why does she have a key, and I don't?" Tears formed in the young woman's eyes. She turned the full force of her sorrow on Erin. "You said you loved me. But she has a key, and I don't? You love her more than me, don't you?"

Collin swallowed her smile. "I'll talk to you later." She walked out. *Oh, A-One. What have you gotten yourself into?*

Collin walked back to Erin's truck. She pulled out of the parking lot, got on the freeway, but headed downtown rather than to Erin's. There would be no way she could drive this truck all over town with this stiff and unyielding suspension. The babies complained. Okay, so they hadn't actually said anything about it. But bouncing on her bladder like a mini-trampoline could be considered translation enough. And the last thing she needed to do was make the babies unhappy.

Collin drove to a rental agency in the Barrows. Good people. Trustworthy people. People she knew from her "living downtown amongst them" days. She rented a comfortable sedan. Easy to get in and out of. And a smooth ride. Yes. It would make her very happy. She made arrangements to leave the truck on the lot until Erin would be able to retrieve it himself.

She drove the car to Erin's house and parked in the driveway. As she got out, she noticed a black sedan parked in front of the neighbor's house. Unusual, as the neighbor drove a bright pink SUV. *So they have company. So what? Not your concern.*

Collin also noted Tom stood in his accustomed place, looking out his window. Watching. Always watching. She waved at him. He didn't respond. *He never responds.* She walked in the front door. She took two steps in when something hit her in the head from the side. Collin fell to her knees. Arms grabbed around her. She smashed her head against the chest of her assailant. She heard the 'oof' and felt the arms loosen. Seizing the moment, Collin slipped out of her captor's grip and rolled sideways. She came to her feet and put her back to the door.

Her brain registered there were two assailants; men dressed in black jumpsuits. Both were medium height and build, fair-skinned, and fair-haired. Any other details would have to wait. Collin ducked under one man's blow to her head, swung her way into the living room, and kicked over a table. *Noise. Make noise. Tom will hear. He hears everything.*

Attacker number two went low, grabbing for Collin's legs. Collin side-stepped the attempt to bring her down but couldn't avoid the first attacker's two-fisted blow to her side. She curled in. Both men jumped on her. Collin went down, still kicking and fighting and biting and, as a last resort, screaming.

The scream earned her a fist across the jaw. Collin weakened. The men grabbed her, one at her legs, the other at her arms. Collin twisted and struggled to no avail. Her attackers carried her to the mudroom next to the garage. One of the men grabbed a roll of duct tape while the other forced Collin's hands behind her back. The first man taped her mouth, wrapped her still-writhing hands, and kicked her sharply in the side. "Lay there. Don't move."

Collin gathered any strength she had left. There would be another chance to escape. They had to take her out to put her in the car. She would make a break for it. She would. Maybe it wouldn't succeed, but someone might see it. Someone would know.

Attacker one disappeared. Collin leaned against the wall trying to anticipate the next move. She heard the garage door open, heard a car drive in, heard the door close. *Okay, so is there a plan B?*

Not yet. We're thinking, we're thinking.

Attacker one came into the mudroom. He had his phone out and spoke into the receiver. "No, we didn't find anything. Place is clean. We are bringing in a witness. Yeah, she walked in on us. Had a key. Maybe she knows."

He pocketed his phone, motioned with his head, and he and his partner picked Collin up. Collin didn't try to fight as they shoved her in the back seat of the car. A better escape opportunity would present itself later. She needed to be patient.

The garage door opened, the sedan backed out. Collin stared out the window at Tom's house. She couldn't see the man but knew he watched. She rolled her face as close to the window as she could so Tom would see the tape across her mouth. The car turned at the corner.

* * *

Jeff worked until nine a.m. *Wonder if she's telling everyone at church I accused her of having an affair?* The phone rang. Jeff answered. "Yeah, Mater. What can I help you with?"

"We didn't see Collin this morning. Is she okay?"

"She's fine."

"It's not like her to miss Coffee Service and not call in. We were worried."

"I'll have her give you a call and explain later."

"No need. We were worried, that's all."

"Thanks for checking on her, Mater."

Jeff returned his focus to the papers on the desk.

Fifteen minutes later, the phone rang again. Jeff closed his eyes. "Patsy."

"Did Collin forget she had nursery this morning? We haven't seen her."

This would be a problem. "Uh, she may have forgotten, Patsy. Her brother's in the hospital, and maybe she didn't remember."

"Oh, of course. Of course. I heard Erin had been in an accident. Is he going to be okay?"

"He'll be fine, Patsy. Thanks for asking. And I'll tell Collin you called."

"Well, I tried her number first, and she didn't answer. Not even a voicemail."

"Maybe her box is full." Jeff marked the ledger sheet on the desk. "Patsy, when I see Collin, I'll tell her you were looking for her. Thanks for calling."

Jeff set the phone down. *Who else will call looking for her?* People cared about Collin. Her not being at church would be a big deal. *Unlike me, who no one calls about.*

Jeff shook his head. *They did, at first, but I kept putting them off. Not really their fault.* He went back to work. He reconciled two more accounts before his phone rang again. He checked the ID. Mom. Jeff sighed and picked it up. "Yes, Mom, I know Collin didn't come to church this morning. I assure you, she's fine."

Mom's voice sounded guarded. "Did something happen with Erin? Is that why she missed?"

Jeff flipped over the receivables pile and began shuffling through it. "I'm sure Erin is fine, Mom. Collin said he seemed good when she left him last night. If there had been a problem, someone would have called."

"You haven't talked to him today? You haven't checked in on him?"

"He's a grown man, Mom. He knows how to use a phone."

An extended silence followed. "Jeffrey, this attitude you have stinks. I won't speak for anyone else who's asked about it, but I will speak for myself. You're hurting the people who love you, and you're driving them away. Whatever this is, you've carried it long enough. I want my son back."

Jeff scowled. "You talked to Collin, didn't you?"

"No, I haven't. Why would I call you asking where she is if I had spoken to her?

Jeff watched a bug run across the floor. "No reason. We had…a…fight. I thought she went to you for support."

Mom's voice sounded crisp. "Collin would never come to me with a complaint about you. Just as you better never come to me with a complaint about her. We made an agreement. Collin is a woman of discretion."

Jeff snorted. "Right. I gotta go, Mom."

"Consider this, Jeffrey. Collin arranged a lunch date with your sister today. Leesa told me Collin would call her about eleven to decide what restaurant they should go to. Collin hasn't called. It's eleven-thirty. That is not like your wife, and if you don't care, you should."

The call went dead. Jeff tossed the device across the desk. He stood, stretched, and went outside to the back patio. He stood silent for several moments. "You're enjoying this, aren't You, God? Is this Your punishment for me trying to usurp Your authority? Letting her have an affair and not calling her on it? I lie one time, and You're all over me. She has an affair…an affair! Do you make her feel guilty? No. She waltzes through life like everything is perfect. And You don't do a thing."

Jeff let out an angry sigh. He walked back into the house as his phone ran once again. He confirmed the number. Uncle Rich. Maybe… Jeff answered the call. "Uncle Rich? Did you think of something?"

"Think of what?"

"Some reason why Collin would be pregnant."

Silence. "Jeffrey, there is only one answer. Collin has had an affair. It's the only logical answer. I called to see how you're doing. Collin didn't show at church this morning, which tells me you confronted her, and the sham is over."

Jeff stared out the window. "Yeah, I confronted her."

"Did she admit it?"

"No."

Rich sighed. "I'm sorry, Jeff. I liked Collin. She fooled me. She fooled a lot of us. We all thought she was a wonderful woman. If I had known she'd do this, I would never have suggested the surgery for you. And I certainly wouldn't have performed it. In your next marriage, I'm certain you can adopt."

"'Next marriage?' What are you talking about?"

"She committed adultery. Adultery is clear grounds for divorce in scripture. God has no tolerance for sin of such magnitude."

Jeff gaped at his phone. "Doesn't what we did bother you? I mean, we lied to her."

"We didn't lie. I certainly didn't. I performed surgery to save a woman's life. God has no quarrel with me about that, and you shouldn't feel guilty either. You made a choice to protect your wife. You did nothing wrong."

"No? Why have I felt so distant from Him? If I did nothing wrong, why does it eat at me?"

Rich's voice became placating. "Perhaps you're a tad over-enthusiastic about your relationship with the Lord. You need to learn to compartmentalize your life. My work is one area. My family is another, and the two do not commingle. My devotion to the Lord is another area. Again, it doesn't spill over into any other compartment. When I keep all the parts of my life separate, I find balance and peace. Maybe you should try it too."

Jeff scowled at the phone. *Good thing this isn't a video call.* "Right. I've gotta go, Uncle Rich. I'm expecting another call. Thanks for checking in on me."

He didn't wait to hear his uncle's reply. He threw the phone on the desk. "Compartmentalize. What garbage. You don't put God in a box and take Him out when you want Him."

Every teacher, every pastor, every message Jeff had ever heard echoed in his mind. *"God is either Lord of all, or He's not Lord at all."*

Jeff smashed his empty coffee cup against the wall. "You did this! You let her go behind my back. And she prances to church and back like everything is great. But me, I lie once to save her, and You chase me down with guilt every day! What about her? What about what she did?"

Jeff's jaw clenched hard. Tears burned in his eyes. "It's not fair, God. It's not." The pain in his heart tore at him. Collin. His Collin. The love of his life. The one God had picked for him… "Right. You picked her. You knew she'd do this. Why did I have to marry her? So she could rip my heart out? Leave me unable to have kids ever? It's not fair."

The phone rang again, and Jeff's shoulders drooped. Erin. Of all people. He picked up the call. "Yeah, man."

"Hey, Jeff. The hospital is throwing me out. I tried to reach Collin, but she's not answering her phone. You think you could stop by my place, get me some clothes, then come get me? I don't want to go home in my BVDs, man."

Jeff stood. "Yeah, I'll be there. See you shortly."

He walked out, got in his car, and drove to Erin's. He let himself in from the back and grabbed enough clothes to cover his brother-in-law's dignity. As he left, he noticed a drawer open in Erin's desk. Jeff's eyes narrowed. Erin never left drawers, doors, or cabinets open. Jeff scanned the living room. A table was overturned with chairs broken and knocked askew. He walked carefully back out the way he'd come in without touching anything. He dialed the police. "I want to report a burglary."

"What's your location?"

Jeff gave Erin's address. "The homeowner is at the hospital. I have to pick him up. We'll be back in another hour."

"We'll notify the department and get someone out to speak to you." The dispatcher paused. "Or we'll get someone out to take pictures, and the officers will contact you later."

Jeff snorted. "Burglary low on the priority list?"

"I wouldn't say that. But you probably could."

Jeff walked back to his car. He studied the dark blue sedan in the driveway. *Wonder whose car?* Jeff saw Tom standing in the picture window. Maybe he should ask Tom about it.

A small nudge in his brain whispered, *Ask him. Now.*

Jeff dismissed the idea. No. He'd get Erin, bring him home, and be done with it. Of course, he might have to wait and talk to the cops. He climbed back in his car. Jeff tensed as he drove. He didn't need the extra annoyance with Erin's business. He needed time to think things out. Alone.

The accuser gloated. *With Collin gone, you'll have all the alone time you ever wanted. Great job.*

Jeff turned on the radio. The Christian network had on a song about forgiveness. He changed the station. Secular rock and roll came on, playing a track about hard, unrequited love. Better. He left it there.

He reached the hospital and took the clothes to Erin's room. He called from the hall, "Got your stuff, man."

A young woman stuck her head out from behind the privacy curtain pulled to prevent anyone from seeing in the room. She smiled a wide smile. "You must be Jeff. Erin talks about you all the time. You're his best friend." She took the clothes and walked back behind the curtain with them.

Jeff heard a strong, "Thanks, I can do the rest of this myself."

"But you may need help."

"I've been getting dressed for twenty-nine years. I think I can handle it. Out."

"Oh, alright." The woman came out of the room and joined Jeff in the hallway. She smiled at Jeff again. "I'm Franny. I bet you're nicer than your wife. She was here this morning. And last night. She's jealous Erik and I have a thing going on."

Jeff gave her a sideways glance. "Erik?"

She laughed. "Oh, it's just my name for him. It sounds much more manly than Erin."

"I see."

"And, of course, your wife didn't like it. I know she's jealous." The woman's voice filled with scorn. "She is mean and hateful, and she calls herself a Christian. What a joke. I think she's pretending to be a Christian." She gaped at Jeff, and her eyes widened. "I'm sorry. I didn't mean to say those things." Her eyes filled with tears. "It's just she said mean things, and it hurt me."

Jeff muttered a non-committal, "Yeah." *Even she saw through Collin's Goody Two Shoes act.*

Erin called out, "I'm ready."

Jeff and Franny walked into the room. Erin sat, fully dressed, looking washed out and pale. Jeff eyed him closely. "You sure about checking out so soon?"

"Yeah. Hospital says there's no reason to keep me. Nothing broken, nothing torn. Everything bruised but functioning. I need my own home, my own bed, my own pillow, and my own kitchen."

The woman draped herself on Erin. "Are you sure you don't want to come to my house? I can take good care of you there."

Erin repeated. "No. I'll be fine at home."

She pouted. "Because you told your sister to go there. She'll love taking care of you, won't she?"

She directed her gaze at Jeff. "But if your wife is staying at Erik's place, who will take care of you? She should be home with you, and I should be caring for Erik. I'll go home and get some things."

Erin untangled himself from Franny's hold. "No one is going to take care of me. I'm perfectly capable of caring for myself. Collin isn't coming over to care for me."

The woman huffed. "Why is she staying there?"

Erin cleared his throat. "It's…uh, complicated."

"And you don't think I can understand it? Do you think I'm stupid?" Franny's bottom lip began to quiver.

Erin touched her arm. "No, I don't think you're stupid at all. This just isn't the time to go into it."

Medical transport stuck their head in the room. "Someone need a chair to the front?"

Erin raised his hand. "If it's the only way I can get out of here, yeah. Me."

Transport laughed. "It's the rules. Have a seat."

Erin complied and sat in the wheelchair. Jeff and Franny trailed behind him and his escort. Erin and Franny waited at the curb for Jeff to retrieve his car. When he pulled to the curb, Franny leaned into the open passenger window to speak to Jeff. "You can take him home, but I'm going to come over to make sure he gets settled in. That's what girlfriends do, right?"

Jeff noted the stiffness of Erin's gait. The way he maneuvered his frame into the seat. The care with which he belted himself in. The sigh once he stopped moving. Erin hurt.

Erin closed the door. "Get me out of here. Please. Now."

Jeff chuckled. They headed north. "Collin saw you at the hospital this morning?"

"Yeah." Erin focused his gaze straight ahead. "She told me you two had a fight. She told me what you fought about." Erin turned and faced Jeff. "I made a commitment to stay neutral in your fights. Collin did the same with any of my fights. I'm honoring it."

Jeff eyed Erin. "But you're mad."

"I'm human, Jeff. I said I'd stay out of it, and I will. I offered her my place so she'd have somewhere to stay other than rec center parking lots."

Jeff's head snapped around. "What?"

"There's where she spent the night. In my truck, in a rec center parking lot. I got the feeling she's not thinking straight, so I told her to go to my place and stay."

Jeff faced the road ahead. "What time?"

"Before eight."

"Are you sure of the time?"

"Yeah. Why?"

"When I went by there, it looked like someone had been in the house. Some things were left open. A couple of drawers, a closet, filing cabinet. The table and some chairs in the living room were knocked over. But Collin wasn't there." *I should care about this. I should.*

I don't. Why?

Jeff remembered the car. "And I saw a blue sedan in the driveway. Collin has your truck, right?"

"Yeah. I've a feeling…something's bad wrong, Jeff." Erin's face tightened. "I know it."

Jeff held up a hand. "Calm down, man. Everything is fine. We're talking about Collin here. You know she can handle herself in any situation."

Erin said nothing but stared out the side window. Jeff felt the nudge in his gut again. Stronger this time. He dismissed it. The venom in his heart refused to acknowledge anything but the pain. Collin would have to take care of herself.

They rounded the corner to Erin's street. Erin opened his mouth to say something but was interrupted by a resounding explosion, followed by crashes and the sound of debris falling. Erin's house disappeared in a fireball. Erin rolled out of the car as fast as his injured body would allow. Jeff threw it in park and ran after him, grabbing him. "Forget it! It's gone, man! Leave it!"

"But Collin…"

Jeff's training kicked in. He held him back hard, feeling his own stomach bottom out. His tears joined Erin's. His voice strangled."You can't help her, Erin." *COLLIN! God, no. Not like this. Please. COLLIN!*

Within minutes, sirens sounded and surrounded the neighborhood. Fire crews jumped from the trucks and began pouring water on the blaze. Jeff grabbed the first man on the scene. "There might be someone in there!"

The man shoved Jeff back. "Go! We'll do what we can." Jeff and Erin were forced to watch and wait from the perimeter, shielding their eyes from the heat and glare, watching. Waiting. Jeff's gut twisted and gnawed at itself. His hands tremored. His throat tightened.

Only after the fire had been extinguished did anyone go inside what remained of Erin's house. One of the team came out and declared, "No one inside." Jeff began to breathe again. Relief swept over him, and his knees began to shake. *Why do I care? If she'd died in the explosion, everyone could still think of her as a saint…*

Jeff thrust the thoughts out, trying to bury them. *She's still my wife. Still Collin.* He breathed out hard. "Let's go talk to the cops."

Franny screamed from the perimeter. "Erik! Erik!"

Erin turned, and Jeff saw the dismay on his face. He also saw Erin hide it in the same instant. His brother-in-law motioned for the police to let the hysterical woman through. Franny nearly barreled him over and threw herself around him. "Erik! I saw the flames! I was so afraid you were in the fire!" She turned to scan the remains of Erin's life scattered on the lawn. Her head cocked as she saw the burned-out hulk of metal in the driveway. She hugged Erin close but then stepped back. "Where is your truck?

Erin's eyes went wide. Jeff dropped his gaze to the ground. His brother-in-law exploded. "My truck? My truck? Is that what you're worried about? Look at my house! It's gone! The truck doesn't matter!"

Franny began crying. "Don't yell at me! I don't like it when you yell at me." She pointed to the house and sniffed. "I bet your sister did this."

Erin shook loose from her, fury in his eyes, fists clenched, jaw tight. Jeff walked beside him. Jeff shielded the frantic woman from reaching him. Jeff caught her by the arm. "I think you should let Erin alone to deal with this for a while. He's upset and needs to calm down. Give him some time."

Franny's lip quivered. "But I want to help him. I want to comfort him and be strong for him."

"Erin needs time alone more than he needs to be comforted. Trust me."

She gave Jeff a wide-eyed stare. "If you're sure. You wouldn't lie to me, would you, Jeff?"

"No, I won't lie to you."

Jeff caught up with Erin, who remained tense and drawn. Erin walked to the fire inspector. "I'm the homeowner." He gazed at the yard. "The rubble owner."

Inspector Pike, his name written on his shirt, held out his hand. "Sorry for your loss here."

Jeff joined the conversation. "Any idea what might have caused this?"

"Not yet."

Detective Troutman walked up to Jeff and Erin. To Jeff, he said, "We meet again." To Erin, "Is this your car?"

"No. I have no idea whose car it is." His eyes laser-focused across the street. "But I know who does."

Tom stepped out of his house and walked across the street. He nodded to Erin. "The HOA will probably want to talk to you."

Erin rolled his eyes. "Tom, what did you see this morning?"

Tom shrugged. "People coming and going. I don't keep track of everyone who comes down the street."

Jeff knew Tom's statement was, politely put, in error. Jeff probed. "Did you see anyone go into the house?"

"Erin's house?"

"Yes." Jeff kept his tone as even as possible.

"Yeah. Two men came by early."

Detective Troutman pulled out a notepad. "How early?"

"Seven or seven-fifteen. Seven-fifteen."

"Can you give me a description?"

"They drove a black four-door sedan. One of the ones with a cat on the hood. Except this one didn't have a cat. The headlights were rimmed in white and black, not silver."

"Did you get a plate number?"

"FDL8005. It might have been FDL8006. But I'm pretty sure it read FDL8005."

"Can you describe the men?"

Tom went into a lengthy detailing of the men, their apparel, their demeanor, their gait... Impressive how much the man remembered.

Troutman took furious notes. He lifted his head once. "Did you see them go inside?"

"I thought it kinda curious. They tried the front door but couldn't get in. They went around to the backyard. When they didn't come back around, I guessed they got in."

Jeff watched Erin. His brother-in-law rolled his eyes. *I know what you're thinking, bro. I know you wanna say things you shouldn't. Gotta hand it to you for your self-control.*

Troutman continued the questioning. "Can you tell me what happened next?"

"About ten-fifteen, this man's wife drove up in that blue car. She parked it there, in the driveway, and went into the house."

Jeff's eyes flared. "While the two men were still there?"

"I suppose. I didn't see them leave before she got there. So they must have been."

Erin closed his eyes. His words were measured. "And you didn't try to stop her?"

Tom shrugged. "I don't get involved in other people's business."

Jeff caught Erin by the arm. "It won't help her. It'll only slow things down. Keep it together."

Color returned to Erin's face, but his fists remained clenched. He gave Jeff a sharp nod.

Troutman eyed Tom. "Did you hear anything?"

"Not that mattered."

The detective frowned. "Let me be the judge."

"I heard some noise like furniture being moved around."

"Moved? Or knocked?"

Tom lifted his chin and rubbed it. "Maybe more like knocked over. Maybe a thud. Maybe I heard a yell."

Jeff and Erin both started forward. Troutman waved one hand at them to stay back as he spoke to Tom. "What happened next?"

"The taller of the two men came out and got the car. He pulled it to the garage door. The door opened, it went in, and the door closed. After seven minutes, the garage door opened, and the car pulled out. His wife was in the back seat."

"Did she look frightened? Scared?"

"No. She seemed like she always does. There was one thing kind of funny. She looked like she had something in front of her mouth. She seemed like maybe she wanted to say something to me, but she didn't roll the window down or try to speak. She doesn't usually speak to me."

"But she looked like she had something over her mouth?"

"Maybe."

Jeff asked before Erin could, "And you didn't call the police?" His voice shook in time to his fists.

Tom said, "No. It wasn't my business. I like to keep to myself." Tom turned and walked away from the group.

Erin's whole body shook. Jeff held him back. Just desserts would be to let Erin loose on Tom. And Jeff could have the leftovers. But it wouldn't help Collin. Jeff turned to the detective, got his voice under control. "What now?"

Troutman pointed to Erin. "Stay where we can reach you."

Jeff offered, "My place."

"And if you think of any reason someone would want you dead or would kidnap your sister…"

Erin breathed out heavily. "I'll let you know."

As Detective Troutman and Inspector Pike walked away, Franny returned to bear hug Erin. "You could have been in there. You could have been killed! What would I do without you?"

Erin stared past the woman. "Jeff, did you say I could stay with you?"

Jeff put a thumb up. Franny pouted. "His place? Why not my place? You'd be safer. Whoever took Jeff's wife may come after you, too. My house would be safe."

Erin pried himself from her clutches. "Someone has tried to kill me twice. I'm not going to put you in danger."

The woman's lower lip stuck out and quivered. She kicked at the ground then asked, "Where's your truck, Erik?"

"My truck? Why does it matter?"

"You gave it to her to drive. But she drove the blue car. Where did she leave the truck?"

Jeff's gut twisted. *This is real. Collin's been kidnapped and is out there, somewhere, in trouble. And she's worried about Erin's truck?*

Erin said Jeff's exact thought. "Why is it important? She protected it for me, okay? She didn't bring it here where it would have been destroyed. When we find her, we'll ask her."

The pout returned. "I care about your truck because it's yours. It's all you have, now, and it's important. I worked hard to clean it and shine it and have it detailed. That's why it matters to me."

Erin remained patient. Far more patient than Jeff would have been. "After we find my sister, we can find my truck." He turned to Jeff. "I need to go shopping, man. I need pajamas."

Franny smiled. "Oh, you sleep in pajamas? That's so funny. When you move into my place, you won't need—"

Erin's eyes flared. "Long ones. With feet."

Jeff swallowed his chuckle. "I hear you. Let's go, man."

Erin squeezed Franny's hand. "I'll talk to you later. Be careful going home."

"I love you, Erik. Please stay safe and alive." She went in for another hug, but Erin side-stepped her and got away clean. He and Jeff climbed into the car and drove away.

Jeff said, "I don't know about her."

Erin closed his eyes. "I don't either. Right now, I don't want to know."

"I hear you. We'll get the things you need in the short term."

"A phone would be good."

"We'll get you a phone."

"Pajamas. Definitely pajamas."

Jeff nodded. "We'll get you pajamas."

"Will you get me a pony? I always wanted a pony."

Jeff grimaced. "At least your sense of humor is intact. But no, no ponies."

"That's what my father always said."

They drove to the local "we have it all" store, and Erin got clothes, pajamas, footwear, and sundries. A second stop and Erin had a phone with his old number. As they drove home, Erin stared out the window. He didn't turn to face Jeff. "I promised Cane I would never get between you two, and I would never take sides. I'm going to stick to my promise until we find her." Erin paused. "Then I want an answer from both of you why you are tearing each other apart."

Jeff frowned. "Thanks, brother. This isn't something…something either of us wanted." *She wanted to be pregnant. I never expected her to have an affair to get that way. Not my Collin.*

Jeff kept the thoughts to himself. Erin's phone began buzzing before he hit the door. Jeff said. "Answer it. We can talk about it later."

Erin shrugged and put it on speaker. "Talk to me."

"Erin, this is TJ at the body shop. I thought you were going to Fort Newton on Thursday. Your lady had your truck prepped and ready to go." Erin side-eyed Jeff. Jeff rolled his eyes. "You were supposed to drop off a package at her Aunt Beela's. Now Franny tells me you took someone's car? Why would you do that when she—"

"TJ, I took my sister's car because the ride is smooth. Okay? What is it with this concern about the truck? I don't care where it is. My sister is missing. Someone blew up my house. Those are things I'm concerned about right now. Not my…truck."

Jeff smiled inwardly. Impressive restraint on Erin's part.

TJ's voice came back. "I didn't know about your sister. Someone blew up your house? When did this happen?"

"About two hours ago. In front of my eyes."

"I'm sorry, Erin. I didn't know. I didn't mean to upset you."

Erin sighed. "It's been a long few days. I got stuffed in the trunk of my sister's car, the car got compacted, I got rescued and spent the night in the hospital. On the way home, someone blew up my home. I'm a little stressed. Okay?"

TJ's voice sounded shocked. "You were what? Stuffed…compacted? Before they blew up your house?"

"Yeah, that's about what happened."

A long silence followed. A very long silence. "Erin? I gotta go. I'll catch you later. Bye."

Erin stared at Jeff. "Was all that weird to you?"

"Yeah. A little. Why is the body shop concerned about your truck? And you never said anything about delivering a package."

Erin sat in Collin's recliner. He lay his head back and closed his eyes. "Franny asked me to leave a package off at her Aunt Beela's. Said she's a lonely old woman, and Franny likes to find ways to make her happy. Me taking a package and spending time with her would make her happy. So I did it. Why does it matter?"

"Maybe it doesn't. But you didn't tell Detective Troutman about that."

"I forgot. I'll call him and tell him. I'm going to close my eyes for a little bit, then I'll call him."

Jeff chuckled, threw an afghan over his brother-in-law. "Night, Erin."

Silence. Soft snoring. Nothing more.

* * *

Seven p.m. A knock at the door. Jeff answered it. The local news station video truck sat parked across from the house. A reporter, one Jeff recognized from the morning news feed, held a microphone and leveled it at Jeff. "Creighton Barnes, Channel 75 news. Is Erin Winger here? May we speak to him?"

Jeff decided to run blocker on this one. "He's resting. You can understand this has been a trying day for him. Maybe some other time."

"Yes, I understand. You are Jeffrey Farrell, married to his sister Collin Winger?"

"Walker."

"Excuse me?

"His sister's name used to be Walker. Collin Walker. Erin's name is Winger."

Creighton took a breath. "Right. You were with him when the house exploded. Can you tell us what happened?"

"What you said. The house exploded. That's as much as I know. Now, if you'll excuse me—"

Creighton leaned into the door slightly. "Mr. Farrell, do you have any theories as to why someone would blow up your brother's house?"

"Not one. Thank you."

This time, Jeff made sure there were no obstructions to the door, closed it firmly, and walked away.

Erin stood behind the hallway, undetected by the news crew. He tapped Jeff's fist with his own. "Thanks, brother. I owe you."

Jeff shook his head. "Vultures. I know they have a job to do, but still. Couldn't they wait a day or two?"

"Nope. Might miss being first." Erin stopped. "You think they could get the word out about Collin? And maybe help find her?"

"They're more likely to get her killed, Erin. The more people who know about the kidnapping, the more talk, the less likely the kidnappers will want to negotiate."

Erin lowered his head. He stood still a moment. "You're right."

Jeff heard another truck swing around the corner. He peeked out the shaded window. "Great. Here come two more."

Erin shrugged. "Fine. I'll speak to them." His eyes took on an unholy light. "I'll speak to them alright."

Jeff eyed him sideways. "You make me nervous when you look like that, man. What have you got planned?"

"Nothing. I'm going to talk to them. Tell them the whole story." He smiled at Jeff. "I need rest. That's your story, and you're sticking to it, got it?"

Two more reporters came to the door to join Creighton. Jeff heard murmurs through the door as if over a discussion of supremacy. He waited until he heard the knock. Erin disappeared around the hallway. Jeff opened the door.

Creighton smiled. "I'm sorry, Mr. Farrell. I don't mean to disturb you again. My colleagues have a few more questions they would like to address, and after, we will leave Mr. Winger alone. Is there any chance we can speak to him?"

Jeff repeated, "No. Mr. Winger is resting. He's had a long, hard day and needs to unwind—"

Erin's voice floated down the hallway. It tremored and quaked, filled with fear. "Jeff? Is someone out there?"

Jeff glanced around at the trio of slavering reporters. "Yes, but I'll send them off. You go back and lie down, bro."

Erin swung around the corner. His eyes were as wide as he could get them, filled with shock and fear and a wild light even Jeff hadn't seen before. "No! I have to talk to someone. I do. They have to know what is going on!"

His clothes were askew, rumpled. He appeared for all the world a madman. He caught Jeff by the arm and jerked Jeff out of the way. "I will talk to them! The world has to know!"

The intensity of Erin's voice made the three reporters step back. Erin stared at each person in turn. "You want to know what happened? You want the truth? I'll tell you. I'll tell all of you. It started Friday. I drove there to have tea with my girlfriend's aunt. A lovely woman. A kind woman. She fixed me tea. Lemon verbena, I think. But we had a sweet time sitting in her swing and talking. She is so dear to me…"

Erin trailed off, both verbally and mentally. After a moment, he came back to his harried self. "I left. It was dark. I saw…I saw lights coming toward me. Two lights. Then, then four. They blinded me. I tried to look away, but the lights kept coming and coming and coming." His voice began to quaver. "I couldn't avoid seeing them. Over and over. They appeared to circle around and come back again."

A tremor replaced the quaver. "I saw two more lights. They were…red? Red at first. Blinking. Blinking. Endlessly blinking. They got closer and closer…I thought they would crash into me. I pulled over, and the lights shone in my eyes."

His distraught brother-in-law risked a surreptitious glance at Jeff. Jeff put an arm around his shoulder. "It's okay, Erin. You just need to rest, buddy." He glared at the reporters. "Can't you see he's not himself?"

Erin fought him off. "No! I have to tell them! I do!" He turned frantically to the reporters. "You believe me, don't you? You do, right?"

The men exchanged glances. Jeff watched the video team shutting down their units, closing the trucks. One of the reporters suggested. "Uh, maybe Mr. Farrell is right, and you do need to rest some, Mr. Winger. We can come back another time when you're feeling better."

Erin grabbed Creighton by the shirt sleeve. "You have to listen. You have to. I see it in you. You believe, don't you? You've seen them too. The lights. Coming at you. Always coming. And…" Erin swallowed hard, forced himself to go on. "The craft…I don't know what kind. Black. Black as night. So black. I couldn't make out any details except the lights. They were…they were…they changed from the red to yellow. Yellow lights blinking. Blinking in my eyes."

He dropped his gaze to the ground, his eyes still wide, unblinking. "I'll never forget the figure. Standing outside the craft…trying to tell me something. I couldn't understand what it said. The noise…the noise of the engines…so terrible! I reached out to touch the craft…to stabilize myself…and then nothing."

Erin's eyes came back up, and the wildness had returned. "What did they want? Why did they choose me? Why? I don't understand! Why are they here? Tell me! Tell me! You know, don't you? You've seen them, too. I can see it on you. You have to tell me what they want!"

Erin's voice rose to a cry, plaintive and desperate. "Please!"

Jeff carefully pulled Erin off of Creighton's arm. He put an arm around Erin's shoulder and kept his voice calm and soothing. "It's okay, Erin. It's okay. You need to rest, buddy. You go in and lie down, and you'll feel a lot better. Go close your eyes and try to sleep."

Erin's eyes never blinked. He stared at Jeff. "You won't let them get to me, will you? You'll protect me?"

Jeff nodded. "Of course, Erin. I won't let anyone get to you. Go lie down. I'll be in in a minute."

Erin turned away from the porch. "You're right. I'll go. Thank you, Jeffrey."

Jeff turned to the reporters. Creighton cleared his throat. "Uh…I hope he gets to feeling better."

Jeff smiled. "Yeah, he just needs some time." Jeff closed the door, locked it, walked into the living room, doubled over, and exploded in laughter.

Erin lay in the recliner, his eyes closed. "All of it was the truth. All of it described exactly what I saw."

Jeff chuckled. 'I won't argue the 'what.' It's the 'way' you described it." Jeff smiled at him. "Pure genius. I'm glad you didn't stay on the dark side."

Erin frowned. "The dark side didn't have cookies. And soda. I prefer the sweet side of life." He muttered, "G'nite, Jeffman."

TUESDAY

Collin sat still in a wooden chair. Her arms and legs were securely taped to the chair's arms and legs. The only allowance she had for movement would be for fidgeting, which she refused to do. The cloth bag over her head suppressed noise and vision. She could sense light, and she could see shadow. Period.

But the restraints couldn't keep her from praying and praising and worshipping the Lord. Which she did. Without ceasing. She prayed for Jeff. She prayed for Erin. She prayed for Franny. *Lord, You know how much she needs it.* She prayed for her babies. For family. Friends. Her captors. Her enemies. Anyone and everyone she could think of. And when she finished she started over.

She had finished her third round of prayers when someone grabbed the chair and tipped it onto the back legs. They dragged her--and the chair--across the floor. In the darkness of the hood, she felt them maneuver her out a door, across the floor--again--through another door, across a floor, and finally returned her to her full upright position. Under her hood, she could see only darkness.

There's no such thing as darkness. There's only absence of light.

That helps how?

It doesn't. Just thought I'd throw it in.

Throw it out. Please.

A voice in front of her ordered, "Remove the hood. Let me see who we have here."

The hood came off, along with several strands of hair. Collin decided now would not be the optimal time to lodge a complaint. She forced herself to relax, to be calm, to appear unrattled. She breathed in. She breathed out. A day at the park. Nothing more.

A light came on, shining directly in her eyes. Collin blinked once. Period. No problem. Everything cool. Peaceful, even.

The deep male voice spoke. "Who are you? Do you know me?"

Collin slumped her shoulders in an exaggerated sag. She bobbled her head side to side, sat upright again. And waited.

"Remove the tape from her mouth."

A hand appeared and grabbed a corner of the tape. Collin tensed all the muscles in her face. The hand ripped the tape off her mouth. Collin let the muscles relax slowly, hiding any urge to scream or complain. Nothing. She would give them nothing.

The voice demanded. "Again. Who are you? And do you know me?"

Collin prayed, then spoke. "My name is Caitlin Winger. You're a man sitting across from me in a dark room. I will assume it was your people who kidnapped me and brought me to you. Beyond that, no, I do not know you. Should I?"

"Do I know you?" Curiosity tinged the voice.

"I don't know many kidnappers. The odds our paths have crossed before are not good."

"But the name Winger rings a bell. Why do I know it?"

Collin remained silent. *Lord, this is all You. If he knows Robert Winger, this could be bad.*

"Robert Winger. I remember now. Are you related?"

Okay, now what?

The Shepherd's Voice in her soul. *Speak the truth.*

"Yes."

A tone of curiosity heightened. "Daughter?"

"Yes."

"I didn't know he had a daughter. He never mentioned you."

"There's a reason why. He never wanted me."

"But you are his daughter?"

"Biologically, yes. By any other standard, no."

"If I held you for ransom, he'd pay to get you back, though."

"He's not in a position to be able to make any decision. He's in Federal prison, doing life for murder. Among other things."

"He had brothers."

"And they're in prison with him."

"Hmm. Well, wouldn't your aunts want to see you safe? Surely some relative would want you."

"Considering I'm the one who put Robert and his brothers in prison, no, I don't think they care."

"I see your point." The voice turned to the side. "Turn the lights on."

Collin prepared her eyes to receive the light without squinting or blinking. She needed to be in control. Cool. Calm. Collected. Like she controlled the meeting, not whoever held her captive. *I fear no evil men because You, God, are with me. Always.*

The man in front of her didn't look familiar. Didn't look like anyone she had ever seen in passing, even. He may have known Robert, but never at a time when Collin had been around. *Thank You, Lord.*

He studied her. "Nope, you don't look familiar at all."

"Neither do you. Since we've established we're strangers, can we keep it that way, and you let me go home? We can let this go as a case of mistaken identity, laugh about it, and go our separate ways. Sound good to you? It does to me."

The man chuckled. "I like your sense of humor. Robert never had one, as I remember."

"So you'll let me go?"

"No. Not until you explain what you were doing in the house Sunday morning."

Collin cocked her head. "This isn't still Sunday?"

"No."

"Hmm." Collin swallowed all of her fear. *Lord, speak. Show me what to say. Help me.*

"It's my brother's place. I went in to get some of my dishes back. He borrowed some for a date he had. He wanted it to look like he actually kept a house instead of living off take-out and paper plates."

"Ah, so you have a brother. Would he pay a ransom?"

"My brother can't pay his electric bill. No, he can't pay a ransom."

The man's eyes crinkled at the corners. "I do like you. You're not afraid of me, are you?"

Collin stared him full in the face. "Should I be?"

He motioned to her taped body. "I have you prisoner."

Collin smiled. "Not really."

He sat back in his chair. "No? Look where you are."

Collin shrugged her shoulder. "You have the body. Everything else belongs to the Lord. He's the One Who decides my status."

"Really." The man slumped one arm over the arm of the chair. "The Lord. That's who you think is in control of this? Not me? Not my men who kidnapped you? Some invisible, imaginary spirit is in control. I was beginning to think you might be a worthy adversary. Or at least someone interesting to speak with."

"Maybe I am. Maybe I'm not. When I die, I know where I'm going. Do you?"

The man's face slackened. "What a waste of brilliance."

Collin shrugged again. "I'm still me. Haven't changed. Same mind. Same sense of humor. Same lack of fear. What makes me less brilliant? Because I believe in God? Who do you think made me this way?"

The man's eyes narrowed. "Take her back to the room…no, wait. Take her to the studio. Let her loose in there. But keep her locked in." He smiled. "I'm not ready to let you go. I have a feeling I may still find a use for you." He laughed drily. "Unless your god stops me." He motioned his head sideways.

The hood went over her eyes again. The chair tipped back, the dragging began again. Inside, Collin sighed. *Thank You, Father. Stay with me. I need You. And I love You.*

WEDNESDAY

Erin's voicemail pinged. "Detective Troutman here, Mr. Winger. We managed to pull the VIN off the car in your driveway. We traced it back to a rental agency. Seems your sister rented the car before she drove to your place. Your truck is sitting in their yard, and you can retrieve it at your convenience. Our forensics team would like to check the interior before you take it home. Call my office at 555-614-2000 to coordinate a time. Will wait to hear from you."

Erin hung up. "Franny will be happy."

Jeff coughed. "When are you going to do something about that relationship? Where did you fi…I mean, meet her?"

Erin sat at the coffee bar in the kitchen. Jeff occupied the stool two seats down so he could spread out his ever-present pile of paperwork. Erin guessed it kept his brother-in-law busy while the search for Collin continued. Without progress. Erin swirled his coffee. "Met her at church. She came to a single's mingle. Friend of a friend of a cousin. I thought it would be a safe place to meet people, you know?" He snorted. "Or a place to meet safe people. Bad assumption on my part."

"Truth."

Erin dodged the "what are you going to do" part of the question. "Can I rip you away from your work overload to take me to get my truck?"

Erin watched Jeff through narrowed eyes. How the man reacted would tell Erin more about Jeff's state of mind than anything Jeff might say.

Jeff pushed the papers away. "Any time, Erin. These papers aren't going anywhere."

Bingo. Busy work to keep his mind off Collin. There's hope. Before Erin could hit redial, his phone rang again. Erin closed his eyes and breathed out. *Franny.* He drew in a deep breath. "Hi. No, I don't have my truck back yet. I'm working on it. I promise."

The woman's voice flooded with tears. "Oh, Erik. You have to find your truck. You have to. You don't understand how important it is to me."

Erin stretched still-cramped muscles. "No, I don't understand it. Explain it to me. Why is it so important?" His voice toughened. A little. Not a lot. But it did. "Don't tell me because you cleaned it. I want the truth. Why?"

The sobs continued. "You're not with anyone, are you? No one else can hear this?"

"I'm with Jeff. He can hear anything and keep it private. I trust him with my life." *Trusted him with my sister. Questionable move. Jury still out on that one.*

Hesitation. Sniffle. Sob. "Okay. I made a bad mistake. A really, really bad mistake, Erik. It could ruin the rest of my life, but I wasn't thinking at the time. The photographer said it would be fun, you know? No one would ever see the pictures." The sobbing started in earnest. "I was only twenty-two. Still a baby. He took advantage of my innocence. I agreed, and he took some pictures…some pictures… I'm so ashamed." Erin heard the nuclear meltdown of sobs.

He rolled his eyes; Jeff followed suit. Both men shook their heads. Almost as if synchronized. "Now he's trying to expose the pictures to the internet, right?" Jeff sneered and tossed a wad of paper at him. Erin shrugged. "And he wants money. I see your problem. But how does my truck tie into it? No one blackmails someone for a truck."

Franny half-laughed. "No, silly. He doesn't want the truck. He wanted money. Lots of money."

"How much?"

"What?"

"How much money did he want?"

"Oh…uh…$100,000."

"Wow. It must have been hard for you to come up with so much. How did you manage it?"

"I…uh…I begged everyone who cared about me for help. And they did. My…sister gave me the money she's been saving for her wedding. And…uh…my brother gave me his adoption fund. No one had enough, but they all said they didn't want me to have the rest of my life ruined. They gave me everything they had."

Erin closed his eyes and rubbed his temple. He could feel a headache coming. "Why didn't you ask me?"

"I couldn't ask you. I didn't know you well enough yet. I didn't. I thought you'd dump me if you found out I made such a bad mistake." Sniveling.

Erin rested his head on his hand. "What does this have to do with my truck? I still don't understand."

"The man is in Fort Newton. I had to get the money there somehow, and I had to send it with someone I trusted. When you told me you were going to go there, I hid the money in your truck." Erin opened his eyes. Jeff's eyes were narrowing as he leaned in to listen with increased interest.

"You hid the money in my truck? Where?"

"I can't tell you. The man who's blackmailing me made me swear I wouldn't tell anyone else. He didn't want to take chances it could be stolen."

"Stolen by who? Me?" Erin rolled his eyes. Jeff covered a smirk.

Sudden contrition. "No, no! Not by you. Never by you, Erik. I…uh…I don't know who he thought would steal it. But I had to promise, and I don't want to have to lie to him."

"Okay, I get it. You hid the money in my truck. Then what?"

"You were going to drive the truck to Aunt Beela's. He would sneak over and get the money, and everything would be fine. Except you didn't take the truck, and he thought I tried to double-cross him. That's why he crushed your car. He didn't know you were in it. He swears he didn't. He just wants the money."

Erin raised his hands in submission. "I get it. I do. I know there's only one way to deal with people like him. He says he wants the money, and he'll never bother you again. Except once his bankroll runs out, he'll come back and ask for more. And more. And more. The only way to get him of your back is to tell the truth."

"What?" Shock and horror. "Tell the truth?"

I know. What a concept. "Yeah. You get it all out in the open. You admit you screwed up, accept the consequences of your lapse of judgment, get on with your life. It's what my sister did."

Self-righteous sniff. "I bet your sister never had bad pictures taken of her."

"What do you want me to do, Franny? Once I find the truck, what do I need to do?"

"I need to check to see the money is still there. You need to drive to Fort Newton like you said you would. He'll get the money out of the truck and leave the pictures for me. Then he'll leave me alone. I know he will."

"Why can't you tell him I'll drive the money over in a car? It would be so much easier on my back. The suspension in the truck is killing me."

Explosion of tears. "No, no. It has to be the truck. He made me swear you would come in the truck."

Erin sat. He glanced at Jeff. Jeff's eyes narrowed, and his head cocked. "What's special about the truck?"

"Nothing! It's not about the truck…it's…uh…it's I told him what you were going to drive, and now he insists you bring it. So he knows it's really you. And you're bringing the money."

"Uh-huh." Erin raised an eyebrow at Jeff. Jeff waved him off. "I have to go. There's a call on another line. It might be the detective about my sister. And the truck. Bye."

Erin put the phone down. "Okay, what do you make of it?"

"Something's in the truck, and I don't think it's money."

"Suggestions?"

"Call Detective Troutman. Fill him in and see what he suggests."

Erin's gaze fell to the floor. "This might solve my side. Wish it could help with finding Collin."

"I'm with you, Erin. I wish it every day."

Erin's thoughts went dark. *You wish it. But you won't pray it, will you? Can't admit your part in this. Not yet. Lord, open his heart. Don't make Collin the ransom for his stupidity. Your will, not mine. But You want our requests, so You got mine. Thanks.*

Erin made the call. Detective Troutman listened, agreed, referred him to a contact in the DEA. Erin repeated his suspicions to three people before he finally heard, "Very interesting, Mr. Winger. I'd like to inspect your truck with you. Can you tell me where it is and when you'll be there to retrieve it?"

Erin did a visual check with Jeff, who nodded. Erin turned back to the phone. "We're headed to the rental agency to pick it up. I'd prefer not to do all this inspecting in front of a crowd of onlookers. I also don't want to take the chance my 'girlfriend' gets wind of it."

"Understood. We'll have an undercover agent meet you at the lot, and you can drive it to our garage for inspection."

"At the DEA building? How does that work for not making her suspicious?"

"We have a local body shop we use. It makes for good cover. Trust us, we've been doing this awhile."

Erin chuckled. "I gotcha. Okay. We roll now, we'll be there in forty minutes. Will that give your agent time to meet us?"

"She'll be there. Her name is Agent Vy Johnson."

Erin wrote the name. "Vy Johnson. Got it. Thanks."

Jeff picked up his keys. "Tough way to meet women, bro."

Erin tossed the paper wad back at Jeff. "Degenerate."

"Cretan."

"Ooo. You and Cane must have been playing Scrabble."

Jeff smiled. "You should see what I can do with a q-u combination."

Jeff's phone buzzed. Erin watched his face for emotion. He read disappointment, frustration, resentment, resolution. All in a matter of three seconds. "Hi, Mom. No, there haven't been any new reports. Erin and I have called the police so much they told us not to call anymore, they will call us. Yeah. I know, Mom. It's killing us, too. But Erin is convinced she's alive, so we're going with his gut. Right. Uh-huh. Okay. I will. Love you, Mom." Jeff pocketed his phone. "Mom says she loves you."

Erin didn't trust his voice. He gave Jeff a 'thumbs-up' sign. They climbed into the car and left.

Forty minutes brought them to the rental desk of the lot where Collin had exchanged Erin's truck for a smoother ride. Erin and Jeff walked into the rental agency building. A woman of mahogany complexion and unadorned beauty greeted them. Erin noted her full-face smile. And her eyes. Dark brown with flecks of gold and tan. Her black hair was cut short and curled in soft waves around her face.

Erin wanted nothing more than to stand and stare at her. Jeff hit him in the back, and Erin returned to earth. "Uh, hi. We're Erin Walker…I mean…Farrell…" Erin slapped his head. "I am Erin Winger. This is my brother-in-law, Jeff Farrell. We're here to pick up my truck."

The beautiful woman with the entrancing eyes extended a graceful hand to him. "I'm Vy Johnson. I'll be assisting you." She wore the rental agency's uniform, but Erin recognized her name as the DEA agent he should meet.

Erin's heart thumped hard in his chest. He took her hand. "Pleasure to meet you."

He reluctantly released her. Jeff stepped forward and shook hands as well. "We appreciate your help."

Vy smiled at both men. "That's what we're here for. Let me take you to where the vehicle is parked. Did you bring a key?"

Erin's eyes widened. "Uh…Jeffman?"

"I don't have it."

"Well, I certainly don't have a spare. Everything I have got blown up."

Vy interrupted. "It's fine. We have the set Ms. Farrell left when she picked up the rental. In case the owners had to move the truck. But can you describe the truck you're looking for?"

One with you in it… Don't say it. Don't say it. "Ten-year-old green crew cab short bed with Motor City tires and a Disney World sticker in the back window." *My gift to myself after I got my mobility back. Jeff, Cane, and me. Best time of my life. Until now.*

Vy's eyes sparkled. "I've never been. Still on my to-do list."

"Really? What else is on there??" *Getting married? Oh, wait…okay, no rings on her fingers. She's undercover; she wouldn't wear one anyhow. How do I ask?*

The woman led the men to the back of the car lot, where Erin's truck had been parked. Vy unlocked the driver's door. Erin checked inside. "Yep, this is my truck."

Vy smiled. "Which we verified already. It will look less suspicious if you drive the vehicle from here, following Mr. Farrell and me."

Jeff started to raise his hand, but Erin beat him to the punch. "Uh, he can't. He's married, and they have this thing about not riding alone with someone from the opposite sex. Keeps things safer."

Vy approved. "I understand. Our church encourages the same practice." She smiled at Jeff. "I'm allowed some leeway considering my job, but even so, it makes good sense."

Erin jumped in. "I'm not married, so it's not as big a deal for me." *Use your leeway. Please.*

Ooo...she said she goes to church.

So did Franny.

Spoilsport. Who asked you here? And besides, Franny said she went to church sometimes, not all the time. Friend of a friend of a cousin, remember? That's how she was introduced. This could be different.

Erin stepped away from the argument in his head. "If you want, you can ride with me. If it's allowed. I mean, your husband won't mind, right?"

Vy's eyes crinkled with laughter. "Well, if that wasn't a fishing opportunity, I don't know what one is. No, Mr. Winger, I don't have a husband. But thank you for considering his feelings in the matter."

I like this woman! She's sharp. Too sharp to like me, maybe? Nothing ventured... "So, you'll ride with me, and Jeff can follow us. Jeff, you okay with those arrangements?" He turned to his brother-in-law.

A thought crashed his elation. His voice caught. "I don't know if this will help bring Cane back, but it might. So will you come with us?" He played what he hoped would be an ace. "Paperwork will still be there tonight, bro. I could help you with some of it if you show me what you're doing."

Jeff drew in a deep breath. "Shuffling it mostly. Yeah, I'll follow you. Shouldn't be hard." He grinned at him. "You drive like a granny anyhow."

Erin rolled his eyes. "Thanks, man. I appreciate the vote of confidence." Erin ran around and opened the door for Vy. Well, he didn't run. He trotted. Three days home from the hospital had helped his recovery. Helped being the operative word. He had a ways to go before he would declare himself "healed." But every day saw some progress.

Erin climbed into the driver's seat, started the car. "Which way out of here?"

"Take the Market exit and go left."

Erin waited for Jeff to get mounted, fall in behind him, and signal he was ready. The two vehicles drove off the lot.

Vy directed Erin to a converted gas station, now without pumps, a few blocks from downtown. He pulled into the parking area and tapped his horn lightly twice according to Vy's directions. A jumpsuited mechanic opened the roll-up door and waved him in. Erin pulled the truck into the repair bay, over the lift racks, and stopped. He turned the engine off.

The mechanic had "Tobias" embroidered on his coveralls. He extended a hand to Erin. "Hi. Welcome to Uncle Sam's garage. What are you here for today? Oil change? Check engine light on?"

Vy gave Tobias a mock scowl. "Once over lightly, please. Heavy on the lightly."

She slid out of the truck before Erin had time to get around to open the door. Vy's manner became all business. "We don't know there's anything to find, Tobias. But we've got some really good suspicions."

Tobias reached under the wheel well, felt along the side, and dropped to the ground to get a better look. He used both hands to wiggle something loose from the side panel, held it out to Vy to hold, stood. "I bet your suspicions are good ones, too. And I'll bet this block has brothers."

Erin's eyes widened as he gawked at the brick-sized object Vy held. It had been wrapped heavily in plastic to keep the contents safe. Who knew what manner of contamination might have been kicked up on the drive from Oakton to Ft. Newton?

Erin flashed a wide-eyed look at Jeff; Jeff returned the favor. Vy retrieved a pair of vinyl gloves from a box hanging on the wall, slipped them on, and used a box knife to surgically dissect the wrappings from the material packed inside. She picked up a few grains of white powder, rubbed them between her fingers, blew the slightest puff of air over them. She nodded at Tobias, her eyebrows raised. "Not bad. Not pure, but not bad. We'll send it to the lab for confirmation."

Erin wanted to lean in and also examine the powder but refrained. It would accomplish as much as looking under the hood of a car did. Yep, there's an engine. Yep, Vy held white powder. After that, he got nothing. He did ask, "Cocaine?"

"Horse."

Erin put on his most innocent face. "Powdered horse? Why would they powder—"

Jeff slugged him in the arm. Erin flinched. "Okay, I've been around Franny too long." He grew serious as a thought settled in his brain. *Has she been playing me all this time? Not the dumb female, but a calculated performance knowing I'm the gullible one?* Erin felt heat in his face.

Vy touched his arm. "Don't." He gazed into her eyes, colored in compassion. "Don't feel hard on yourself. These people are very good at what they do, and that's how they stay in business. Where'd you meet her?"

"Church on Sunday night."

Vy set her mouth in a straight line. "Church people are the easiest to manipulate." She gave him a small smile. "We always try to see the best in people. It's also why we get sucked into co-dependent relationships. We're always trying to help everyone."

She motioned with her head to the sales office. "Why don't we wait in there while Tobias goes over this truck carefully. You can give me all the details on your friend."

Erin pulled out of his self-flagellation for the moment to nod. He and Jeff followed Vy into the waiting room. Two more DEA agents were already there, ready to record Erin's information. The fivesome got seated, then got to work.

It took Tobias nearly three hours to finish doing what he needed to do before he walked into the main room. He wiped his hands before reporting to Vy. "All done. We found around 10 kilos total. All of it cut by about 1/10th. I'd say the supplier is trying to skim the distributor."

"Not surprised. Business as usual for this bunch." She smiled at Erin and Jeff, however. "Thank you for bringing this to us. Street value is around $2.75 million. That'll put a dent in someone's bank account."

Erin didn't know whether to feel sick he had been used or angry, embarrassed, outraged… He let the feelings battle it out for supremacy while he attended to something more helpful. "What do you want me to do now? Tell her I found the truck? See what she suggests from there?"

Vy's eyes hardened. "I know what she'll suggest. She'll want to check out the merchandise herself, then may offer to drive it over to save you the extra trouble. You won't see her or your truck again."

Erin snorted slightly. "Good riddance to both of them."

Vy smiled again. "Understood. But we have a backup plan just in case she has other ideas." She outlined the plans, the details, and what needed to be done.

Erin listened. "But how do you catch the bad guys at the other end?"

"We put a tracker on the truck and a team on the road. When she stops at Aunt Beela's, or wherever, we sweep all of them." She gave Erin a satisfied smile.

"Can you find out who stuffed me in the trunk of my sister's car?"

She cocked her head. "Stuffed you in the trunk, Mr. Winger?"

"Erin, please." He shuddered. "Please."

Jeff chortled but didn't say anything.

Vy glanced from man to man. "What?"

"Franny never would call me Erin. She called me 'Erik.' Said it was a more manly name. I've had Erin for twenty-nine years, and I'm proud of it."

Vy chuckled. "Some people." Her face straightened. "We repacked the bricks with harmless powder and put them back where we found them. We also put trackers on them and the vehicle while we had it." A small smile tickled her eyes. "I would remember that when you think about where you go for the next few days."

Now. Do it now. Say it and get it over with. Erin smiled in return. "The Lord has been tracking me for some time now. I go where He sends me." Pause. "Mostly."

Vy's eyes exploded with light. Erin felt her joy wash over him. "Oh, I do know that one, Mr…Erin. He and I have walked together for a few years ourselves."

Erin silenced the chorus of hallelujahs his brain launched. "I'd love to sit and talk with you about Him." He turned his head to the side. "And about other things. If it's permissible. Sometime."

Vy reached in her shirt pocket and handed him a card. "When this case is over, we will, Erin. I'd love to sit and talk about the Lord. And other things." Her gentle smile radiated all over her.

Jeff caught Erin's arm. "Come on, dude. I need to get back to work on my own case. Finding your sister?"

Vy's eyes darkened. "Your sister…you mean your wife is missing?"

Erin nodded. "She was kidnapped Sunday morning."

Vy turned from Winger to Farrell. "Why didn't I hear about that part of the case?"

Jeff's tone carried more heat than Erin thought necessary. "Because the authorities haven't made a definitive connection, yet. Other than she got snatched from his house before someone blew it up."

Vy's eyes narrowed. "Mr. Farrell, will you sit and tell me everything about your wife's disappearance?"

"City police say they're working on it. You might not want to interfere with something they're already looking into."

Vy remained polite but firm. "There are details here the City Police, as fine as they are, may not recognize. Please."

Jeff sat, but Erin could see his face and knew he didn't want to go over it all again. It didn't get any easier with the retelling, Erin knew. "My wife…Collin Farrell…and yes, I know there's an actor with the same name. Bad planning on our part, we know now. Anyway, she went to Erin's house Sunday morning. A witness saw two men go into the house early. My wife arrived a few hours later. The witness said he heard some commotion from the house. One of the men brought their car into the garage. When the car pulled out, the witness saw my wife in the back seat with tape across her mouth. He didn't call the police, however, because he doesn't like to interfere in other people's business."

The vitriol in Jeff's voice was palpable. Erin didn't blame him. Except… *If you hadn't accused her of having an affair, she wouldn't have been at my house to begin with. First causes, Jeff. Accountability.*

Erin leaned into Jeff's arm. Enough to let the man know he had a friend. Jeff dropped his eyes and lowered his head. Erin turned to Vy. "Jeff picked me up from the hospital around one. We drove to the house and reached it the same time someone blew it to kingdom come. No chance for forensics to track the kidnappers. And no word from her for three days now."

Vy asked one of the agents to move away from the laptop and began typing furiously. Erin noted how beautiful her hands were while she typed. Long, elegant…

Erin shook his head to clear it. "You think there's a connection?"

Vy continued typing. "I think there are patterns that look surprisingly familiar."

One of the agents, identified as only "Ron" grunted. "Dead ten years, Vy. It's not him."

Jeff looked up sharply. "What did you say?"

Ron cocked his head. "I said the guy she's looking for has been dead ten years."

A cold, dangerous light came in Jeff's eyes, and his face hardened. "Rudy the Red?"

All eyes in the room trained on Jeff. "Yeah. That's who Detective Troutman mentioned. Erin"--Jeff jerked his head at him--"took some drone footage out near his grandfather's farm. Abandoned real estate, actually. I saw a shot of a man standing in front of a building that shouldn't have been there. Detective Troutman said it resembled some guy, Rudy the Red. His organization used to stuff people in cars, too."

Vy questioned Erin. "Do you have that footage?"

Erin pointed to his feet. "Only footage I have. Everything else got blown up."

Jeff corrected him. "The detective took the laptop to have it analyzed." Jeff managed a small sideways grin. "So you got something, man."

Vy continued her typing. "Which gives me more to look at."

Ron peered over the monitor. "Hacking the city is frowned on, Vy."

She smiled. "They'll never know." She shrugged. "Besides, if it helps solve a case, who cares who gets the credit?"

"Department heads. Bureaucrats. Politicians."

"We won't tell them, right?"

"Not unless you get caught."

"You worry too much."

Erin watched the interplay between the two agents. A nagging sense of jealousy tugged at him. *He's honing in on your girl.* Followed by an equally nagging sense of the absurd. *Your girl? You barely know her. A little reality check on the emotions, okay?*

Hmmm...I wonder if Cane's hormones are making me crazy, too?

You're crazy all on your own.

Thank you for the reminder.

Erin dragged himself out of the inner conflict. He and Cane had definitely been together too long. Despite the twelve-year separation. He gazed around the room rather than stare at Vy. While he preferred the view, he refused to look like a stalker.

A dagger of pain shot through his back and down his right leg. Erin buried all outward reactions. He reached out to steady himself against the desk, pushing his fingers harder and harder against the unyielding surface. He needed to move, to walk, to do anything except stand there. Yet to excuse himself, he'd have to say something. And he couldn't guarantee his voice would hold.

Jeff cast a glance over at him. He tapped on the desk. "I need air. Come on, Erin. Let's walk outside." He directed his gaze to Vy. "Is it allowed?"

"Of course. You're two guys at a garage. Nothing to see here."

Jeff reached over and took Erin's arm. "Come on, brother. You can stop ogling the scenary."

Erin felt Jeff's firm grip on his arm and leaned into the support. Erin willed his feet to move. After a moment, they responded. Appropriately. Jeff led him out of the bay into the parking lot. They walked short lengths, stopped, turned, and walked back.

After the third pass, Erin felt the cramp loosen. The pain disappeared. Well, except for an annoying tingle which traced up his leg, into his back, and down again. A hint not everything in his body had healed yet. He relaxed his muscles. "Thanks, Jeffman. I owe you."

Jeff shrugged. "I've been around you and Collin so long it's not hard to spot when one of you is in pain. I think you've been on your feet too long. We need to get you home."

Erin sighed. Deep sigh. "You're right. But I like the scenery here."

"You. I thought you and Vy were going to start a revival when you found out you both know the Lord."

Erin held his gaze. "Used to be a time the old Jeff would have joined us. I miss that Jeff."

Jeff grunted. Erin walked back into the room under his own power. Jeff addressed Vy. "Is there anything else you need from me? If the kidnappers are watching my place, I want to make it easy for them to find me. In case they leave a ransom note. Then I can get my wife back."

"No, Mr. Farrell. We appreciate your help here today. You've helped take a major cache of heroin off the streets. We might be able to shut down a supply line as well. That's plenty, and we thank you."

Jeff nodded. He pointed at Erin. "Get off your feet."

"I'll be right behind you."

Jeff walked out. Erin sighed. He turned back to Vy. "Do you think these cases are connected? And could help us find my sister?"

Vy lay a hand on Erin's arm. The nerves tingled, but in a different way than before. She smiled at him. "Anything we come up with, I'll let you know." She dipped her head. "I promise I'll stay in touch. And when this case is over, we'll see if we can have that talk about the Lord. And other things."

Her eyes sparkled and twinkled and reflected and refracted and bounced light back in a million different ways. Erin smiled. "I look forward to it." He turned to Ron and extended his hand. "Thank you for your help. I appreciate your work." He shook the hand of the other agent and walked out. *See? I acknowledged there were others in the room. I'm not blind.* He got in his truck and drove back to Jeff's house.

* * *

Jeff drove home, his mood dark. He mocked Erin's words. "'Used to be a time the old Jeff would have joined us. I miss that Jeff.' Yeah, well, talk to your sister. She's the one who made me this way."

Go ahead, blame her. Whatever helps you sleep at night.

Jeff growled at the accuser. "Nothing helps me sleep at night."

A beer might. You could try a beer. Just one. See if it helps.

Jeff let the thought linger. And linger. And linger. He gripped the steering wheel tighter, peeked into his rearview mirror, and saw Erin's truck three cars behind him. No chance to stop and pick up a six-pack.

"But with the temptation will make a way of escape…"

The Scripture filled Jeff's mind. He hit the steering wheel with his fist. "Even if we don't want one, right?" He exhaled, relaxed his grip, and kept driving.

Once at the house, he went straight to his office and dragged out as many incomplete purchase orders, invoices, and requisition sheets as he could find. He set them all on the breakfast bar in the kitchen and waited for Erin to come inside. He would keep them both busy. No time for questions about what happened and why.

Except he knows what and why. He wants to know what I'm going to do about it.

I don't know what to do about it. I don't know what to think about it. I hurt so much inside. How could she do this? How could she have… Lord, how could You let this happen? How? She was the love of my life! I want…

I don't know what I want anymore. Except I don't want to feel this.

The door opened, and Erin came in. Jeff noticed the stiffness in Erin's gait. *Bad suspension, huh?* Jeff poured himself a glass of tea, held it up to Erin. "Tea?"

"Soda."

Jeff snorted. "You and your sugar."

"Hey, I've only been in the free world for three years. I've got a lot of missed culinary indulgences to make up for. Starting with sodas."

"Have you tried anything harder than plain soda?"

"Alcohol? No. Well, once."

"Yeah? How did it go?"

"Not well. I fell a lot. Swore never again."

"Hmm." *Aww…no drinking buddy here.* Jeff ignored the thought. "How about you sort through these, pull out the requisitions, and match them to the purchase orders. Make sure we've got everything ordered."

Erin shuffled through the stack, pulled out half the papers, and set them aside. He frowned at the mound. "Why are you still going old school with paper?"

"Because it's what Dad is comfortable with. Once he steps back permanently, I'll get a program written to integrate all this. But not for a few years yet."

Erin examined the sheets, compared several pages to one another. "I could write it now, and it would be ready to implement as soon as Pop Harmon is ready to let go of all of this." He paused. "I could start it now and still be able to print out anything he wanted to look at." Erin's voice became unsure. "If you trust me. And if you want."

Jeff mulled it over. "You sure you can do it? I don't mean 'do you have the expertise'? I mean, do you have the time?"

Erin grunted. "It's all I have right now."

"You and me both. Go for it."

"After I match these."

They worked for about two hours, mostly in silence. Jeff set his phone for all calls from his 'church contacts' to go straight to voicemail. *I can't have them tying up the line if the kidnappers call.* He didn't need the "we're praying for you and Collin" well-wishers reminding him she had a very loyal fan base out there. Would they be so loyal if they knew the truth? *Which truth? She's pregnant? Or she committed adultery?*

You don't know that. No one knows that. But you keep thinking it. Erin's cell pinged. He growled. "Franny." He gave Jeff a sideways frown. "Here we go." He picked it up and put it on speaker phone. "Great news. I got my truck back."

"You did? When? Where is it? Is it safe?" Her voice picked up an octave in her excitement.

"Yes, I did. Yes, it's safe. My sister left it at a rental agency when she got the car. They'd been storing it for her. It's been in a locked yard. No one has been able to access it or disturb it in any way."

"Oh, Erik! I'm so happy! Do you have it back now?"

"Yes. I've got it, and it's safe."

"Where is it?"

"It's safe. What do you want me to do?"

"I need to make sure the money is still there, Erik. I can't have another mix-up. I don't know what the blackmailer will do if he doesn't get the money this time."

"I understand." Erin's voice remained cordial and restrained. Jeff gave him credit. His brother-in-law did know how to stay in character. "What do you want me to do?"

"If you tell me where the truck is, I can go and make sure the money is still where it's supposed to be. You can drive it over to Aunt Beela's like before."

The demand caught Erin off-guard. His eyes widened, then narrowed again. "I can drive it? I thought maybe you would want to deliver it yourself, so you know it's safe."

"No, no! I don't want to be anywhere near that man! I don't. And I told you, he expects you to deliver it. I told him it would be you, and that's who he wants to see."

"The last time I went out there, I nearly got killed. It's only by God's grace I didn't. What's to keep him from trying again? And succeeding this time?"

The woman's voice drowned in tears. "Erik! I need you to go. I do. I need you to do this for me. He won't hurt you if you bring the money. I know he won't."

Erin raised a hand palm up, inquiring. If he wanted support, Jeff had none to give. Nothing in his experience trained him to outsmart blackmailers, drug runners, or kidnappers. He shrugged. *I know I'm taking my frustration out on Erin. Guilt by association. She's his sister after all.*

Erin scowled at him but spoke to the phone. "Fine. I'll go. I would tell you the truck is in my garage, but since my garage doesn't exist, I'm at my brother-in-law's."

Jeff waved his hands back and forth. He didn't want anything to do with this exchange.

He got the point. "Except he needs his garage. Tell you what. I know a place near downtown. It's a service garage. You can come there, I'll bring the truck, and you can check to your heart's content. How about that?"

Long pause. "I don't know, Erik. It might be too out in the open. Too many people may watch what I'm doing."

"All they'll see is you climbing around the truck, just like the rest of the people at the garage."

Tears and sobs. "Oh, Erik! You're making this hard on purpose, aren't you? You want to punish me for the pictures. I know you do."

Erin rolled his eyes. "I don't care about the pictures. I don't want to see the pictures. I'm sorry I can't make it any easier. It has to be the garage downtown. I don't know what else to tell you."

"Could you bring it to my place? I could look at it here."

Jeff could hear the hesitation in Erin's voice. "I'm not comfortable with that idea. Your place is in a tough neighborhood."

The woman laughed, her voice high-pitched. "Oh, you silly! I live here. How scary can it be? Are you so afraid of my neighbors you won't bring your truck here? You're braver than that, aren't you?"

Jeff saw Erin's jaw tighten. "I'm not afraid."

"I know you're not, silly! So you'll bring it here, and I can check it out, and you can drive it to Aunt Beela's. You're the best boyfriend a girl could ever have. The address is 1550 Kingsford. I'll see you in about an hour. Love you, Erik."

Erin stared at the phone, his eyes narrowing even more. He swung to Jeff. "This feels like a set-up. I don't like it."

Jeff shrugged again. "They need you to take the truck. Nothing's going to happen." He ignored the nudge in his gut. And the one in his brain.

Erin cocked his head. "You don't think this is a bad idea?"

"She said she needs you to drive the truck. She's not going to let anything happen to her mule."

"I'm not so sure."

"If you're afraid to go, call her back and have her meet you here. I'd rather a bunch of drug runners didn't know my address, but it's up to you."

Erin picked up his keys and walked out. His phone remained on the counter. *He'll come back for it. He wouldn't head into trouble without it.* The engine revved on the truck, and Erin backed out of the driveway.

I should wave him down and give him his phone. He might need it.

He's a grown man, and I am not his keeper. Besides, his sister cheated on me.

And that justifies throwing him to the wolves? You're better than that.

Jeff scowled. He went back to the invoices in front of him. Why was it so hard to stay angry? Why did he keep caring what happened to Erin? Or Collin?

The nudge in his brain grew. *Why would Franny insist Erin drive? Why him? To get rid of witnesses? He drives, blackmailer kills him, no one knows anything. Or, she has him come to her house, he's killed there, and again, no one is the wiser. No loose ends.*

Jeff threw off the idea. She had no reason to kill Erin. Except…

Except he knows the story about the blackmailer. And knows she climbed around the truck. If somehow he were to "find" the drugs, he could implicate her. Might be reason enough for murder. But I'm not his…

Jeff pushed the papers across the bar, picked up the phone, and started for the door. Only to have it ring in his hand. He didn't recognize the number but picked it up anyway. "Erin's phone."

Pause. "Mr. Farrell?" Vy sounded confused.

"Yes. Erin forgot his phone. I'm chasing after him to give it to him."

"Where did he go?"

"He's taking his truck to Franny's house for her to inspect it. She insists he has to be the one to drive it to meet the blackmailer and asked him to come to her house so she could inspect the money."

Vy's voice became rich with concern. "You need to stop him. They may have changed plans and decided to eliminate him as a witness. We got lucky the first time, but I don't want to take any more chances."

Jeff ran to his car. "I'll catch him. He can't be too far."

"Hurry, Mr. Farrell. Give me the address, and I'll see if we can send someone out there. We may lose this bust, but better than losing an innocent life."

Jeff gunned his car down the street. He stopped at the corner. Which way? Which way? Shortest route? Or longest? "Lord…"

Will He answer me? After all this time?

"Lord, for Erin's sake, please. Which way did he go? Which way?"

The sure conviction Erin had turned to take the shortest route swelled in him. Jeff turned left and dodged and weaved through traffic. He kept his eyes glued to the road ahead, looking for the green truck. Three stop-lights down, he saw one. On closer inspection, it wasn't Erin's. He slapped the steering wheel in frustration. "Lord, please. For Erin. Please. Don't let my pride cost him his life."

Another three lights, another green truck. Still not Erin. Jeff yelled it. "I'm sorry! I'm sorry. I've been wrong, okay? I admit it. I'm wrong. I'll confess everything to everyone if You stop him from getting killed." Jeff sobbed. "It will be my fault. Like Collin being kidnapped is my fault. I admit it. Don't make them pay for my arrogance. Please."

Tears threatened to blur his vision. He shook them from his eyes and kept driving.

Two more lights, three more turns, and Jeff spotted the truck. Pulled over on the side of the road, a front tire flat on the pavement. Jeff pulled in behind him, wiped his face on his shirt, and got out. He walked beside Erin, who stood staring at the tire, tire iron in his hand.

Erin motioned to the tire. "Flat."

Jeff shrugged. His voice trembled. "Only on one side." He sniffed, then handed Erin's phone to him. "You forgot this."

"You chased after me to bring me my phone?"

"Yeah." He scuffed the ground. "Vy called."

"She did?"

"Yeah. She said don't go to Franny's."

"Really?"

"Yeah. She seemed to think they would kill you to eliminate witnesses."

Erin lifted his chin. "I see."

"Yeah. Probably why Franny wants you to drive the truck. So they can kill you when you get there."

Erin cocked his head sideways. "Imagine." He nodded. "Good thing you stopped me."

Jeff grabbed the tire iron. "Give me that thing. All you're going to do is hurt yourself with it."

"Probably true." Erin let go. "Good thing I had the flat tire, huh?"

Jeff kneeled, put the wrench on the tire, and strained against the lugnuts. "Yeah. Good thing." *God thing. I know it. Let me get him home. We'll talk. I swear we will.* He grunted and busted the first one loose. "Maybe give your crazy friend a call and tell her you can't make it. The truck is being towed to the garage."

Jeff yanked hard on the second lug. He heard the grinding of metal. "Flat tire. And busted lug." He threw the lug wrench on the pavement. "You need to oil those things once in a while, dude. Keeps 'em from freezing up like this."

Erin's eyes held more than a glint of light. His face wrinkled to a grin. "Thanks, Jeffman." He ignored the passing traffic and hugged Jeff in a manly bear hug. "Good to have you back."

Jeff grunted. "Yeah, well, I couldn't let you get killed and have to face Collin or Mom and Dad. I'd a' been joining you beyond those Pearly Gates."

Erin put in a call to Vy, then to Franny. He left it on speaker so she could hear the road noise. "I can't make it to your place. I got a flat, then busted a lug."

"What's a lug? It doesn't sound serious. People get flat tires all the time. Can't you change it and still come?"

"A lug is what holds the tire on the axle. It's not something I can fix out here."

The woman's voice sounded put out. Very put out. "Well, you have others, don't you? It takes more than one or two, right? So you could still get here missing one."

"Not safely, I can't."

Silence. "What are you going to do?"

"I'm having it towed to the garage downtown. You can meet us there, make sure your money is securely in place, and I'll drive the truck to Aunt Beela's tomorrow."

"Where will the truck be tonight?"

"Locked in the garage. It will be safe, believe me. No one will touch it."

Long pause. Snippy and curt described the answer. "Fine. I'll meet you there."

Erin gave her the address and hung up. He smiled at Jeff. "I think the bloom is off the rose."

Jeff chuckled. "Ya think?" He slapped a hand on Erin's shoulder. "Let's wait in my car. Might make us less-inviting targets."

"Truth."

* * *

Vy and company retrieved the wounded truck and towed it to the garage. Tobias, who actually did work on cars, fixed the lug and replaced the tire. He also found a second tire that needed to be changed and had everything ready to go when Franny pulled into the lot. Erin waited beside his vehicle until she walked over to him. Her face had become frozen into a permanent pout. She glared at the truck, then at Erin.

"I can't examine the money with you standing here. The same goes for all the people around here. No one can see me. Those are the rules."

Erin shrugged. "If that's the way it has to be, fine." He turned and walked into the office area of the station. Tobias followed him, leaving Franny to check out the payment to the blackmailer. Closed-circuit monitors recorded every move the woman made. They watched her feel under the side panel, under the rear wheel well, and underneath the bumper mounts. Satisfied the bricks were still where they should be, she got off the ground, dusted herself off, and walked into the office.

Erin started the conversation. "Is everything still where it should be?"

The pout didn't disappear. She jerked her head to the side, summoning Erin outside. He followed her out into the empty bay. She peered around to make sure no one was listening. "I don't like leaving this here. I don't think it's safe. I think it would be safer at my place, and you could come get it in the morning. I'd feel much better about it, Erik."

"I can't. I can't ask Jeff to drive me to your place in the morning. He's got a job, and he's got meetings all day. He's worrying about his wife being missing. It's not fair to him to keep dragging him out to take me places."

She sniffed. "He has to bring you here."

"It's on his way. Jeff is doing us a huge favor by just driving me around today so I can help you. I don't want to take advantage of him. We leave it here tonight, and I get it in the morning. Have you talked to the blackmailer and told him there is a change of times?"

"He called this afternoon. I told him you would be there before noon." She eyed him coldly. "You will be there by noon, right?"

He nodded. "Yes. I'll be there before noon. And I will go in and visit with Aunt Beela." He stepped back a bit. "Does Aunt Beela know what is going on at her place?"

The woman waved a hand. "She knows both of us. It's why he chose her place for the exchange. He knows Aunt Beela isn't going to call the police if she sees him sneaking around. He had to tell her about it, or she might have gotten her shotgun and killed him. She's a feisty old lady."

"I liked her. I enjoyed having tea with her."

She laughed. "Oh, Erik. That's what I love about you. You only see the good in people."

"Eh, not always. But I try." Vy had warned him they would not make the actual bust until they could get the 'blackmailer' wrapped up, then they would sweep Franny and her cohorts. Jump too early, and they risked losing one of the halves of the equation. With Franny changing the plan, Vy had offered Erin an alternative arrangement.

Erin hesitated. "Would it be okay if someone rode along with me?"

Franny's eyes narrowed, and her voice became sharp. "Who?"

"A cousin. My sister did one of those DNA registry things. We found some cousins on our mother's side we never knew existed. Two of them live right here in Oakton. I promised one of them, Vy, I would show her the farm our grandfather owned the next time I went to Fort Newton. It's right on the way to Aunt Beela's."

She pouted. "I don't like you stopping before you get to Beela's. Can't you stop after? That way I know you won't be late. You never know what might happen if you stop. You could be robbed. You could get another flat tire." The sarcasm dripped from her voice.

Erin remained calm. "The technician checked all the tires for me. I had to replace two of them. So no more flats. I promise I'll get your money to your blackmailer on time." He paused. "We'll go after we see your aunt. Will it be okay with you? And I can introduce Vy to Aunt Beela. Your aunt said she'd like to have more company visit. Vy's a great cook. She can bake a pie and take it with us to give to Beela. How does that sound?"

The woman snipped, "Oh, she can bake a pie, can she? How delightful."

Erin sighed. "Franny…she's my cousin. Okay? Not a romantic interest." *Not yet.*

She sniffed but seemed pacified. "Well, since you promised…I suppose I can let it go this time. And Aunt Beela will like having other people there. This once."

Erin stared at her sideways. "So your blackmailer will be okay with me having another person with me?"

The woman shrugged. "I'll call him and tell him. Since it's a woman and your cousin, he won't mind."

"Okay."

Franny climbed back in her car and gunned out of the parking lot. Erin walked into the waiting room. "Well, that went better than I expected."

Jeff chuckled. "Yeah, she left your manhood intact."

Vy's eyes crinkled at the corners. "What type of pie should I bake, Mr. Winger?"

Erin held his hands up in defense. "I don't know why I said half the things I did. Feel free to overrule any or all of it."

Vy laughed. "I'll have to see what I can whip up that's pie-shaped."

Jeff raised a hand. "The 'Pie Shop' is having a two-for-one sale. We'll stop on the way home and pick one—or two—up." He smiled. "You have a preference?" His eyes lost their light. "Collin loved—loves the place. She orders the dark chocolate cream with chocolate whipped cream." Erin noted the moisture in his brother-in-law's eyes.

Vy's voice was gentle in response. "Blackberry."

Jeff drew in a deep breath. "Blackberry it is. Come on, Erik, I've still got all those papers to get through."

Erin smiled at Vy. "Thanks for humoring me."

"I'll see you in the morning, Erin." Her eyes twinkled.

Erin tore himself away and followed Jeff out the door. They climbed into the car and left the parking lot at a speed well below Franny's. Jeff's voice was dry. "Your taste in women is improving."

Erin snorted. "After this last one, it could only go up." He punched Jeff in the shoulder. "Thanks for letting me drag you all over town today. And for stopping me from going to Franny's. And maybe getting killed."

Jeff kept his eyes on the road. "I set you up for it, Erin. Calling you scared for having misgivings. Forgive me?" He risked a glance at Erin.

"Of course."

He watched Jeff struggle with some internal thought. Finally, Jeff said, "I've been a jerk. Not the word I want to use, but it's the closest acceptable one."

"I can relate. To being one, I mean."

"Since the wedding. Before the wedding. When I thought I could pull a fast one on God and keep Collin safe."

Erin sat and said nothing. Jeff had to move through this at his own pace. "I can't excuse what I did…okay, I can excuse it, and I did. But I was wrong, I am wrong, and I'm sorry." Jeff's voice caught. He held out his hand to Erin, and it shook. "This is the first of many apologies I owe to people. Including your sister. If we find her."

Erin watched Jeff's eyes widen. *Reality must be hitting him. Hard.* "What if I don't?"

Erin took his hand, corrected him. "We'll find her. She's alive, Jeff. Wherever she is, she's alive. And we will get her back. I know it."

"I'll go with your gut. Mine is all screwed up with thinking taking her will be God's punishment for my arrogance." He glanced over at Erin. "That's what I thought when you took off today. My arrogance, my thinking I could play God, would get you killed. And probably Collin as well." Tears filled his eyes, and he brushed them off on his sleeve.

Erin drew his mouth into a straight line. "I can see it. From a 'God is a petty, vengeful god' mindset. Which He isn't."

"No, but He does let us suffer the consequences of our own actions and stupidities."

Erin pointed. "Pie Shop. In case you forgot."

Jeff chuckled. "I expected you to remind me."

The discussion went on hold until Erin and Jeff got home. And had consumed half the chocolate banana cream pie for dinner. Not dessert. Dinner.

Erin decided to reopen the talk as they sorted invoices. Paid, not paid, partially paid (the most frustrating of the piles). "So what do you believe about the pregnancy? Deep in your gut? Did my sister cheat on you?"

Jeff closed his eyes. Erin could see him struggling not to let the tears escape. His voice broke. "Lord, forgive me for ever thinking Collin would do something like have an affair. I am so sorry I ever thought it. I knew better. I knew it. But there was all the anger, the jealousy… I owe her everything." His eyes pleaded. "Will she take me back? Or did I screw up beyond repair?"

Erin reached out and put his hand on Jeff's shoulder. "I know one thing about my sister. She will forgive. And she will love you the rest of your life. Jerk though you are." Erin harrumphed. "And that's not the word I wanted to use, either."

Jeff laughed once. "I deserve it." He stared at the floor. "I don't know how to make it up to her."

"Love her. Raise those babies right. Let me spoil them and send them home."

Jeff gave Erin the side-eye. Erin grinned. "Thought while you were feeling repentant, I'd throw that in there. We can scratch the last one."

"You. I should make you move in with us to help be nanny to them."

"I believe the proper term is 'manny.' At least for now. Subject to change."

Jeff crinkled a wad of paper and tossed it across the room toward the trash. "Missed."

Erin decided to follow suit. "Swish."

Jeff grinned at him. "Oh, it's on."

"Bring it, big guy."

Half an hour and a floor littered in paper wads later, emotions were sufficiently released. While Erin scooped up the misses, Jeff made a pot of coffee. Erin cocked his head and studied his brother-in-law sideways. Jeff shrugged. "Figured it would help me stay awake while I'm praying for Collin. I've got a few days to make up for."

"Make two. I'm not sleeping tonight either. I'd rather be praying with you than lying in bed, creating bad endings to scenarios for tomorrow."

Jeff poured two large mugs out. "Has Vy told you whether she still thinks these cases are connected?"

Erin took the coffee. "She told me she was certain that Franny and her connections aren't the ones who kidnapped Collin. She can't tell me how she knows. That's a company secret. But she's certain enough it won't impact Collin that she is letting the case go forward." *I want to believe that, Lord. Help me believe. Or at least act like I trust Vy about it.*

Jeff changed subjects. "How do they pull you out? They're not going to let you drive all the way into the meet-up, are they?"

"Vy says we will stop somewhere convenient. I'll ride with the recovery team. A fake me drives the rest of the way in. She said there were too many variables beyond that. But her team can handle any of them." Erin smiled but felt anything but joyous. "She reminded me she does this for a living."

"Can't fault her dedication."

"No." Erin drew in a deep breath. "Anyhow, I get a free ride home, the bad guys, including Aunt Beela, I guess, get a ride to jail. And we take $2.75 million worth of heroin off the streets of Fort Newton."

"A good afternoon's work."

"If it all goes the way it should."

Erin prepared a place in the living room by the couch. Jeff kneeled beside Collin's rocking chair. Erin grabbed a Bible and laid it beside him. The thought of replacing his after the explosion hurt. All those notes. All the cross-references. All the maps painstakingly drawn. How do you recreate it?

You don't. You start over. New notes. New highlighting. New insights. Which is why the Scripture says His Word is new every morning.

Erin lowered his head. "Fine." He kneeled on the carpet, leaned his elbows on the coffee table. And so storming the gates of Heaven began.

THURSDAY

Jeff woke first and made coffee. He'd stayed up until nearly three; Erin had fallen asleep sometime before then. Jeff hadn't bothered waking him to send him to bed. He'd thrown a blanket over him, tucked a pillow under his head, and left him on the couch in the living room.

The smell of fresh-brewed coffee gave Jeff strength for the day. An idea began brewing with the coffee. Maybe not a good idea, but it gave him something to go on in his search for Collin. He needed to find her, apologize, and bring her back. Period.

Erin drifted into the kitchen on the smell of the elixir of life. He took a seat at the bar and lay his head on the table. "Wake me when it's ready."

Jeff chuckled. He felt lighter today. The veil of shadow he'd lived under the past few months—three years—was gone. The weight of Collin's absence remained, but now he had hope. He poured two mugs of coffee and slid one to Erin.

Erin lifted his head high enough to get his first sips of liquid starter fluid. He sat straight, stretched, cracked his neck and shoulders. "Thanks for the coffee. And the pillow. What time do you want to head to get the truck?"

"What time do you need to be on the road?"

"Takes two hours to get to Aunt Beela's. We should leave the garage no later than nine-thirty. Nine if we have to stop and make a driver change."

Jeff checked his phone. Google maps said his destination required one and one-half hour's driving time. "Nine should work. I'll trail you as far as your grandfather's farm."

Erin's eyes narrowed. "What are you thinking?"

"If the drone footage got Collin kidnapped and your place blown up, searching the area should be a good place to start looking for her."

Erin shook his head. "Um…did you think this all the way through? Have you run it by Detective Troutman?"

"I'm going to call him before I leave. If he can't tell me he has someone out searching the area already, I'm going to do it for him."

Erin drew in a deep breath. "Okay. But can you wait until I can help? Like, get done with the drug bust? Or we can switch drivers there, and I go with you?"

Jeff stayed firm. "Erin, you have your mission this morning. This is my mission. I'm not saying you can't help, but finding Collin is my responsibility. I'll leave it to you to call the police if I don't come out of the woods."

Erin let out the breath he'd been holding. "I knew you were going to say that. Okay, brother of mine, we're both in it. And trusting God for the outcomes."

"Amen."

The men changed clothes, loaded the car with essentials which might or might not help them in the coming battle, Jeff put in the call to Detective Troutman, and they drove to the counterfeit garage.

Franny waited outside the door. Jeff grunted. "Bet she wants to ride along."

"No bet. She doesn't want to be tied in with this shipment. Plausible deniability. Or something along those lines."

"Probably right. She's your problem. And good luck with her."

Erin grumbled something unintelligible and got out of the car. He grabbed his backpack and smiled at his former girlfriend. "Good morning."

Franny's face retained the pout from the night before. "It will be if you get this money to Aunt Beela's on time."

"It'll get there. No mix-ups this time." Erin motioned to a car pulling in. "There's Vy, my cousin. She said she'd be here on time, and she is. Everything is going to go exactly as planned."

She snorted. "I'll believe it when I see it."

Jeff made sure to intercept Vy before she got out of her car. He carried the all-important blackberry pie in front of him so Franny wouldn't see it. He handed it to Vy as she sat behind the wheel. "Don't forget this."

Vy smiled at him. "After all the hard work I put in to make it? No way. Do you know how hard it is to harvest enough blackberries to put in a pie?"

Jeff chuckled. "I'll bet. But only the freshest ingredients for Aunt Beela, I'm sure."

Vy slid out of the car, took the pie from Jeff. "Of course." Her eyes narrowed. "What are you doing today?"

"Going looking for my wife."

Vy's lips drew into a straight line. Her head went down. "I thought as much. Please be careful. Just because they kidnapped your wife is no guarantee they won't kill you."

"I know. I'm willing to take the chance. I need my wife. I'm not complete without her." *Which I should have figured out before this.* Jeff smiled at Vy, but a sad smile. "Whatever it takes."

Vy nodded. "I understand."

They walked over to join Franny and Erin. Erin made the introductions of Vy to Franny and Franny to Vy. Vy extended her hand. Franny didn't. Her eyes narrowed as she stared from Erin to Vy and back again. "Cousin?"

"On my mom's side. Her sister's daughter."

The woman continued to eye Vy with suspicion and distaste but said nothing. Vy held the pie. "See? I remembered. I hope it's edible."

Erin chuckled. "I'm sure it will be."

The garage bays were full, and technicians were busy examining under the hoods of cars, surveying undercarriages, draining oil… Jeff approved to himself. *You'd think this really was a garage. I'd bring my car here. I'd bring all the company cars here.*

Erin's truck sat by itself in an empty bay. Erin dangled the keys at the drug runner. "Are we good to go, or do you want to check it out one more time?"

The woman's eyes narrowed further as she stared at the truck. She walked around it twice then sneered at Erin, "You can take it. But you better be there by noon. I won't take any responsibility for you if you're not there by noon."

"I know. This isn't a man to play with. He tried to kill me once before. I'm not going to give him a chance again. Vy and I will be at Aunt Beela's by noon, and he can get his money. I'm assuming you will know where he puts the flash drive."

"Of course I will. I'm not stupid."

"I never thought you were." Erin turned to Jeff. "I'll see you later."

Jeff clapped a hand on Erin's shoulder. "Be careful, Erin. I don't want to lose you." Jeff's throat tightened unexpectedly.

Erin hesitated. "Can we pray before we go?"

Jeff smiled. "I think that's a great idea."

Erin extended the invitation to Vy. "Join us?"

Vy smiled. "Of course. I never turn down a prayer meeting."

Erin turned to Franny. "You in?"

"I have important things to do. I just came to make sure you were here and going. I'll wait to hear you got there." She climbed in her car but didn't leave the parking lot. Jeff guessed she would wait until the truck actually pulled out. *Suspicious to the end.*

Jeff, Vy, and Erin huddled together, hands on each others' shoulders. Erin started. "Thank You, Lord. Just thank You. You know, You see, You are here. Guide us. Your will be done. It's all we can ask."

Vy's voice was soft. "If there's room in it, see us all through safely. Protect us. Help us be and do all You would want."

Jeff finished simply. "Thank You. Amen." He hugged Erin, grinned at Vy. "Not on a first date, I know."

"Not 'til I'm off duty. Be safe, Jeff."

Jeff pointed at Erin. "You, too. No heroics."

"Moi? No chance." Erin raised a thumb to Jeff. "Same to you, man. Kids need their dad."

Jeff raised his thumb in return. "I know."

The group climbed in their respective cars and dispersed. Jeff took the short way to the beltline, so he could fall in line behind Erin. He held back far enough to see Erin but not be right on his bumper.

Traffic slowed them around the off-ramp. After that, they had clear sailing all the way to the Benton Bridge, separating Indiana and Ohio. The little convoy turned north and headed to Ft. Newton. Erin, Vy, and any company Vy had, would pass on through Ft. Newton to the northern side, while Jeff's target, the Mudd property, lay on the south end. He turned off the highway, followed the GPS directions to a fork in the road. Jeff followed the right fork around Chapel Hill, over Duke's Creek, past Finnigan's barn, to a dirt road with fencing and a gate saying, "KEEP OUT."

He parked in front of the gate, then sat and stared at the overgrown stretch of trees, shrubs, tangled moss, and willow. This was the spot. Erin had launched his drone from here. Jeff verified he still had no response from Detective Troutman. *Okay. Here we go.*

Jeff opened the door, swung his feet out, and stopped. *Do I know what I'm doing? Really, really know what I'm doing?*

I'm looking for my wife. For Collin. God, be in this, please. I can't do it without You. I've always known that, but I wanted to do it my way. I screwed it all up, and I need You to fix it. Help me, Lord. Please.

Jeff stood, grabbed his backpack of essentials, and closed the door. He climbed over the fence and began walking to the tree line. He followed the line as it grew from two trees thick to three to four to he couldn't tell how thick the grove might be. No property markers indicated he'd crossed the boundary into the neighboring fields. Jeff continued walking the stand of trees, looking for disruptions of any kind. Footsteps. Wires. Poles. Anything of human origin.

The land dipped and rolled, but not so severely he ever lost sight of the car. Jeff walked half an hour, stopped for a break. Walked half an hour. Stopped for a break. Walked half an hour…

At the two-hour mark, he stopped and tried to judge the distance he'd walked. He tried to match what he remembered from the drone video to what he saw around him. If he guessed right, the building would be where the grove dipped away from the natural curve of the land. Right about…there.

Jeff entered the woods and searched for the building. Nothing. He tried walking further in. He pulled a pink flag on a tall spike from his backpack and shoved it into the ground. "Better than breadcrumbs." He marked his path every five yards or so, confident he would be able to retrace his way out. So long as no one moved the flags.

He walked and flagged and walked and flagged and walked and flagged for another hour. No building. No footprints. Nothing of any kind to lead him to Collin. Jeff sat at the base of a tree and took out the lunch he'd brought. He snorted. "No, I will not take a nap and let the leprechauns play with my flags." He rested long enough to eat his sandwich (PBJ, the only thing he could think of not requiring refrigeration) and an apple, climbed back to his feet and started off again.

Two more hours of walking led him nowhere. Well, it led him somewhere, but not to any mysterious building. Nor to the whereabouts of Collin. Jeff could feel his hope failing as the day wore on. He checked his watch; he'd been searching for five hours. Time to turn around and go back, or he'd lose the light and be walking in the dark. This far from civilization, it would be dark indeed.

Jeff bowed his head. "Lord, I thought this would be a good idea. I thought You would let me find her. It's hard, and I don't want to leave. I want Collin back. Please, Lord. Help me. Give me some way to know what to do next. In Your will, Lord."

He stood with his head bowed for several moments. No inspiration came. No voice or light gave him any hope. He sighed and started back, picking up his flags as he returned the way he came.

Or was it? The flags were still there. But he didn't remember planting one so close to a stump. Maybe he just didn't remember correctly. The next two seemed fine…or close to it. As close as memory served.

The ones after seemed to follow a straight course. But did they? Or were they curving, and he couldn't see it? *I'm getting paranoid. Fool.*

Jeff stopped. "Lord, lead me. Show me which way to go. Help me."

With nothing further to go on, he continued following the markers. The feeling they were not leading him out of the forest grew in him. Confirmation came when he walked into a clearing in the middle of the stand of trees. One of his flags stood tall in the center. A good many others, if not all of the rest of them, lay in a pile beside it.

Jeff walked into the circle, picked up his flag, then the others, and put them in his backpack. He scanned the area. "Okay, you've got me. Now what? You leave me here to wander around, digging grubs and hoping somehow I find my way out before I die of starvation or old age?"

No one answered. He glanced around the circle again. "If you're going to kill me, do it and be done with it. I can't stop you. The Lord can, so it's really up to Him." He turned in small circles, trying to see someone, anyone.

No one. "I'm going to climb the tallest of the trees here, and tonight, when the stars and the moon come out, I'm going to find my way out of here." He gave a half-chuckle. "Once a scout, always a scout."

He walked the perimeter of the clearing, examining the trees for a likely candidate. He continued to talk all the while. "This one looks like you could get a good start up it. Limbs are low. But it tapers too early to get you high enough to see anything." He tapped a second trunk. "This fellow is tall enough, but he doesn't have any way to get to the upper limbs." Jeff bypassed the next few. He came to a large, fat, stately sycamore. He smiled. "This one. This one will work. I can even cross over to the taller one next to it."

He circled one last time. If he was being watched, he couldn't tell it. He put his backpack securely over his shoulders, pulled the straps tight. "No time like now."

His back to the clearing, Jeff reached for the lowest branch. As he caught it, he heard the snap of a twig breaking. He spun around.

His brain had one instant to register a man in camo behind him. He held a rifle. The rifle butt snapped Jeff's head up as it whacked him in the chin. Consciousness lasted seconds long enough to feel the blow to the back of his head. And then darkness.

* * *

Erin and Vy followed the highway around Ft. Newton to the north end and off to the west for three miles. From there, the direction said to pass three stoplights, two schools (one elementary, one secondary), then turn left at the convenience store. Drive another five miles, turn right on Barnam Road. The third house on the left belonged to Aunt Beela.

Vy and Erin talked about nothing more important than what sports she liked, which ones she participated in, how long she'd been with the DEA, and why. Erin grew more and more enthralled with the younger woman. He liked driving and talking. He could do this all day.

When they reached the convenience store, Vy motioned for Erin to stop. Her eyes narrowed, and her face drew into a frown. "Samish should have called by now. He said he'd tell me when to make the switch." She checked her phone. "I expected it to be sooner." She punched in a number. No answer. "No bars. There's no service here." She scowled. "That's weird. We're not that far from civilization."

Erin pulled his out of his shirt pocket. "Try mine. Maybe it's your carrier."

Vy frowned. "No. You don't have any reception, either."

"Hmm. Okay. What do you want to do?"

Vy checked the time. "We've got half an hour leeway. We can wait here for the team to catch up."

"With only half an hour, I'd rather wait closer to the house. No chance of being late. But this is your mission. Your call."

Vy's eyes narrowed and moved side to side. She nodded once. "Agreed. We can make the switch closer. But this not having cell service bugs me. I don't like it."

Erin shrugged. "I see it a lot around here. The towers are stretched far apart. People don't want an ugly mass of steel obscuring their scenic view of the neighbor's cows. Or their own soybeans and corn. Come on, Vy. Do you want a tower in your yard?"

Vy laughed. "If I had a yard, I might object. My apartment has plenty of towers around. Towers and skyscrapers and the cement jungle." She smiled at him. "I imagine you live somewhere with more scenery."

Erin shrugged. "Right now, I'm living with my brother-in-law and my sister. They have a nice place, and yes, it's surrounded by trees and nature and some wildlife. Very comfortable. Needs kids, but…"

Erin trailed off. *Yes, I forgave him. But those are my nieces and nephews she's carrying. I want to spoil them and give them all the things Cane and I never had. But we have to find Cane first. And she still needs to beat the odds and survive. If that quack physician is right. He probably knows as much about obstetrics as he does urology.*

Vy touched his arm. "You—we—will find your sister. I know it. God loves her, and He's with her."

Erin let out a small sigh. "I know He is. And I have hope He will bring her back."

They drove on. Vy's efforts to contact her team failed. Without cell service, there was no answer and no way to flag them. By the time they reached Barnam Road, Erin could see the muscles in Vy's jaw tighten. Her hands, beautiful as they were, were clenched in fists. Vy motioned for Erin to pull to the side of the road.

"I don't like this at all, Erin. You shouldn't be anywhere near this house. You shouldn't be within ten miles of here. This is all wrong."

Erin felt the tension as well. "I don't know what to do, Vy. We have to deliver this truck in the next half-hour. We can sit here and wait fifteen minutes, but we have to go. If I have to drive it all the way, I'll drive it. Didn't you say there would be a team surrounding Aunt Beela's place?"

"There should be. I wouldn't take a team into a bust like this without knowing the area had been secured."

"Which means you have to trust you have back-up, right?"

Vy growled. But slightly. "I know what you're driving at, Erin. I have to trust what I can't see. That works with God, but in this line of work, we need the assurance our people are in place. I've known too many good agents who got hung out to dry when their backup didn't show, or went to the wrong house, or had a million and one things go wrong. If it were just me, I'd go for it. But you're a civilian, and I'm against the idea of taking you in with me."

Erin smiled. Small smile. "I'm a volunteer, Vy. You're not taking me anywhere I don't know about. I know the risks, and I'm not stupid. I want to see this through. I want these guys off the streets and behind bars. Including Franny. Especially Franny."

Vy sniffed. She checked her gun at her waist. "You're not carrying any weapons, are you?"

"Nope. Didn't want to learn." He smiled crookedly. "Might be nice to have about now."

"It's better you don't. Your job is to stay out of the line of fire, got it? I do not want to write paperwork on why a civilian got shot during my raid. You hear me, Mr. Winger?"

"I hear you. Stay out of the line of fire and keep my head down. No heroics. I leave everything to the professionals."

"That's what I want to hear." She checked her phone. "Fifteen minutes. We have to go now." She bowed her head. "Lord, watch over us. In Jesus's Name."

Erin added, "Amen."

He pulled the truck back onto the road, turned down Barnam, and drove to Aunt Beela's.

They pulled into the dirt driveway with five minutes to spare. The drapes and blinds were open, but Erin's feeling went from uneasy to bad. No car in the driveway. He remembered seeing at least a couple the last time he'd been here. "No cars. There were cars the last time." Vy shifted the pie to her left hand. Erin took it from her. "Let me carry it. I can use it as a weapon if I need to." He grinned. "Probably be lethal if I cooked it and they ate it. But I'll do what I can."

Vy laughed. "You are good for my soul, you know? Thanks."

Erin shrugged. "Hey, I'm always good for a laugh at inappropriate times. Now seemed like one of those."

Vy slipped out of the truck. "It is."

Erin stepped out and called, "Aunt Beela! I brought company."

An unshaven man peered out from behind the drapes. He let the drapes fall back into place. No sound came from the house.

Lord, now would be a great time for some direction. Do I pick up a rock? Five of them? Help, please?

Fear knocked, peace answered. Erin raised his brows and turned to Vy. She shrugged slightly, put on her best smile. They walked to the doorway together. Erin stepped on the landing and knocked. "Aunt Beela! It's Erin. Franny's friend. I brought my cousin with me for a visit." He grinned at Vy. "And she baked a pie. Can we come in?"

The door opened. Aunt Beela wore the same size double X dress and paisley pinafore she'd had on the last time Erin came. Her hair, gray and thinning, fell uncombed around her face. Her eyes were red and puffy, swollen from obvious crying. She shuffled back to let Erin in. "Come in, son." She eyed Vy up and down, up and down. She snuffled, but added, "You too, young woman."

Erin scrunched to study her level in the eyes. "What's wrong, Beela?"

She sniffled. "Bad news. Worst news ever."

Erin continued to stand on the landing, unwilling to go inside without an explanation. "What news, Aunt Beela?"

"My son. Wilbur? The one I told you about?"

"The one in prison, yes."

She sniffled hard. "He's been killed. Someone killed him in his cell. I got the letter about an hour ago."

Erin reached around and gave Beela a strong hug. "I'm sorry, Beela. It's terrible to hear news like that. Is there anything I can do? Do you need a ride anyplace?"

Beela hugged him back. "No, no. I'll be fine. It's a shock, that's all. Just a shock. They said he'd be getting out in another year. But now…"

Her entire body began to shake with the sobs. "Now I don't know what I'm going to do! He was my baby."

Erin continued to hug Beela, hold the pie, and try to stare over her shoulder. The man who had been in the window had disappeared. Erin let Beela go and caught her eyes again. "Are you going to be okay? Maybe this is a bad time for us to visit. We can leave and come back another time."

Beela blew her nose on her apron. "Nonsense. You drove all the way out here. The least I can do is be hospitable. Even in my sorrow." She stared at Vy, and her eyes narrowed slightly. "You say she's a cousin? Really?"

"On my mom's side. My sister did some genealogy and found we had a whole raft of aunts, uncles, and cousins we didn't know we had growing up. It's been fun getting to meet them. Vy is related to my mom's sister's husband's first wife."

If Beela followed Erin's explanation, her eyes didn't show it. She smiled instead. "Come on in, both of you. I got coffee in the kitchen. It'll go good with pie." She opened the door wider. Erin and Vy walked in carefully. Erin noted Vy's eyes searching behind doorways, looking down halls, trying to see around corners. Still on high alert. Not that he blamed her. His own "flight-or-fight" sense had him on edge as well. The man he'd seen still needed to be accounted for.

The kitchen remained stuck in 50s décor. Black and white checkered floor. The red metal table and four chairs. The white vinyl-covered, flannel-backed tablecloth decorated with roosters and chickens. Valance curtains sporting singing coffee cups. Wood cabinets painted yellow. Gas range with a tea kettle on it. Erin heard it whistling in his mind.

Beela poured three coffee cups—not mugs, cups—of coffee and set them on the table. She got out plates and forks, cut and served pie to Erin and Vy, served herself a generous portion, and sat. After everyone had tasted the pie and declared it wonderful, Erin returned to the matter of Wilbur. "Do you have someone to stay with you, Aunt Beela? Someone to help you out with Wilbur's affairs?"

Beela gave out a deep, deep sigh. "My middle son, Bertherd. You might have seen him in the window. He's here for the month. He's been out on parole for a few weeks and is still looking for work. I told him he could stay with me until he found a job. He stays in his room most the time. Says he's job hunting by looking through magazines. I don't know anyone that's got hired that way, but he keeps promising me he's gonna do it."

Erin cocked his head. "What's he doing for wheels? I didn't see any cars out front when we came in."

Beela laughed. "My other son Harold borrowed the car to go to Fort Newton. He's got a job interview today."

Vy slid into the conversation. "What does Harold do?"

"Nothing until he gets a job. All my sons had a tough upbringing. My late husband was a good man but lazy, you know? Couldn't keep a job to save his life. Spent most of his money before he earned it."

Beela took another sizeable bite of the pie. "I worked odd jobs to keep the roof over our heads and put some food on the table, but the boys saw their father living free and decided they wanted to try living that way, too. I tried to teach them differently, but you know how young people can be. Life had to teach them the hard way."

Erin suggested, "Sometimes it's the only way a person learns."

Beela nodded solemnly. "Don't I know it."

Vy moved the pie around on her plate. "How do you keep the house, Ms. Beela? Do you have help paying the bills?"

Beela smiled, and her joy reached to her eyes and beyond. "Oh, my oldest, Mason. He works in town. He's a salesman. A pharmaceutical representative. He pays the mortgage and the electric. I grow some herbs and plants in the greenhouse and sell those and fresh eggs to get cash for food and the like. Of all of them, he's the only one turned out decent." She buried a chuckle behind a withered hand. "Don't tell the others I said so."

Erin felt a knot in the pit of his stomach, and it had nothing to do with the pie. *Great. We're going to bust her son, and this poor woman will be left out in the cold. Lord, I hate this.*

Vy's eyes reflected interest. "Oh? Do you know what company he works for?"

"No, honey, I don't. Are you looking for work around here, too?"

"I'm always looking for work, Ms. Beela."

"Call me Aunt Beela. The rest of the world does."

Vy smiled. "Okay, yes, Aunt Beela. I'm always interested in new opportunities. Especially in the Fort Newton area."

"Well, I can give your name and phone number to my son. If he knows of any opening, he can call you."

"Does he have a business card? I'm between phones, and it would be easier if I called him to tell him what I can do rather than wasting his time."

"Very considerate, Vy, dear. Let me see if I can dig one out of the drawer there."

Beela stood and walked to the kitchen counter. She pulled open the drawer.

An impulse from outside himself ordered, *Down! Now!*

Erin didn't question the impulse but dragged Vy with him. A shotgun blast came through the door, blowing all the place settings off the table. Erin pulled the table over the top of himself and Vy, angling it to provide some element of protection.

Beela screamed. Vy rolled to the right, gun drawn, to return fire. Erin rolled to the left to grab Beela and shoved her behind the table. Beela's eyes were wide as the pie plates. She looked from Erin to the holes in the table back to Erin. He patted her shoulder. "Don't move and keep your head down." He placed himself between the table and Beela. Wouldn't be much of a shield for him, but would be for her. He peered out behind the edge to find Vy.

Vy crouched behind the doorway, her eyes swinging back and forth. She fired twice and moved from the right to the left. Another blast from the shotgun tore through the wallboard. Beela stuffed her fist in her mouth and screamed again, but muted this time. Erin put his hands on the woman's shoulders to look her in the eyes. "Do you have any firearms in the house?"

She pointed to a lever-action rifle sitting in the corner of the kitchen. Erin looked. "Good. Is it loaded?"

She whispered, "Have to keep the gophers and the possums out of the garden."

Erin smiled. "Good woman, Aunt Beela." Erin watched Vy to see where her head was looking. Vy began firing to give him cover. He counted, *1 – 2 – 3*, rolled, retrieved the rifle, and rolled back to shelter Beela again. He checked the cylinder to see how many rounds were available, then hustled Beela down the hallway to the back. "Where is Bertherd?"

The woman sobbed. "Being smart. Hiding under his bed, I bet."

Erin opened a bedroom door. He pushed her in gently. "Close this door. Get behind the bed or the dresser or something really sturdy. Don't come out until you hear Vy or me call you, got it?"

Beela's eyes hadn't lost their deer-in-headlights look, but she nodded. Erin reached in and kissed the woman on her forehead. "Good. We'll be right back." *Keep this woman safe, Lord. And protect Vy. Your will, Lord.*

Erin returned to the kitchen. He placed himself at the opposite side of the doorway as Vy but did not peek outside. "What's it look like?"

"It looks like too many of them and too few of us. I don't hear my backup anywhere." She shook her head. "I'm sorry, Erin."

Erin shrugged. "We're not dead yet. And hey, if it goes bad, I get to enter Heaven with a beautiful woman on my arm. What more could a guy ask for?"

Vy rolled her eyes. "You are a mess, you know that, Erin Winger?"

"Yeah, I've been told a time or two." He risked a quick look around the doorpost. "What do we do?"

"Pray for backup."

"Been doing that. What's next?"

"I'm going to draw their fire. See if you can tell where from and how many."

"Let me draw the fire. I'm a bigger target. They'll see me better." He didn't wait for Vy to argue. Erin popped into view and as quickly dropped back down again. He slid down as flat as he could manage as bullets and shrapnel from a shotgun blew through the wall. He felt something strike him in the hip. The muscles reacted; Erin didn't. He called to Vy. "How many?"

"Two. Behind the truck."

No sooner had Vy finished when another firearm sounded from further up the lane. Instead of shooting at the house, however, the shot ricocheted off Erin's truck. *Cavalry?*

Competition, more likely.

Vy risked a glance out the door to see who the new shooter might be. She ducked back into her position. "New guy is behind the yellow van. Do you remember it being there when we came in?"

"No. Didn't look. Opinion?"

"The enemy of my enemy is my friend. Until he isn't."

"But we gotta live to find out."

"Granted. I say concentrate on the two behind the truck, then we worry about new guy."

Erin pumped the lever twice, shouldered the rifle, and expertly placed two shots, shattering front and back windows simultaneously.

For a single moment, both shooters were exposed. Vy rolled out, fired, and the odds went from two to one. She rolled back to safety. "I thought you said you couldn't shoot."

"No, I said I didn't want to learn. I learned, but I didn't want to." Erin popped off two more shots. "Best advice I ever got: 'aim for the middle, you're bound to hit something.'" Erin jerked his head to the side. "New guy is moving up."

The man behind the yellow van redeployed to a vantage point one tree closer than he had been. His movement drew fire from the shooter behind Erin's truck. Vy slipped out the door, came in behind the right side of the truck, and drew down on the man. "Hands! Show me hands!"

The culprit showed his hands by attempting to shoot at Vy. She was quicker. The man lay still. Dead. Vy pointed her gun at the man behind the tree. "Hands!"

The man lowered his weapon, lay it on the ground, and stepped out, smiling. "Nice shooting, lady. Very nice."

Vy didn't put her gun away. "Who are you? What do you have to do with this?"

The man continued to smile but kept his hands in the air. "That's my mom's house they were shooting at." He lost the smile. "She okay?"

Erin rolled to his feet. He felt the sting in his side but forced himself to walk down the hallway. He called, "Aunt Beela! It's safe. You can come out now. Are you okay?"

Beela's head peeked around the doorway. "Is it over?"

"Yeah. There's someone out here saying you're his mom. Will you vouch for him?"

Beela came into the kitchen, took one look at the man outside with Vy, and collapsed into a chair. "Yes! That's my oldest boy, Mason."

Bertherd ambled in from the back, none too steady on his feet. He leaned against the refrigerator, looking lost.

Vy holstered her gun. Mason ran into the kitchen and threw his arms around Beela. "You okay, Mom? You're not hurt?"

"No, and it's thanks to these two." Beela did a quick introduction of Erin and Vy to Mason. "I don't know what I would have done if they hadn't been here. Who were those two hooligans? What did they want?"

Erin started to speak, stopped. Even now, he still felt a check in his gut. He deferred to Vy, who said, "I don't know, Aunt Beela. Maybe Mason will recognize them." She smiled at the older woman. "Perhaps you better call the police."

Mason held up a hand. "Let's see who they were. Maybe I can figure out what they wanted." He motioned his head to have Vy follow him outside. Vy raised an eyebrow at Erin. She walked outside and followed Mason around the truck.

Erin examined below his shirt. "Aunt Beela, do you have a first aid kit handy?"

Her eyes went wide again. "Are you hurt?"

Erin shrugged. "A scratch. Don't want to get blood all over your house, though."

The woman jumped to her feet and went to the back of the house. She called as she walked, "I have one back here. I've never used it. Mason got it for me from his company. He says they were passing them out as promotional items, and who better to promote it than his mother?"

Beela returned with the kit. It did indeed look like a bonafide first aid kit, with a logo and everything. Erin tried to reverse his thinking about Mason. Beela handed him the case. Erin noted the plastic around the kit to prevent tampering had been removed. *Okay, maybe. Maybe not.*

Erin thanked her and went to the back to patch his side without observers. The shrapnel had lodged deep in the crook of his hip. There would be no extracting it on his own. *There go the Olympics. Oh, well.* He staunched the blooding with a gauze pad, taped another one on top of it, added a third one for good measure, then returned himself and the kit to its owner. He handed it to Beela with a smile. "Thank you. I think I've got it taken care of."

Before Beela could leave to put the first aid supplies away, Vy and Mason walked back into the kitchen. Vy's eyes were somber, but she said nothing. Mason hugged his mom again. "I don't know either one of them. My guess is they were trying to steal the truck. They didn't expect anyone to fight back." He picked up his phone. "I'll call the sheriff. Bertherd, come outside with me."

As Mason spoke on the phone, Erin slipped his phone partially out of his pocket. Still no bars. Things were not looking up. He held Vy's eyes a moment. She waved him off. He didn't understand what she was trying to tell him. Erin turned to Beela. "I'm sorry we brought those crooks on you, Aunt Beela."

She threw her hands in the air. "Pshaw. If it wasn't your truck, it would have been Mason's. Crooks are crooks. They were just looking for a quick buck."

Mason got off the phone. "Mom, the sheriff is tied up over in Quincy right now. He asked if I could take the bodies to the morgue for him. Otherwise, they'll have to stay there until tomorrow, and I don't want you being upset every time you look outside. I'll take pictures of everything, all the damage, where the bodies are, then Bertherd and I will load them into the van, and I'll drive them in. Won't take us very long."

Erin glanced at his truck, then at Vy. "I guess it will make it back across the river."

Mason argued. "No, no. You two will need to give your statements to the sheriff tomorrow. He's going to want to hear from you about what happened and when. Could you spend the night here with Mom if you don't mind? I'm sure she will feel much safer having company. I have more runs to make this afternoon and tonight, but I will be back in the morning, Mom. With the sheriff. Okay?"

He waited for Beela, who nodded. "Of course. And I want to fix you two a good meal for dinner, for helping me out. I wouldn't feel right letting you drive off with no thanks. Please? Humor an old woman?"

Erin eyed Vy; she tipped her head yes. Erin said, "I guess we can stay. The least I can do is help patch the holes those men put in your house. Wouldn't want the possums and the gophers coming in looking for a handout."

Erin waited until Mason and Bertherd had reached the back of his truck. "I think I've got some tools in the hatch. Let me go look."

He limped out, waited until the two brothers loaded the first man in the van, then came for the second one. Erin called Mason over. "Got a second, man?"

Mason appeared suspicious. "Yeah. What's up?"

Erin pulled out his phone and showed Mason no bars. "Been the same all the way here. You weren't talking to the sheriff. Now you're moving evidence. What's up is what I want to know."

Mason stepped away from the house a little further. "Phone service has been down for three days now. Mom lives out here by herself, and she gets scared if she can't get in touch with people. She only has a landline, so I convinced her it was just her phone and not the whole area being out. I've been pretending to have service here at the house, then calling when I get into range." He motioned his head to Erin. "I appreciate you not challenging me about it in there."

"Your mom is a sweet woman, and she deserves to be treated well."

Mason chuckled. "Sweet woman? Mom? Of course she is. How'd you meet her, anyhow?"

"A friend in town. Franny Landsford. She sent me this way a week or so ago, telling me she had a package for her Aunt Beela." Erin stopped. "It's a long story after that."

Mason's face darkened. "Franny. She's no relation to Mom. She's a drug runner and a…well, let's say she's not well-liked here."

Erin held up his hands. "Sorry. Not fond of her myself these days."

Mason clapped Erin on the shoulder. "It's summer, and these boys aren't going to smell any nicer than they do now. I know I'm 'moving evidence' but I can't let them lay there all night and into tomorrow. I will call the sheriff when I get in range. Then I'll get them into the morgue's icebox, and we can discuss Franny, and everything else, tomorrow." He motioned toward the house. "You'll keep her safe?"

"Like my own mom." *If I had one.*

"Thanks. I'll see you in the morning."

Erin walked back into the house. His hip told him too much more activity, and he would be operating on one leg. He took the complaint under advisement and went back into the kitchen.

Vy and Beela had found some ¾ inch plywood particle sheets and were placing them against the wall. Erin grumbled, "Jeff must have taken my tools again. I don't know why. He only knows how to hurt himself with them." He motioned to the boards. "Aunt Beela, can you show Vy where the hammer and nails are? I want to take measurements in here and make sure we have enough to cover everything."

Beela moved out, more than happy to help. Vy's eyes narrowed as she studied Erin. He shrugged. "Okay, so I got nicked in the side. I plugged it, it's fine. I think. I'm guessing. Or hoping anyhow. Go with Aunt Beela, or she'll get suspicious."

Vy's eyes narrowed even further, and her face scrunched into anger. Erin held his hand up. "Later, okay? Chew me out later. Let's get this woman's house back together so we don't fight mosquitos for the beds. Some of them are big enough to carry you off. With the bed."

Vy rolled her eyes but went with Beela to the back. Erin leaned a board against the wall. "Good enough. It'll work."

Vy and Beela came back in a few short minutes. Beela picked up a broom and began cleaning the kitchen, sweeping away the broken crockery, splinters, and bits of wallboard. Vy muscled Erin aside, hammer in her hand and nails in her mouth. "Move, mister. Let me show you how a woman swings a hammer."

Erin slipped out of the way of any backswing. Vy pounded the nails quite expertly. Better than Erin would. "You do that like you know how."

"My father was a carpenter. He has four daughters. We all learned how to swing a hammer and nail a nail in straight. Didn't do it right; we had to pull it out and try again. No matter how many times we had to do it over."

She drove the fasteners in, tested to make sure the board wouldn't pull loose, moved to the opposite side. "My sisters and I built them a house for their 40th wedding anniversary."

Erin whistled. "That takes some serious skills."

Vy pounded the last nail in. "Yep. Hard work supervising all those builders and contractors. But they got it done, so that's all that mattered." She smirked at Erin.

"Cute."

Beela hugged Vy. "Oh, honey, thank you so much. Thank you both. I don't know what I would have done without you here."

Erin stood. "I'm sure the Lord would have helped you, Aunt Beela."

"Oh, He did. He sent me you two." The woman smiled at Vy. "And you having a gun and all. You must have a pretty important job to be able to pack heat wherever you go."

Vy tossed her head. "I don't always carry it. We were lucky."

Beela waved her hand. "No luck about it. It was all the Lord." She turned to stare in the refrigerator. "What can I fix you for supper?"

Erin kept his voice low so Beela wouldn't hear the question. "Any prohibitions?"

Vy responded in kind. "Does this frame look like it turns down food?"

Erin smiled. "Well, since you give me permission to look…" Erin studied her up and down. "Yes, yes it does. Either that, or it handles what you consume very well." He could feel some heat in his cheeks. *Must be shock setting in.* "You're a beautiful woman, Vy. God did good."

Vy's eyes twinkled, and the corners of her mouth twitched. "Thanks, cuz."

Erin addressed Beela. "We'll eat anything you fix. Unless it's gophers or possums."

Beela laughed hard. "You are special, you know, Erin? I'll leave the gophers for another day and fry some venison steaks. How does that sound?"

"Great." Vy and Erin chimed in at the same time.

Beela nodded. "Okay, I'll go get some out of the fridge on the back porch." Beela headed outdoors.

Erin quickly shared all Mason had told him outside.

Vy's face drew down. "I want to see the 'nick.' No arguments. No modesty. Now."

Erin gave her a tight-lipped smile. "But will you still respect me in the morning?"

Vy's eyes narrowed. "Enough with the jokes, Erin. Let me see now."

Erin pulled up his shirt. From the amount of blood he saw, his patch job had held.

Vy pulled the patch away, then seethed, "You idiot." Vy glared at Erin. "Nicked? Why didn't you—"

"Tell you? I didn't want to scare Beela. Poor woman has been through enough."

"And you think dying in her house won't scare her?" Vy's anger was palpable.

Erin shrugged. "It's a nick, Vy. I'll rest tonight, we'll be home tomorrow, and I'll have it taken care of. I'm fine. But I need to sit for a while, so if you could help me to the back..."

Vy let him lean on her. "You're hurting bad, aren't you?"

"Either that or I'm trying to put a move on you."

"Lame. Pretty lame."

"So am I at this point." *I know, I know. If she hears the jokes, she won't know how bad it is.*

They stopped at the end of the hallway and tried to decide which bedroom of the three might be the spare. One room had walls and windows covered in matching print with farm animals in bows and ribbons. The one across from it had big green tractors on the walls and the curtains. The shag carpet mirrored the green on the walls. The third room smelled of stale alcohol. Vy looked at Erin; Erin looked at Vy.

"Bertherd." Unanimous.

Erin motioned back towards the living room. "I'll sleep on the couch. Wake me when dinner is ready."

Vy supported him to the sagging, frayed couch with the purple flower motif. She helped him down. Erin gritted his teeth and swallowed hard. "Thanks. I'm sorry, Vy. I am."

She grabbed a throw pillow with a crocheted covering and stuffed it under his head. "Lie there and get some strength back."

Erin closed his eyes and concentrated on controlling the pain. He'd settle for reducing it by half. He slowed his breathing, slowed his heart rate, slowed his thoughts...

To be shaken back to reality. Vy handed him a glass of water. "Drink this. All of it."

"Yes, Mother." Erin rolled on his side so he could chug the contents. He turned back flat. "Thank you."

"Mmhmm..."

Erin sensed more than a hint of disapproval in Vy's tone. *She'll have to get over it.* He went back to his pain-reduction protocols. *Lord, thank You I learned this early. I know You could zap the pain away. I'm using what You gave me.*

Erin slowed his breathing, slowed his heart rate…

And woke to a hand shaking his shoulder. "Drink."

He opened his eyes. "Didn't we just do this?" The room seemed darker than he remembered. The drapes were closed. The lights in the kitchen were out. A single floor lamp with a faded shade lit the corner of the room where Erin lay.

"Three hours ago." Vy held out the glass again. "You've been asleep all the time. Aunt Beela and I agreed you needed rest more than food, so we didn't wake you for dinner." She smiled. "You missed a great meal, Erin. Beela can cook! We saved you the leftovers."

"Thanks. Later." He downed the water. "What time is it?"

"About nine-thirty."

Erin sighed and handed the glass back. "Right. I'm sorry this drug bust went bust. I don't know what we do from here."

Vy shrugged. "It happens. We don't always catch the bad guys. But we did keep the drugs off the street. That's a win in my book." Her eyes twinkled even in the dim light. "And I got to meet an interesting man I'd like to know better."

Erin smiled. "Really?"

"Yes. Your brother-in-law strikes me as a unique person. I'd like to find out more about him."

Erin ran the comment through his mind a time or two. "He is spoken for, you know. Thus the 'brother-in-law' status?"

Vy grinned. "I did consider that. Seeing as how I can't have him, I'll take getting to know you better instead."

Erin sighed. "Always second choice. I suppose I'll have to live with it."

Vy chuckled. "We all have a burden to bear." She lost the levity. "How are you feeling?"

"Better. I might be able to take on one bad guy. Not two. One. Who won't fight back."

"My kind of bad guy. Unfortunately, there aren't many of those around. How about we hope for no bad guys tonight, and we see what tomorrow brings?"

"Agreed. Can I skip the midnight feeding? You can get your rest without having to get up to take care of me. If you escort me to the water closet now, I promise not to go anywhere unaccompanied for the rest of the night. Deal?"

"Deal." Vy helped him down the hall, waited for him, then escorted him back to the couch. She grabbed an afghan and handed it to him. "In case you get cold. Or want to keep the bugs at bay."

"Summer in Indiana. Can't beat it for biting insects. Thanks, Vy."

"Good night, Erin."

He watched her walk to the back of the house. He covered with the afghan and muttered, "I may be second choice, but for her, I'd take third or fourth. I don't even care if I'm in the top ten. So long as I'm in the running." He settled in and closed his eyes. "Or the walking. Walking is good. Good night, Lord. Thanks."

Outside, a dog barked.

FRIDAY

Jeff woke to a throbbing in his jaw and a pounding in his head. He moaned but didn't try to open his eyes. He didn't have a clue where he might be, and didn't care. All he wanted was the hammering to stop. Through the fog and haze in his brain, he realized he sat in a chair, his forearms fastened down. From the feel of it, a damp towel had been wrapped around his neck.

A sharp female voice seethed, "Were you trying to kill him? Why didn't you simply shoot him and be done with him?" The speaker turned her fury in another direction. "Or are those the rules? Someone gets lost in the trees, and your men automatically assume they have to eliminate them?"

A man's smooth voice declared, "He trespassed in my woods."

The words did nothing to pacify the speaker. "Excuse me? Trespassed? Where do you think those woods are, hmm? Who owns the property the woods stand on? *Your* woods?"

Jeff knew the words mattered. The voice mattered. If the pounding would stop for one minute, he might be able to figure out why.

The woman turned back to his direction. "I'm sorry this happened to you. Strangers don't fare well around here. But keep your eyes closed. It will help the headache and maybe help you get out of here alive."

Jeff tried to speak. He had to. The voice…the voice. He knew it.

The woman patted his shoulder. "Don't. Don't talk. Save your breath." She leaned in and whispered, "And your life."

Her voice turned away again. "What do you expect to do with him? If you brought him to me to see my reaction, there will be none."

The smooth voice seemed unimpressed. "So I see. But you are caring for him."

"He's wounded. He's human. If your places were reversed, I would treat you the same. I might not want to, but I would. That's one of those differences about being a Christ-follower. We don't yield to our base nature. Much."

Jeff sensed the male voice moving. Leaning forward? "You are saying if he had kidnapped you and I had been wounded, you would help me? Hardly commends your Lord to me."

Impatience filled the woman's voice. "No, I'm saying if you kidnapped me, and he hit you, I'd take care of you. I'd still escape, but I'd make sure you had the help you needed first."

The man chuckled. "We'll never know, will we?"

"God knows. Don't discount Him. Ever."

"Your faith in this unseen, unknown, and unknowable deity amuses me."

"You're wrong, Rudy. He is knowable. Step outside tonight and look at the stars. All of creation sings for Him. You know it, I know it, the whole world knows it. You can choose to deny Him, but there will come a reckoning."

Rudy sounded bored. "So you say. What would you like me to do with this trespasser?" He snorted. "Other than let him go. Which will not happen."

"Keep him. Treat him well." She snorted herself. "Or as well as you treat me. Perhaps you can find a use for him. Like the one you're still looking for with me?"

"I keep you around because you amuse me, and you have a brain. His walking in the woods alone says he has none."

"I beg to differ. He had equipment to lead him out of the woods, correct? That shows planning, foresight, and a strategy."

"Maybe. We'll see when his head clears." Rudy laughed. "I'll have him taken to your room. You can care for him properly." Jeff could imagine the gleam in the man's eyes. "We'll see what happens in a day or two."

"My Lord tells me to say 'thank you.' So I will. Thank you for demonstrating you still have a spark of the divine in you."

"How so?" Rudy sounded genuinely interested.

"Mercy comes from the Lord. You've shown you still have the mark of the Maker on you."

Jeff felt his chair being tipped and dragged. The motion sent his brain spinning in directions a brain shouldn't spin. He stopped trying to follow the rotations and let himself fall back into darkness.

When next he opened his eyes, he wasn't sure they were open. His vision couldn't penetrate the total blackness. He sensed he lay on something softer than a cold floor. Blankets were under him. And over him. He wiggled his toes and realized his boots were missing. Might be a good thing if he were lying on a bed. Might be a bad thing if the bed happened to be in the woods.

Yet he'd never been anywhere outside where it got this dark. The only place light could be shut out this tightly had to be indoors. He remembered Rudy… Rudy? Was that the name he'd heard?

Wait…were the voices real? And if they were, then the female voice…

Jeff sat straight. He whispered, "Collin. You're here." Wherever here might be. Again he whispered, "I found you. I found you."

A voice beside him whispered, "Well… not exactly. But we won't argue the point. And it's Caitlin."

Jeff felt an arm snake around his waist and a furtive hug given. He wanted to grab her and hold her and kiss her and tell her…

Collin's voice whispered, "Later, Farrell. Later. Now, we need to get out of here. Alive. All four of us."

Four? Four…oh, the babies.

The accuser jeered in his mind. *The ones who aren't yours?*

Jeff kicked the thought to the curb. *She's my wife. Those are our babies. Period.*

Collin stepped away from him. "I'm going to light a lamp. I have to conserve the light. Rudy, our 'host,' believes in being frugal. He also prefers I don't know how to count the time. Giving me short candles is his way of keeping me in the dark. Literally."

A snap of a match, then a dim glow illuminated a portion of the room. Jeff could see barely in front of him. But in front of him…stood Collin. He reached for her. Collin moved slightly away to put the candle in a holder. It gave a soft light to the room. Jeff's eyes flooded with tears. "Collin…"

"It's Caitlin. Caitlin Winger. And you're who?" She pointed to the corners of the ceiling and various spots along the wall. "There is constant surveillance. Remember it. Always. Your life depends on it. So does mine. Got it?"

Jeff dashed the tears from his face. He got his voice under control. "Got it. Caitlin Winger? Okay. Thank you for saving my life out there."

"You're welcome. I see no reason stragglers should be accosted in the woods for no reason. You can tell me why you were there later. But a name would be good. It will be researched, I'm sure, but that's beside the point."

"Jeff."

"Jeff is good. I can go with Jeff." Collin sat on the bed beside him. "What brought you to the woods?"

"I uh…lost a friend. He went missing around this area. I thought I would look for him myself since the police aren't having any luck finding him."

"Where are the police looking?"

"Not here. They don't have any clues except one eyewitness, and his story is changing every time he's asked. It's very frustrating." Jeff breathed in slowly to keep his emotions in check.

Collin folded her hands. "Must have been a special friend for you to come out here alone looking for them."

Jeff felt his throat tighten. He wasn't sure he could say what needed to be said. "We…we had…a fight. All my fault, and I was wrong. I know it now. But he went missing before I could tell him."

Jeff choked, not caring if anyone heard or not. "I want to tell him how sorry I am. And ask him to forgive me and be my friend again. Because I can't live without him being…being around, you know? I…I had a long talk with God. I told Him I regretted the lie I had been living. I couldn't live without Him, and I needed Him to forgive me."

Collin unfolded and folded her hands. "I'm certain your friend will forgive you. It's what best friends do. They love, and they forgive."

Jeff pulled himself together. "First, I have to find him."

Collin nodded. Her eyes sober, her face drawn. "Right. First, we have to find him. And if he's around here, we have to keep him alive by convincing Rudy he has a brain and can match wits with him." Collin smiled a tight smile. "Rudy believes all Christ-followers checked their brains at the church door when they accepted Him. He finds my faith amusing. Having you here will double the odds of him learning the truth. Or hearing it, anyhow." She glanced at the corner of the room. "Have you gone outside yet, Rudy? Seen the stars? Count them, Rudy."

She checked her candle. "I need to blow it out. I don't want to assume I will receive another one. I will make a bed on the floor, and you can—"

"No. The floor is mine. Since you've been here longer, you deserve the cushioning. I planned to sleep on the ground if I had to. The floor at least won't bite me. Right?"

Collin's eyes sparkled for the first time. "It hasn't yet."

"The floor it is."

Collin handed him a blanket and a pillow. "How's your head?"

"It's still there. The headache is better."

Collin blew the candle out. Pitch blackness returned to the room. Jeff slid off the bed to the floor and made himself as comfortable as he could. He could hear Collin shifting on the bed.

"Jeff, right?"

"Uh-huh."

"What day did you come to the woods?"

"Thursday."

"And your friend went missing when?"

"On Sunday."

"Oh." The reply sounded small. Vulnerable.

"I had complications. My…my brother got out of the hospital on Sunday. I had to pick him up. Before I could get him home, his place…well, his place blew up."

"Blew up?" Shock.

"Yeah. Maybe a faulty water heater. The police are looking into it. No clues so far."

"Did…did he lose everything?"

"Yeah. Lost all of it. Not even a stud standing."

The shock continued. "That's so…so awful for your brother."

"But thank the Lord, no people were injured."

"I understand why you had complications."

"It got more complicated in the afternoon. My brother's girlfriend is a drug runner."

"A what?" Shock mixed with anger.

"Yeah. My brother…well…anyhow, we discovered his girlfriend had placed a sizeable shipment of heroin on his truck. He was supposed to take the truck to Indiana last week. When he took a friend's car instead, he got sent home in the trunk. The car had been through a compactor."

"Okay, now that's all wrong. He didn't know about any of this?"

"No. But we found out after we located his truck. We…" Jeff trailed off. Did he mention the DEA? *Lord?*

No.

"We found the heroin. My brother decided to take it to Fort Newton and deliver it, to get rid of it."

Now she got mad. "Your brother did what?" Each word spaced dangerously.

"Right. He went there, and I came here. He promised he'd come search for my friend with me when he got done. Since he's not here, I guess something happened in Fort Newton. I don't know what. I couldn't get any phone reception to check on him. I'm wondering if he had the same problem."

The door opened. Light spilled into the room. A silhouette of a guard with a weapon ordered, "Out. Now. Both of you."

Collin slipped off the bed. Jeff climbed from the floor. In the light, he noted Collin had no footwear. The soldier had boots. *Okay…*

They walked through a maze of short, sharp corridors, some barely a door long. If the purpose was to confuse the uninitiated, it did it very well.

Eventually, they came into an expansive semi-lit space. Curtained windows gave no evidence of light. There were short tables, stiff-back chairs filled with soldiers, and several standing guards with side-arms.

Jeff made out the figure of a large man lounging in a wooden desk chair. The chair had a high back, curved arms, and wheels rotating in all directions. Jeff had no idea how tall the man would be if he stood, but from the looks of him, he weighed well into the high two-hundred-pound range. His head bald, his face heavily jowled. His eyes had a look of keen interest: sharp, focused. Nothing would get past him. *Be alert. Wise as serpents. Harmless as doves. But mostly wise.*

Collin stood before the man. "To what do we owe the sudden summons, Rudy?"

Rudy's eyes narrowed. "I want to hear the tale of this man's brother. I hear he is a drug runner?"

Jeff mirrored Collin's even, almost bored tone. "No, he isn't. Someone put drugs in his vehicle and tricked him into taking them north to Fort Newton."

"And what exactly happened when he arrived?"

Jeff repeated the sequence of events his "brother" experienced. As he finished, Collin took a step forward. "Were you behind this, Rudy? You told me you had retired from your past exploits."

Rudy snapped his fingers. A guard appeared at his side. "Check it out. All of it. See who is running in my place."

The guard retreated from the room. Jeff offered, "I have the woman's name if you like. Franny Landsford. Anyone you know?"

Rudy slapped his hand on the arm of the chair. "That thieving little…" Rudy went off on a rampage about Franny, which didn't bear repeating or remembering, so Jeff ignored it. When Rudy finished expressing his displeasure with Franny Landsford, he turned back to Jeff. "And you say they stuffed your brother in the trunk of the wrong car, sent him to a car crusher, then delivered the remains back to his house?"

"That's about the size of it."

"And how exactly did your brother escape being flattened with the car?"

Jeff swallowed his smile. "Seems the car had a flat tire earlier in the week. What with one thing and another, the spare never got replaced in the trunk. When the drug runners threw him in the back, he landed in the hollowed-out area. It left just enough room for him to be safe. Because they taped him into a fetal position and left him for three days, he needed hospitalization. Beyond that, he's fine." *I hope. Lord? Watch over Erin.*

Collin clicked her tongue. "Nice of God to protect him. Sending a flat tire first so there would be room in the back." Her eyes shone. "That's the God I serve."

Rudy eyed Collin not with anger but almost frustration. "Coincidence."

"Not in my world. God. I don't live in a random universe, Rudy. Neither do you. Which means my being here isn't an accident. There is purpose behind it. And it isn't yours."

Rudy glared at her. "You are…" He trailed off, unable to find a word to describe exactly what he wanted. He called for one of his guards. "Bring them chairs. Stiff ones."

Collin did a half-curtsey. "Why, thank you, Rudy. I appreciate the courtesy. Another sign of the Maker's mark. Consideration for someone else's welfare."

He growled at her. "Don't push it."

Collin smiled, her eyes twinkling. Jeff wondered at her behavior. She appeared to be taunting the man. For what?

Whatever the reason, she had survived this long and saved Jeff's life. He should pay close attention and follow her lead. *If I knew where she was going.*

The chairs arrived. Collin and Jeff sat. Time passed. Rudy's men came and went, jobs were assigned, reports were made, food appeared for Rudy. Jeff watched to see how this would play out. Rudy eyed Collin for several moments. He seemed to debate within himself. "I will have food brought for you and our newest guest *if…*" Rudy came down hard on the condition, "…you do *not* tell me how it makes me like 'my maker.'" He sneered at her. "Do you want to eat or proselytize?"

Collin rubbed her chin. "You'll give us food if I don't tell you how doing so makes you reflect the image of God? Agreed. I won't tell you."

Jeff knew what came next. Collin smiled at Jeff. "Did you know kindness is one of the attributes of God? Being considerate of another person's needs or wants. Treating others the way you would want to be treated. A very God-like thing to do, don't you agree?"

"Of course. I see it all the time. People who claim to be mean-spirited and selfish can perform some of the most selfless acts. They have to get a spark from somewhere."

Rudy stood. He handed his tray to one of the henchmen at his side. "Make sure they get fed. I'm going to go eat where I can have some peace." He walked out.

Collin glanced at Jeff, her eyes and tone full-on innocence. "Did I say something to upset him?"

Jeff mirrored her attitude. "I don't know. You'll have to ask him when he comes back."

A soldier brought them trays with cheese, crackers, some hard something which might have been salami, and water to drink. Jeff ate sparingly, not sure if he should stuff the crackers in his pockets for later.

Collin noticed his hesitancy. "Eat. Rudy does feed his prisoners." She smiled, tightlipped. "Maybe not well, but he does feed us."

He still moved some of his crackers and a piece of the cheese to the side of his plate. He handed them to Collin. "You need to eat extra."

Collin gave him a raised eyebrow. "Why? Because I look thin and wasting away?"

She held his gaze without blinking. Jeff studied her face. "Of course. Why else would I give you my food? You need to eat to keep your strength."

Collin smiled. "Why, thank you, kind sir." She took the cheese and two of the four crackers. "I still have to watch my figure."

I love watching your figure. Probably shouldn't say that right about now.

The trays were removed. Collin and Jeff sat and waited for something to happen, for someone to tell them what to do or where to go. In what Jeff figured took about half an hour, Rudy came back into the room. He resumed his place in the chair and stared at Collin and Jeff.

"You lied to me. You do know each other. In fact, you're married."

Collin lifted her chin. "Deception isn't the same as lying. I didn't say I didn't know him. I said you would get no reaction from me. And you didn't."

Rudy snarled. "Stop. The victim of the car incident and whose house they destroyed is Erin Winger." He pointed at Collin. "Your brother." He jerked a thumb at Jeff. "Not your brother."

Jeff stared back. "He is. Erin is her brother, which makes him mine. He's also my brother by blood. Jesus's blood runs in both our veins."

Rudy rolled his eyes. "Spare me." He turned on Collin again. "Caitlin Winger ceased to exist at fourteen. Is that when Collin Walker came to existence?"

Collin twisted her lip. "About then, yeah." Collin stared evenly at Rudy. "Safer to be known as a nobody, or the daughter of someone in jail, than to be known as an heiress." She tipped her head to Rudy. "In some circles."

"So your brother can pay a ransom."

"I told you the truth. My brother can't pay his electric bills." She shrugged. "Not because he can't afford them. He never remembers he has to. He's terrible about details."

Rudy didn't roll his eyes, but Jeff could see the man wanted to. Rudy shifted in his chair. "So I have Collin Walker and Jeff Farrell in my company."

Collin held up a hand. "No, you have Jeff and Collin Farrell in your company. And no cracks about my married name. Lack of forethought. Leave it go."

Rudy glared at Collin. "The fact remains I have you both here. Both of you are worth a great deal of money if I chose to ransom you." He studied the walls on either side of him. "Which I don't choose to do."

Jeff peered sideways at the man, waiting to see what he had in his head to do with them.

Rudy leaned forward to stare at Jeff and Collin. "I came to this compound so I could retire in some semblance of peace. I told you I had given up my former exploits. That is the truth. But with this incident, with this imposter using my tactics, my name has resurfaced, and interest in my whereabouts will no doubt be rekindled. That is unacceptable."

He scowled. "I need to bring down this fraud. The police must be convinced I had nothing to do with this, that I am still 'dead' and not worth looking for."

He leaned forward again. "You two are going to help me. Since it is your brother who, I'm assuming, blundered into this chaos, you will rectify it."

Collin held her hands out wide. "I would be happy to rectify my brother's blunders. If I knew where my brother is. I don't."

Rudy pointed to Jeff. "But you do."

"I know he went to Fort Newton. Franny Landsford gave him directions to an 'Aunt Beela's' house. No GPS coordinates. She gave him a list of instructions to follow. I don't know more than that."

Rudy eyed them. "I need you to bring in Franny Landsford. I would think you would know how to contact your brother's girlfriend. Correct? All good sisters keep tabs on the girls dating their brothers."

Collin laughed. "Uh, no. We made a pact when we were kids not to interfere in each other's love lives. I don't judge his—within his earshot—and he doesn't judge mine."

Rudy's eyes narrowed. "But you do know how to contact her."

Jeff spoke. "She's called my phone searching for Erin." Jeff thought it would be prudent to mention a small fact. "But I don't have my phone. I had it in the woods, but I don't have it now."

Rudy snapped his fingers. An aide exited the room. He reappeared with Jeff's phone and handed it to him. Collin pouted. "Why does he get his phone, and I don't get mine?"

Rudy raised an eyebrow at her. "Because he has information I need. You don't."

Collin huffed. "Unfair."

Rudy scowled at her. "You are still the prisoner here, remember? You do not dictate what is fair and what isn't."

Collin bobbled her head. "Fine."

Rudy glanced at Jeff. "You really married this?"

Jeff nodded. And wisely said nothing.

Rudy's eyes narrowed. "I want Ms. Landsford's address and phone number."

Collin cocked her head. "Do you play chess?"

"Of course."

"You ever win?"

Rudy's eyes narrowed to tiny slits. "Would you like to challenge me?"

Collin shrugged. "Of course. Right now, I'm more interested in how you intend to bring Franny into the open so you can prove to the cops she is the one operating, not you."

"You have a plan, I'm guessing."

"I have an idea that will bring her and the cops out at the same time and place. There is one piece missing, however."

Rudy drew in a short breath. "Let me guess. Your brother?"

Collin drawled, "If he's loose and shows where he's not supposed to be, the whole plan goes up in smoke. If, however, he's brought here, I can manipulate Franny to come out. The police will be waiting, and all will be well."

"How?"

Jeff wondered if Collin had a plan or was making this up as she went along. He hoped the former. He also hoped she remembered this man could end all their lives in a heartbeat.

You are in the Father's hand. Nothing touches you except what He allows.

Jeff kept any doubts to himself.

Collin rose from the chair. "I tell her I have the shipment. She already doesn't like me. She'll believe it coming from me." Collin paced around the small space between Jeff and Rudy. "I tell her my brother died delivering it, and I took it from the ones who killed him. I want blood money. And she's going to bring it to me. She comes, the police come, and your problem is solved. Most of it, anyhow."

"How does that get the police off my back?"

"Franny admits to using your tricks. She'll be happy to boast about it, I'm sure. We record her confession, have the evidence they need to convict her. Your 'seeming part' is explained and waved away as the fraud it is."

Rudy sat back in his chair. He rocked back and forth for several moments, considering the floor, considering the ceiling, considering Collin. "And for this, you need your brother brought here."

"And the shipment. Or, at the very least, my brother's truck."

"You seem to believe I am capable of intercepting your brother from delivering the goods or stealing it from the ones he delivered it to."

Jeff watched Collin's eyes. They never left Rudy's gaze. "Since I have no way of telling time, I don't know what day or time it is. I don't know how long I've been here, nor how long Jeff has been here. Only you can know if you have time."

Rudy lifted his head and tapped the arm of his chair. "Hmm. I have an old friend in the area who might be able to accomplish what we need. I'll get in touch with…them." He stood and dipped his head to Collin. "We should play that game soon. I have a feeling you will be a formidable opponent." He walked out.

Collin sat back beside Jeff, leaned into his shoulders. "What am I thinking?"

Jeff put his arm around her. "You're thinking of ways to get us out of here alive. You, me, the babies, and Erin." He hesitated. "There is one other joker in the pile, though. Erin took a friend with him." He lowered his voice. "Her name is Vy. She works for our uncle."

Collin stared at him, chewed her cheek, thought a moment. Her eyes widened as she caught his drift. Jeff's mouth drew into a straight line. "Yep. You got it."

Collin dropped her head on Jeff's chest. "Oh, no."

"We'll make it work, Collin. Vy is smart, witty, sharp. She's more than a match for your brother. If anyone can help bring this to pass, I'm sure she can."

"Does she know the Lord?"

"She does. And she's not shy to tell you about it, either."

"That's a good thing." Collin sat. "Help me here. If, and that's a big if, we got the shipment back—"

"You won't. You'll get the truck and the bricks planted on Erin's car. But the shipment itself has been removed by Vy's employers."

Collin stared at him. "Not good. What if she demands proof I really have the goods? I can't fool her with baby formula."

Jeff squeezed her shoulder. "You're trying to think too far ahead. First, we have to get Erin and Vy and the truck back. Until it happens, don't worry about what comes next."

"That may work in life but not in chess. You have to be able to think four or five moves ahead, my love. Which is why you can't beat Erin. You're not thinking far enough ahead."

Jeff lifted his head. "Now I understand why he always wins. He never taught me that skill."

Collin chuckled. "I'm sure he mentioned it to you."

"He did. He told me I needed to learn how. But he never taught me."

Collin lay her head on Jeff's shoulder. "I love you."

His voice caught. "I love you, Collin. I am so sorry for everything I've put you through. I'm an idiot, and I'm sorry. Will you forgive me?"

Collin's smile was sad. "I do. I did. I think I understand how Mary must have felt when she told Joseph she had 'tidings of great joy,' and he didn't believe her. She's carrying the Savior of the world, and he's looking to divorce her. I can imagine how crushed she felt."

Jeff added, "But an angel spoke to Joseph and straightened him out." Jeff frowned. "The one person I talked to didn't help at all."

Collin's mouth formed a hard, straight line. "I have more trouble forgiving that one." She studied the floor, too. "But I'll work on it."

"We both can work on it."

Rudy walked back into the room. He appeared pleased with himself, sat in his chair, and beamed at Jeff and Collin. "My friend is happy to assist us. They will arrange everything at their end."

Collin leaned forward. "What time is it? What day and time? Please? Since we're working together now?"

Rudy called an aide. "What day and time is it?"

"Friday. Zero four-thirty."

Rudy waved a hand, palm up, at Collin. "There. You have the time and date. Now, do you feel better?"

"Yes, I do. It gives me a foothold back in reality. Makes me feel in sync with the rest of the world."

"Why would you want to be?"

Collin stared at Rudy, her jaw open. After a moment, she closed it, sat straight. "Excellent question."

"I do manage a few."

Jeff watched Collin give Rudy a genuine smile. A jealous twitch struck him. He struck it back. *No. None of that. Period. Lord, not by my power, but by Your Spirit. Clean out the garbage. Don't leave even a hint. Please.*

Jeff asked, "What do we do now? Wait? Join him? Move to a rendezvous point?"

"We wait. My friend will inform me when things have been wrapped at their end. Then you can safely approach Ms. Landsford with your proposal."

Rudy motioned to an aide. "Bring the chess set. Let's see what kind of player you are, Ms. Farrell."

The man carried in a portable table and a hand-carved wooden chess set. He placed the pieces on the board then stepped back to await any further orders.

Collin pulled her chair to the table. She picked each piece and examined it in her hand, twirling it as Jeff had seen Erin do. She raised an eyebrow at Rudy. "Very nice. Did you carve these yourself?"

"Why would you think so?"

Jeff hid his amusement from his face. If Rudy hadn't figured Collin out by now, the retired dealer was about to be schooled. Collin shrugged. "Hand-carving is an art which takes considerable time and skill to master. Not the thing today's world sets much store in. I also see very few creature comforts around here. You didn't come here with a moving van of valuables. And you've had, by your admission, plenty of time to devote to learning a new skill. Plus, wood is easy to come by. I'd learn to whittle if I had time."

Rudy's eyes narrowed. "Whittling makes toothpicks from tree limbs. Carving requires precision and an eye for beauty."

"And pride in one's craftsmanship. These are exquisite."

Rudy smiled. "Why, thank you."

"I can be kind." Collin pointed at the board. "But it will be the last time until this match is over."

Rudy's eyes gleamed. "I would expect no less."

Jeff rose and moved away from the combatants. He figured as long as he stayed in the room and didn't make noise, he'd be unrestricted. He could sense the aide's eyes on him. Jeff made no move toward any of the three exits from the room. He simply stretched his legs. It would be a long couple of hours.

Or not. Jeff heard Collin tsking… "Rudy, I should slap your hand. Would you like to reconsider that move?"

"Why?"

"Checkmate."

Jeff looked over at the table. Rudy had his head down, still studying the board, probably trying to figure out where he'd gone wrong. Jeff could empathize. *Yes, yes I can.*

Rudy chuckled. "No. Call it a lesson learned. We shall begin again. And score one for comeuppances."

Jeff realized he'd been holding his breath. A little. Maybe. He let it out and resumed walking the room.

He heard Collin snipe, "If he's distracting you, tell him to sit. I don't want you to have any excuses to repeat your performance."

Rudy stared at Jeff. "Why did you marry this?"

"Seemed like the only logical thing to do at the time."

Collin rolled her eyes. "Play the game. Play the game."

Rudy moved his king's pawn. "Checkmate in fifty moves."

Collin smiled. "I'll hold you to that."

* * *

Vy didn't sleep well in the green tractor room. She would have preferred the couch, but Erin wouldn't allow it. Vy smiled. Erin was unique. Lying in bed, thinking about him, wasn't getting her to sleep, so she directed her thoughts elsewhere. *Lord, You are in control of all that is, of all that will be. Father, please, help Jeff find his wife. And Lord, I would like to get to know this man better. I love his dedication to You. There is so much else about him I like. But I want Your will, not my own. I dedicated my life to serve You and only You. Lead me.*

Praying brought peace. Peace brought sleep. Until…

A clank, so soft she couldn't be sure she'd actually heard it, woke her. Instinct told her to investigate. Vy shouldered her weapon and walked on silent feet into the kitchen. Erin lay on his back, asleep on the couch, a pillow on the floor beside him. She hadn't remembered seeing the extra pillow before but didn't have time to wonder at it. She moved to look out the tattered curtains, staying hidden in the shadows.

A dusk-to-dawn light over the chicken coop cast long shadows in the front yard. Alongside Erin's truck, furtive figures dived and rolled and crossed over under the vehicle, retrieving the shipment of fake drugs. She counted four of them. *Pretty spry…and small.*

Vy stepped outside without making a sound. She crouched in the darkness, waiting for the group to gather in one place. If they scattered, she would have to settle for tackling one. One would be enough. It would have to be.

She watched as one of the shadow figures began shoving the blocks into the backpacks each person held. As the blocks were loaded, she heard a voice complain, "They're too heavy."

Vy's breath caught. The voice was of a child, a girl most likely, and maybe only ten or eleven. *Are they all children? What is going on?*

Vy moved in behind the group, pulled her weapon, and ordered, "Federal Agent. Everyone freeze."

Three of the four shadows obeyed. The fourth shadow turned into the light. Vy clearly saw a child. A child with a gun. Pointed dead at Vy. In one motion, Vy dodged to the side, and the culprit pulled the trigger. The bullet grazed Vy's left arm. She jerked back to knock the gun aside. The thief fired again, and one of the shadow figures crumpled to the ground with a whimper. Vy kicked the thief in the knees; the shooter went down, losing the gun. Vy punted the weapon into the ditch and tackled the shooter. Two other figures disappeared in the shadows.

Vy grabbed the shooter by the neck of their shirt and dragged them to where the wounded companion lay in a heap. The DEA agent dropped her prisoner to the ground and ordered, "Don't move. Don't breathe. Don't think." She kneeled beside the child who had been shot, checking for the bullet wound. She found it in his leg, a clean through-and-through. And it missed the bone, too. *He'll have a scar to tell a story, but that's the only thing he'll have.*

Aunt Beela's voice sounded from the porch steps. "What is going on out here?"

Vy motioned to the two children in her custody. "They were…trying to steal Erin's truck. Two of them ran off. This one got shot."

Beela stepped off the porch and into the light. She held a large caliber handgun and had it pointed at Vy. "Put the gun down, Vy."

Vy stared at Beela in confusion. "Aunt Beela? You?"

Beela repeated, "Put the gun down." Vy complied. The older woman crossed over to the child who held his leg and moaned. Beela's eyes narrowed as she glared from one child to the other. "You two are worthless! Worthless! See what you've done?"

She pushed the ex-shooter in the shoulder. "Go get the first aid kit. Bring it out here." She waved at the child, still moaning. "Shut up, Fitter. You're not hurt bad."

Vy held her injured arm, watched as her former captive pounded up the steps, stomped through the kitchen and living room, returning at the same decibel level. *Why didn't Erin wake? Why…*

Her eyes widened as possibilities filled her mind. Her voice came out hollow. "Beela, what did you do to Erin?"

The woman focused on the small boy she bandaged. "It wasn't supposed to happen like this. If those two crooks hadn't tried to poach my territory, you and Erin would have been able to drive back to Oakton, and everything would have been fine. I really did like him."

Vy repeated with more heat. "What did you do to him?"

"I smothered him on the couch. He slept so sound, poor man. He never even tried to fight me off. Hated to do it to him, but with all the commotion out here, you didn't leave me much choice."

Vy felt her stomach lurch and her heart fall. *Oh, Erin…* She stared at Beela, her eyes hard, her face harder. "Now what? You shoot me, too?"

"No, it won't work. Mason will be back here in the morning, and I need to have a good story for where you went and why there's blood on the ground. Can't clean it all tonight since I can't see it. I'll put you in the garage where you'll be safe and out of sight." She cuffed the shooter in the back of the head. "Lou, get Fitter into the house. I need you to help me drag the poor man out behind the chicken coop, and take these bags to the garage. Stack them in the middle of the floor. You can keep watch over her and them."

Lou lifted Fitter to his feet. He pointed at Vy. "She said she's a federal agent."

Beela snorted. "Of course she did."

Vy snarled, "What am I supposed to say? 'Stop in the name of the law?' Would that have gotten your attention?"

Beela laughed. "I haven't heard that old line in years! Of course, it wouldn't stop anyone." She motioned for Vy to walk to the back of the yard, to the garage outbuilding. Inside, Beela zip-tied Vy's hands behind her back, made her sit, then zip-tied her hands to the leg of a four-by-four workbench. "Sorry about your arm. And sorry you'll have to spend what's left of the night out here, young woman. I really did like you. You and Erin were a delightful ray of sunshine in my week."

With that, Beela left the garage. Vy settled back against the workbench. *What happened? Lord, what did I do wrong? How did this come apart like this? Erin...poor Erin. How can Beela be so evil as to offer to feed a man dinner, and smother him with her own hands as he sleeps on her couch?*

Lou shuffled through the door, dragging the backpacks with him. He dumped them, then glared at Vy. "Don't try anything." Lou sat along the opposite wall, curled his knees to his chest, and stared across the room.

Vy ignored him, doubting he'd be awake long. Her suspicions were correct. Lou fell asleep inside of ten minutes.

Vy still had precious little time to plot an escape. But how? *Lord, what do You want from me? What am I supposed to do? Help me, please. Help me get justice for Erin. He didn't deserve to die.*

You didn't deserve to die, either, Lord, but You did it for me. And for Beela and for Franny and whoever wants these drugs.

She smirked. *Someone is going to be very unhappy about the quality of this product.*

Vy twisted and turned her wrists, trying to loosen or break the cable ties. She worked her hands raw, but nothing. She tried sawing the bands up and down on the workbench. Splinters, nothing else. She tried to work the tie holding her to the bench down the leg, thinking maybe she could slip it under the four-by-four. Nowhere. The restraints didn't move.

Vy felt frustration and anger and bitterness and disappointment and shame pour over her efforts. Hot tears filled her eyes, but she tossed them off. Beela would not see her cry. No one would. She cried out to the only One Who could help her. *Lord! Please! Help me. I don't know what to do. Everything I've tried hasn't worked. I don't want to die here. Please!*

Vy felt peace seep in over her fear. Nothing changed around her. She remained tied to the bench. But something in her soul felt peace. Live or die, she would be with the Lord. She breathed in and out a long, slow breath. *Father, thank You. You have this, I know. You have Me. Have Your way. Your will be done.*

She spent the rest of the night in communion with the Lord. If He would not release the physical bonds, at least her soul and spirit were free. Nothing would change that.

Dawn came, but the garage remained draped in shadow. Vy noted her warden slept deeply. She offered a suggestion. *Now would be a good time for a miracle, Lord. A "Peter, get up, put on your cloak, and follow me" moment.*

A hand covered her mouth. A voice whispered in her ear. "Hi. Don't panic."

Vy breathed in sharply and turned to look at the speaker. *Erin!*

He smiled at her. "Long story. Not dead. Two lives down. Go with it. I'll get you free here in a moment."

She felt him pulling on the bindings on her hands. Vy hissed at him. "Where have you been all night? Leave me, get the backpacks. Hide them, dump them, get rid of them somehow. And be quick."

Erin disappeared. The packs were still shadowed in darkness. Vy heard dragging sounds, followed by silence.

Voices from the driveway caught Vy's attention. Overhead lights flipped on. Beela talked as she and an unknown man walked into the garage. "You don't have any idea how much trouble this shipment has brought me. I need you to…"

Beela stopped midsentence. Her mouth fell open, her eyes widened farther than eyes should. The packs were gone. Vy kept her smirk to herself. Beela did a frantic search around the garage. "Gone! How? How can..." Beela spotted the sleeping Lou. She marched over to him and kicked him sharply in the side.

Lou's eyes opened. Fear colored the boy's face as he focused on Beela. The woman seethed, "Where are the packs? Where? You were supposed to be watching." She punctuated her frustration with a second kick to Lou's hip.

Lou went pale. "I...I closed my eyes for a moment. No one came in here. I promise."

"Where are the packs? What happened to them?"

"I...I don't know. I don't know."

Beela turned to the man beside her. "Give me half an hour, Brice. I'll have it all for you, I swear it."

Vy studied the man. Her eyes narrowed as she tried to determine if she'd seen him before. Average height. Dark brown hair pulled into a ponytail reaching below his shoulders. One eye appeared less open than the other. What people called a "lazy eye." Longish sideburns. Dressed in a dark gray business suit with a light raincoat over it. No. Vy was sure she'd not seen him before.

Brice shook his head. "I'm disappointed in you, Beela. You called me to come because you had a shipment for me. You said someone's trying to poach my territory, but you had the goods. But where? I drove a great distance, and you have nothing to show me." He kicked a rock. "Very disappointed."

Beela's face became red, then purple with anger. "I will find the shipment." She walked over and slapped Lou. "You! You get up and start searching the area. Look everywhere." The boy took off in a heartbeat. Beela marched over to Vy and glared at her. "You know, don't you?"

"Know what? Where the backpacks are? I've been tied here the whole time. How would I know what happened to them?"

Beela raised her fist to strike Vy, but Brice stopped her. "Slapping your prisoner isn't going to locate anything. I suggest you search along with your helper." Beela continued to glare at Vy but turned on her heel and went out.

Brice walked over to stand in front of Vy. "I do apologize for this unnecessary violence. I see the management at this outlet is in need of...replacement." He smiled at Vy. "I don't suppose you would be interested in saving your own life and taking over the position?"

Vy cocked her head. "Excuse me? You kill my friend, threaten me with violence and murder, and now you want me to work for you?"

Brice kneeled on his haunches. "I did not kill anyone. We take a dim view of killing in general. Bad for business. Scares off employees and customers. Nor did I threaten you with violence. I prevented it from being used against you, in fact."

"Yes, you did. I appreciate it."

"Beela tells me she had to kill the man you came with. I am sorry I couldn't be here to prevent that mishap. I do promise he'll have a full and decent burial. If it matters."

Vy hung her head. "It does." She imagined Erin listening with glee. "Why would you even think of putting me in Beela's place?"

Brice shrugged. "My organization covers this territory. Beela's home makes a convenient drop-off location. It becomes a most efficient distribution point from here to our northern and western vendors. We're a business. Not a band of cutthroats and brigands as in days past." He added, "You could make a nice asset to our operation."

Brice's eyes smiled. "And if you say no, we will allow Beela to kill you as she has planned. Of course, she doesn't know we are planning her funeral as well. It'll be our little secret."

She glared at him. "I thought you took a dim view on killing."

"We do. But when it is needed, we don't hesitate. In this situation, it's needed."

Vy met his gaze. "I will have to think about it. You make it hard to say no."

He raised an eyebrow. "That's what we hope for. Persuasion, not violence. You have until Beela locates the shipment." He stood, stopped. "You do know where it is, don't you?"

"No, I honestly don't."

"But you know what happened to it?"

"I know it's not here. I know it disappeared. Beyond that, I have no more clue than you do."

"Um-hum. I see." What Brice saw would remain with him, however. The man turned and walked out of the garage, closing the door behind him.

Vy leaned back against the bench. *Lord! Help me! If I say yes, it gets me into an organization I'm not sure we even knew existed. That could be huge for us.*

But at what cost? Can I live and act like they do and still honor You? Just as a job? Make Yourself clear, Lord. Please. Show me what You want me to do.

Erin reappeared behind her and whispered in her ear, "Soon as I can figure out how to hotwire a car, we're out of here."

Vy cocked her head. "Hotwire? Why not take yours?"

"I disabled it before Brice got here. If I'd have known he was coming, I would have left things alone. As it is, the truck may never run again."

"What did you do?"

"Reversed some of the wiring. It'll start, short out, and probably suffer a meltdown."

Vy nodded her head. "Nice. Creative. Unfortunate." She pointed at the door to the garage. "Did you hear Brice?"

"His offer to you?"

Vy started to get excited at the possibilities. "Do you know how long it would take us to get someone on the inside of an organization like this? How many years, how many men and women it would take to infiltrate to this level? Erin, we could put the whole thing out of business."

Erin's face became sober and drawn. "Or die in the process."

"I accepted the risk when I signed."

"Did you accept having to lie? To cheat people?" Erin's face grew hard. "To arrange someone's death, so you're not discovered?"

Vy lifted her chin. "If the job required it…yes."

"What kind of witness for Christ can you be while you're hustling illegal drugs?"

Vy argued sharply. "This isn't about the Lord. This is about doing a job that needs to be done. Jesus' law doesn't matter when it comes to the job…" Vy trailed off as she heard herself speak words she swore she never would.

Erin stared at her, and his eyes lost their light. "Your job is your god. I hope you're good at it. I do." He cut the ties binding her wrists. "I won't take Brice's car. I'll find another way back."

Vy watched him turn away. "Erin…wait."

He didn't turn around, but he did stop. Vy swallowed hard. "I'm an agent of the US government. I swore an oath to serve. It's who I am."

Erin said quietly, "No. It's what you do. It will only be who you are if you make it that way." He turned back to meet her gaze, and his eyes…the pain in his eyes… Erin turned around and disappeared into the shadows again.

Vy watched him go. *He's wrong, Lord. I know he is. He doesn't understand what this job means. Someone has to do it. Someone has to make the sacrifice.*

An image of Christ on the cross, his head covered with the crown of thorns, his body beaten and bloodied, crossed her mind. Jesus lifted his head and gazed into Vy's eyes. No condemnation, no disappointment, no anger. Love. Forgiveness. Freedom. That's all she saw. She heard the words echo in her mind. *"Jesus doesn't matter here."*

Vy sat still, her heart and mind at war.

The job.

The Lord.

Look at all the lives I could save.

Lives, yes. But souls?

With the distributors off the street, I could tell more people about Jesus.

I tell people now.

But it would be better. People wouldn't need drugs, and they'd hear the message and get saved.

How many addicts have you seen come to Jesus off the street? Five? Ten? How many well-to-do? How many "have it all together" people come?

Vy bowed her head. *No one comes until they know they have a need. The Lord came to call the sick to repentance, not those who think they have it all.*

Vy sat with her back to the workbench and studied the floor. *I took this job because I thought it would be a way to make a difference. To help others. Isn't that what I'm doing?*

If I have to use the enemy's tactics, does it make me any different from him?

My motives are pure.

How long can you dance with the devil and not get burned? Do you really think you're strong enough? Do you know the depths of evil you will be called on to experience?

Vy let the battle continue. She had until Beela found the shipment…

The shipment which had been replaced with not-heroin.

Vy sat straighter. What would happen when Brice discovered his drugs were bogus? Would he believe Beela had swapped them? Would Vy stand by and watch Beela die for something Vy had orchestrated? Could she really be that cold inside?

Vy stared off into nothing. All the arguments were done. Reckoning due. Decision?

"I can't." She whispered it again. "I can't. I can't do it. You matter, Lord. You're all that matters." She closed her eyes. Vy's lower lip trembled. She clamped down hard on it, squeezed her eyes shut against the tears. *I'm sorry, Lord. I'm sorry. You will always matter. Always and forever. Forgive me.*

A hand brushed away a tear off her cheek. Vy opened her eyes, and through the wash of moisture, saw Erin sitting beside her. He touched her cheek. "I couldn't leave without saying goodbye. Then I couldn't leave without you, period."

Vy bumped her forehead against his. "Thanks, friend." She smiled at him. "Without telling me how or where, did you dispose of the powder?"

"Yes."

"I say we get out of here as fast as we can."

"You have any ideas about how to manage it?"

"Not yet."

Beela's heavy steps could be heard on the driveway. The older woman came running into the garage and slammed the door behind her. She locked it, ducked behind the windows. Erin disappeared behind the workbench.

Vy stared at Beela. "What are you doing?"

"Hiding from Brice. He's out there with Lou still looking for the drugs." Beela's eyes were wide with fear. "You took them, didn't you? Where did you put them?"

Vy retorted, "You left me tied, Beela. I couldn't go anywhere if I wanted to."

Beela scooted closer to Vy, still staying low and out of view from the outside. "But you know, don't you? You know what happened to them. You had someone else follow you, right? And they came and got the stuff. You want to make a bargain with Brice for yourself? Is that how it is?" Beela seemed even more terrified. "Don't leave me to Brice, please. He'll kill me."

"Like you did Erin?"

Beela sagged. "I'm sorry about that. I am. He's dead. And we're alive, but we won't be much longer if Brice doesn't get his drugs." Beela scooted a bit closer. "You can help me; I know you can. Tell me where the drugs are. He'll take them and leave, and we'll be safe."

Desperation made the woman's eyes wilder and wider than Vy had ever seen. "Please, Vy. Tell me where the drugs are."

"I can't, Beela. I don't know where the shipment of heroin is." *Truth, Lord. I don't know where the actual drugs are.* "I'm in as much danger as you are. What makes you think he'll leave me alive? I'd be bargaining with him myself if I knew. But I don't."

Beela breathed out heavily. She scanned around the garage, her eyes darting back and forth. "He can't get in through the big door. Been boarded up for years. He's going to try to shoot his way in. I know it. We've got to get something against the side door to stop him." Her eyes landed on the workbench. "The bench. It's heavy. He won't get past that."

Vy remembered the ties around her wrists were gone. Beela would see she was free and think Vy had somehow moved the drugs. She felt a sense of panic, followed by a sense of calm. She picked the pieces of the bands Erin had cut and placed them back around her wrist with the cut pieces between her palms. Beela pushed Vy forward and cut the bonds. "There. Now help me push this thing over to the door."

Vy's eyes widened. Erin had gone back there. He'd be found out, and Beela…

Beela yanked at her end of the bench and seethed, "Help me!" She pulled the table clear of the wall, far enough for Vy to see empty space behind it. Vy squelched the desire to search for Erin and instead added her momentum to Beela's. In moments they had the furniture braced against the only exit to the garage. Other than the window, of course.

Vy motioned to the opening. "What about that?"

Beela squinted around the area, grabbed a lethal-looking pitchfork. "Anyone comes through there, I'll impale them!"

Vy raised her eyebrows. "That oughta do it." She lay her hand on the trembling woman's arm. "He could simply set fire to the garage, you know."

Beela threw one hand in the air. "Never. He'd risk burning his shipment. He doesn't know if it's in here or not, so he's not gonna take that chance."

Vy wasn't as convinced but didn't bother arguing. She preferred to spend the time figuring out how Erin got in and out of the room without detection. No skylight, no backdoor, no side hatch… How was he doing it? Magic?

She swallowed a smile. *He does have that. A little.*

Brice's voice walked up the path beside the back of the garage. "Okay, we moved the dead guy, and there's nothing there."

Vy's eyes widened. *Not only is Erin magic, but somehow he can perfectly mimic a dead body? Who is this crazy man?*

A knock sounded at the door. "Beela, I know you're hiding in there. Come out, and let's talk about it. I want the shipment. Give it to me, and everything returns to business as usual."

Beela snapped with sarcasm in her voice, "Sure it will! And you've got beachfront property in Arizona to sell me, right?

Brice sounded almost tired. "Beela, there's no sense getting ugly about it. You know the way things work. I get the shipment, I pay you your cut, and we both go away happy. Why did you think you had to change the arrangement without telling me? Do you want a bigger cut, is that it?"

"No, I want you to go away and pretend this never happened. I don't know where the drugs are. I stole them off the truck last night, and someone stole them from me. That's the truth. Killing me won't get you your stuff back."

"Leaving you alive won't either. And it looks bad to the business owners. Makes them think they can't trust me to take care of my territory. I don't like looking bad, Beela. If I can't give them the merchandise, I have to show them I took steps to prevent this from happening again. How do we work this out, Beela?"

Vy heard the sound of a car pulling into the driveway and stopping. She risked a quick look and saw Brice's car backed to the garage with the engine running. She watched him shove a garden hose into the exhaust, then slide it to a crack below the door. Vy grabbed some rags and stuffed them into the hole. She yelled at Beela. "This isn't going to stop all the fumes."

"He's bluffing. This old building is so full of holes, it'll never fill with gas."

Vy swallowed a chortle. *You have no idea, Beela. There's a hole big enough for a man to get in and out. Somewhere.* "What do you suggest we do? We can't stay in here forever, and I doubt he's going to just go away."

"Are you a praying woman? If so, I suggest we pray and ask the good Lord to help us out of this situation."

Vy felt the stab in her soul. *You move drugs, you kill people, and you think the Lord will simply wave a magic wand and let you go? Father, forgive me for thinking I could work with these people.*

I know, Lord. You came and died for "these people" as much as for me. I'm sorry. But this is beyond me. Who do people think You are?

Vy heard another car pull up, and a voice shouted, "What is going on here?" *I know, I know. That's not exactly what he said. But the translation's the same.*

Beela's eyes widened. She smiled as wide as her eyes. "Mason! He'll save me."

"Me?" *A moment ago, it was "we"! Every woman for herself, right?*

Vy couldn't hear the words being exchanged between Brice and Mason. She didn't need to. As long as no shooting started, she'd be happy for the two dealers to work out their differences. As long as Beela and Vy came out alive. *See? I'm thinking of her, too.*

The negotiations lasted longer than Vy thought necessary. *Where is Erin? Is he lying in the dirt behind the coop? Breathing in formula and horse? Lord, protect him, please.*

A car pulled away. Mason called out, "Mom, you can open the door now."

Beela called back. "What's the password?"

"Mom, I can't say the password when there are other people around to hear it."

"We'll change it. What's the password?"

Mason cleared his throat. "I love my mommy."

Vy put her hand over her mouth to hide the giggle. *Yeah, no one is going to say that one by accident.*

Beela crowed. "Okay, we're moving the bench." Vy helped drag the worktop out of the way of the door. Beela unlocked it and rushed outside to bear hug her son. "I so happy to see you! That man wanted to kill me!"

Mason pushed his mother away gently. "Mom! You have a whole lot of explaining to do. What in the world are you doing? Are you running drugs? What?"

Beela shook her head. "It's all a mix-up, Mason, I swear it is. It's her and the fellow she brought with her. They had the drugs. They brought them here. I...I...I was trying to stay alive. I'd say anything so they wouldn't kill me."

"Where is Erin?"

Beela pointed to Vy. "She killed him. They had a falling out, and she smothered him in his sleep. She made me drag his body out behind the chicken coop to hide it. I'll show you where it is."

Mason hugged his mom. "Okay, Mom. Fine. I can find it on my own. You go in the house, and we'll figure this all out. I want a word with Vy here." He glared at her, his eyes fire.

Vy waited. Mason would set the tone for this.

Mason looked over to see his mom had gone into the house. He turned to Vy. "I ran your ID last night." He held her gaze.

Vy lifted her chin. "Uh-huh. Found something interesting?"

He nodded. "Erin is the odd read. How did he get roped into this?" He paused. "He's not dead, right? You staged that for a reason."

Erin's voice as he exited the garage behind Vy startled her. "She didn't stage it."

Vy turned around and scowled at him. "How do you keep doing that? How are you getting in and out?"

"Cat flap?"

Vy's eyes narrowed.

"Doggie door?"

"Erin Winger…"

"Hole in the roof about my size. Happy?"

"Yes. Very."

Erin glared at Mason. "Your mom tried to smother me. She thought she'd succeeded."

Mason sighed. "This gets worse with the moment. Okay, tell me all of it."

Erin leaned against the garage. Vy eyed him. He appeared tired. Pale. Of course, climbing up and down and in and out would tire anyone. Vy motioned to Erin. "You may as well start this marathon." She held his gaze. "From the beginning. The very beginning."

Erin looked confused. She motioned with her head. "Tell it all."

Erin drew in a deep breath. "Okay, it all started when my sister and I were born—"

"Not that far back, you idiot!" Vy laughed.

Erin sighed. "Fine. It started when I met Franny Landsford."

Erin filled Mason in on all the past events leading up to contacting Vy. Vy filled in from then until the shoot-out.

Mason frowned. "Those two were after Mom's crop. We checked them out. And yes, the sheriff'll be here later to take statements and look at the evidence. So what happened after that?"

Vy filled in the rest of the details as she experienced them. Mason's face turned dark and even darker as he listened. He hung his head as Vy finished the telling. "I'm sorry. I am. I didn't know Mom would be the middleman in anything like this." He cursed softly but soundly.

He finished his expression of frustration and smiled at Vy. "So the real drugs are under lock and key in Oakton?"

"Right."

"And the fake stash?"

Erin jerked his head toward the backyard. "The chickens are enjoying it."

Mason exhaled. "This just gets worse and worse. Okay, do you still have the wrappings of the bricks?"

"Yeah. Why?"

Mason raised his head to the sky. "Because I promised a friend I would bring the shipment, and you, to him."

Erin's eyes narrowed. "Me? What do I have to do with any friend of yours?"

Mason's shoulders slumped. "It's a very long story. Longer than the one you just told me. But connected." He exhaled again. "I need to retire. I'm getting too old for all this."

He waved his hand. "Come on, let's go inside and talk to Mom. It's gonna be a long day."

SATURDAY

Jeff lay on the bed in the room he and Collin occupied, staring at the ceiling. Rudy had relented and turned on the electricity in the compound. He had also given them a floor plan so they could find their way around. But not leave. Jeff retained his phone, but there was no cell service out of the underground bunker. Rudy also claimed surveillance had been shut off. All in the interests of promoting cooperation. *Sure it is.*

Jeff's mood darkened as he stared at nothing. Collin seemed far more interested in their host than in him. She'd spent the past few hours playing chess with Rudy. Or talking with him. Arguing Scripture. Making the older man read Scripture.

Of course he has a Bible. Don't all drug smugglers carry Bibles around? And know them by heart? Lord, this isn't fair. I came out here to rescue Collin, and she seems happy to stay right here. Like being a prisoner in this dungeon doesn't bother her at all.

Why should it? She's got You, and she's got Rudy. Someone who can finally offer her a challenge at chess. What more could she want? I wonder if the babies' father plays che—

Jeff sat straight. *Where did that thought come from? I'm the father of the babies. We settled it. Over. Done with.*

Okay, so Collin had been spending a lot of time with Rudy. She was trying to figure out a way to escape. To make her plan work so everyone would get out alive. And stay alive. Shouldn't that be worth a few alone hours?

Jeff rolled off the bed. He walked back to the central living space to see how the players were faring. Rudy sat alone at the chessboard, staring at the pieces. Jeff swallowed a chuckle. "How'd it go?"

Rudy didn't look up. "As expected."

Jeff eyed Rudy sideways, trying to figure if he should ask or not. *Oh, why not? Live dangerously.* "What's the score?"

Rudy still didn't look up. "Five-two." He frowned at Jeff. "Your wife is a brilliant strategist. She must be a great asset to whatever endeavors the two of you have going."

Jeff snorted. "I haven't begun to tap her potential, I'm sure." *Of course not. I haven't included her in anything. Then I wonder why she'd have an—* "How long have you been here, Rudy?"

"Ten years, I believe."

"Did you know Collin's grandfather, Fenton Mudd?"

"No. Why would I?"

"He owned the land we're on."

Rudy stared off to one side. He didn't look at Jeff. "Someone offered me this place. I never inquired about who it might belong to."

"And yet you built this compound without anyone knowing about it? How did you keep the workers from talking about it?" *Do I really want to know where the bodies are buried?*

Rudy shrugged. "That wasn't my concern either. Someone constructed this before I took residence."

"How often do you get out?"

Rudy turned his gaze on Jeff. "I don't. I haven't left in ten years."

Jeff's eyes widened. "What? Why?"

"I prefer solitude." Rudy snorted. "Some might call it just desserts. Others might call it penance. I call it being a hermit."

The man stood. Jeff could see the discomfort he experienced in rising. His face contorted in momentary pain. Jeff had to ask. "What's wrong?"

Rudy shrugged. "Nothing anyone can fix. I'm going to my room now. If your wife comes looking for another challenge, tell her she will have to practice on you." He glared at Jeff. "You do play, I take it."

Jeff nodded. "I play." Rudy had no need to know how poorly.

"Good. Someone should challenge that woman. Keep her humble." At that, Rudy walked out.

Jeff stared down the hall. *What did all that mean?*

Why does it matter? He's a criminal. He kidnapped me, kidnapped my wife—

Jeff turned on his heel and practically ran over Collin. She startled back. "I'm sorry, Jeff. I wasn't trying to sneak up on you." She peered over his shoulder. "Where is Rudy?"

"He went to his room. He said you'd have to practice on me. Won't give you any real challenge, but if you want to play…"

"No, thank you. I'm tired of playing chess. My brain hurts."

Jeff put his arms around her. "Give it a rest."

Collin stepped out. "Walk with me. I've been sitting too long, too. I need some exercise."

They walked arm-in-arm down the corridors empty of guards for once. Jeff noted the lack. "Where did everyone go?"

"I don't know. Unless it's the crew's night off? Fourth of July?"

"That's next month."

Collin grimaced. "I keep losing track of time. It all runs together here. It's frustrating to keep asking what day it is.."

Jeff stopped and moved her away from himself for a moment. "What's wrong?"

Collin studied the floor. "I need to know for the babies' sake." She glanced at Jeff. "Viability. With twins, it's crucial. With one of them having a heart murmur, the longer I can go, the better for them."

Jeff didn't respond. Collin cocked her head. "My turn to ask what's wrong?"

"I miss our time together, you and me."

Collin buried her head in his chest. "This is you and me time. And I love it."

Jeff held her close, feeling the warmth of her arms, the beating of her heart. "But it's not. Not really. We're captive in this underground labyrinth. You're either thinking of ways to beat Rudy at chess or worrying about the babies."

Collin glanced at him and held his eyes. "Do you not believe I'm trying to find a way out of here?"

"Yes, I do. I do." He frowned at her. "But I know you're also scheming to get Erin brought here so you can make sure he's safe, too. As if us and the babies being safe isn't enough. You won't be happy unless it's all of us, will you?"

Collin stepped away from him. She searched his face, his eyes. "What are you saying?"

"Nothing. Never mind. I don't know what I'm saying. I'm getting claustrophobia here, and it's affecting my brain."

Collin's eyes held vulnerability in them. He kissed her on the forehead. "I'm sorry. I am. This has been the longest week in my life, and it's not over yet."

Collin chewed on her lower lip. "I know what you mean. It has been for me, too." She hesitated. "Did you really think…think I would…cheat on you?"

Jeff closed his. "No. I knew you'd never do that to me. You'd never betray the Lord, either. I'm sorry, Collin. Will you forgive me?"

The hurt in her eyes belied the words. "I have. I did." Her gaze hit the floor. "I suppose with my past, it—"

"No! It had nothing to do with your past, Collin. You have to believe me. It was my fault. Mine. You did nothing to deserve anything I thought."

Didn't we have this discussion once? How many times do I have to say I'm sorry?

Jeff slashed at the accusation. *As many times as she needs to hear.* He started them walking again. "Has Rudy said anything about when his friend is going to bring Erin and Vy?"

"No. He said there had been a complication, but he didn't say what. Only we might need to be a little patient."

"When did he tell you?"

"This last match. Maybe the one before. They all run together."

For you, maybe. I'm the one cooling my heels with nothing to do except watch you fawn—

"Okay. We'll let it go for tonight."

They walked in silence.

Collin cleared her throat. "I know this is putting your projects in the hole, with you being gone. And I'm sure your parents are going nuts wanting to know where you are. I will make it up to you. Somehow."

Jeff didn't stop walking. "We're a team, Collin. You don't owe me anything for work delays. It's all community property, right?"

"It used to be. You got aggravated when I would ask you about them, so I stopped asking. I wanted to help, but you kept telling me you had everything under control, and you didn't need my help." Her voice became softer. "After a while, I took it to mean you didn't need me."

Jeff stopped walking. He turned Collin to face him and kissed her as warmly as when they had been almost-weds. Before the lie.

They broke. Jeff whispered, "I never meant to hurt you, Collin. I never meant to shut you out. Can we start over? All over? From the beginning?"

Collin laughed. She patted her stomach. "Almost the beginning. There's no going back on these two."

Jeff smiled. "Agreed." *Sure there is. You—* "Have you thought about names yet?" They started walking again.

Collin frowned. "Do you have any naming traditions in your family you want to follow?"

"No traditions I know of. We did stay away from juniors or seconds and thirds. Easier when you're playing football not to have to call 'William the Third catch.' Takes some of the stress out."

"Agreed. And let's not make one a derivation of the other. Tim and Tom. I hate that."

"Erin and Caitlin weren't close."

"I know. But I knew other sets, Tim and Jim, or Bob and Rob. Micah and Michael. Let's not do that to our children."

"Agreed. Total individuals." He peeked at her through one eye. "Do you know if they're identical or fraternal? Boys or girls? One of each?"

"Not yet. I didn't even know I was pregnant when I went to see my doctor. I couldn't understand all the nausea. So the doctor didn't do an ultrasound because he doesn't have one in his office. I was supposed to make a follow-up with an Ob-Gyn as soon as I could get in to see one. But then all this happened… It was enough he heard two heartbeats."

Jeff pursed his lips. "Hmm. Which grandparent has to fight Leesa for the right to hold one first?"

Collin laughed. "Oh, no, I'm not getting into that battle royale. You can make the decision."

"Two out of three falls? I make no bets on who will win."

They arrived full circle back at the living area. Rudy hadn't returned. Collin chewed her lip. "I don't think he's healthy. I think there's something wrong with him, and he's just waiting out his time here."

"Yeah. I saw him get up, and he was in pain. But he said it's something no one could fix." He hesitated. "Did you know he hasn't been outside this place in ten years?"

"Really? No, I didn't. He doesn't talk to me much."

Jeff's face screwed up. "You're kidding? All the time you two spend together?"

"We're playing chess. We don't talk when we're playing chess."

"I heard you talking Scripture with him."

"He asks about different passages as a way of arguing with me about God. But we never talk about anything personal." She shook her head. "You've got more out of him than I have."

"Hmm."

"What does that mean, 'hmm'?"

"Just, hmm. Interesting." Jeff booted the attitude one more time for good measure.

They took chairs opposite the chess table, where they could sit comfortably. Collin leaned forward. "Will you listen to my plan as far as it goes and tell me where the holes are?"

"Go ahead."

"We get Erin, Vy, and the shipment…well, the pretend shipment…here and off the street. I contact Franny. I tell her Erin died trying to deliver it, and it's her fault. I intercepted the runners who killed my brother, have the shipment, and am holding it for ransom. I want the street equivalent value, and I want it delivered here."

Collin shifted in her chair. "Or this area. When she comes to try to kill me, I get her to confess her contact's the one who had Erin stuffed in the trunk of the car and planted the photo of Rudy on Erin's computer."

She chewed her lip again. "There's part I'm not sure about, though. If Erin really did catch a photo of Rudy…"

"No. Rudy said he hasn't been outside in ten years. I doubt seriously if he posed for pictures. Safe bet she photoshopped and planted it to make it look like Rudy was alive and active after Erin was crushed." Jeff tapped the table. "Which the police immediately thought of Rudy. Especially with the M.O. of stuffing him in the trunk, then blowing the place up to prevent anyone finding any evidence."

Collin glanced sideways at Jeff. "But the police have the computer and can tell the picture wasn't real."

"If they evaluated it. And that doesn't incriminate Franny. The only way to get the heat off Rudy so he'll feel safe enough to let us go is to put the matter to bed. Franny gets busted, and we make it happen." Jeff thought a moment. "Franny doesn't know the police have the computer. She probably thought she disposed of it when they blew Erin's place up."

"Okay." Collin finished her plan. "The police take Franny, sweep her contacts and her coworkers, and everyone is happy except the bad guys. We get to go home to live the rest of our lives." She tapped her chin. "What did I leave out?"

Jeff took Collin's hand. "What about the fact we know a wanted criminal is alive, and the police should be looking for him?" Jeff squeezed her hand. "I know you care about him, but he's a criminal. One who more than likely had people murdered. He may be sparing us, but his other victims deserve justice."

Collin stared at the floor. "That's the part I'm having the hardest time with." She stared Jeff in the eyes. "I can't figure how to work with him, not betray him, yet still turn him in. I don't know how to do all that, Jeff. I don't."

Jeff put his arm around her shoulder. "We'll think of something. Together. We'll figure it out, milady."

Collin's lip quivered, and a tear trickled down her nose. "That's the first time you've called me milady in a very long time."

Jeff kissed her forehead. "Get used to it. I intend to use it often."

MONDAY

By Collin's reckoning, two days and nights passed before Erin and Vy arrived. Accompanied by Rudy's "friend." Absent anything resembling a shipment of drugs, fake or otherwise.

Collin hugged her brother hard, letting all her emotions travel to Erin in one embrace. She released him and checked him over. He looked horrible. To anyone else, he appeared tired but otherwise fine. But Collin could see beneath the exterior. She knew Erin was not only hurting but sick.

He smiled at her. "Hey, Cane. Long time no see. How you doing?"

She hugged him again and whispered, "Better than you. What's wrong?"

Erin shrugged. "Eh. When this is over, we can talk about it."

Vy stood close to Erin. "I'm Vy. You have to be Collin."

Collin took Vy's appearance in stride and hugged the woman. "I've heard good things about you. Nice to put the face to the myth."

Vy chuckled. "I hope I don't disappoint."

"You're watching out for my brother. How can you disappoint?"

Vy introduced Mason around the room. Collin noticed Rudy seemed more energized with Mason there. Or faked it well.

Chairs were provided for the war room to bring everyone up to speed. The who, what, when, where, and why of the week were discussed. Mason deferred to Erin, who deferred to Vy to detail the last few days.

"Mason arranged for Beela to be admitted to an independent living facility where she can be monitored and kept safe."

Mason added, "And harmless."

Collin eyed the man. "And she agreed to this?"

"Between going there, being murdered, or serving life in prison, she chose the living facility. Clearly the wise choice."

Jeff turned to Erin. "She tried to kill you. There were no charges for that?"

Erin shrugged. "She failed. I can forgive. Especially when it means not having to go through a trial and all the mess."

Collin asked, "I still don't understand who Franny is working with on this end. Who actually stuffed Erin in the trunk?"

Vy pointed to Mason. He cleared his throat. "We're working on that now. It appears Franny is poaching territory belonging to someone else."

"Brice's territory?" Collin couldn't quite make the connection.

Mason nodded. "So it would seem. Brice gave me a few likely candidates of people wanting to expand their reach. He's looking for them. So am I. They can't hide for long."

Jeff glanced from Mason to Rudy back to Mason. "You and Brice aren't part of the same organization?"

Mason tapped the arm of his chair a few times. "Let's say no, and leave it there. For now."

Collin could see Jeff wanted to push the issue, so changed the subject. "The two men who tried to shoot their way in. What happened with them? I know they were killed, but who were they with?"

Vy took the question. "The sheriff ran their IDs. Turns out they were small-time pushers who wanted to steal Erin's truck for a fast buck. Not related to the shipment at all."

Rudy leaned forward. "The question now is, what are you planning for Franny?"

Collin detailed her plan as she had explained it to Jeff. Rudy and Mason listened, nodding to each other at points. Collin noticed Vy's eyes were glued on Mason. *Is she trying to figure how to take him as well as Rudy? Will she try to sabotage the plan to get both dealers arrested?*

When Collin finished, Mason stroked his chin. He asked Rudy, "What do you think?"

"It might have worked if we had the shipment. Or something to pass as the shipment. As it is, we don't. However, we do have something she will want more than the drugs."

"What?" Mason waited for Rudy's answer.

Rudy eyed Jeff. "Your phone has her contact information on it, doesn't it? Address, phone number?"

Jeff answered slowly. "Yes…"

Rudy pointed to Collin. "What if you were to threaten to give the information to Brice? I believe she would be far more apt to respond to a direct threat on her life."

Collin thought it through. "And we still get the confession?"

"Of course. That is the whole purpose of this stratagem."

Mason cleared his throat. "There is a matter of getting the proper police factions to participate."

The two dealers began discussing the logistics of involving law enforcement. Collin saw Jeff's eyes flare. He wouldn't challenge the two outlaws to their faces, would he? Or refuse to cooperate because it let the guilty go free for another day? Collin touched his arm. She held his eyes. After a moment, he relaxed.

Collin turned her focus to Vy. The woman's face remained focused on the discussion, interested, invested, but non-committal. Collin would have to speak to her privately. *Great. The bad guys sign on, but the good guys don't. Does that tell you something? Like, maybe this isn't a good plan to begin with?*

Lord, I need You to be in this. Yes, I've been praying about it. Yes, I'm asking You to be honored. Tell me what to do. I need You.

Collin checked on Erin. Her brother's eyes were closed. She watched his breathing. And stood and walked over to kneel beside his chair. "A-One, you hear me?"

She touched his forehead. Fever. High fever. Collin swung around to Jeff. "He's sick. He needs help."

Jeff swung into paramedic mode. He crossed over and kneeled beside Erin. He eased her brother's eyes open and examined them. Erin didn't respond. Jeff motioned to Mason. "Help me get him somewhere I can check him over."

Mason and Jeff carried Erin to a spare room with a bed. They lay him down. Collin wrang out a wet cloth and handed it to Jeff. Vy caught Jeff's arm. "I checked it and it didn't look that bad. He told me he got nicked in the side."

Jeff growled. "Which means he probably took a direct hit from a howitzer."

Collin snatched the cloth back from him and wiped her brother's face and neck. Her face burned with anger. Tears dripped on his chest as she worked. "He did what needed to be done. You'd do the same."

Jeff searched Erin's side. "I know you both have a martyr complex a mile wide. Everything always depends on you." He exposed the wound, now purple and angry red. Jeff called to Rudy. "First-aid kit? Alcohol? Anything antiseptic?"

Mason tapped Rudy's arm. "I can get it faster. Stay in here and referee."

Collin glared at Jeff. She swallowed as many of the hormone-fueled emotions as she could and let loose the protective-sister anger. "Sometimes, Mr. Farrell. Sometimes it does depend on us. Us and the Lord. Erin knows it. I know it." She wanted to add, *Do you?* but didn't. She went back to cooling Erin's face.

Jeff looked at Rudy. "I need a knife. A small, sharper-than-sharp knife."

Rudy reached in his pocket and pulled out a very small, very illegal switchblade. He handed it to Jeff by the blade. "You want a flame to clean it?"

"I'll wait for the antiseptic." He frowned at the knife. "Carving knife?"

"Dinner. Steaks aren't as tender as they used to be."

Jeff chuckled, touched Collin's arm. "I wasn't trying to start a fight. I'm sorry. Poor choice of words."

Vy stepped forward. "Erin kept us alive. He never said how bad he was wounded." Tears filled her eyes, but she choked them back. "I'd never let him go running around like he did if I'd known."

Jeff stared at Collin, his eyes stern. Collin frowned. "Vy, he didn't want you to know. He…we…we both came up hard, okay? You never admitted pain." Collin turned to Jeff. "Even now. You never let someone know you're hurt. We had it drilled into us being injured gave the enemy an opening he would exploit. Any weakness had to be buried and denied. Hard to let it go." She swallowed hard and kept her head down.

Do not start the fight again. Do not start the fight again. Let it go.

He hurt me! He said I cheated on him. I have done nothing but love that man, nothing but try to please him, and he accused me of cheating on him!

Collin left the bed and rinsed out the towel, cooling it once again, wringing out the excess, then wiping Erin's face and chest.

Jeff went to look over the contents of the first aid kit Mason retrieved. Collin heard him whistle in amazement. "You could stock an ER with some of this stuff."

Mason's voice tinged only slightly with sarcasm. "No, we didn't hijack it from a hospital."

Collin glanced at the "we" comment. *Just how close are Rudy and Mason? Does Mason keep Rudy supplied with…with what? Something isn't right here.* Collin put her head down again to concentrate on Erin. She watched her brother's eyes flutter. "Bad time to wake up, A-One. Jeff's going to open the wound. It's infected."

Erin grumbled. "Yeah, I thought so." He gave her a wan smile. "Give me something to bite on?"

Vy stepped in. "You can bite on my hand."

Erin declined. "No, that won't work. I need something I can't hurt." His grin seemed forced. "Your hand is too inviting."

"That's the second lame move you've tried to make, Erin." Vy's voice shook slightly. Collin could see the woman trying to keep herself under control.

Erin pointed to Collin. "Both of you get out of here. Go pray. I can join you from here. We'll start with praying Jeff knows what he's doing."

Collin read her brother's intent. She lay the wet cloth across his face. "Chew on this. It'll take the punishment." She kissed him on the forehead, turned to Vy. "Let's get some air."

Vy glared from Erin to Collin back to Erin. He smiled weakly at her. She turned and followed Collin out of the room.

Outside, she caught Collin's arm. "Why did we come out?"

"Because Erin doesn't want you to watch Jeff operate."

Vy's face hardened. "Why? He doesn't think I can handle it?"

"No, I think he knows you could. He doesn't think you should have to." Collin drew in a deep breath. "And if something goes wrong, he doesn't want your last memories to be of him in crisis."

Vy cocked her head. "Is that something else you two were taught?"

"No. It's something we promised each other. We wouldn't watch each other die. We didn't want it to be our last memory of each other." Collin shrugged. "Of course, we didn't know the Lord, so maybe it won't be the same." She held her hands out, palms up. "Maybe."

Vy took hold of Collin's hand and squeezed it. "Your brother is a gentle and caring soul, Collin. I'm going to pray the Lord lets him stick around longer so I can get to know him even better. If it's alright with you."

Collin smiled even as her eyes filled with moisture. "Of course it is."

The two women joined hands and began praying silently. Collin heard a muffled grunt of pain and switched to praying aloud. "Lord, please. We want Erin to live. I'm selfish. I want him to be around to play with the twins and love them and spoil them like a good uncle should. I want to watch him get married and have kids of his own and grow old in You. All that is what I want. You love him more than I do. You died for him. You know what's best. Your will, Lord."

Vy echoed Collin's prayer. "Father, You said to bring our requests to You. We have because we know we can trust You. You are good, You are God, and all You do is right. Have Your way, Lord."

Together they finished, "In Jesus's Name. Amen."

Collin realized Rudy was standing in the doorway, watching them. He shrugged. "Don't like the sight of blood not my own."

Collin grinned. "No wonder you retired from your line of work."

Rudy pulled the door closed to the sick room. He motioned for Vy and Collin to sit as he did himself. Collin eyed him sideways.

Rudy studied Collin and Vy. "Explain what you prayed just then."

Collin asked, "What? Asking God to save Erin?"

"No. I understand that part. You would quite naturally want your supreme genie to save his life. But saying 'have your way' and 'your will'? Why would you ever create a god that doesn't do what you want?"

Collin raised her eyebrows. "Why create one that does?"

Rudy's eyes narrowed. "I lost you."

"If I create a god who only does what I want him to do, I've created something in my own image. It can never be any smarter nor know anything more than I know. If it is my reflection, it will have no more power than I do myself."

Rudy's eyes scanned the floor, then the ceiling. "Maybe."

Vy raised an eyebrow. "May I?"

Collin waved to her. "Be my guest."

"In Isaiah, the prophet told this parable. A man goes into the woods and cuts a tree. With some of the wood, he builds a fire to keep himself warm. With other of the wood, he roasts food to eat. And with the rest, he carves the image of a god and says, 'Save me.' How foolish is that? You use it to stay warm, you use it to cook your food, and you're going to worship it as a god?"

Rudy stroked his chin. "I see the point. If you're going to create a god, you need to create one better than you are."

Collin smiled. "But how do you create something smarter than yourself or that knows more than you can know? Not talking about artificial intelligence, okay? Sure, you can *say* your god is smarter, but how does it tell you something you don't already know?"

She pounded on the chair in which she sat. "Might as well ask the chair." She looked at Rudy. "But God, the God of the Universe, knows. He wasn't created. He is the Creator. He made all things, knows all things, holds all things together."

"I could ask him what's behind door number two, and he'd tell me?"

Collin shrugged. "He could. But He isn't a magic genie, and He doesn't answer to us. He gave us the Scriptures to reveal most of His wisdom and what we need to know. Sometimes He may speak through other means, like a circumstance, or a friend, or a feeling. Or a still, small voice in your soul." She smiled. "Like telling me to trust you in spite of all appearances to the contrary."

Rudy grunted. "That's just good sense on your part."

The door to the sickroom opened, and Jeff walked out. Collin eyed him closely. "Well?"

Jeff shrugged. "I think I've saved him from himself once again." Collin's scowl must have raised a red flag. Jeff cleared his throat. "I mean, I think he'll be fine after some rest. But someone needs to keep an eye on him so he doesn't try to go over the wall."

Vy raised her eyebrows at Jeff. "I don't think that's going to happen. But I'll volunteer to speak truth into him if he does."

Collin felt a sudden disturbance in the force as something bumped sharply in her abdomen. She placed her hand on her side. A moment, later it happened again. She laughed, her eyes wide and shining. "He kicked me!" She crowed. "He kicked me! The little runt kicked me."

Rudy cocked his head. "Excuse me?"

Jeff's eyes narrowed, then shone. Collin had the uneasy feeling the shining was deliberate, the narrowing, the reflex of his heart. He smiled. "Really? Isn't it early for that?"

Collin chuckled. "Maybe there's not enough room in there."

Rudy repeated more strongly, "Excuse me? What are you talking about?"

Collin couldn't suppress the joy. "The baby. Babies. I'm pregnant." She slipped her arm in Jeff's. "We're pregnant. Twins."

Rudy's eyes widened. "Oh? Oh! We need to get you out of here. I'm not birthin' no babies in my home!" His eyes narrowed, and he focused on Jeff. "And you're good with letting your wife challenge Franny?"

Jeff raised a hand. "I'm not good with it. I know Collin, and I know when she decides something, it's useless to argue."

Collin felt her stomach lurch, and it wasn't from the babies kicking it. *I haven't challenged him in three years...and now he says he can't argue with me?*

He's back to his old tricks. Blame you for everything. Always— Lord, help me.

Collin smiled at her husband. "I can be reasonable. And reasoned with." She turned to Rudy. "But I don't think Franny would believe Jeff wants revenge for Erin being killed in a heist gone bad. It would have to come from someone more invested in Erin. Like a sister."

That didn't come out sounding the way I wanted it to.
Leave it go.
Right.

Rudy nodded. "I see. Very well. We still need to get you back to your lives aboveground. And the sooner, the better."

Jeff's gaze narrowed. A little.

Collin read Jeff's eyes, and she didn't like the look of them. She needed to get him alone and soon. Like, now? She gripped her stomach again and smiled at him. "I want to go back to the room for a little bit. Stretch out so someone will quit kick-boxing my bladder." She motioned to Rudy. "Give me half an hour."

"Take your time. Mason and I still have a few details to nail down." Rudy bowed to Collin, then to Vy. "May I ask you to take over nurse duties from Mason so he and I can talk about your release?" He made a circular motion to indicate Collin, Jeff, and Vy.

Vy smiled at the older man. "Of course. I'll send him out."

Jeff opened his mouth, but Collin cut him off. "Thanks, Vy. Jeff and I will sub out for you later. We appreciate your help." Collin took Jeff's arm and led him away before he could say anything else.

In the corridor and out of earshot of the others, Jeff protested, "I wasn't going to say anything wrong."

"And I wanted to make sure of it." She glanced at her husband. "You're getting snippy again. I feel like I'm getting you back, then I lose you again. What bothers you about this plan?"

"Oh, how about two notorious drug smugglers get off scot-free and live like nothing happened? And we help them? That bothers me. It should bother you. My wife, who used to believe in justice, throws away her morals for two nice men. One of whom plays a decent game of chess for her entertainment."

Collin listened without comment. She stayed silent the whole way to the small room they occupied. She closed the door, spun on Jeff, and stared at him. Her eyes narrowed as tears loomed just below the surface of her emotions.

"I believed, Mr. Farrell, we had re-established a measure of trust and faith in one another. At least you were giving me the benefit of the doubt. What happened to change our dynamic?" She spaced her words for effect.

Jeff sat on the bed. "I thought we had, too. Except I see my wife consorting with criminals, and it bugs me. It should bug you. Why doesn't it?"

Collin breathed deep. She stood in front of him and held his eyes. "When you stopped trusting me, did you stop loving me as well?"

Jeff lowered his gaze first. "I'm sorry. I hate being cooped up. The longer we're here, the worse it gets." He reached for her hands. "I love you, Collin. I trust you. I hate who I've become these days. I'm fighting it, but I'm not winning many of the rounds."

Collin sat beside him. "You're still here. You haven't tried to escape and notify the authorities."

Jeff snorted. "It's not for lack of thinking about it. I can't figure out a way to do it, that's all."

"Maybe that's how God wants it."

"It's certainly how Rudy wants it."

Collin kissed his cheek. "I imagine I know how God feels. He wants us to trust Him without asking Him a lot of questions about why and how."

Jeff cocked his head. "What does He have to do with this?"

Collin examined her hands. "I want you to trust me because I'm your wife, and you love me, and you know I love you. And I would never betray you or my morals." She raised her head. "But you don't." She breathed out. "I believe Rudy and Mason are undercover. Deep undercover. I think Rudy has retired but is hiding out here to keep the dealers he exposed from finding and killing him. We're thinking Franny wanted to cover her tracks by copying Rudy's old MO, but she wouldn't know that. Neither would the police. No one would, except higher-ups. Rudy wants this resolved because his cover could be blown."

Collin stood and paced the room. "Franny and her partner had likely discussed using Rudy as cover, but her partner jumped the gun on doing it by trying to crush Erin. When it happened, Franny had to follow through. She planted the picture showing Rudy in the woods on Erin's computer to further hide their tracks. They didn't know Rudy really was out there."

Jeff's eyes followed Collin. She didn't know whether he believed her or not, so she pushed ahead. "Mason helped get Vy and Erin out of the situation they were in up north without too much trouble. And he and Rudy are friends. I think they're more than friends."

Collin stopped pacing. "Mason knew right where to get the first-aid kit. Which means he's been here before and knows his way around. Someone keeps Rudy supplied with goods and information. I think it's Mason, and I think he's either Rudy's old partner or someone who knows what Rudy is doing and why."

She pursed her lips. "And Vy as much as told me so. I read it in her eyes."

"When?" The disbelief in Jeff's tone cut Collin.

"The way she has been following their discussions. How she speaks to Rudy. And came here with Mason. The whole thing about Mason's mom being put in a home. That had to take time to arrange. Time Vy and Erin could have used to escape. If either of them were convinced Mason wasn't above board, don't you think they would have tried harder to get free? Been brought here in cuffs and leg irons?"

Collin paced the floor again. "No. They all walked in, and they all talked like everything has been settled. I don't believe Vy would do that if she didn't know Mason and Rudy were law enforcement. Or had been law enforcement. She loves the Lord too much to play games."

Collin's voice became small. "You used to believe I loved the Lord, too. Now I don't know what you think of me."

Jeff tried to take Collin into his arms, but she held back. "No, Jeff. I know you're still struggling. Maybe being cooped up is contributing to it, but this is all still a matter of do you believe me or not? Do you, deep in your heart, believe I betrayed you and the Lord, lied about it, and am capable of living with that lie? That's the question you need to settle."

Collin turned and walked out of the room alone. There a stillness filled her soul. A sense of waiting. Not hoping, not dreading, not trying to imagine the future. Only waiting. And Jeff had to be the one to release her.

* * *

Jeff watched her walk away. *What is wrong with me? Why can't I believe her and make it stick? Why can't I get excited about the babies?*

Because they're not yours. You know it. Deep down, you know she's lying.

Jeff lifted his head to the ceiling. "Lord, help me! I can't keep doing this. I want to believe her. Help my unbelief. Settle this once and for all."

Choose you this day who you will believe.

Water stung his eyes. "I want to believe her, Lord. I do. Why can't I?"

How long will you waffle between two choices? You either believe Collin, or you believe Rich. One trusts in God. One trusts in themself. You can choose one or the other, but you can't choose both.

Jeff stood and mirrored Collin's pacing. "Either Collin or Rich? Is it that simple? One or the other?" He stared at the wall, his jaw open. "I am an idiot. A fool. A… Of course!" He turned and raced down the hall. "Collin! Collin!"

He dodged through the maze and came to the living area. "Where is she? Where is Collin?"

Mason and Rudy sat at the chess table, game in motion. Rudy looked up at Jeff's demand. "She's outside making the call to Franny."

Jeff's eyes widened. "No! I've got to talk to her first. I have to."

Rudy shook his head. "It's too late. The call has been connected." He motioned to the laptop on the table.

Jeff checked where Rudy pointed. A screen appeared to be monitoring an electrical signal of some kind. He could see the frequencies increase and decrease. People were talking. He stared at the two drug smug—two undercover DEA agents if Collin guessed right. Jeff watched the screen. "I have to believe you have a warrant to use that."

Mason nodded. "Any time we need it."

Jeff breathed out. "Yeah. I uh…I owe you both…an apology."

Rudy snorted. "For what? Believing we are what we pretend to be? That's the whole idea, son. We want people to think we're mean and nasty." He shrugged. "Or he is." He motioned to Mason. "I'm retired. But I have an image to uphold on the outside."

Mason chuckled. "Actually, your image on the outside is you're dead. You should stay that way."

Jeff stuck his hands in his pockets. "I'm still sorry. Collin had you figured out, but I didn't." He shrugged. "No, Collin and I don't play chess. I am no match for her."

Rudy waved his hand at the board. "We're replaying her last game. No one is a match for her."

"I am. I taught her."

Erin came into the room, supported by Vy. She took him over to a chair, helped him sit, and ordered, "Do not move."

"Yes, ma'am. I'll stay right here." Erin smiled at Vy. She scowled at him, but Jeff could read her true feelings through the light in her eyes. *Another one bites the dust. Good catch, Erin.*

Rudy's eyes narrowed. "You taught her?" His tone held a tinge of disbelief.

"Sure. We're twins. We didn't have anyone else to play with, so we played against each other. I learned from Grandfather Mudd, and I taught Collin."

Jeff pointed to Erin. "Do not play against him. Do not. Guaranteed." He went to Erin's side. "How are you feeling, man?"

"Like a million bucks. After taxes. And payroll. And profit sharing. And—"

"I get the idea. Look up."

Erin groaned. "My eyes look horrid. I know it."

"Got that right." He turned to Rudy. "How long has she been out there?" He glanced over at the monitor. Soundwaves still bouncing back and forth.

"About five minutes since the call started."

Jeff took a chair across from Erin. "Good at least to see you upright."

"Me too." Erin jerked his head at Vy. "My nurse doesn't think I should be out here. We argued. I won."

Vy scowled at him. "This time, Mr. Winger."

Erin groaned. "Please don't remind me of my heritage. Getting a name change is still on my to-do list."

Jeff stared at the soundwaves. What could Collin be saying? Better not to know, maybe. *Lord, whatever she's telling Franny is for the good of many, many of us. But You already know that. Guide her words.*

* * *

Collin walked to where she had good reception. While the sun felt warm and inviting and soothing and glorious, Collin still shivered. *I'm not sure about this. Lord, in my thinking, in my speaking, in my heart.*

She punched in Franny's number.

Franny picked up. "Jeff! Hi! How are you? How is Erin? Did he get to Aunt Beela's okay?"

Collin kept her tone as cold and deadly as she knew how. "Erin made it there. He never made it back. You owe me."

Franny didn't pretend. She dropped the blonde act. "I take it this is his sister. I don't know what you are talking about. And I don't have time—"

"Brice knows you're poaching his territory."

Silence. Then a cautious, "Who?"

"You know Brice. Director over the northern half of the quadrant. He caught your people taking the shipment when it came off Erin's truck. It did not end well."

Franny returned to her boredness. "Well, I'm sure that was terrible for them. I hardly see how—"

"Beela dimed you out. Brice is looking for you. I'm sure you know what that means. It'd be a real shame if Brice got this phone with your contact information in it."

"What do you want?" No longer bored. Angry.

"Vengeance for my brother. Seeing as how I can't get it, I'll take a million dollars."

"You're insane. I don't have money like that laying around."

"You bought the drugs you put on the truck. Someone fronted you the money. It wasn't your associate; he just moved the stuff along. You have connections. I want a million dollars cash, and I want it delivered to me here in Fort Newton. At my grandfather's farm."

"Even if I could get that kind of money together, it would take me a month to do it."

"You have two days."

"You're insane. I can't—"

"Two days or Brice gets the phone. And yes, I know exactly how to contact him." Collin disconnected the call.

She waited. And waited. And—

Ping. Collin let it ping three times. "What?"

"You're bluffing. You don't know Brice. You heard his name and—"

"Average height. Dark brown hair in a ponytail below his shoulders. One eye closed more than the other. A 'lazy eye.' Longish sideburns. Offered Vy a job. She turned him down. That did not end well, either."

"Maybe you're not bluffing. I still can't get that kind of money in two days."

"That's your problem, not mine. Oh, and Franny? Don't think running will get you off his radar. He may operate north, but he does have operatives all over the tri-state area. Poaching another man's territory is something all dealers detest. You won't find many friends."

"You think you've got this all figured out, don't you? You don't know me at all."

"I know you tried to hide your dealings by implicating a man that's been dead ten years. Using his signature tactics. Even pasting a picture of him in my brother's video from the drone. Neat trick, that one. Almost had the police convinced. Until they had the footage analyzed, of course."

"You're wasting your time. I don't have that kind of money, and I can't raise it in two days."

"That's a shame. I'll have Brice give you a call. Maybe you can work out something together."

Collin disconnected the call again. She waited. Again. Three minutes passed. Collin's eyes narrowed. Would Franny take the bait? *Did I lose her?*

Ping. Ping. Ping. Ping. Collin picked it up. "Next time, the price will go up."

"Where and when do I bring the money?"

"You know where the farm is. Erin showed it to you before. Walk half a mile west from the road. There will be a marker. Follow the flags. I'll be waiting at the end of the path."

"When?"

"Day after tomorrow. Three p.m. I know you're not planning to come alone. So I'll tell you now I will be at a vantage point to see you when you go in the woods. You do what you think you have to do. I'll see you."

Collin shoved the phone in her pocket. She closed her eyes, lifted her chin. "Lord, I'm sorry about this. I lied. I deliberately deceived her. I know it. Forgive me. It's all in Your hands, Father."

Collin stood another minute in the warmth of the sun, then made her way back to the entrance to the underground compound. A single manhole cover, half-buried under leaves and branches strategically fastened together, remained partially open for her. Collin slipped through the gap, pulled the steel cover over her head, and climbed down the ladder to the darkness below.

Collin walked into the common area and found all eyes focused on her entrance. Five faces stared at her, all with the same "Well?" looks on them. Collin found an empty seat, settled in it. "She's coming. I don't doubt she's bringing reinforcements, and there will be no money to exchange."

Mason's gaze was soft. "You did good. Now the rest of us can take over."

Collin cocked her head to look at him. "What do you mean?"

"I mean, we'll take it from here. Someone else will be waiting for her. Someone else can carry the conversation we need to get the goods on her. You're done."

"I don't think so. If she doesn't see me, she'll be long gone."

Jeff touched her arm. "We discussed it while you were up top. There's one other person who could be there and talk to her, and she'll likely carry on the conversation."

Collin felt her stomach tighten. "Who?"

All eyes turned to Jeff. "Me."

Collin shook her head hard. "No. No way. You do not have experience dealing with street—"

"She likes me better than you. And she thinks she can buffalo me. I can use that."

"How? You lie about as well as a two-year-old with his hand in the cookie jar. It's all over your face."

Jeff raised his eyebrows. "I don't want you and our children up there risking all your lives, milady."

She heard the words *"our children."* Looked him in the eyes. Looked him in the heart. Collin closed her eyes to settle the emotions, swallow the tears of happiness she felt. She breathed out, opened her eyes. "One condition."

"What?"

Collin pointed to Mason and Rudy, still poring over the chessboard. "Which of you is better at chess?"

Quick discussion. Mason pointed. "Rudy."

She turned back to Jeff. "You win three matches. One against Mason. One against Rudy. One against Erin. Beat all three, and you can take my place." She gave the men who would be playing against him a stern warning. "No throwing the games, no helping him win. You play your toughest match. His life will depend on it."

Jeff waved at the three men assembled across the room. "All I have to do is beat them? One at a time?"

"Preferably."

"How many chances do I get?"

"As many as it takes until time runs out."

Jeff touched her cheek. "For you and our babies, I'll do it. You'll see."

Vy sidled over to Collin, lowered her voice, and raised her eyebrows. "Any reason you didn't include me in the challenge?"

Collin kept her voice low in return. "No. Other than I figured he's at least got a chance against the other three. He'd have no chance against you."

Vy grinned. "And why would you assume that?"

"Female logic. No man can defeat a woman when she's defending her territory. She never plays by the rules. I didn't figure you would, either."

Vy smiled wide. "Good guess."

Jeff stood, interlaced his fingers, and cracked his knuckles. "Do I have to do these all in a row? Or do I get to take a break between them?"

Collin sighed. "You have until two p.m. day after tomorrow to finish. Franny is coming at three."

Jeff smiled at her, his lips pursed, his eyes narrowed a bit. "Who are you rooting for in this contest?"

Collin closed her eyes. "All of us. For all of us to make it out of here alive and well." *Lord, Your will. If You want him there, give him the ammunition he needs to use against the giants I'm setting in front of him. For all our sakes, Lord. In Jesus's Name. Amen.*

* * *

Jeff's first match with Mason proved a disaster. Ten moves. Not good. Not good at all. *This is for Collin and the babies. Knuckle down. You can do this. Stop thinking game. Start thinking war.*

The second match ended closer. Much closer. Collin retired to the bedroom while the competition continued. Jeff lost but learned. He shook hands with Mason. "Next time. And thanks for the lessons."

"You're welcome. You're a fast learner."

"When I need to be. And I need to be more often." Jeff stood. "I'm going to go hug my wife. I'll be back later."

"Make it in the morning. You lose track of time here, but it's almost ten p.m. in the 'real world.' Call it a night, and we'll pick it up tomorrow."

"Sounds good." Jeff glanced around and realized Erin had disappeared, Vy was missing, and Rudy had fallen asleep in his chair. Jeff turned back to Mason. "When did everyone leave?"

"About halfway through the game. And that's good you didn't notice. Shows you're focused on the game." Mason reached out and tapped Jeff on the shoulder. "You can do this, Jeff. Remember your motivation. Trust me, we're all rooting for you. Not letting up, but rooting for you."

"Thanks. I need to remember a lot of things I've let slide. I'll catch you in the morning." He motioned his head towards Rudy. "Is he…declining?"

"You mean is he dying? Yeah. He is. Cancer. And too many bullet holes, and knife wounds, and you name it. He's tough, but the body can only fight for so long."

Jeff nodded. "I understand." Jeff gazed at the ground, then to Mason. "Did you two work together?"

"Yeah. Ten years before we went undercover. We didn't see much of each other while we were in the field. Once he 'died' and moved here, I could see more of him and help him out some."

Since Mason seemed to be willing to talk, Jeff pushed for more answers. "How did he get this place? I mean, Collin and Erin own the property, but there's nothing in the paperwork anywhere saying this place exists."

"Yeah, I think it's buried way deep in the fine print. The government owns a tiny piece of the property or has it certified as wetlands or some clause saying it can't be built on or over or under."

Jeff stared at Rudy. "What kind of debt does the government owe so it creates a place this secret?"

Mason stood, stretched, motioned to his sleeping partner. "A big one." He waved Jeff off. "Goodnight."

Jeff walked back to the room. His eyes narrowed as he tried to imagine what kind of deal Rudy could have swung to get this. *Must have had the goods on someone. Then again, his part of the bargain is to stay underground the rest of his life. Wonder who really got the best end of this?*

Collin lay curled in a fetal position on top of the covers. Jeff slipped off his shoes and lay beside her, wrapping his arms around her. He snuggled into her ear, kissed her, whispered, "I love you, Collin," and closed his eyes. Collin did not stir.

But when Jeff woke several hours later, Collin was sitting, rubbing her belly. Her face looked pinched, her eyes tired. Jeff sat. "What's wrong, milady?"

Collin smiled on one side. "Your children are fighting already. I'm a little uncomfortable." She smiled full-faced. "I'll be fine."

Jeff glanced at her side-eyed. She looked at her stomach. "Stop it, you two. Mama needs some sleep."

Jeff put his hand on Collin's middle. Collin said, "It feels like one of them has taken their fist, pushed it against my abdomen, and is pushing out for all he's worth."

Jeff felt the tightening of Collin's stomach. He felt the muscle tighten all the way around to Collin's back. He could see from Collin's still-happy-but-tired face she didn't know what the tightening meant. What the contractions meant. He chose his words and his tone carefully. "How long has this been going on?"

He rubbed her side and felt the contraction ease. Collin shrugged. "Eh. Started yesterday."

"How often?"

"Not much. Maybe every couple of hours. Tonight it's been a little more often, but it will happen, then it stops." She touched Jeff's cheek. "Nothing to worry about, dearheart. I'll let you referee the fights when they happen on the outside of my belly. Not before."

Jeff smiled. He put all the conviction into his voice he had. "Sounds like a plan, milady. You want to lay and try to rest some more? I can give you a back rub." He motioned to the bed. "If you lay on your left side, maybe it will help. I'll prop some pillows behind you so you can stay on your side."

"Why? What does that do?"

Jeff thought fast. "It gives the babies more room and keeps them off your abdomen for a while."

Collin shrugged. "If you say so. You're almost the doctor."

Jeff chuckled. "Never. I prefer my building career."

Collin lay back and twisted onto her left side. Jeff tucked the pillows and the blankets behind her, then stretched out beside her to massage her belly. He felt one more contraction, a weak one, but no more beyond that. Maybe it didn't mean anything. Women had Braxton-Hicks contractions, the so-called "false labor" pains, all the time. He'd feel better about the diagnosis if Collin didn't look so pale and tired and washed out. *Father God, please. Take care of her. And please, help us keep the babies. You know everything about being a Father, more than I ever will. If there's room in Your plans for us, please, keep these babies alive and well, and keep Collin well, too. In the Name of Your Son, Jesus. Amen.*

Jeff held her in his arms. He didn't try to sleep but simply lay beside her. *Lord, I can't compete with these guys on my best day, but with worry about Collin and the babies...no way. If You want me to go outside instead of Collin, You have to make it happen. Help me. Please. For Collin. For the babies. For everyone in this compound.*

He went down his list, praying for family and friends, acquaintances, even enemies. And when he finished the list, he went over it again. And again. And again. The rest of the night. It felt good.

TUESDAY

With the morning came renewed determination to do whatever he needed to do to make certain Collin did not go out to face Franny. Leaving Collin sleeping, Jeff went out to the common area, ate breakfast (*nice they deliver weekly here. Haven't got a clue how, but food shows regularly),* then went to find Erin.

He found his brother-in-law stumbling out of his room, looking lost and confused. Jeff took him by the arm, led him to the common area, and sat him down. "Sit. Stay. I'll get coffee."

Erin grunted something that might have sounded like, "Okay," but Jeff couldn't confirm it. He rounded up two coffee mugs, filled them with coffee some thoughtful person had made already, and carried them back to Erin.

He handed one to the semi-conscious man. "Here. It's the last time I serve you today."

Erin received the cup. "Much appreciation." He took a large swallow of the thick brew, stared at the cup in dismay and awe, swallowed another mouthful, shuddered. "That's awful. Is there more?"

"Whole container full."

"That'll about do it."

Jeff grinned. "How are you feeling?"

"Better. Thanks for saving my life again. How many times does this make now?"

Jeff shrugged. "Who's counting? I think it makes us about even. Or I still owe you one. I'm not sure."

"We'll call it even and leave it there." Erin swallowed more of the coffee. "Where's Cane?"

"Sleeping." Jeff looked over his shoulder toward the room. "I don't like the way she looks. Pale. Tired. I know she's carrying twins. But she's not so far along they've gained much weight. They shouldn't be causing much trouble. Yet."

Erin's eyes narrowed. "You're worried something is going on?"

"Yeah. A little. I wish I had a way to check her blood pressure."

"Have you asked Rudy? Seems like he can produce what you need with a snap of his finger. Or send Mason after it. Maybe there's a blood pressure cuff here."

"I'll ask one of them." He swallowed half his coffee. It was as awful as Erin said. But it was hot and black, and that's all it had to be at this point. He pulled a chair, sat, leaned forward, stared Erin in the eyes. "I need help, man. I need you to help me beat Mason. And Rudy. And you. Not cheat. But defeat them. You watched Mason play last night, some. What do I need to know to win against him?"

Erin's eyes searched Jeff's. Jeff stared him levelly. "This is for Collin, bro. No ego. No pride. It's all about not sending your sister and my wife out there to face a killer." He glanced at the floor. "I'll stop her myself if I have to. But I know what she wants to accomplish with the matches. She wants me to be prepared, to think strategically, so I can say the right things, present the right attitudes, and get us all out of here alive. I get that." He stared back at Erin. "Help me."

Erin swallowed the rest of the coffee. He handed his mug to Jeff. "Get me more coffee. I'll set the board."

Five hours of coaching and four long games produced a win over Mason. Jeff moved up the ladder to Rudy, knowing the final challenge—Erin—might be a step too far. But for Collin, he'd do it. He had to. Had to.

Collin wandered in at some point during the day. Jeff remembered to ask about the blood pressure cuff, and yep, Rudy had one, and yep, Mason knew right where it was and went to fetch it. Jeff took Collin's BP. He checked the numbers, kept his face non-commital, and smiled at her. "Yeah, your heart is pumping. Working hard, too. I'd appreciate it if you would try to stay off your feet as much as possible."

Collin gave him a little girl pout. "It's boring back there. I don't want to stay in my room."

He grinned at her. "You don't have to stay in your room. You can come out here any time you want. But when you're here, put your feet up. Up, up. Like elevated."

She cocked her head to look at him. "Why?"

He dissembled. "Women who carry twins can get into trouble if they don't take care of themselves. I want you to be careful, that's all. Got it?"

She leaned back in the chair and put her feet on the rungs of a chair facing her. "Good enough?"

"On the seat would be better."

"Fine." Collin put her feet up. Jeff noted her ankles were swollen. Not "so swollen her toes appeared like sausages," but "swollen enough to leave an imprint if she crossed her feet." He drew in a deep breath and turned back to his chess game.

Rudy's eyes met Jeff's. "You really can't hide your emotions well, can you, son? She's sick, isn't she?"

Jeff glanced at the floor. "I don't want to scare her. And yes, I know I'm talking about my wife, who will face killers and lions and tigers and bears, oh my. She's fearless for herself. I don't want to create fear in her about the babies."

Rudy raised an eyebrow. "Admirable." He motioned to the board. "This, not so much. I'm sorry, Jeff, but checkmate."

Jeff grimaced. "I saw it coming and couldn't get out of it."

Rudy stretched a bit, and his face contorted to one side. Jeff eyed him. Rudy shrugged. "I have to quit. I can't sit still like this for long periods. This game is about the limit."

Jeff held out his hand. "I appreciate you taking time to play. And give me another lesson in how not to play chess."

Rudy chuckled. "You'll get it, one of these days."

"I've only got one of these days left to make it happen."

Rudy stood. He pointed from Jeff to Collin back to Jeff. "Chess isn't the only game there is, you know."

"She set the challenge."

"And she can be wrong. You might remember that."

Jeff gazed at the floor. "I'm afraid I've forfeited the right to call her on being wrong. Probably for some time to come."

Rudy's eyes smiled. "Don't let the past trap you into doing something unwise." He moved off, his limp more pronounced than it had been before.

Jeff studied the board, studied Rudy as he lumbered down the hallway and out of sight. Conviction grew in him. He walked over to Collin and sat opposite her. "Proposal."

She smiled at him. "Sorry, I'm already married. What?"

Jeff smiled at her joke. "Rudy. He told me sitting for long periods is hard on him. The match we just finished? Yeah, he says that's about as long as he can stand to sit. He's hurting."

Collin's face grew solemn. "I didn't know. What's wrong? Or has he said?"

Jeff drew in a breath. "You should ask him, okay? That's all I can say. Ask him."

Collin nodded. "What do you propose?"

"Let me take on Erin. I have to face him sometime. May as well be now. You know he's better than Rudy. You've played both of them."

Collin turned her head to the side. "Erin's ego notwithstanding, they are close to being evenly matched. Not exactly, and yes, I agree, Erin still would beat Rudy two out of three matches. But Rudy would surprise Erin at least once in the three."

"Still leaves Erin on top. Let me work on him. It'll help Rudy."

Collin appeared to think about it for several moments. "For Rudy. Tell Erin he's up. And I'll be watching him."

"You won't need to. Erin knows the rules. He won't let up on me."

Collin smiled. "I know. He's cruel at chess. And yes, he did learn from Grandfather Fenton."

Jeff leaned in and kissed her on the forehead. "Thanks, milady."

She looked at him, and her eyes shone. "Aim."

Which he did. And got him a catcall from across the room. "None of that! There are unmarried people here who might get jealous."

Collin laughed at her brother. "Who?"

Erin would not be pinned down. "Vy."

Vy drew back in mock surprise. "Me? I'd get jealous not being kissed?"

Erin shrugged. "Well, since it could be either you or Mason, and I was going to volunteer to correct the injustice, I had a fifty-fifty chance of coming out a winner."

Mason held up his hands. "Leave me out of this. I'm a married man."

Collin glared over at him, and her eyes reflected concern. "You're married? Does your wife know where you are? Does she know what you do?"

"Yes to both questions. I keep her informed of where I am. Maybe not all I do. I don't want people trying to use her as a target. But she knows."

Collin's eyes filled with moisture. She closed them tight. "Hormones. Worst part about being pregnant. Can't keep them in check!"

Jeff patted her on the shoulder. "They only last for a few months. About nine. You'll be rid of them. And fighting to keep the babies in check."

He walked over to where Erin lounged on a bench. "You're up, bro. Time to face me."

Erin motioned down the hall where Rudy had gone. "He okay?"

"Sitting bothers him. Since I take too long to beat, Collin has graciously decided you can step in and finish the challenge."

Erin waggled his head back and forth. "Fine. When do we start?"

"You doing anything important right this minute?"

"I'm watching Vy read. I think that's very important."

Vy dropped her book. "Don't let me distract you from your mission, Mist...sir. I can read in my own room."

Erin appeared crestfallen. "No. I like it when you read here. You add a certain grace to the room it otherwise lacks."

Collin glared at her brother. "Excuse me?"

Erin smiled. "Cane, I love you. But you're beginning to walk like a walrus. An uncomfortable walrus. Vy glides through a room."

Collin waved Erin off. "Go play chess. Do something."

"I am doing something. I'm trying to compliment this beautiful woman in hopes she'll still appreciate me when we're free from our self-imposed captivity."

Vy chuckled. "I'll always appreciate you, Erin. You saved my life."

Jeff pointed to the board. "Focus, bro. I have just over twenty-four hours to beat you. And I'm going to need at least twenty-three of them to do it."

Erin frowned. "Okay, let's do this." He offered his hand to Jeff. "Good luck. To all of us."

Jeff sat opposite him. "Amen."

* * *

Collin watched the matches without comment but with great interest. She could tell Erin stayed true to his word: he didn't give Jeff any easy passes—or any passes period. He played every game to win. After each victory, he took the time to instruct Jeff on what he'd done right as well as wrong.

But five long contests in, she could tell Jeff had come no closer to defeating her brother. Her husband's frustration level rose with each loss. As the fifth game ended, she stretched. "Jeff, let's take a walk. I'm tired of sitting here, and the babies are tired of being sat on. Will you walk with me back to the room?"

Jeff's face was dark as he turned to her. He stared for several moments. His face lost the scowl, replaced by his features relaxing and a smile finally coming over him. "Yes, milady. I will escort you to your room." He pointed to Erin. "Break time."

Erin sighed. "About time. I need food." He smiled over at Vy. "And a friendly face. A charming, friendly face. And I know just the one I want to look at."

Rudy chuckled. "Sorry, Erin. I'm headed to the library."

Mason threw in, "Don't look at me. I'm a married man."

Erin rolled his eyes. "Vy, would you accompany me to…to anywhere other than here?"

Vy stood. "Of course, Erin. I'd be happy to." Together they left the room.

Jeff chuckled. "He gets worse every time he talks to her." He helped Collin to her feet.

Collin smiled as she took Jeff's arm. "Worse how? She's obviously a match for him."

"Obvious to who?"

They walked to the bedroom. Collin noted Jeff picked up the blood pressure cuff as they left the common area. "Obvious to him. I don't see her complaining much."

Jeff chuckled. "Yeah, I don't either. That's what worries me."

They arrived. Jeff had Collin sit on the bed while he took her blood pressure. She noticed he kept the dial turned away from her. "What's the number?"

"It's a little high. You need to—"

"Get off my feet, lay on my left side, and stay there for the duration of the evening, right?"

Jeff kissed her. "That would be the ideal. I'll bring you something to eat that approximates whatever time it is."

"That would be nice. I haven't noticed any cravings yet. I suppose that's a good thing." Collin waved her hand to indicate the compound they were in.

He laughed. "Yeah, I don't think Rudy has a store of dill pickles or ice cream. Or anything else you might get a weird hankerin' for."

Collin lifted her chin. "When the babies decide what it is they want to eat, I'll let you know." She stopped the disdained act. "Is my blood pressure really okay?"

"It's high, Collin. Higher than I would want to see, but not so high I'm going to strangle Rudy and Mason to get you out of here and to a hospital. Yet."

Collin's eyebrows rose. "Well, I will definitely do my best to keep it under control." She lay on her side. "What does lying on my left side do?"

"They told us in training laying on your left side decreased the strain on the heart and helped keep the pressure down. I haven't seen it, but I know I've heard doctors tell their patients to do it."

Collin let Jeff prop the pillows and blankets behind her. As he finished, she patted the bed. "Sit with me awhile?"

Jeff looked down the hall, then relented. "Okay. For a few."

She rubbed his back. "You're muscles are all tensed."

"I've got to beat Erin if I don't want you to go out there. And I don't. I keep praying the Lord will give me wisdom to beat your brother, but it keeps not happening. I don't know whether this is punishment for those years I ignored Him or what, but it's frustrating."

"You know He's not punishing you. God doesn't punish His children. He disciplines them."

"When you're on the receiving end, it doesn't matter what you call it. It still hurts." Jeff studied his hands. "Now I'm finally back to being a real husband and wanting to protect you, I can't." He lifted his eyes. "You still having those pains?"

"You mean where I get punched in the stomach, and it feels like a belt goes around me? No. Those stopped. Now one of them has decided to reverse the process. The tightening starts in the back and moves around to the front." Collin grinned. "Little snots. They are determined to make my life as difficult as possible, and they aren't even here yet."

She watched his eyes narrow and darken. He took a breath and relaxed his face. "A taste of what's coming. Try to rest. And I'll be back after I beat Erin."

Collin smiled. "I'll probably hear the voice of triumph from here."

"Truth." He stood and walked out.

Collin watched him go. She whispered, "What aren't you telling me, my love?" She patted her belly, rubbed it. "You two need to behave. Your father's got enough stress on him. He doesn't need to be worrying about you, as well. Okay? Okay."

Collin rehearsed Scriptures in her head: *You formed me in my mother's womb. You know all about me. Every hair on my head is numbered. You are great and greatly to be praised, now and forever, amen.*

"Lord, help Jeff. I don't know what You're doing in him, but help him." Collin closed her eyes and tried to sleep.

WEDNESDAY

But the next day brought Jeff no closer to defeating Erin. Nor did it bring Collin any clarity to what the Lord was doing. She had slept in, stayed as immobile as she could for as long as she could, got up and walked (not waddled, thank you very much) to the common room.

Rudy sat at the desk, looking at the computer monitor. Mason talked to Vy in hushed tones. And Jeff and Erin were hunched over the chess table, faces scrunched in concentration, eyes focused like lasers on the board. From the pieces lining the sides, both men had captured several key members of each other's arsenal.

Collin walked over to where Vy and Mason were sitting. Vy's eyes rose as Collin sat. "How are you feeling?"

Collin shrugged. "Eh. I'm awake and alive. I'll go with that." She rubbed her hand across her belly, feeling it tighten again. "How long has this game been going on?"

Mason frowned. "Too long. Erin declared it's the last match. I think his hip is bothering him. He's hung with your husband, but even Superman had to call it after a while."

Collin glanced around the room. "What time is it?"

Mason checked at his watch. "Quarter to two."

Collin's face jerked in surprise. "That late? I didn't think I slept that long."

Vy nodded. "You seemed tired last night when Jeff walked you back." She added, "You still look tired. Washed out. If Jeff can't go, are you positive you can handle it?"

Collin steeled herself. "I'll have to. Three of you are dead, and Mason works for the competition. It has to be me."

A loud bellow of frustration sounded from the chess area. Collin's head whipped to see Jeff jump from the table and bellow. "No!"

Erin had his head down. He didn't move. Jeff did enough for both of them, waving his arms in the air. "I can't do this! I am not a chess player! I can't think like you do! I can't!"

He turned to face Collin, and she read the anguish on his face. He marched over to her. "I'm not a chess player. I never will be. I can't outthink you or Erin or Rudy or Mason. I can't. I admit it. But I am not going to allow you to go there. I'm going."

Collin bit her lips. "We agreed—"

"You agreed. You set the challenge, the terms." He kneeled beside her. "Listen to me, milady. Please. I'm not analytical like you are. You think in terms of chess or what pieces can and will do. Fine. It's logical. It's strategic. It's warfare. I get that. Your opponent has predictable capabilities and can move in predictable ways. You analyze what he can do with the possible ways he has to maneuver. But it's all according to a set of defined rules."

Jeff's eyes pleaded with her. "I'm not a chess player. I'm a fireman. I think like a fireman. And the one thing we know about fire— it doesn't play by any rules. It doesn't. Yes, if you starve it of fuel, it goes out. That's the only rule it obeys."

He took her hand. "You expect to outthink Franny. To anticipate what she's going to do and have strategies ready to counter her moves. But she isn't going to play by the rules, and that's why I can beat her. Because I don't expect her to.

"I'm not going out there thinking, 'she'll do this or that, and I can do this…' I'm going out there with no expectations. I'm going to treat her like a wildfire. I'm going to watch and learn and see which way the wind is blowing. Then I can move against her. And I will beat her. Just like we beat every other fire we've faced. I can do this, Collin. I can't do it your way, that's all."

Collin felt her gut shift, and it wasn't from the babies. She turned to face her brother. "You agree with this?"

Erin's mouth drew into a line. "Yeah. You're pushing Jeff to think like you because that's the only way you can conceive of beating Franny. Maybe he's right, and his approach will be better." Erin nailed Collin with his glance. "You have no business going there. You know it. Admit it. Step back, step down, and admit it."

Collin closed her eyes to keep the water from spilling over the dam. "I'm sorry, Jeff. I never thought of it as forcing you to be like me." She ran one hand in his hair, the other along his cheek. "I'm sorry. Forgive me?"

Jeff took her hands into his and kissed them both. "Oh, milady. I love you. There's nothing to forgive." He got off his knees.

Collin noted Rudy and Mason were watching the scene closely. Did they disagree with Jeff? Disagree with her? Had they thought of a different plan?

Mason held his hand out to shake Jeff's. "Brilliantly played, Jeff. I think Rudy and I may have some equipment you can use to fight the fire. And put it out for good."

Jeff smiled. "Thanks." Collin read all the tension melting from Jeff's face, his shoulders, his body.

The three men left the common area for parts unknown. Collin watched Jeff walk away, lifted her chin, and closed her eyes. She felt a hand on her shoulder, an arm around her. Erin's voice sounded gentle. "You can't control him, Cane. You think you can keep him safe by doing everything yourself. You can't." He chuckled. "You two. Both of you are trying so hard to protect the other one, and neither one of you is fully trusting God."

Collin sniffed. "I trust God." She looked at her brother. "I don't trust Him to work things out the way I want, that's all." She leaned against Erin's chest. "I honestly didn't realize what I was doing. It's not my fight, is it?"

"Nope." Erin grimaced. Collin caught his sigh under his breath. She jerked around to look at her brother. "What? What's wrong?"

He shrugged. "The hip. Where I caught the shrapnel. It hurts."

Collin's jaw fell open. "You never admit pain."

Vy slipped her hand around Erin's arm. "Yes, we've been having discussions about that. Honesty in relationships matters." She smiled at Erin. "Honesty in everything matters."

Erin sighed. Slightly. Very slightly. "Vy is teaching me Superman wears a cape and has a big S on his chest and can fly. Until I learn the flying part, I can't claim to be him. Can't even think I'm him." He snorted. "Lots to unlearn."

Vy bumped his shoulder. "We both do." She pointed to the bench. "Now go stretch out."

"Yes, ma'am." Erin smiled at Collin. "I like her."

The others returned closer to three. Mason talked as they came in the room. "We've got the two goons she brought with her misdirected into the west side of the woods. They won't be helping anyone with anything." He snorted. "Crying for their mamas after dark, but that's the best they will be able to do until the police pick them up. And usually, a night alone in the forest is enough to make a man talkative."

Rudy added, "A city dweller, yeah. And I suspect that's who she brought with her. Thugs from her part of the hood."

Jeff nodded. "Yeah, I know how easily I got confused once you started moving markers."

Rudy continued, "There will be someone tailing Franny, moving her flags as well. She may make it in, but she won't make it out. She'll have some time to think about the error of her lawless ways."

Mason caught Jeff's gaze. "Remember, it's up to you to get her to talk about framing him. Vy will give the police a record of it all, but you need her to say it, not just agree with you."

Collin watched Jeff nod. "Right. I've got it." He patted his chest, then pointed at Collin. "Let me kiss my wife goodbye, and we'll go."

Jeff walked over to her. Collin stilled her hands from shaking, her voice from trembling. Something in her snapped, and she caught Jeff around the neck with both arms. She kissed him like a newlywed, lay her head on his shoulder, and whispered, "Don't get killed. I love you, Jeff Farrell."

He hugged her tight. "I'll be back, milady. I love you, Collin Farrell."

Jeff turned to Mason. "Show me how to get out of here." The two men walked down the hall.

Rudy went to the computer on his desk, turned the monitor around, and said, "We can watch it if you want."

Collin's eyes widened. "We can watch him? Of course, I want! Can we talk to him, too?"

"No. Like with you, we can monitor the frequencies, play it back later for sound, but can't get audio here."

"Visual is better than nothing."

Erin held up a finger. "Uh…visual without context can be misleading. You might remember that."

Collin started to snap at him but stopped. She counted to ten, counted again. "You're right. I'm still going to watch."

Erin snorted. "I knew you would. I thought I'd at least try."

Mason joined the group as they positioned themselves around the monitor to watch. Erin quipped, "You should consider wide screen the next time you invite a crowd to a showing."

Rudy growled. "I'll remember that. Just for you."

They watched as Jeff entered the small clearing prepared for the meet-up. Mason commented under his breath, "She'll be late. Ten minutes. She thinks she's meeting you, so she's pulling a power trip."

Collin snorted. "Yeah, no. My biological father used to pull that stunt. I am way past being rattled by people not showing on time."

"Will he be?"

Collin wasn't sure who asked the question. She had no answer. Only God knew.

* * *

Jeff paced around the small clearing. He resisted the urge to look at the phone to check the time, how late Franny might be, and whether she would come at all. After an undetermined amount of time, Jeff parked himself on a tree stump to wait her out. *I remember Collin's biological father would do this…show well past the time, so his competition would be rattled or off their game. This one I'm wise to. Thank you, milady.*

A nudge hit him. *Are you doing this in your own brains and brawn? Thinking you'll beat her on your own?*

That bore examination. Jeff looked at the ground, lifted his head to the sky. *Forgive me. I need You to lead all of this. Not just this meeting but everything in my life, Lord. I tried living without You, and it didn't work. Help me, Father. Be in me, directing and guiding.*

Tree limbs rustled as someone brushed through them. Jeff heard aggravated, "Ow!" "Let go, stupid branch" and "Great. Another rip. You so will pay for this," mutters, getting closer to his location. He put on his best "serious face" and stood.

As Franny fought her way through the last few brambles, he moved to help her. "Here, let me." He pulled back the thorns trying to grab at her and made a clear path so she could enter the circle.

Franny stared at him. "Jeff! What are you doing here? I thought Collin—"

Jeff hardened his tone. "Collin isn't part of this anymore. When I found out what she was doing, I took the phone away from her."

Franny smiled. "You did? So she isn't going to use it against me?"

"No. Or against anyone else, either."

Franny eyed him sideways. "What did you do with it?"

"I've got it. What's on it you would come all the way out here to buy it back?"

"Didn't Collin tell you?"

"She told me her side. I want to hear your side."

Franny shrugged. "My personal information is in there. I asked her to delete it, and she said no. She wanted to use it to blackmail me."

"How? Over what?" Jeff let incredulity tint his tone.

"Oh, she thinks I tricked her brother into moving drugs for me. Then he got killed, and she blamed me. But I didn't put the shipment on his truck."

"There were drugs on Erin's truck? How did that happen?"

"How should I know?"

Jeff eyed her sideways. "Franny, you were the last one to do anything to Erin's truck, remember? I saw you there at the service station. You said you put money on the truck. What's going on? Really?"

Franny shrugged. "It's nothing. Really. Can I have the phone?"

"Not until I hear the truth. Did you plant drugs on Erin's truck?"

"No. I didn't."

"Did you have someone else put drugs on his truck?"

"No."

"Why are you out here? Why would you come all this way? Why not simply call the police and have my wife arrested?"

Franny glared at him. "Are you going to have me arrested?"

"For what? Trying to pay my wife off? I don't understand any of this. Make me understand, Franny, please. Does this have anything to do with Erin's car being crushed with him in it?"

Franny smiled at him. "I like you, Jeff. You're nice to me. I'm sorry your wife got you mixed up in this." She pulled out a handgun.

Jeff's eyes widened. "Franny! What? Why? What's so important you'd want to kill me?"

"I don't want to kill you, Jeff. I wanted to kill your wife. I need the phone. Now."

"Why?"

"Because I did plant those drugs. And if Erin had done things right the first time, none of this would have happened."

"So it's Erin's fault, now?" Jeff continued to stare at her wide-eyed and frightened.

"Yes. I had my guys put the drugs on Erin's truck. He was supposed to deliver them to Aunt Beela's, and my contact there would get them while Erin and Beela had tea on the veranda." Franny snorted. "My sweet aunt…who's taking a cut out of everything I send through her."

Jeff shook his head. "Franny…I…your aunt is helping you smuggle drugs? Why? Why are you doing this? But…but Erin drove Collin's car instead of his truck."

Franny kicked at an offending root. "Right. My man contacted me to tell me about it. I had to think fast, or my buyer would think I stiffed him."

Jeff held his hand out, palms up. "Franny…you're going to kill me. Is that why you're telling me all this?"

"You wanted to know."

"But not if you're going to kill me! What good does that do?"

"Get's it off my chest. I can confess it to you, and I don't have to feel bad about it anymore."

Jeff sank on the stump. "Telling me, then killing me, lets you sleep at night?" *Lord, please. Make sure this is all recorded clearly. No breaks in the wire. We have got to get this woman off the streets.*

"Yeah. It does." Franny smirked. "I thought that's what Christians do. They break the rules, tell someone about it, and that makes it all better."

"That's not how it works, Franny. It's not."

"Works for me. That's all that matters. So yeah, I figured if I could make my buyer think someone else stole the drugs, I'd be off the hook. I remembered hearing about this smuggler who operated around this area. He used to stuff people in their cars and have them crushed. He's been dead for a few years, but I thought, why not? So I had my crew intercept Erin on the way home—"

"Your crew? You have a crew working with you?" Jeff lifted his head skyward. "Franny..."

"Oh, get over it, Jeff. Yes, I have a crew. They caught Erin before he left Fort Newton, beat him, and stuffed him in the trunk. I don't know how he survived it, but he did. Which left me with a bigger problem. Which I solved nicely if I do say so myself."

Jeff sagged. "How bad does this get, Franny? What else could you do?"

"Oh, I planted a picture of the dead guy on Erin's computer, so the cops would think that's why he got stuffed."

Jeff dropped his eye to the ground. "I suppose you're going to tell me the dead man's name?"

Franny smiled. "Of course. Rudy something."

Jeff glanced sharply. "Rudy? Rudy who?"

Franny laughed. "Rudy the Red. That's him. Or used to be him. I didn't think he would care if I used his MO and let people think he was still alive. I bet the cops are still looking for him."

Jeff looked up, looked around, looked down. "Franny, is there any way I walk out of here alive? Any way at all, you don't kill me?" He begged her, pleading in his eyes. "Collin is expecting a baby. Two babies. Twins. Please. I'd like to see my children born. Start school. Go to college. You know, those special moments in a kid's life?"

Franny laughed lightly. "Oh, Jeff. I do like you. I am sorry you got caught in this. I'm going to have to cover this meeting up, of course."

Jeff threw his hands in the air. "You're going to make it look like I attacked you? Is that the legacy my kids will have of me? If you're going to stage this, can't you stage it I tried to save you, not kill you?"

"I'm sorry, Jeff. I am. But we'd need another person, and we don't have anyone else around. So it has to be this way." She pointed the gun at him. "Give me the phone." Jeff hesitated. She motioned. "If you don't, I'll rifle through your pockets to find it. You want to be spared that indignity while you lay dying? And if you throw it, I'll kill you, then go find it. Except I might make you suffer first. Kneecap? Both kneecaps? Make it easy, hand me the phone, and I promise to make it clean and quick."

Jeff reached in his pocket and pulled out the phone. He handed it to her. She pointed to the ground. "Lay it down." Jeff complied. He stared into her face, her eyes. Franny smiled. And fired point-blank at his middle.

Jeff felt the bullet tear into his shirt, the impact crushing the air from his lungs. Franny fired again. And again. And again.

Jeff folded to the ground, twisting, turning, silent. Still.

* * *

Mason raced out of the common room. Rudy followed with a pronounced limp, leaving Erin, Vy, and Collin staring at the monitor. Collin lifted her eyes but saw nothing. She felt nothing. No words. No comfort. No peace. Only the bullet ripping into her husband. Again. And again. And again.

Erin gripped her shoulder tightly. "Visual without context, Cane. Hold on."

She lifted her eyes. His words didn't register. Erin shook her sharply and repeated himself. "No context, Cane. Watch and wait. Trust."

Collin stared blankly at her brother and turned back to the screen. Franny nudged Jeff's lifeless form with her foot. She seemed satisfied with what she saw. The woman on the screen picked up the phone, checked it, stuffed it in her pocket. She turned around and located the first flag to lead her out of the clearing.

The monitor continued to track Franny from camera to camera. Collin could do nothing but watch with stunned obsession. Hate seethed in Collin's veins. The smuggler picked up a flag and waved it in her hands as she walked, humming to herself, batting the occasional leaf out of her way.

Even if I walk through the darkest valley of death, I know You are with me. Your shepherd's rod and crook will comfort me.

The small Voice whispered the old Words. Collin didn't question. Didn't ask what or why or how. Unable to do anything else, she watched Franny walk further and further away from the spot where Collin's forever after ended.

The cameras followed the drug dealer from behind, looking from strategic placements in the trees. Franny strode with confidence and purpose. Backward-facing cameras caught the simpering smile on her face. Not a care in the world.

Until the flags stopped. Franny searched around for another flag but apparently didn't see one. She checked low among the bushes, high under the tree limbs, even got on her knees to look in the dirt. No flag. Collin watched as the woman jumped to her feet and backtracked…

Only to find the marker she had left behind gone. Collin watched Franny spin in circles, watched her clench her fists, nail them to her sides, throw her head back and scream. Silently, of course. No sound monitors. Franny faced every direction she could, screaming with every fiber in her being from the way her face was contorted. Nothing happened. No one came for her. No one called back.

Franny fell to her knees. Collin watched her body sob. When she lifted her head, ugly tears and snot covered her face. The smear-proof mascara wasn't. The wash of foundation and eyeliner and blush and toner melted and blended to paint an abstract portrait of utter desperation and fear.

Do not gloat when your enemy falls…

I'm not gloating, Lord. I want to feel bad for her. I know You died for her as much as for me. Collin caught her breath. She closed her eyes and whispered, "Forgive her, Father. I'll forgive her because You forgave me… But not if I have to see her now."

Collin turned away from the monitor. She stared at her brother. "Now what? What happens next?" Her voice came out barely above a whisper.

She heard the commotion of Rudy and Mason coming into the room, laughing and congratulating someone in no uncertain terms. Daggers pierced through Collin's heart. *How can they? Jeff is…is…*

…walking in the room with them. Laughing and crowing and holding Mason by the shoulder. He saw Collin and yelled, "Lady! We did it! Did you see me?"

Collin's eyes closed. She breathed hard. She heard Jeff move in front of her. His voice became questioning. "Lady? You knew we set this up, right?"

Collin opened her eyes. She could feel the shockwaves reverberating in her system. Wave after wave… *Don't faint. Don't faint. Looks tacky when you faint. Trust me.*

Collin stepped into Jeff's embrace, placed her head on his chest, and began pounding him as hard as she could and not suffer bodily injury. "No! No, I did NOT KNOW you set this up! No one told me. No one told any of us. I thought you were dead!"

She glared at Rudy and Mason. "Someone is going to be! Who forgot to tell me, huh? Who's assignment was it to assure me you had this covered?" No one spoke. Collin shouted, "WHO?"

Jeff scrunched down and looked her in the eyes. "Let it go, milady. I'm sorry you had to go through that. But it's over, and I'm alive. You're stuck with me from here to eternity."

Breathe. Say, "thank you" and "I love you." And mean it. There's still work to do.

Collin stepped back, found her composure, and nodded. "Right. I love you, Jeff. If I ever learn you were the one who forgot to tell me, I will kill you, but right now, I love you." She embraced him as hard as she could without crushing the babies. She broke, glared at Mason and Rudy. "Sleep with one eye open, gentlemen, until I get to the bottom of this." She swung on her brother. "And you…"

Erin threw his hands in the air. "Me? I sat here with you the whole time. How could I know?"

Collin mocked, "'Visuals without context…' What did you know, huh?"

Erin shrugged. "His shirt seemed thicker when he came out of the room, that's all. I didn't get to hug him like you did, so I didn't know for certain he had a vest. But I had a good guess. Just didn't want to say anything if I was wrong."

Collin pointed to Vy. She'd accused everyone else, may as well include Vy, too. "Vy?"

"No. I didn't know." She sniffed a little. "Not that I would have been able to tell you. We don't disclose details of the operations to civilians before the bust goes down." She glanced at Erin. "Civilians who aren't directly involved in the operation, I mean."

Collin's jaws fell open. "Thanks a lot! The one person I thought would have my back!"

Vy smiled. "I'm sorry, Collin. It's a DEA thing."

"Fine! Fine!" Collin threw her hands in the air. "You all knew about it, no one told me, and I had to watch him die. I'm over it now, and I won't mention it again." She kissed Jeff again, leaning into his chest. "I am so glad you're okay."

He nuzzled her hair. "Me, too."

Rudy clapped Jeff on the back. "Great job there, Jeff. You had me convinced you were scared of dying."

Jeff chuckled. "No acting. I was afraid. But I thought I could use it to my advantage."

Mason sat opposite them. "You did. Now, we call the local boys and make sure they got the confessions. We give them the information where to pick up the suspects and the crew, and we're good for another fifteen or twenty years."

Rudy shrugged. "Or so."

Jeff asked, "So we can go home now, right?"

Mason threw a glance at Rudy. Rudy raised his eyebrow. Mason faced Jeff straight on. "No. We have to come up with a cover story for why you disappeared and where you've been." He motioned to Vy. "Since she's part of the company, she's expected to disappear and reappear at will."

Vy shrugged. "Comes with the territory. I 'travel for work.' I'm an IT troubleshooter and get called away at a moment's notice. I'm too busy to check-in, or I schedule messages to post at specific times."

Mason picked back up the conversation. "You three, however, have been missing a good week. There is also the matter of your 'kidnapping' and the police report. We can close the case, but we can't hide the fact you've been missing. We need to come up with a plausible explanation for where you've been."

Silence. Lots of silence. Erin chuckled. "How about an implausible one?"

Collin peered at him sideways. "What?"

"Aliens."

Jeff lifted his head and rolled his eyes. "Not again."

Rudy pointed to Erin. "Explain. Slowly."

Erin shrugged. "There were reporters who wanted a story about me getting stuffed in the trunk. I gave them one. All of it true."

Jeff raised his eyebrows. "Well…"

Erin smiled. "It's all in the delivery. I sort of implied that I believed I was accosted by aliens. They stopped asking questions."

Rudy smiled. "I would have loved to hear that."

"Encore's at eleven."

"I'm sure."

Collin waved her hands, palms down. "Uh-uh. Aliens would work with reporters but not with Mom Lacey. Or a board of directors." She nailed Erin with a stern glance. "Not all of our clients think you're balanced as it is. Floating a story about believing aliens kidnapped us won't help any."

Erin scuffed a shoe. "It would be fun."

Collin sighed. "Erin…"

Vy turned to Rudy. "Before I leave, I want you to answer one question. Why are you here, Rudy?"

Rudy held her gaze. "I told you. I'm retired. This is a safe place to do it."

"No. I can accept there might be criminal forces after you. But I've watched you. You're not a man to run away from a fight." Vy continued to eye Rudy. "And families can get witness protection."

Mason cleared his throat. "Halfway across the country."

Vy looked from one man to the next. "Families move all the time. Even without being chased." Vy circled to stand directly in front of Rudy. "I keep thinking about it. And the more I do, the more questions I have. What kind of deal sends a man into exile underground for the rest of his life? Who benefits from that?"

Collin watched the corners of Rudy's mouth twitch. Whether up or down, she wasn't sure. He dipped his head slightly. "It's your story. You figure it out."

Vy's eyes narrowed. "I think you're here because someone needs you to be available. Like, for a trial, maybe? One that's been postponed and postponed and moved back and postponed. High-profile trials can drag out for years. Ten years? Rare, but not unheard of."

Vy glanced at Mason. "Especially if it's an international affair." She turned back to Rudy. "But why would you agree to it? Unless…" Vy's eyes narrowed even more. "Unless the powers that be were holding something—or someone—over you."

Collin saw the minutest flare in Rudy's eyes. Did Vy see it?

Vy's tone stayed gentle. "Who is it, Rudy? Family?"

Rudy shrugged. "Does it matter? Dance with the devil long enough; he snares you." The man lowered his eyes and stared at the floor for a long time. "My kid. My daughter. She just turned sixteen. Wrong place, wrong time, wrong crowd. Someone brought a gun to a knife fight. Things got heated, things got out of control. When the dust settled, and the shooting stopped, she had the pistol. She swears she never fired a shot, in the screaming and confusion, someone shoved the gun into her hand. She didn't know she had it until the police drew down on her."

Collin's heart ached. She wanted to hug him, to tell him it would be okay… The Voice inside cautioned, *Listen. Don't speak. Listen.*

Rudy sneered, "The powers that be made the deal. I'd hang around and testify when they needed me, and she would be cleared of all charges. Except if I ever showed my face above ground, or if anyone got wind of my being alive, they'd reinstate the charges."

Collin watched Vy's eyes burn. "And your daughter knew about this? As a juvenile charges could—"

"She didn't know anything about it. She was five when her mother divorced me, took the kid, and left town. I don't think my daughter knows I exist."

Now. "Why, Rudy? Why would you do that for someone who doesn't know you? Your daughter doesn't deserve it."

Rudy whirled on Collin. "She's my kid, okay? I love her. I want the best for her. You'll understand when you hold those babies in your arms."

Gently. "I do understand, Rudy. You sacrificed yourself for someone you love, even though they don't know you and certainly don't love you. Maybe don't even know you exist."

Rudy's eyes glowered. Collin asked, "But what would happen if someone told her that her father loved her? Told her what he'd done for her? You think it would make a difference to her?"

The man's eyes widened. Collin continued. "You think maybe she would want to tell others about him? Tell them he loved her so much he took her punishment?" One question remained. "But what if they told her, and she said she didn't care? Would you stop loving her?"

Rudy stared at Collin. And stared. And stared. Collin kept her voice as soft as she knew how. "Now you get it. You didn't have to take the penalty, but you did. Because you love your daughter. And you always will. No matter what she does or doesn't do. Even if she doesn't believe you exist."

Rudy scowled from Collin to Vy. "You two set this up, didn't you?"

Collin raised her hands in innocence. "I'm just asking questions, Rudy."

He frowned at Vy. Vy shook her head. "I'm trying to decide if I go back to the office and bust this injustice wide apart or walk away and pretend it never happened."

Rudy snorted. "Walk away."

"I can't do that. Not and be true to my Lord." Vy pointed to the laptop on the table. "Does that thing connect to the outside world?"

Rudy glared at her. Mason agreed. "Yeah, it does." He turned to Rudy. "Maybe it is time to end this. You've been here too long. They could have made their case and cut a deal, and you wouldn't know."

Erin objected. "But why wouldn't they recall you?"

Rudy walked over to his chair and sagged into it. Mason answered for him. "You're in this business long enough; you ruffle feathers and step on toes. You find out where the bodies are buried. And you make powerful, vengeful enemies on your own side. Some that would be thrilled if no one ever heard of or from you again."

Erin huffed. "Sounds like our family. Except, Cane beat 'em."

Collin corrected her brother. "We all beat them. It was a joint effort."

Vy stretched her fingers and sat in front of the laptop. "Maybe we can beat this 'family' as well. I'm certainly going to give it a try." She smiled at Rudy. "Password?"

Rudy stared at the floor for several moments. "Deidra. One word. E before I."

Vy turned to the computer. "Deidra it is." She began typing.

Erin moved over to watch her. He pulled a chair beside her and sat. Jeff cleared his throat. "Not to be selfish, but does this help get us out of here as well?"

Vy smiled, her lips in a tight line. "If I'm as good as I think I am, if the system will cooperate, and the Lord wills it, yes."

Collin touched her husband's arm. "Maybe you and I can put some prayer behind this effort?"

Jeff smiled at her. "I believe that would be a wonderful idea, milady."

Mason glanced at his former partner, pulled a chair beside Vy. "If I can help, let me know."

Rudy harumphed. "I get final veto on any scheme you come up with. Just so we're clear on who's in charge here."

Collin laughed. "Rudy, you haven't been in charge since the day your men brought me here. God's been doing all of it. And bringing you along for the ride."

Collin heard his muttered, "I still get to say no."

* * *

No one kept track of the time. Mason and Vy traded off working the computer. Collin could have sworn she saw smoke coming from the keyboard, but it might have been her imagination. Or a hallucination from lack of sleep. Even Rudy relented and joined the team, adding his knowledge to the increasingly complex cache of information on the case. The more they dug, the deeper the hole went. And the uglier it became.

At some point in the marathon, Collin looked from her prayers. Rudy was gone, presumably to his room. Mason had confiscated the rolling chair but had fallen asleep in it. Erin's head lay on his folded arms on the desk next to the computer. Jeff had succumbed to weariness and fallen asleep on the floor. Only Vy continued hammering away at the keyboard.

Collin stood, tiptoed over to the tireless woman, and put her hand on her shoulder. "Give it a break, Vy. We're not going anywhere."

Vy pushed back from the desk. "I'm close, Collin. I know I am."

"Hit pause and get some sleep. It'll be there when you get up." Collin waved around the room. "You'll have lots of company. Everyone else has surrendered the field."

Vy scanned the area and chuckled. "Yeah, I see that." She stretched her back, cracked her neck. "They did him wrong. Bad wrong."

"Deliberate?"

"No question. They set him up for it." The DEA agent rolled her shoulders. "The biggest question now is what do we do about it?"

"If Rudy says walk away?"

"I can't. Not now. Not knowing what I do." She studied her fingers. "This field requires walking the fine edge between deception and lying. Some people don't have a problem crossing the line. For them, the end justifies the means. I'm not one of them."

The woman interlocked her fingers, stretched her arms over her head. "They inserted Rudy into a South American drug cartel. A cartel with contacts high up." Vy dropped her arms. "I mean way high up. On both continents. He worked his way to the top. What he found out could have been enough to bring down prominent government officials."

Collin echoed. "On both continents?"

"Exactly. Negotiations were made, broken, re-made, warrants were issued, warrants were canceled. All the while, Rudy is sitting in a hideout, waiting to testify. After a couple years of waiting, he gets fed up and says he's going to the press with his information. Tragically, his estranged daughter gets into trouble, and now the feds have what they need to keep Rudy on ice for however long they need him."

"Why not kill him?"

"Because they really do want and need the information he has. Rudy is cagey enough not to tell everything all at once. And he does have some champions. Enough so, he's still alive but out of harm's way in a hole in the ground."

"How do we get him out?"

"That's the part I'm stuck on."

Collin jerked her head to the side. "Go. Sleep. Everyone will be sharper in…in whatever time it will be in a few hours. We're still not going anywhere."

Vy pointed to Collin's belly. "What about them? Are they content to stay put?"

"They don't get a choice. They'll stay put until I tell them they can leave."

Vy chuckled. "I wouldn't be so sure."

Collin sighed. "Me, neither. But I thought I'd try to convince them Mama knows what's best."

"Maybe after they're born. Until then, I doubt it." Vy stood and stretched once again. "I'll go grab a fast nap and be back in a couple of hours. Maybe by then, some of the help will be more helpful." She chuckled at Erin's sleeping figure. "Except him. He's no help at all. He just sits and smiles."

Collin swallowed the smirk. "I think when you get to tactics, he'll be more helpful." Collin debated, then said, her voice almost a whisper, "He doesn't have a lot of experience with women. He's somewhat in awe of meeting a sister in the Lord who honestly loves the Lord and puts Him first in her thinking."

Vy matched her volume to Collin's. "Where's he been all his life?"

Collin's face lost the smile. "In a hole not unlike this one. Except his was above ground. With our father."

Vy's eyes widened, then narrowed. She gazed at Erin with more intensity, turned, and left the room. Collin touched her brother's sleeping head, brushed it with a kiss. She moved back to where Jeff sprawled on the floor, his head propped on a chair cushion. Collin debated getting down to his level to wake him, but if she did, she might not get back again. She nudged him with her foot. "Jeff. Jeff."

Maybe shout fire.

That's cold.

But it would be effective.

Collin prodded him. "Mr. Farrell."

He rolled over. "Hmph?"

"Jeff. Wake up. Get off the floor, anyhow."

His eyes opened. "Off the floor?"

Collin made circles with her finger. "Yeah. The floor. Get up. Walk with me to the room. I want to stretch out, but not here."

Jeff curled to a sitting position, rolled onto his hands and knees, and forced his way to standing straight. Collin heard but didn't comment on all the grunts. She waited until he stood and put her hand around his arm. "Come on, dear. The little ones need me off my rear. Walking or laying is fine. Anything but sitting."

Jeff managed a smile. "Right. You woke me because you want to sleep. Seems fair."

"We may as well practice tag-teaming now."

"Truth." Jeff and Collin walked out.

THURSDAY

Collin returned to the war room some five hours later. She would have loved to sleep more, but the twins seemed of a different mind. Between the tap-dancing on her spine and the kickboxing on her bladder, she couldn't get any rest. Better to be up and moving. At least she could rock them to sleep, right? *Or sit on them. Either way, they're quieter.*

But not too quiet, right, little ones? Keep sending the reassurances you're alive. I'll take 'em. Got it?

The room was devoid of life, save her brother still sitting at the desk. He had his head up, and he leaned back in his chair. His eyes were closed, his face contorted, sweat beaded on his brow. Collin watched him a moment. "What are you doing?"

Through gritted teeth, "Trying to move my foot."

Comprehension snapped Collin's head around. She tore to his side and kneeled on the floor beside him. "Here." She tapped his right foot sharply.

Erin jerked the foot sideways. Collin tapped the left foot. Erin stared at it, stared at it. Collin tapped it again, harder. Erin shifted his heel off the ground, dragged the toes to follow, and lifted his foot off the ground. All the air went out of his body, and he relaxed. Erin moved his feet freely. "Okay, that's frightening. I woke and couldn't find them."

"Couldn't feel them?"

"Couldn't find them. My brain didn't know where they were. No pathway." His eyes were haunted. "I think I'm losing it again."

"No. You are not losing anything. You sat there too long and cut off the circulation, that's all. You're fine." She squeezed his shoulder. "Got it?"

"I told you about the spasms, right?" Erin bent gingerly to one side, then to the other.

"Yes. All this can be fixed when we get back to the real world. Dr. Rich can…" Collin trailed off. *Rich. Did Rich do the surgery on Jeff? He sure made it clear he thought I should never have kids. And at the reception…he sat there with that smug look and told everyone he had given us the best gift of all. He gave us the gift of life.*

Collin's eyes widened. *I thought he meant from the aneurysm. But maybe that wasn't what he meant. Maybe he meant… Is that why Jeff wouldn't tell me who did the surgery?*

"Cane? Are you okay?"

Collin shook off the thoughts, but not the conviction. She squeezed Erin's shoulder again. "We'll get it fixed. If it can be, we'll do it." She hesitated. "The Lord willing."

Erin grinned. "Of course." He lost the smile. "Don't tell… " He stopped. "Um… I'll tell Vy."

"Good choice."

Erin pulled the computer to his side of the desk. "Where are we?"

"Vy has all the information she needs about who, what, when, and even why. It's the 'what do we do about it' part we have to figure out."

"And?"

"And I don't know. We need to get everyone together and work it out."

"But Rudy still has veto power?"

"God has veto power. Rudy will have to go along with Him. Or not. I know, free will."

"Yeah, strange how that works. Literally. Strange. Can't figure it out. Just know it happens and trust Him."

Erin examined the information Vy had accumulated and tabulated. His eyes narrowed as he read further and further. Only when he finished did he raise his head to hold Collin's gaze. "That's it? That's what we have to go on?"

"Unless you know something they don't. Vy said all that remains is to decide what to do with it."

"Is it a chess game or a fire, right?"

Collin gave her brother a wry smile. "Right. Whose strategy do we use?"

Erin stood to his feet. Carefully. Gingerly. As if not convinced all the parts would stay connected. He stretched. "I'm going to walk around and plan our out. You can do the same." He took a few trial steps. Seemingly convinced he could walk, he began circling the room, staring at the floor, muttering.

Collin watched him and chuckled. *Only Erin. Okay, but what have I got? Lord? Any suggestions?*

Jim Russo.

Detective Russo? What does he have to do with this?

She tried to dismiss the thought, but it wouldn't go away.

Contact Russo.

He's got no bearing on this.

Erin circled over to Collin's side of the room. "You still have Jim Russo's number?"

Collin grimaced. "What does he have to do with this?" She couldn't keep the exasperation from her voice.

Erin shrugged. "Just a thought. Maybe he can locate Deidra, see what she's doing these days. Fill her in on what's going on. See how she reacts. Maybe help us know what next steps to take."

Collin sighed. *I hear You. Now. Thank You.* "Yes, I have his number. Yes, it's a good idea to see if he can help. If anyone can find Deidra, I'm sure it would be Jim."

She sat at the spot Erin had vacated. "Let me hear the rest of it."

Erin laid out his moves, his contingencies, his attacks, and his defenses. Collin typed them into the computer, leaving room for discussion and questions. They brainstormed and hashed and re-hashed and *ooo…hash browns…*

Focus.

Spoilsport.

They worked for an hour before Mason reappeared. He looked over the plan, added a few helpful suggestions. Jeff made it a foursome half an hour later. Vy came in about an hour later, and Rudy made his appearance shortly after to bring the squad to full strength.

His would be the final vote, Collin knew. All eyes were on him as he read over the notes, snorted, harrumphed, groused, deleted assorted steps, inserted his own. No one spoke a word until the exile pushed back from the desk, scanned around the room, nodded. "I think it will work."

Collin released a breath she didn't know she'd been holding. From the sounds in the room, she hadn't been alone. She massaged a twin that had an elbow or knee in her ribs. "Vy, it's up to you now."

* * *

Vy held up a hand. "One detail we forgot." Four heads turned her way. "How do I get back to the city? Hard to hail an Uber from here."

Mason smiled. "Got you covered. Come on, I'll show you the parking garage. You can take your pick."

Rudy grumbled. "Except the V-Twin."

Vy laughed. "No worries, Rudy. I am not a biker." Vy returned to her room to gather her things and put them in the small bag Mason had given her before they arrived at the compound. It had seemed strange at first there were laundry facilities this far below ground. But it made perfect sense once she thought about it.

Preparing to leave, she realized the possibility she might not see any of the "squad" again. Vy sat on her bed, then kneeled on the floor. *Lord, You orchestrated all of this. Meeting Erin. Finding Collin and Jeff. Now trying to break Rudy loose from his prison. Direct my steps. Keep my mouth shut from saying anything that doesn't honor You. Your will is all that matters, Father. In Jesus's Name, amen.*

Vy returned to the common room. She went to Collin first and hugged her. "I want to see those babies before all the 'new car smell' wears off."

Collin laughed. "I'm sure you will. Thanks for keeping Erin alive." Collin's eyes teared. "He's not much, but he's all I got."

Vy hugged her and whispered, "I think he's pretty special." She smiled at Jeff. "Second date, maybe."

Jeff grinned. "Of course." He hugged her quickly and let her go.

Erin waited. She eyed him, wondering how he would handle this. He leaned in for a warm kiss on the cheek, stood back, and held her hands. "I intend to see you again, Vy Johnson. Remember that." His face was sober, his eyes deep. "Take care of yourself. All of yourself. And I will see you again."

He stepped back. Vy felt a tightness in her throat but swallowed it. "Of course." She turned away and caught Rudy staring at the floor. "We will make this work, Rudy. And I'll see you on the outside."

Rudy lifted his head. "You better. I've still got some questions for you about that God of yours." He motioned his head towards Collin. "That one thinks she has all the answers. I want a human to talk to."

Collin spun on Rudy. "That is cold, sir. Very cold."

He shrugged. "Live with it." He pointed at Vy. "Do not get yourself killed or fired or anything on my account, got that?"

Vy swallowed any thought of a smile. "Of course not, Rudy. I will be very careful. I know what's riding on these next few days."

Mason escorted her to a basement floor where several vehicles, including his yellow van, were parked. He waved at the selection. "Your choice."

Vy thought several moments. Non-descript would be a plus. She pointed to a dark blue coupe. Nothing stood out about it. No fancy tires, no extra trim. Plain. "That one."

Mason seemed pleased. "Good choice." He pulled a set of keys off a board and handed them to her. "Take care of it. It's my mom's."

Vy eyed him with horror. He smiled. "Not really. I wouldn't do that to you." He motioned to the glovebox. "Paperwork is in there. It's registered to a rental agency we own. Any calls will come back with your name and license number."

"You do think of everything, don't you?"

"When you're in the field as long as we have been, we have to think of everything." Mason put a hand on Vy's shoulder. "Don't stay in the field, Vy. This company will eat you alive. You're good at what you do. But you deserve a life, too. Away from all this."

Vy gave the man a quick hug and slid into the driver's seat. Mason handed her three pieces of folded paper and a map with directions how to get out of the garage. He showed her where the exit would bring her above ground and how to get to the highway. "Be an hour and a half to Oakton from there. Should put you into town before rush hour."

"That would be nice." She started the engine. She lifted her head one last time. "You think we have a shot?"

"One. Maybe two. No pressure, Agent Johnson."

Vy smiled at him. "Of course not." She closed the door, adjusted the seat and the mirror. "God does the impossible all the time." She drove out of the garage.

* * *

Traffic remained light until Vy reached the south of Oakton. She drove to her apartment, let herself in, and threw the bag in the closet. As she changed clothes, she dialed the number Collin had given her for Detective James Russo. Vy had her own sources she would call on if the detective couldn't—or wouldn't—help them out.

She got his answering service. Vy debated, then left a message. "I'm a friend of Collin and Jeff Farrell. They told me to give you a call when I came to town. I have a matter requiring assistance. Collin says you are only the man for the job." She left her number. "Okay, Lord. That's step one. Next, step two." She pulled out a conservative light-colored skirt and jacket combination, swept her hair high, pinned a hat on top. She examined the outfit, decided against the hat, and nodded. She added some jewelry to her fingers and wrists. "That's the ticket. Give them what they expect to see, and that's what they will remember."

Vy looked at her watch. Five-thirty. Time to make the second call. "Brother Golding? My name is Vy Johnson. I attend the Fifth Street Chapel, and we've been partnering with you and the street mission? Right. Brother Golding, I need your help." She outlined what she wanted to do and why she needed his help. "Do you think you can assist me with this? Thank you, Brother Golding. You're an answer to my prayers." *And a few others' as well...*

A thought nudged her. *The look needs a hat. The feathered one.* She ignored it. Vy slipped on a pair of comfortable pumps to complete the outfit. She smiled at her reflection. "Just the right look. Official church compassion business."

Vy picked up a stack of card envelopes, wrote a quick note, stuffed the papers she'd been given into the top one. *You need a hat. The feathered one.* Vy growled at the intruding nudge. "I do not need a hat." She grabbed her study Bible, the large fat one, and locked the door behind her.

You forgot the hat. Vy ground her teeth. "Fine." She unlocked the door, donned her black hat with the feathers, locked the door. "Now, are you happy?" *Very.* Vy shook her head.

The drive to the Farrell home took forty minutes. Time enough for Vy to rehearse both speeches. The first one, to get her around any news crews. The second, to get her into the Farrell household. Preferably the kitchen. With a cup of coffee. And plenty of time for explanations.

Vy spotted the news vans parked across the street from the Farrell's house. Her eyes narrowed. "Can't miss a story, can you? Got to be first in line."

A thought nudged her. *I understand, Father. We all have jobs to do. And Your Son died for them as much as me. I will remember.*

She pulled in behind the last truck in the caravan, parked, and got out with her Bible and the stack of cards. She marched down the center of the street, her head up.

Vy saw the reporter before he slid out of the car. She pretended not to see him until he called to her. "Miss. Ma'am. Excuse me?"

Vy stopped and addressed the man. "Yes? May I help you?"

"Uh, yes, ma'am. Are you going to see the Farrells?"

She smiled but kept a solemn look in her eyes. "Why, yes I am. The brothers and sisters at the Fifth Street Chapel wanted to send cards of encouragement to Mr. and Mrs. Farrell. They support Brother Godling's street mission, same as we. We want to come alongside them in this trying time."

The reporter handed her a card. "Brian Inskeep. Channel 11 news. You think I could go with you and speak with them myself?"

Vy feigned surprise. "Mr. Inskeep, are you a praying man?"

He hesitated. "I can be."

Vy lifted her chin. "I am here to render the aid and comfort of our congregation on behalf of Brother and Sister Farrell. This is the Lord's mission. Can you say the same, sir?"

Mr. Inskeep dissembled. "Maybe I can help if they will talk to me about what they know."

Vy put up a hand to stop him. "This would not be the proper time for questions, sir. This is a time for the Lord to comfort and console. You will have to seek your own audience. Good evening, Mr. Inskeep."

She dismissed him by turning away and marching on up the street. She heard, more than saw, the man slide back into his car to wait. Vy smiled. "Thank you, Auntie Viola. You handled that perfectly." *I watched you do it enough times. I should have it down pat.* Now came the real hurdle. Would the Farrells answer the door? She rapped at the door and called, "Mr. Farrell, Ms. Farrell, I'm not a reporter. I am Viola Johnson, and I'm here from the Fifth Street Chapel. Brother Golding said you might appreciate some cards and some comfort from the Lord."

Vy stepped back to allow room to be seen when the door opened. An older man, probably Mr. Farrell, opened the door slightly. He peered down the street at the news teams. His eyes were clear, non-threatening, and far more welcoming than Vy would have expected. She kept her voice quiet and even. "I am not part of that pack of coyotes, sir. I really am from Fifth Chapel. And I really do have cards for you."

Mr. Farrell gave her a sad smile. "I apologize for any inconvenience you may have had navigating the street."

"Oh, no problem at all." She gave him a conspiratorial wink. "Me and the Lord simply walked on through." She handed him a card off the top of the stack. "There are notes in here you'll want to see, sir." Mr. Farrell's eyes narrowed in suspicion. Vy held up a hand to stop any protest. "Please, sir. Hear me out. The Lord and I are working together." She held his gaze firmly. "And with your children. But don't let the coyotes see a reaction, please."

Mr. Farrell seemed to catch himself, smiled, opened the door. "Viola Johnson, was it?"

"Vy, if you don't mind, sir." She stepped into the entryway.

Harmon shut the door firmly behind her but did not lead her further into the house. He cleared his throat. "I am not unaccustomed to receiving nudges from the Lord. But receiving a message from Him to expect a young woman bearing a Bible, cards and wearing that hat…" He smiled. "That's specific even for my Lord. Come in, Vy."

Vy followed the gentleman into the kitchen. A table had been set with coffee service for three. An older woman, late fifties, maybe sixty, sat at one of the places. She'd pulled her hair back into a messy bun. She eyed Vy with curiosity but not hostility. She stood and waved to a place at the table. Her eyes held a hint of mischief. "The Lord told us you would want coffee. He didn't specify cream or sugar."

Vy laughed. "Both, please."

Mrs. Farrell fetched the sweeteners, then all three sat. Vy began to speak, but Mr. Farrell stopped her. "Please, Vy. I believe it would appropriate to ask the Lord to lead this proceeding since He seems to have orchestrated it." Vy nodded. Mr. and Mrs. Farrell took her hands, held each other's, and Mr. Farrell prayed, "God, Lacey and I aren't understanding any of this. But You told us separately to expect a young woman in a cream suit and a black hat—"

"With feathers. He was quite specific about the feathers, Harmon." Lacey's voice all but laughed.

Harmon continued, "A black hat with feathers. And she would have word about Jeff, Collin, and Erin. She's here, we're here, the coffee is here. You're here. Have Your way, Lord."

Vy added, "Amen." She looked into the anxious eyes of her hosts. "Yes, I've been with those three. They are alive, they are safe, and they are fine. They will be home soon." She had practiced not saying "free." No connotation of harm in any way. She pulled out the notes Jeff, Collin, and Erin had written, handed them to the Farrells, and waited as they read them.

When they were done reading, Vy pulled out her DEA badge and ID. "Your son, his wife, and Erin have been instrumental in bringing to light an injustice done to a citizen of this state."

Before she could continue, Lacey snorted. "Pshaw. Erin stumbled into it, Collin insisted Jeff and she rescue him, and that's how they got involved."

Harmon waved her off. "You don't know that, Lacey. Jeff could have just as easily been the culprit. With his attitude of late…"

Vy held up both hands. "Erin stumbled, Collin was snatched, and Jeff went in after both of them, okay? But the Lord directed the whole thing, so He's the one to blame." She smiled. "Or gets all the credit, anyhow. We need your help to close this 'case' and get everyone home with a minimum of questions and fuss. Ideally." She studied both Harmon's and Lacey's eyes. "If not, there will be a maximum of questions certain people will have to answer the 'why' of. And it could be uncomfortable. For them."

Harmon's eyes narrowed. "When you say 'certain people' in that tone of voice, my fighting sense comes to attention. Powerful people?"

"The world might consider them so. They might consider themselves so as well."

Harmon smiled. "But our Lord has a different standard of power, you mean."

"The only standard that means anything."

Lacey tapped the table. "Can we speak plain? Name names and get it over with?"

Vy laughed and touched Lacey's hand. "Erin said I would love you, and I do. Yes, ma'am. But this may be the only time we can. Once we start moving, we have to expect the bad guys not to play fair. Or nice."

Lacey's face grew fierce. "If I'm fighting for my children, I don't play nice, either."

She snuck a look at Harmon, then added, "Or my grandchildren."

Vy refused to comment, though she knew Lacey was fishing. Vy assumed her most innocent expression. "Do you know something I don't, Mrs. Farrell?"

Lacey lifted a finger to point at her. "Do not 'Mrs. Farrell' me with that tone of voice, young woman. It's Lacey, or if that's too disrespectful for you, Mom Lacey. And the only ones who don't know Collin is pregnant have to be my son and Collin herself." Lacey chuckled. "Those two."

Vy smiled. "I can't tell you anything about that, Mom Lacey. I can say Collin has a healthy glow and has put on a few pounds."

Lacey held her hand out to Harmon. "Pay up."

Harmon rolled his eyes. "Women's intuition." He turned to face Vy. "Now, tell us the full story."

Only when Vy finished explaining all she needed to—and could—say, did Harmon stand. He walked to the kitchen, refilled his coffee, offered her more (which she politely refused), sat back, and said, "Tell me what we need to do. And what we need to be prepared to do."

Vy outlined the next steps that would follow. She added, "I am still waiting to hear from a Detective Russo before I can go much farther."

Harmon raised his cup. "Jim is a good man and a brother in the Lord. He'll give you all the help he can."

"If he's available." Vy studied the notes she had. "Collin asked me to contact Rob Sider, but she didn't know where he might be staying right now."

Lacey stood and pulled a sticky note off the refrigerator. "This is his cell. I know he's working at the Southside rec center for the summer and staying at the mission. He starts OSU in the fall." Lacey's eyes beamed. She pointed to a senior high school graduation picture on the counter. "Our first grandson in college."

The picture of a young man of mixed parentage, in cap and gown, standing between Collin and Jeff with Lacey and Harmon behind the threesome, stood in a place of honor. All five radiated joy and pride. Vy guessed there were still some stories Collin hadn't shared yet. In time.

Lacey asked, "Would it help if I contacted him? What did she want to tell him, besides she's alive, and she's 'not' pregnant?"

Vy laughed. "Um, that would probably be sufficient. She also wanted me to tell him to watch himself."

Lacey offered, "I'll tell him. You won't have to keep waiting for your phone to ring."

"Thank you. That will be a help."

Harmon leaned forward, his face somber. "What can we do to assist you, Vy? Specifically?"

Vy glanced down to the table then raised her eyes to both Farrells. "Pray? Courage for me. That my steps are guided and my words precise. God's will in all."

Harmon squeezed her hand. "Starting tonight and going forward, it will be our pleasure and duty to lift you in prayer. Beyond prayer?"

"Be prepared. The opposition may try to discredit everything we say. Which usually means discrediting us. If there is dirt to be found, they'll find it. If there isn't, they'll create it."

Lacey pursed her lips, raised an eyebrow. "I am not afraid of anything they can bring. My security is in the Lord."

Harmon squeezed his wife's hand. "All this"—he waved around the room— "belongs to the Lord. If He chooses to take it back, we'll praise Him anyhow."

Vy glanced from one Farrell to the other. "I'm convinced you really believe that."

Harmon smiled. "We do. The Lord is our life, Vy. Job said it best—"

Lacey threw in, "Along with thirty-some chapters of complaining…"

Harmon grimaced at her. "He said, 'Even if God kills me, I will still praise Him.' Daniel's three friends facing death by fire knew God could save them but also determined to die for Him if need be. Win, lose, or draw, we belong to Him."

"Amen." Vy stood. "I've got to go. I need to be in the office early tomorrow."

Harmon and Lacey followed her to the front door. Vy peered out, saw no one. "Thank you for your hospitality."

"Thank you for the encouragement. Take care of yourself, young woman." Lacey gave her a quick hug and a kiss on the cheek.

Harmon hugged her as well in a fatherly embrace. "God keep you, Vy."

Vy pulled herself back into "church matron" character, straightened her hat and her Bible. She marched out to the street, walked with determined steps to her car, dipped her head once to Brian Inskeep as she passed him, got in her car, and drove away. She relaxed and smiled. "Black hat with feathers, Lord? Really?" She laughed for the joy of it.

FRIDAY

Vy hit the archives by six in the morning. It took all her creative research techniques and flat-out snooping to find what she needed, buried so far back in the records even she almost couldn't find it.

All the information had been deleted, of course. But a ghost of a trail remained for those trained—and gifted—enough to find it. Like Vy.

At seven, her phone rang. Detective Russo. She kept her voice a notch above a whisper as she detailed her credentials with Jeff and Collin. She explained what they needed from him. Could he do it? Reassured by his answers, she went back to work.

Her phone showed eight-thirty when she finished. She tucked the files she needed under a ten-page report she'd been working on before Erin Winger's case interrupted her. She carried it in with her. It would go out with her as well, providing her cover for why she had gone into the records room so early. The room was monitored. But legitimate searches were rarely questioned beyond, "What case were you investigating?" She could flash the report to whoever asked and be clear.

Reviewing the files, however, required a different level of misdirection. And covert scrutiny. Annoying as it might be, she set her phone to alert her every five minutes to keep from being too engrossed in her reading. Otherwise, she would lose all track of time or miss what happened around her.

Like Agent Hasbro coming past her desk. "Boss wants to see you and your report on where you were last week."

"What time?"

"How long do you need to put it together?"

"And wrap the bow around it? Another two days. But I can give him the bones now." *Especially the one I want to pick with him…the "where was my back-up?" bone. He better have a good answer.*

"After he's done with Carmine. Say, another hour?"

"Sounds good. You want to come get me or should I watch his office door?"

"I'll come. I've got some requisitions he needs to sign. Once I have his undivided attention and his signature, I'll let him know you're ready."

"Thanks, Has'. I appreciate it." *Has' because he always thinks he has the answers.*

Vy diverted from working on Rudy's files long enough to cobble together the facts of who did what to who and when from Erin's case. She ended with the telling of Mason's involvement and Beela's "incarceration." She skipped over exactly how they brought Franny down, choosing to say Franny's organization had been swept and closed with civilian assistance. If the deputy director wanted more information, he would have to wait for her full written report.

With a bare-bones report to keep her boss happy, she switched back to Rudy. She made a list of all the agents who had been around at the time Rudy had gone undercover. She cross-referenced it with all the agents still active when he disappeared. Narrowed the inquiry field to those working in the Mid-West region, then and now.

Looking for malcontents who had been drummed out would be more difficult, but Vy worked until just past noon getting the list of those who might still have an interest in the case from the DEA's side. Less than a handful.

Of course, she had to contend with the political side, and that would be harder to navigate. *Not harder. More complex. But only for me, not for You, right, Lord? Show me where to look, how to look, and lead me. And You will get all the glory for it, I know.*

Agent Hasbro swept past Vy's desk. "He's free. Unless you want to wait until after lunch, and hope he's in a better mood."

Vy raised an eyebrow. "Really? Carmine left him in a bad mood? Is that possible?"

"When he takes the whole morning, yeah. Boss loves Carmine's stories of the 'good ol' days,' but a full morning's worth? That's too much for anyone."

"Especially Carmine's wife. Which is why she sends him in here at least once a week since he retired."

Has' smiled. "Yeah, I know. Poor woman."

"I'll chance it. Boss could get called away or into a meeting or want to see me right before quitting time."

"Your choice."

Vy gathered her papers, including those belonging to Rudy's case. She shuttled those to the bottom, walked to the open office. She rapped once on the door frame. "Deputy Director Lyons? You wanted my report?"

Deputy Director Lyons pushed the top drawer in on his desk. He palmed three white pills, took a glass of water, and washed them down. He held out his hand for Vy's papers.

Vy asked, "Headache, sir?"

"Carmine. The man can talk the hind leg off a mule. I'm trying to convince him he needs to come out of retirement and get a job. Greeter at a big-box store. Talk to vets at the hospital. Teach gardening at a rec center. Anything but sit in my office all morning." He scowled. "I know his wife sends him here. It's her revenge for the long hours Carmine put in all those years. She doesn't want him home either."

Vy kept her face from showing any pleasure at her boss's discomfort. "Retirement can be hard on people."

Director Lyons grumbled. "Tell me about it. My dad retired, and he did nothing but sit around. Didn't know what to do with himself. No hobbies. No interests other than his job. Once he lost that, he lost his reason to get up in the morning."

"I've heard of that happening."

Director Lyons lifted his head. "Which is why I am leaving the office when you and I are through here and going to play golf. Nasty game. Hate it. But it's better than staring at the lawn."

"Yes, sir."

"So tell me, Agent Johnson, what happened on this raid that took you two weeks and four days to finish?"

Vy kept her cool. "My final report will have all the details. We left town having everything buttoned up and coordinated and planned out. Thirty minutes from the rendezvous spot, I noticed something missing."

"Oh? What?"

"My backup." Vy's eyes narrowed. "We lost communications, but that hasn't stopped the team before from meeting at the designated place. I waited as long as I could, but no one showed. And they didn't show from the Indiana side, either." Vy leaned forward and placed her fists on the director's desk. "Why did I get hung out to dry, Director Lyons? I had a civilian with me. You drummed it into us. We never endanger a civilian if we can help it. Where was my backup?"

The director held Vy's glare for several moments. "I expect my agents to be able to improvise, Johnson. Which you did. And admirably, from what I'm told."

"Told by who?"

"The field office over in Indiana. An agent they refuse to name said you acquitted yourself in an exemplary fashion. Even with a civilian tagging along. They would like to see you commended for your actions."

Vy's eyes narrowed further. "Well, isn't that just fine. It doesn't answer the question of what happened to my backup. Who pulled them off? Why wasn't I intercepted and told the situation had changed? Why did I get hung out to dry, Director Lyons?"

Lyons leaned back in his chair. "Shut the door, Agent Johnson."

Vy closed the door, turned, sat. Waited.

Lyons tapped his pencil on the desk. "I could assure you it was nothing personal. I could say there had been a mistake, say these things happen sometimes. And I could promise you it will never happen again." He stopped tapping the pencil. "And I would be lying through my teeth. Except the part about it not being personal. That much is true."

Lyons dropped the pencil. "The way our superiors see it, we are a small unit in a backwater part of the country. Ohio, Indiana, Kentucky? Drug cartels? Kingpins? Not to their way of thinking. Someone up the food chain thought"—Lyons sneered the word—"thought they had a bigger bust requiring more people. People I had deployed with you."

Lyons jerked his thumb towards the ceiling. "I got outvoted. No one knew about the phone issue. You were far enough ahead of the team they didn't have eyes on you. They had no reason to think you didn't get the same message they did."

Lyons's face hardened, his eyes narrowed. "You can believe Agents Mather and Foster were both livid and ready to go rogue. I talked them off the roof. They calmed down and joined the other task force."

A look of almost pleasure tinged his eyes. "Which though they had far superior numbers, still managed to lose a shipment on the order of five million dollars. And the seller. And the buyer. In fact, the bust netted them nothing. Big fat nothing."

He waved his hand at Vy. "And there's you, all by your lonesome, hung out to dry with a civilian anchor. You manage to intercept the drugs and clear two organizations off the street. And if that wasn't enough, you provide us with an opening to a group we didn't even know existed there."

Deputy Director Lyons smiled and extended his hand to Vy. "Congratulations, Agent Johnson. You made my month. And probably the rest of my year."

Vy accepted the handshake. "Thank you, sir. I appreciate your confidence in me." She handed him the second file. "You might want to reconsider, however. Here's the rest of the story."

Lyons's eyes narrowed, widened, narrowed... Vy waited without comment until the director looked back up. "Where did you get this? Why did you get this?" He growled. "I'd ask how, but I figure I know that answer."

Vy nodded. "Yes, sir. That's what detained me the extra week." She gave him a shortened version of how exactly her case had intertwined with Rudy's. "You are one of the five active agents who were around when this went down. Do you remember the case? And what can you tell me about it?"

The director pointed to the paperwork. "You've got it all there. That's what happened. That's why it happened."

"But why didn't he get brought back?" Vy felt frustration growing.

"Because of a national drug crisis, an agreement between nations, and politicians who could be bought." Lyons shifted in his chair. "Anyone who objected got reassigned to other districts, most out in places so remote they had to pipe in sunshine." The director stared off into space. "If he wanted to live, he only had one compromise. Being buried underground, yeah, but left alive." He held Vy's gaze. "I don't expect you to understand, but that's the best we could do at the time."

"Has the political climate changed any? The ones in power aren't still in control, right?" Vy stood and paced. "Ten years. That's two presidential terms. A senate election. Who knows how many firings and hirings. It can't still matter, can it?"

Director Lyons snorted. "You'd think that. You'd be wrong, but you'd think that. People who have that kind of power don't go away. They have legacies to protect. An image to preserve."

"Okay, but what about the actual case? The legal proceedings? If charges were filed, then dropped, why is he still being held prisoner?"

"He's not a prisoner, he's—"

"His daughter's life is being held over his head. He's a prisoner."

Lyons cocked his head. "What'd you say?"

"His daughter. Rudy agreed to the plan because his daughter had a murder charge against her. They promised no action would be taken as long as he stayed quietly gone until they needed him."

Lyons drew in a deep breath. "I never heard that part of it."

Vy flipped over a few pages of her notes. "I had to dig deep for this one. But here. Here's the agreement." She stepped back while the director read.

"Those…" Vy let the Holy Spirit filter his responses. Lyons glared at the papers. "This, this I can do something about." He held Vy's eyes. "I can get this taken care of. Convenient, this department was the one set to testify against her. We held all the evidence. Wanna bet she got set up just for this?"

"No bet." Vy felt her stomach tighten. "I'm beginning to believe they would do anything to get what they want."

Lyons sagged. "Yeah, it's about like that." He studied the papers in front of him. "I know these people. I'm as likely to get my head handed to me if I try to bring this up." He straightened his back. "It's about justice, right?"

"Yes, Director. It's about justice. That's what I thought when I joined. I want to believe it still is."

Lyons's mouth drew into a hard line. "Me too." He tapped his lips with his index finger. "I am guessing you have a backup plan if this doesn't go the way you want?"

Vy smiled without mirth. "I cannot confirm or deny that, Director Lyons."

The corner of his eyes crinkled. "That's what I thought. Give me two days. I'll let you know."

"You have until Monday." She did not disclose why. Director Lyons didn't need—or want—to know the details her squad still needed to work through. Everything would be in place, and the full board in play by then.

She reached out and offered her hand. "Thank you, Director Lyons."

"For what? I didn't do anything."

"You listened. That is enough."

"Right. I'll see you on Monday." Vy turned to go. "Oh, and Agent Johnson…" Vy turned back. "Good job. You're a good agent. I'd be sorry if anything happened and we lost you."

Vy lifted her chin. "Thank you, sir. I appreciate that." She exited the room.

At her desk, she sat and let all the emotions rattle around inside her. Nothing would show on the outside. At least not yet. Vy told anyone who wanted to hear it, "I'm going out to lunch." She walked to the elevator, slipped in, waited until the door closed, slammed her fist against the metal wall. She stomped her foot. "God! These people! How can they be so self-righteous? No, don't tell me. I know how. I know why. But this is so wrong. So very wrong."

What are you willing to do about it? What price will you pay for Rudy's freedom?

The thought cooled her anger. Vy walked to her car, slid inside, closed the door. She picked up her cellphone and stopped. She stared at it, stared at the building, stared at her phone. She talked it out softly. "I wanted to be a DEA agent from the moment I heard Iris ran off to the streets. I remember Mama crying she'd lost her baby. I wanted nothing more than to find the dealer who hooked my sister and bring him in."

Her eyes teared with moisture. "Except it didn't go down that way. Dad would find her, bring her home, she'd stay a week, a month, a year, off she went again. I realized I didn't want just the street dealers. I wanted the big fish, the smugglers, and the kingpins, and the cartel bosses. All the Iris's of the world didn't matter to them as long as the money kept flowing in."

Her voice cracked. "But I fought the good fight, Lord. I knew we were battling against the tide. Playing whack-a-mole. Shut down one organization, two more pop up. But it was worth it knowing someone else's little sister might be spared. A father, a mother, a child…someone got some good out of it."

She swiped at her cheeks. "But this…this is wrong. I'm not naïve. I know how the game is played." Bitterness painted her tone. "This went beyond playing the game. This is ten years out of someone's life. For what? Expediency? Political goodwill? Huh-uh. No. Not right." She shook her head. "It's wrong, Lord. I know it. You got me involved, and this is where it stops."

Vy checked the time on her phone. Mason would be above ground and hopefully in a place with cell reception. She waited for his "Speak to me."

"The long suit is red. The short suit is green in three."

"Heard."

She pocketed her phone. "Dumbest conversation ever." There would be no chances taken.

MONDAY

Collin waited for Jeff to come back inside from the outdoors tunnel and his "walk." Yes, he would scout the forest for any signs of intrusion. No, he didn't have to. That's what Rudy's security teams were for. But Jeff benefited from the fresh air, sunshine, and the proximity to a forest not unlike at Camp Grace. Claustrophobia was a real problem for him.

As soon as he and Erin returned from outside, Collin pulled her husband by the arm. "Come on. I need some help." She noticed the gloomy look in Erin's eyes and added, "You too. I've got an idea, and I need you both to help me see it."

"What? What's this about?"

Collin tugged on his arm. "I'm trying to layout the bedroom for the babies, and I can't seem to make the dimensions work."

Erin laughed. "You're not even close, and you're worried about rearranging the furniture?"

Collin nailed her brother with a glare that would strip paint off the furniture. "Do not remind a pregnant woman how much longer she will remain in a fattened condition. Especially if you value your manhood."

Jeff waved a hand at Erin. "Bad move, bro. Apologize, say, 'yes, Collin,' and let it go."

Erin bowed. "I'm sorry. Of course, Collin. What do you want us to do?"

She snorted. "Better." Collin led them to the common room. "This is about the size of the main bedroom. I want to know if we can fit two cribs in with the king-size bed, or should we downsize to a queen?"

Jeff's eyes filled with horror. "Give up my mattress? You're joking!"

Collin lifted an eyebrow. "Do you want your children sleeping in that king-size bed with you at all hours of the night?"

Erin shrugged. "You'll be the one feeding them. I don't see why it would bother Jeff any."

Collin raised a fist to her brother. "I will make you regret those words, A-One. The first time I leave you babysitting the two of them and forget to put out formula for you."

"You wouldn't do that to your children."

"Wanna bet?"

"Jeff! Your wife is contemplating child neglect."

"Which child? You or them?"

Erin rolled his eyes. He turned and studied the room. "I don't think this will be big enough for the four of you. You need to buy a bigger house."

"We can make it work."

"No. You need to get a bigger one. I'll take yours off your hands, and you guys can buy another one. Or build one to suit. Everybody wins."

Collin sighed. "Erin, will you stop? What is with you?"

"No one. No one is with me. And I miss her."

Collin leaned into his shoulder. "I'm sorry. She'll be back soon."

Loneliness colored her brother's eyes. "If things don't go according to plan, she will. I'm not sure what to hope for."

Jeff placed a hand on Erin's shoulder. "We're all praying things go according to God's plan."

"I know. I am. I miss hearing her laugh. Watching her smile. Listening to her fume at me."

Collin grinned. "And she did that quite well."

"And often too. I deserved it."

Jeff asked, "Has anyone talked with Rudy today?"

Collin nodded. "Yeah, I did. He's getting anxious about getting this over with. And he's still nervous about what his daughter may say. Or do."

Erin added, "I think he's afraid of what his ex-wife may say as well."

Collin grimaced. "Russo hasn't managed to find her yet, has he?"

Jeff smiled at his wife. "He will." He turned his palms up. "Or not. I'm not sure having the wife there is going to make that much difference."

"The more witnesses, the better."

Erin corrected Collin. "The more witnesses, the safer for all of us." He lifted his chin. "And I do mean all of us…everyone at the reveal."

Collin felt the uneasiness in her gut. Vy's message, cryptic as it was, meant the short suit—having the DEA recall Rudy—had been put in play. And would culminate today.

She rubbed her stomach. "God has this. He has us, and He has this." Conviction rose in her voice. *I know You have us. You brought us here for this.*

Did he really? Or did you come up with this plan on your own? Collin the Mighty, rescuing helpless people again. But they aren't helpless, and they don't need you interfering in their lives.

Collin shut her ears to the accuser. Would be nice if she could shut her mind as well. Redirect. "I think if we put the cribs at the bottom of the bed, we could get both of them in."

Jeff eyed the space. "Why two cribs? They're twins. They're used to being on top of each other. Let them sleep together until they're big enough for regular beds."

Collin grimaced. "Because I want to be able to keep one from waking the other. Or from starting the other one crying at the same time. I need at least a fighting chance at this."

Mason walked into the room. Collin turned to him. His eyes were guarded, but she could read the anger in them. His face had become dark. Collin dropped her hand to the babies' head. *Or whatever.* "What's wrong?"

Mason spaced his words. "Message from Vy."

Jeff stared at Mason side-eyed. "What did she say?"

"'Short suit null. Long suit green. Now.'"

Erin stared at the floor. "That's bad."

Jeff's face became as grim as Mason's. "Well, we know what we have to do, don't we? Let's get after it."

Collin breathed. *Lord, protect us. Save us. In Your will. Always.*

* * *

Eleven a.m. Monday, Vy finally got to the office. She'd been at the courthouse, waiting to testify, waiting for motions to be made, hanging around while the lawyers and the judge discussed matters behind closed doors, then cut everyone loose for a postponement. Waste of a morning. Except it was the court system and had to be done.

As she entered, the tension in the air practically slapped her in the face. Vy stared around the room, trying to decipher what had happened. No one called to her. No one glanced her way. Heads were all down, studying the paperwork on the desks. Vy went to her desk, fighting the urge to draw her gun. The room bristled with watchfulness, with apprehension. Vy scanned the room and noticed Deputy Director Lyons's door had been closed. She could hear voices…loud voices… several bangs, as of drawers slamming.

The door flew open, crashing against the wall. Director Lyons raged out of his office, flanked by two stern-faced men, each with a hold on the director's arm. Lyons marched through the desks, silent in his wrath. He turned at the exit door, shook off the two men holding him, faced the office, and barked, "Good luck, people. You'll need it." The guards caught his arms again and escorted him from the room. Vy watched as the three men disappeared from view.

The office exploded with voices. "What just happened?" "What's going on?" "Who were those guys?" "What did he mean, 'Good luck?'"

Agent Hasbro waved his arms for quiet. His face looked pale, drawn. He faltered as he spoke. "Uh, I think… I've seen this before. They are…replacing him."

Murmurs and mutters. "Why? What's he done?"

Has' stared at the floor. "I think he…" He looked up. "He brought up an old case. He told me he would be making waves with it. But he wasn't afraid." Hasbro stared at the door. "I think he got fired."

Vy drew in a long breath. Water stung her eyes, but she blinked it back. No tears. She knew what she had to do. *Am I ready for this? Ready to give this up?* She stood and muttered, "Think I left my phone in the car." No one noticed her leaving.

Back in her car, doors closed, locked, and the radio playing, Vy sorted out her emotions. *Two paths ahead. Say nothing, do nothing. Keep my job. Rudy is nothing to me.*

Except he could be me. Could be any of us. Is that what we signed up to be? Expendable commodities to be used by others for personal gain? Tossed aside or buried when we become a liability? Look at the Director. He's been with them what, twenty, thirty years? Don't tell me this isn't related to Rudy's case. And nothing he did before mattered.

Vy looked skyward. *What do I do, Father? Stay? Quit? Pretend none of this happened?*

She knew one thing she had to do. She had to tell Mason and the others. She pulled out her phone and sent the text. "Short suit null. Long suit green. Now." They would know what it meant.

Now what? What do I do now?

A strong impression flooded through her to call Mason before she took any next step. He would know what to do next if anyone knew. *Okay, Lord. I'll talk to him. After I call my folks. Dad at least will want to know. Mom will only worry, but Dad will understand. He will.*

Vy speed-dialed her father's phone. She smiled as he answered. "Hello, daughter."

"Hello, Father."

"Why the honor of a call in the middle of the day?"

Vy chuckled. "I call you all the time, and you know it."

His smooth voice calmed all her nerves. "And I answer all the time. What can I do for you?"

"Nothing." Vy faltered. "Be there. Always be there."

"I am. Is something wrong? Did something happen?"

Vy lifted her chin. "Not yet. I have to make a choice about something." She paused. "I know what your answer will be, but I still want to hear you say it."

A deep but gentle chuckle went straight to her heart. "I will love you no matter what choice you make. You are my daughter, and you'll never be anything else but."

Vy closed her eyes. "I'm afraid. Afraid this could end up hurting you and Mama as well."

"Would the Lord Himself do it?"

"Yes."

"Go and do likewise. We'll weather any storms He brings. Just remember, if He allows the storm, He'll see us through it to the other side."

Vy drew in a deep breath. "Thanks. I love you, Dad."

"I love you, too. Now, which daughter is this?"

Vy laughed. "Vy, Dad."

"Oh." His voice ran the scale. "That daughter. Well, forget what I said. Doesn't apply."

"Nope. Gonna hold you to it every day."

"I hope so. Love you, girl."

Vy put her phone away. She would call Mason tonight. From a burner phone unable to be traced. The department had a surplus of those. They could issue one for the night. Vy climbed out of her car and went back to the office.

* * *

The group dispersed to their appointed tasks. Collin walked to the nearest flat outdoor exit. The half-hour stroll did her nerves good. Didn't help her know what to say to Rob. But it did cue her in on all the things not to say. She pushed back the heavily camouflaged entrance, stood in the sunshine, and let it warm her.

She pulled out her cellphone and speed-dialed his number. He answered after the second ring. "Hey, Collin. I got the message from Brother Golding. Are you okay? Are all you guys okay?"

Collin stripped her tone of any anxiety or stress. Not the time. "Hey, my man. We're all fine now." She glanced and saw the text message from Jeff. Collin pushed through. "This will be the last time I can talk to you freely. I don't know what Vy was able to tell you."

"Mom Lacey called me instead. You're in trouble, right?"

"Not yet. We're about to make public an injustice that happened a long time ago. Certain people don't like being exposed. Makes 'em nasty. They will try to dig up anything and everything on us. What they can't find, they'll make up. My life is an open book. I know what I did, and I know who I am."

Collin felt her throat tighten. Rob's voice came back firm. "Nothing anyone can say will make a difference, Collin. I don't care, and no one I know's gonna care, either. We know you. That's all that matters."

Collin closed her eyes. "I love you, Rob."

"I love you, too. Does this mean I gotta go hide at the mission or something?"

Collin chuckled. "No. Not unless you feel threatened. I won't call Battle Code Red just yet."

Rob groaned. "I hope not. You being Zena never has worked."

"Tell me about it. Just watch the calls, okay? I won't ask, and you don't tell."

"Got it. Be careful, Collin. I expect to see you on move-in day."

"I'll be there." *Whole lot more of me gonna be there than you expecting...but I'll tell you that later.*

Collin broke the connection. She scrolled through her contacts until she found the name she wanted. No speed dial for this one.

Ken Paxton answered. "My phone recognizes your name. Remind me why I know you?"

Collin smiled. "We worked together on the Southside Rec center project. You were the lawyer I asked to keep us on the straight and narrow. I've followed your career and saw you stepped away from corporate law and are working as a Public Defender."

"Oh, that Collin Farrell. Nice to hear from you again."

"You might want to withhold judgment on that until you hear what I need."

"Fair warning. How can I help you?"

"I have a man, a friend, who needs representation. But not against the law. He needs someone who will back him in the court of public opinion, in the political and international arenas, and possibly against the US government."

Silence. Slow drawl. "You don't want much, do you? From a public defender?"

"You were a brilliant lawyer. When you stepped away from your seven-figure career, you did it as a matter of conscience and principle. Conscience and principle are the only reasons anyone should take this case. That, and if the Lord says so."

Silence again. "Tell me about the case."

Collin described the ten-year case as succinctly—but as briefly—as she could. "We're going into this knowing who we might be up against. We're not worried. The Lord will be our defender, or He won't. We want to see this man get a shot at life again."

"And he's willing to risk it all?"

Collin hesitated. It would all come out in the end, so get it out now. "My friend has cancer. He's failing. He'd like to see the sun again. And maybe his kid. Just once. We want that for him."

"I can appreciate that. How soon do you need to know?"

"Is now too soon?"

Paxton laughed. "Yes. I need time to think about it, to look into what I can, and weigh all the pertinent factors." He paused. "Give me fifteen minutes to convince my wife our lives being over as we know them is a good thing. I'll call you back."

Collin found a stump to sit on. She would have been more comfortable sitting on the ground with her knees drawn to her chest, but that wasn't happening anytime soon. She rubbed her belly. "Can you two behave a bit longer? Another month? At least until we get back to Oakton? I don't think Rudy wants to meet you in this compound." She said sternly, "I don't want to meet you two here, either. I'm sure your father could deliver you in exemplary fashion, but there's no NICU here, and I'm afraid you're going to need it."

She hummed to herself, got up and walked around, sat again, checked her phone, walked around…and killed all of three minutes. She groaned. "God, You are Lord of time and space. You're outside of all of it. Can you make fifteen minutes disappear? You drag 'em out while I'm waiting for the coffee to be ready in the mornings."

Complaining didn't make the time go any faster. Neither did walking, singing, weaving in and out around the trees (always careful NOT to lose sight of the doorway…) But fifteen minutes did pass. So did twenty. Twenty-five. Thirty.

At the thirty-five-minute mark, Collin started scrolling through her contact list again. Who to call? Paxton had been her first choice. Frankly, the only person who had come to mind. With him out of the picture, she'd have to—

Her phone beeped. Paxton. She tried to keep her voice even. "Yes?"

"I'll take it on. You can pay me if we survive. If not, well, it was fun while it lasted."

"Your wife is okay with this?"

"Not immediately. It took a little longer than the fifteen I promised you. But she finally saw it my way. And she's with us."

Collin breathed out a sigh. "Great. That's fantastic. You have no idea how wonderful that is. We'll be back in Oakton within three days. Sooner if I can arrange it. We'll meet when we get settled in again." She ended the call. *And after I see an obstetrician…and go shopping for baby items. T-shirts and diapers. That's all they'll need. They're going to live in them 'til they're old enough to start school. I don't care what anyone says!*

Uh-huh. I'll believe that when I see it. Every store you pass will have the cutest little shirts or pants or dresses or onesies…and you'll buy them all.

No, I won't.

Erin will. So will Jeff. And Leesa. And Lacey. And Rob.

Rob won't buy baby stuff!

Betcha both babies are decked out in Scarlet and Gray with a Block O on them before they can walk. The Ohio State University. Go, Bucks!

Collin rolled her eyes. Thoughts of baby clothes, Buckeye or otherwise, provided a pleasant distraction from the nightmare the squad would face. Of their own making. Collin closed her eyes as she walked the corridor back to the main living space.

Jeff eyed her. "And?"

"We have counsel."

He nodded. "We have reporters."

Erin walked in. "We have the tech we need."

Mason followed Erin. "And we have a group to put the presentation together."

No one spoke. Collin could guess the thoughts going through everyone's head. *Are we sure about this? Is this really what we want to do? Are we ready for what could happen?* And at least in Jeff, Erin, and Collin's heads, *God, be in this. And if You're not, stop us, please.*

Erin did a 360⁰ scan of the room. "Suppose we should pack?"

"The chess set. Everything else can stay behind."

Rudy's voice came from around the corner. "You're not leaving my chair. I love that chair."

Collin wagged her head. "Fine. We'll take the chair. But we're not taking the tables."

Rudy walked in. "What's wrong with my tables?"

"Did you build them?"

"No."

"They're ugly and old, and we're leaving them here. You can send for them later if you really want them that bad." Mason walked out of the room.

Rudy's eyes narrowed. He glared at her. "Who put you in charge?"

She waved both arms wide. "Forgive me, sir. This is your domain. You may decide what stays and what goes. Remembering, we have no moving van nor any other conveyance to transport the greater part of your belongings. What shall we pack for you?"

He shook his head. "Nothing. I can come back and get anything I want." He paused. The gaze in his eyes went far away. "If I'm alive to do it."

Collin kept her voice soft. "You've got a lot of living left to do, Rudy. Don't quit on us now."

"I never quit." He continued to gaze off. "I didn't quit back then, either. She did. She thought what I did was important and vital. She thanked me for working to keep drugs off the street so our daughter could live a good life. And then she took the kid and disappeared."

He turned and gazed deep at Collin. "Don't you quit on him, no matter what he does." He glared at Jeff with the same intensity. "And don't you ever quit on her, no matter what she does." The heat of his words crackled in the air.

Erin quipped, "Good thing I'm not married."

Collin hung her head. "Erin…"

"What?"

"Never mind."

Mason entered the fray. Or the ring. *Counseling session?*

Give it a break.

I will if you will.

Collin studied his guarded expression. "What is it, Mason?"

"Vy called." Collin noted Erin's head lift. A little. Mason continued. "Her director got escorted out of the building permanently today. She wants to know if she should stay where she is for reconnaissance's sake. Or should she quit and make the opening statement?"

Erin murmured, "And then get out of Dodge."

Rudy turned to Erin. "You're the strategist among us. Can you render an opinion that isn't colored by your feelings about Vy?"

Erin held Rudy's gaze. "My feelings for Vy are no greater than my feelings for my sister, Jeff, you, or Mason, here." He grinned. "Maybe a little greater than for you, Jeff and Mason. But I can work through that."

Jeff groaned.

Rudy rolled his eyes.

Mason smiled.

Erin stared at the floor. "Do we benefit from any information Vy may gather over the next day or so? My gut says no. Do we benefit from her tipping our hand?" Erin's eyes turned to the side, but only he knew what his gaze saw. "Is she in more danger making her statement before we get to town?" He held his index finger up to stop Rudy—or anyone else—from making any comments. "Does she endanger us?"

He stood silent for several moments. "The director tipped our hand already. Tell Vy to stay where she is. But staying here will present a risk we shouldn't take. It's time to bug out, and now. We need to get away from here before our opponent remembers where he left you and cuts off the exits."

Erin looked to Rudy. Rudy's eyebrows arched. "Agreed." He smiled at Collin. "Guess you win the round on the tables. And the chair."

"But not the chess set. Bring it. I want it if you don't. It's too beautiful to leave behind."

Rudy nodded. Collin couldn't read the expression on the man's face. Gratitude? Appreciation? Embarrassment? There wasn't time to find out. With the others, Collin grabbed anything electronic, anything mission-essential, anything incriminating, and hustled it and herself to the pre-assigned vehicle.

She and Jeff took the sedan parked nearest the exit, in deference to Collin's "condition." Erin and Rudy would take the SUV stationed nearest the farmhouse exit. And Mason would pull out in a late model truck. With the beloved chair.

Jeff and Collin headed directly home. Jeff called his older brother Ren. "Hey, man."

"What's going on, Jeff? Where have you been? Mom and Dad are worried—"

"I know, Ren. I know. Collin and I are on the way home now. Will you open the lake house, make sure the electric and a/c are on, and the fridge is running?"

"Why? Who's using it? You disappear for who knows how long, come back, and now—"

"Ren, I'll explain it all when we get home. Collin's brother Erin needs a place to stay for a while, and I told him he could work from there." Collin sensed the tension Jeff tried to restrain.

"Yeah, I heard his house blew up. Faulty water heater? Is that what they found?"

"I don't know, Ren. We'll find out when we get home. That's all I can say right now, okay? Mom and Dad know we're coming, and they're expecting us. Give us a day or two to get resettled, and we'll have a family meeting and explain everything. Can you do that?"

"You better have a good explanation, kid."

Collin watched Jeff wince. *Kid. He hates that.* "We will. Thanks, brother."

Collin laid her hand on his arm. "I'm sorry he rags on you. Brothers…"

Jeff smiled at her. "Yeah, he does it to remind me he's the oldest. And the smartest. And the most successful. And the best looking. There's absolutely no ego in our family. Ren got it all."

Collin giggled but covered her mouth. She stared out the window as the miles clicked off the highway. "Do we have a shot at this? I mean, a real shot Erin can convince them to admit guilt, accept responsibility, and we live happily ever after?"

"With Erin and Paxton talking, we've got as good a shot as we can get. Do I think it will work? I'm praying, milady. That's all I can do."

She lay her head on his shoulder. "At least we can pray together." She sat and studied him. "Right?"

"Right. The babies are mine, Collin. I will never doubt you again. It's settled."

Collin lay her head back where it'd been. "I'm glad." They rode in silence for several minutes. "Do you want a DNA test?"

Jeff's voice carried frustration. "No, Collin. I said no, and I mean it. I know what the DNA would show. They're my children, and that's the end of it."

Collin dropped the matter. She went back to something more playful. "So, what names are you thinking of?"

Jeff drawled, "Well… If it's a boy and a girl, maybe Justis and Grace. Or Mercy."

Collin gave him a jaundiced eye. "Really?"

"Sure. Why not?"

"Because when roll gets called at school, they're going to be teased."

"You asked what names I was thinking of."

"What about after your dad and mom?"

"No. Both of them said no namesakes. Neither of them was fond of their name in school."

"I get it. Okay, I like Justis. Justin would be better. No chance of being misspelled. J-u-s-t-i-s versus J-u-s-t-i-c-e."

Jeff shrugged. "We'll think about it."

A sharp kick to the ribs made Collin sit straighter. "Ow. I'm thinking we better be thinking about it sooner than later."

Jeff's head spun to check her out. "What?"

"The kicking. These two are not happy in here."

Jeff's eyes sparkled. "Awww…poor babies. Cramped? Be patient. It's not time to come out to face the world yet." Jeff reached a free hand over and caressed the baby bump.

Lights and sirens flashed behind them. Jeff pulled over to let the car by, but it followed him to the berm. Collin and Jeff exchanged concerned looks. Jeff let out a breath. "Nothing. We were doing nothing wrong. I wasn't speeding. Let's see what they want."

Jeff put both hands on the steering wheel so the Highway Patrol officer could see them clearly. The officer leaned in the window. "License, registration, and proof of insurance." His partner stepped behind the car and waited.

Jeff kept his tone even. "All that is on my phone. May I reach to retrieve it?" The phone Mason had given him after Franny took his.

"Slowly, yes." Collin noted the patrolman kept one hand on his sidearm.

Jeff picked his phone out of the holder. He pulled up the screen with the information on it. "This is it."

The officer took Jeff's phone back to the patrol car. Jeff turned to Collin. "Should I have given him the phone?"

"I don't know. We'll ask Jim Russo when we have a chance."

They waited twenty minutes before the patrolman came back. Collin noted Jeff seemed as calm as before they were stopped. *Good man.*

The officer handed Jeff the phone. "Here you go. Sorry I pulled you over. We had a 'be on the lookout' for a vehicle like this, but you don't match the driver we're looking for."

Collin turned to Jeff, wide-eyed. She raised her head to the officer. "Is there a criminal loose? Someone we should be watching for? Jeff…" She put her hand on his arm.

Jeff patted her arm. "It's all good, Collin. It's all good. I'm sure the police can find who they want without our help."

The officer touched his hat. "Yes, sir, we can. You two can go now."

Jeff pulled onto the highway. No one said anything for ten miles. Collin broke the silence. "You think they're already looking for Rudy? This fast?"

"I have no way of knowing, Collin."

Collin's eyes narrowed. "Guess. Please."

Jeff turned, then turned back to the road. "Maybe. I think it would be too quick. But I don't know."

Collin gritted her teeth. "That's the worst part of all of this. Not knowing anything as fact. It's driving me crazy."

She watched Jeff's jaw tighten. "Me too, milady."

No one spoke the remainder of the way home.

* * *

Erin and Rudy arrived at the Farrell lake house just after dark. They drove the backroads, skirted traffic, circled the beltline from beyond the beltline. Anything to keep from arriving before dark and before Ren could "open it for Erin."

In the dark, Erin knew Rudy couldn't see the cabin sat alone at the end of a small peninsula. The smell of pine perfumed the air. Erin heard the gentle lap-lap-lap of the water on the dock. A billion-billion stars twinkled overhead. Owls hooted in the oak trees; four antlerless deer scattered as the SUV pulled into the driveway and stopped.

Rudy pulled the computers from the back of the car while Erin gathered the rest of the equipment they carried with them. Erin showed Rudy the "trap door" under the front steps where phones, i-pads, laptops, and other media-connected devices were stowed upon entry. The Farrells maintained a "no electronics policy" for family vacationers. You turned them in when you entered, you got them back when you left. Period.

Erin watched Rudy give the house the once-over. The older man raised an eyebrow. "Nice. Very nice. For a cabin."

Erin smirked. "And above ground."

Rudy snorted. "Right."

"At least the view is better."

"But at my place, I know no one is looking back at me."

Erin held up both hands. "Truth." He pointed to the trees and fence line. "They have a pretty decent alarm system. We should have an early warning if anyone wants to come visit."

"I'll take your word for it." Rudy glanced around. "Which room should I take?"

"You like stairs?"

"After ten years underground? No."

"Pick one on this level." Erin thought about the spasms he'd been having. "I'll join you."

Rudy eyed Erin. He shrugged. "Don't want to chance falling unannounced. Makes for bad entrances."

Rudy moved off to store his belongings. Erin took the suite to the left of the front door. Rudy selected the one on the right. There were three bedroom/bathroom suites on the main floor, two upstairs, along with four bedrooms. Erin knew the cabin had been built for the expanding Farrell Clan. Plenty of room for everyone, and feel free to bring a friend.

Erin thought about Vy and how she would fit into the family. Granted, he wasn't a "Farrell" as such, but you didn't get close to them and not get adopted. Which gave you all the rights and privileges of any other family member. He measured Ren, Mike, and their wives, against Vy. No, there would be no problem. Leesa accepted everyone. Especially females.

Erin stuffed the few clothes he'd been provided in the compound into a dresser. From a multi-millionaire to a man with the clothes on his back. *How the mighty have fallen. Yeah, well, you can't take it with you.*

"We can rebuild him."

I hope so.

He went to the kitchen and looked into the refrigerator to see what staples there were. A little digging around in the freezer and, "Jackpot! We've got bacon! My life is complete."

Rudy ambled in, following the yell of delight. "Boy, you don't need much, do you?"

Erin grinned. "Bacon, chocolate, a soda, and I'm happy." He stopped. "Well, having Vy here would make it complete. But since she's not, I'll have to settle."

Rudy sat at the center island. He stared around the massive kitchen. "Farrell's pretty well off, then."

"This is the one concession to wealth for the family. Lacey and Harmon's way of keeping the family in touch with each other. They still try to plan whole family gatherings here, but it's getting harder with people's schedules."

"Humph."

Erin chuckled. "About how Harmon feels about it, yeah." He pointed to the drink fridge. "Once you cross the threshold, you're automatically given drink refrigerator privileges. Anything you can find is yours."

"I'm gonna like them." He fixed his gaze on Erin. "Unless they're not as accepting and understanding as you and your 'squad' are."

Erin smiled. "More. Even more. You'll see."

"Let me guess, they're Christians, right?"

"No. They're Christ-followers. Like Jeff and Collin. I'm a work in progress. They're the real deal."

Rudy grabbed a soda and sat. "So tell me, Mr. Work in Progress, what makes a Christ-follower different from a Christian?"

"Christianity is a religion. An organized way of believing and living. Christ-followers look at the words of Jesus and try to do everything His way. We follow the "Way" of Christ. Do things the way He would do. Love our enemies. Forgive people who hate us. Be peacemakers. Give our lives to serve others. If Jesus did it, we try to do it."

"So who writes the rules?"

"Jesus did."

"And who gets to interpret them?"

"The Holy Spirit."

Rudy mocked. "I bet that's easy."

Erin didn't rise to Rudy's taunt. "If you sit and read the Scriptures, it's all pretty clear what Jesus said. Even more clear what He did. There's no mystery in it. When we have questions, we go to Him, and He explains things."

Rudy growled. "Your sister talked about hearing from your god." Rudy glanced around the room. "What do you have to do to hear from him? Go to church? Donate money? Make a big show of how sorry you are for being the miserable person you are?"

"No. No. And no. All you have to do is ask."

"Ask what?"

For all the belligerence in Rudy's tone, Erin sensed there was honesty in the inquiry. "Ask Him to love you. Which He already does. And to forgive you. And He's done that, too. Ask Him to make you into a new person. One that wants to follow Him. He's always ready and willing and happy to answer those prayers."

Erin watched Rudy mull that around. He glared at Erin. "Can't be that easy. Can't be."

Erin shrugged. "I can show you where He wrote it all down for you."

Rudy took a long swig of his soda. "I may let you do that. After this is all over."

"Any time you're ready."

Slight beeps sounded in the entryway. Erin stood. "Means we've got company."

Erin and Rudy moved to the front room and watched as Mason, in his non-descript truck with the chair in the bed, pulled in. Rudy chuckled. "He brought it. I figured he'd toss it the first chance he got."

Mason didn't unload the chair but carried in his bag of belongings. He nodded as he walked in the door. "Very nice. Very nice. A man could get used to a place like this. I bet it's got great views of the lake."

Erin ignored Rudy's eye roll. "It actually sits out on a peninsula of sorts, so you're surrounded by water on three sides. Fantastic views all the way around. Even up. Great place to count the stars at night."

Rudy glared at him but added nothing to the conversation. Mason looked around. "What room?"

Erin pointed up the stairs. "Let's leave the last one down here for Collin and Jeff. They may spend a night, and she shouldn't be climbing stairs."

Mason smiled. "True." He headed up the stairs.

Rudy's face darkened. "Why do all of you want to get involved in this? It should be my fight."

"God made it our fight by bringing us to you. We're not going to walk away."

"God didn't bring you. I brought you. Or I had your sister brought." Rudy glared at the floor. "That was my biggest mistake."

Erin chuckled. "I know how you feel."

Mason slid down the banister. His feet hit the floor with a thump. His eyes were bright and full of laughter. "I have always wanted to do that but never lived anywhere I could. This place looks like it's designed so a kid could have a great time."

"That's the idea." Erin waved the way to the kitchen. "Dinner will be served as soon as I cook a pound of this bacon. And mangle some eggs." He pointed at the cabinets. "Dishes up there somewhere. Look around. Make yourselves at home. This will be for a few days, anyhow."

He pulled a large skillet out. "And anything you don't see we might need, write it down, and Collin will bring it when they come tomorrow."

Rudy and Mason explored the cabinets. Mason turned to Erin. "How many are coming tomorrow for the meeting?"

"Paxton and his aide. Or two. Vy will bring her research. I've got a couple of guys that want to manage the 'hearing-seeing-believing' details, and they'll be here. Everyone is coming at staggered times, so it's not a traffic jam, nor does it warrant a lot of extra attention."

The bacon started sizzling. "Think about a main course."

The entry bell dinged. Erin handed the fork to Rudy. "Do not let that burn." He went to the front.

Two sheriff's department cars pulled into the driveway. Erin shook his head. "Ren, you were supposed to call them, too." He opened the door before the uniformed officers could knock. "Hey, guys. What can I do for you?"

"Tell us you have permission to be here. This place belongs to—"

"Lacey and Harmon Farrell, 3675 Motson Lane. Phone number is 555-719-2341. It's a landline. Leesa is their daughter. Three sons, Ren, Mike, and Jeff, who is married to my sister Collin. I'm Erin Winger."

He watched one officer writing the information. The man walked back to a car, sat, and began calling in the report. Erin continued, "Ren opened the cabin for me. My place…well, let's say it's uninhabitable. The Farrells said I could stay here until I get a new place."

One of the deputies looked around the yard. "Why would you want one?"

Erin grinned. "My thoughts exactly. Commute to work is a bit of a problem from here. I don't want to leave in the mornings."

The deputy smiled. "I can understand. Beautiful property."

The second deputy returned after a few moments. "He's legit. Harmon Farrell verified him. Enjoy your stay."

Erin smiled. "I intend to." He waited until the cars drove around the traffic circle (no backing up) and pulled off the property. "As long as you leave us alone, we'll have a fine time."

* * *

Collin stepped out of the shower, wrapped a towel around her hair, slipped into a robe, and collapsed on the bed. She let out a long sigh of relief and satisfaction and pure pleasure. "Finally! All of me clean at the same time. Rudy, I love you, but those three-minute showers just don't cut it."

Jeff stretched beside her. "I hear you. It's nice to not have to pick a quadrant and leave the rest for another day."

Collin snuggled under his arms. "Oh, I have missed you. I have missed us."

Jeff pulled her close. "Me too. I love you, Collin Farrell. Will you marry me?"

Collin half-grinned at him. "I already did. Remember?"

"Yeah, but I want to do it again. When I can make my vows and not be lying about them. And we can take communion with the whole church. We—I— can start over and be the husband I meant to be, not the one you got stuck with. Will you? Can we?"

Collin watched the light grow in Jeff's eyes. *He's serious about this.*

Like it will make up for calling you an adulteress. For thinking—

Collin ran her hand through his hair. "I'd like that." She looked at her belly. "I don't think I'll fit in my wedding gown, but…"

Jeff laughed. His eyes crinkled, the smile reached ear to ear. "Oh, we can wait until these little ones get here."

'These little ones.' Not 'our little ones.' He's still dodging—
"That's a great idea."

"When is our next appointment with the OB?"

'Our.' So shut up.

"He can see me Friday. Four days is a quick opening for him. His office said they'd do the ultrasound, possibly get the sexes for us. And a definite due date. Plus a c-section date if I need one."

"What time?"

"Nine." Collin felt her gut nudge. "It shouldn't conflict with Rudy's coming-out announcement, should it?"

Jeff caressed her cheek. "If it does, they will have to announce it without us there. You've put everyone else's needs ahead of the babies for long enough. It's their turn to be looked after. Got it?"

Tears stung Collin's eyes. "I didn't mean to. I wasn't trying to neglect them…" She buried her head in the crook of Jeff's neck. "I hate these hormones!"

He wrapped his arms around her. "It's okay, milady. They won't last forever."

Collin and Jeff lay together for several minutes. Suddenly, Collin felt a sharp kick to her stomach. Jeff jerked back. "He kicked me! Hey, none of that."

Collin laughed. "Welcome to my world. Now you know what it's like."

Jeff rubbed the protruding baby body-part bump. "Soon enough, little one. Soon enough. Keep growing in there. Both of you. Got that?" He leaned over and kissed the bump. "Love you, baby Farrell. Now be good and let your mama get some sleep, okay?"

The bump moved back and disappeared. *If I could freeze time, I would freeze this moment. Jeff, me, the babies…loved and cared for and adored. This. This moment. Forever. Thank You, Lord. I love You.*

Collin drifted off to sleep.

TUESDAY

Morning at the cabin. Erin rose early, started coffee. He pulled the computer out of hiding, linked to the Wi-Fi hotspot, and set to work. Objectives: primary, secondary. Demands. Compromises. Strategies. Who. When. Where. Timetable. Alternate plans. Who. Where. When. Timetable. Contingencies. What. Where. How. When.

Lists. Flowcharts. Resources. People. Remember the Objectives.

Erin worked for three hours, pushed back from the table. "God, if You're not in this, I'm doing this for nothing. I don't need You to approve my plans. I need You to write my plans." *A hand writing on the wall would be nice. Freaky, but nice.* "Show me how to make this work, Lord. I'm still a novice at the 'You tell me' communications. I trust You. Give me Your wisdom, Your knowledge, Your whatever so I know what to do."

Erin lowered his head and his eyes. "Yeah, we want it to be all nice and neat and uncomplicated. Rudy gets cleared. The U.S. ambassador gets arrested, the South American cartel leader gets extradited. Both men stand trial, get convicted, go to prison. Rudy meets his daughter. She tells him she loves him, they get back together. Collin has the babies, and everyone lives happily ever after. That's not much, is it, Lord?"

A thought nudged Erin. "Oh, and God, while I'm asking for everything, can Vy and I start a relationship that ends in our happily ever after?" Erin shrugged. "Well, I thought I'd ask. You told us to."

Erin opened his eyes and stared at the ceiling. "There's a lot I don't know, Lord. What I do know is You love all of us. Your Son died for us. You're good, You're God, and that's all that matters. All these plans are nothing if You're not in them. Lead me, Lord. What do you want us to do?"

Erin sat still. Listened. Waited. Listened. Waited.

Rudy hobbled into the room, his breathing uneven and strained. Erin could feel the man's eyes on him. Rudy pulled a chair out, sat, and looked at Erin. "What are you doing?"

"Waiting for answers."

Rudy's eyebrows lifted. "Oh? Just like that, huh?"

Erin hesitated. He opened his mouth, shut it. His eyes widened. "Of course!" He smiled wide at Rudy. "Yeah, like that."

He turned, opened a new file on the computer, and began hammering away. Without looking, he said, "Breakfast is a rerun from last night. Don't burn the bacon."

Mason wandered in. Out of the corner of his eye, Erin noted Mason looking from Erin to Rudy and back again. He poured out some coffee, leaned against the refrigerator. "What's going on in here?"

Rudy jerked his head towards Erin. "He's transcribing his god's plans on how to accomplish our objectives. I hope his god knows what he's doing. And is on our side."

Mason stepped behind Erin, reading over his shoulder. Erin didn't stop to acknowledge him. He continued typing.

After a few moments, Mason stepped back. Erin saw him nod to Rudy. "I think his god has a good plan. I'm actually feeling hopeful again."

Rudy snorted but moved over to take the place Mason had vacated behind Erin. He stood for several minutes. Finally, he pointed to the screen. "You misspelled extradition."

Erin chuckled to himself. "Thanks, Rudy."

"You're welcome. Always here to help."

* * *

Collin and Jeff spent the day briefing Harmon and Lacey on what was going on. Shopped for essentials as requested by Erin and his team. Ordered dinner from the BBQ house located on the way out of town. *Family dinner for twelve. Extra sauce. Spicy. Additional order of corn muffins. Pick up at three-thirty. Thank you and have a nice day.*

All the running left Collin worn out. Sitting for an hour and a half on the ride to the lake house helped restore some of her energy. Now, if only the twins would quit wrestling for position under her ribs. She rubbed her side, trying to ease some of the tightness.

Jeff glanced over at the motion. "Problem?"

"No. Yes. Nothing having these two on the outside instead of the inside won't fix."

Jeff chuckled. "Sorry. I shouldn't have asked."

"Hmm."

Three cars lined the driveway at the lake house. Jeff pulled to the front of the circle rather than risk getting blocked in at the back. Erin came out as they drove in. He helped gather the supplies and the dinner, carrying boxes and bags into the house. It might have been faster if the other attendees had helped. Collin guessed they would have if they weren't warned off. No unnecessary exposure. Low profiles. Can't be too careful. Remember who we're dealing with.

Everything got unloaded and dispersed to rightful want-ers. Reunions with Vy and Ken Paxton were made. They laid dinner out family-style. Help yourself, but leave some for the next person.

Dinner finished, the serious business started. Ken Paxton drew up the list of demands aided by Mason and Rudy. From there, discussion got lively about how best to present them, where, when and to who. Three lists formed. What we want. What we will settle for. What is non-negotiable.

Erin introduced the backup plan. The press conference. The announcement. The fall-out and kick-back. Collin watched her brother marshal his forces, position players, assemble his offense and defense. Like the chess master he'd become.

The floor opened for critique. What had he missed? Could there be a better advance? Retreat? All-out attack, or test the defenses first? Hit 'em with our best shot, or hold something in reserve? Questions and questions and questions. Everyone got to participate. Everyone's opinion counted.

Collin got immense satisfaction seeing Rudy involved and fighting for his future. Maybe seeing twelve strangers come together to fight for him, maybe seeing a chance—slim as it might be—of victory, or at least acknowledgment of his sacrifice, gave him energy. He moved around the tables, looking at computer screens, reading releases, enacting scenarios, arguing with Erin about tactics.

Satisfying as the evening might be, she could sense a growing tension in her body. Like a strap being pulled tight around her middle. She'd felt it before, but it always loosened after a few moments. Or minutes. This didn't feel like that. This felt wrong.

She slipped a hand under the table, massaged her rock-hard abdomen. *Stop it, you two. Give me one more day. Tomorrow you get to be the center of all the attention. And everyone will see you and ooo and aah. Tonight I need cooperation—*

Pain like she'd never experienced ripped through her, taking her breath away. Collin froze, unable to move. She dug her fingers into the bottom of the chair to keep from screaming. She sat. And sat. *Lord! Help me! I don't understand. What is this? Why? Why right now? Help me. Please. Please, Father. Oh, help me.*

Five minutes and the pain began to ebb. But inch by inch. Like the tide going out, wave after wave. Collin sat frozen in her anguish, waiting. Waiting. Waiting…

The pain disappeared, leaving echoes of pain to come. Collin pushed back from the table, stood, caught Jeff's eye. He cocked his head in question.

The babies answered. Fluid washed down Collin's legs, soaking her pants. Fear seized her. *NO! It's too soon. God, help me. Help my babies!*

Jeff jumped to his feet and scrambled to her side. "What happened?"

"My water… Jeff…it's too soon."

Rudy spun around. His eyes widened, then narrowed. His face hardened. But the corners of his mouth…the corners of his mouth…did she detect a smile? Joy in her pain?

Rudy grabbed a set of keys off the table. "Taking whoever's this is. Jeff, bring Superwoman there. Let's go."

Jeff caught Collin below the knees and lifted her. The protest that started in her mouth died in the second wave of pain. She closed her eyes and narrowed all consciousness to fighting the pain. She felt Jeff bump through the front door. Felt him negotiate stuffing her into a back seat. She curled in his lap. Buried her head in his chest. Whispered, "Please."

* * *

Erin stepped into the dining room. He'd gone to loosen the cramp in his back. He scanned the room. "Where did Collin go? Where's Jeff? Where's Rudy? I leave for five minutes, and everybody takes off?"

Mason's eyes narrowed, and his jaw set hard. "Your sister's water broke. Rudy and Jeff are taking her to a hospital."

Erin felt his stomach lurch. "Without me? I…" He closed his mouth. *Not about you. About Cane and the babies.* He nodded. "Okay, that throws a wrench in things."

He sat hard and stared at the floor. *God, You saw this. You knew this. Yeah, I know; You didn't need to tell me. What do I do now? What do we do now?*

He sensed Vy coming alongside him. She sat, putting her hand on his. She prayed softly, "Father God in Heaven, I ask You to help Collin and Jeff and the babies. You Alone know the plans You have for them. Good plans, Lord. Plans to bring You glory and honor, but also plans for their good. Only You know what those plans are right now. Have Your will and Your way, Father. I ask in Your Holy Son Jesus's Name, amen."

Erin drew strength from her prayer. He lifted his head. "Amen." He pulled his heart and mind and soul together. "Right. God is in control. He has this. He has them. Right." Erin drew in, then let out, a deep breath. "Okay, we shuffle things around." He looked at the silent crew around him. "Rudy will be back. Jeff is a maybe. Collin is a no."

Someone muttered, "She better be. Or I'm turning in my man card."

Someone else added, "Amen to that."

The tension broke. Erin rested his head in his hand. "Okay, okay. Let's see what we can do with this."

And then they were back at it.

About eight, Vy left to go home. That left Mason, Ken Paxton, his assistant, two reporters, one from the wire services, one from a network affiliate. Two techies, who were still working on the best systems to use, rounded out the eightsome. Erin watched the time, anxious for some word from Jeff. *No, I don't want to hear from Cane. I want to hear she's fine, the babies are fine, and I have nieces, nephews, or some combination of the two.*

At nine-fifteen, the driveway alarm went off. Erin went to look. He backed up and yelled, "Ken. We got company we don't want."

Ken scrambled to the door as several unmarked cruisers kicked dirt and gravel as they rounded into the drive. Ken instructed, "Hands on the table in plain sight, everyone. And no sudden movements. Everything nice and slow. Don't give them any provocation at all."

Erin ground his teeth. "We don't need this. Not tonight." *Not ever, for that matter. Who tipped them off? For what?*

Erin called back to the crew, "Close the computers." He turned to Ken. "Meet them at the door, or wait until they knock?"

Ken motioned for Erin to follow him. The two men stepped out onto the porch. Ken jerked the door shut with a snap, pulled his phone out of his pocket. He motioned for Erin to mirror him.

S.W.A.T-garbed men spilled from the cars. Each had DEA in black letters across the front and back of their uniforms. Each had an AR-15 style rifle in hand. Weapons were trained on Erin and Ken. A lone man yelled, "Federal Agents! We have a search warrant. Stand aside."

Erin held his ground. "I'm the designated homeowner. Let me see your warrant."

"I don't have to show you my warrant. Step aside."

Ken stepped forward. "Unless you can show probable cause why you are threatening unarmed men standing on their own porch, I suggest you lower your rifles."

Lead agent snorted. "What are you? A lawyer?"

"As a matter of fact, yes. You didn't chase anyone up the driveway here, so you can't claim to be pursuing a felon onto the property. The homeowner has asked to see the warrant. Who or what are you looking for?"

The lead agent dropped his arm in signal to his men. They lowered their weapons. The man snarled. "We don't have to have a name."

"So it's a person. You are required to have a physical description. Man, woman, tall, short, fat, thin, dark hair, bald… There must be a physical description of the suspect. And I want to know what judge issued the warrant."

"Move aside or be arrested for interfering with an investigation."

Ken moved his phone close to his mouth. "Adrian. Peters. Have everyone start filming. We have federal officers here who want to search the place. They are refusing to show us the warrant. We are not going to allow them in, but we're also not going to make them break down the door. Got that?"

Lead agent sneered. "That's so old." He muscled past Erin, pushing him aside, and shoved open the door.

To be met by six men with phones recording, all standing a respectful distance back from the door. He glared at them and hollered, "Turn those things off!"

Ken smiled but his gaze was hard. "The Supreme Court has ruled filming the actions of a law enforcement officer is protected as free speech under the Constitution. As long as they don't impede your search, they are legally allowed to follow you and film what you do."

Peters, the local news affiliate, announced himself and asked, "Is it true you have refused to show the homeowner the search warrant?"

"Turn those cameras off!"

No one complied. No one backed up. Or down, for that matter. Erin wanted to jeer and caw at the DEA agent but didn't. *I do have some sense of decorum. And self-preservation.*

The agents, all wearing masks, crowded into the entryway, waiting for instructions. The leader pointed at two of his men. "Anything you find, I want brought back here. Go."

Erin followed suit. He motioned to his two tech assistants. "Follow them. Don't get in the way. But film everything."

Four men moved off. Leader waved three fingers at two more. "Upstairs." Mason and Ken Paxton's assistant followed them. Leader waved two more fingers. "Search the grounds." Peters and Adrian shadowed them. Leader narrowed his eyes and glared at Ken. "We will search here."

"In places large enough for a human to hide. We are watching." Erin lifted his phone to make clear the man knew they were serious.

Erin watched as the leader threw open cabinets, yanked cushions off the couches, dumped out the contents of closets, and generally trashed the place. His anger burned at the injustice, but good sense kept him in check. *Patience. Follow Ken's lead. Do nothing rash. Don't give them the slightest provocation to make this go catastrophically wrong. Be cool.*

The search lasted fifteen minutes. And produced nothing. No fugitives of any height, weight, age, skin tone, or sex were located. The DEA group reconvened in the dining room. Still masked, the leader's eye burned with fury. "I know you're hiding him. Where is he?"

Ken raised his eyebrows. "Oh, we have our first clue. You're looking for a male. What other descriptors were you given?"

The leader jerked his head to the door. "This isn't over." The agents peeled off, exiting stage front. Leader joined his men outside. Erin watched them climb in their vehicles and roar out of the driveway into the night.

He turned around and faced the crew. "Well, that was enlightening. Good job, everyone. I need a break to stop my knees from shaking. Anyone else?" Four hands raised. "Good. Let's take a few minutes, then we can compare notes."

Adrian and Peters didn't wait but began reviewing their footage. Ken walked over to his assistant and clapped a hand on the young man's shoulder. The haunted look in the man's eyes told Erin this had been his first encounter with opposition. Erin empathized. Shadowing angry men with rifles and a will and want to shoot should make anyone scared.

Erin busied himself straightening and putting things back as best he could. It helped him refocus and calm the nerves. And kept his mind off what might be going on with Collin. And the babies.

The group reassembled in the kitchen. Erin gazed around the room. "I appreciate everything you all did tonight. I really appreciate no one got shot or arrested, and this place is still in one piece. Thank you, all of you. Go home. I think we have what we need, and we can assemble it all on Monday. Anything we've forgotten or neglected, well, it's too late to worry about that. We're go for Monday."

Erin shook hands with each man as they left. Ken hung back to be the last one out. "We can hang on to this footage and use it if we need it. It will up the stakes for them. But I have a gut feeling they'll capitulate."

Erin nodded. "I hope so. I've got a life to live that doesn't include hiding from drug runners or the DEA. But until Rudy is free, we push on through."

"You got it." Ken fist-bumped Erin and left.

Mason tossed a cushion onto the couch. "We want to clean the rest of this tonight or tomorrow?"

"Tomorrow. I've used enough brain cells tonight. I want to collapse in a familiar bed and be done with it."

"Yeah, I'm going to take a walk outside and listen to the frogs. Then I'm going to crash for the night."

"I hear you."

Erin watched Mason step outside the backdoor. He turned to pick up an errant broom. Mason called, "Erin. Come out here."

Erin set the broom down. "What is it?"

Mason pointed to small lights circling above the treeline. Another set seemed to float on the water just off the end of the boat dock. A third set hovered over the house. "Drones."

Erin's jaw tightened. He glared at Mason, then relaxed. "Let 'em watch. Nothing to see here. Nothing at all."

Mason watched the small flying objects for a moment. "Wonder what they can hear?"

Erin felt his eyes widen. "Phone tap?"

"I've never heard of anything that sophisticated. But pays to be vigilant, right?"

"So when I talk to Jeff, I'll be careful what I say."

Erin walked into the house, followed by Mason. They shut the door on the spying eyes. "Night, Mason."

"Night."

Erin got comfortable, then dialed Jeff's number. *Please, please, let them be okay. All of them. Babies, Collin, Jeff… Please keep them all safe. Make a liar out of that quack doctor, whoever he was. I love you, Lord.*

* * *

Jeff held Collin's hand. Doctor Wellman explained, "We were able to stop the labor. The ultrasound shows there is sufficient amniotic fluid present to…" Wellman stopped. "Let's make it simple. We stopped the labor. The babies are safe."

His eyes narrowed as he fixed his gaze on Collin. "You're going to stay in the hospital until these little ones are ready to deliver. Considering the lack of prenatal care you've given them, I'm surprised they're in as good a shape as they are."

Jeff started to protest, but Collin squeezed his hand. He stopped. "Agreed. God has kept them. Were you able to determine a sex?"

"Not conclusively. The twins are pretty well tangled around each other, so it's hard to tell. But the other one is definitely a girl."

Jeff's eyes flew wide. Collin's did as well. "Three? There's three of them?" Her hand flew to her belly. "Triplets?"

Dr. Wellman cast his eyes from Collin to Jeff and back again. "You didn't know?"

"No. We knew there were two." Collin thought hard. "Does that explain why the doctor thought there was an echo? He said there were two heartbeats, but one had an echo…"

Dr. Wellman smiled. "Could be. All three heartbeats are strong. I'll have a technician come in later to repeat the ultrasound so you can see them for yourselves. For now, rest, stay quiet and let the babies grow. We'll get you into a room as soon as one opens."

Collin reached out. "Thank you, Doctor. I appreciate all you've done." He clasped her hand then left.

Collin grinned at Jeff. "Three. Three babies. That's enough for both grandparents and Leesa to hold. No fights." She lifted her head and chuckled.

Jeff lay his head on hers. "That settles it. I'm done with everything but the Billings project. And I'll hire Jacobs and Weiskopf to handle the west side rec center. We are going to have our hands full."

Collin reached to kiss him. "I love you, Jeff Farrell."

248

"I love you, Collin Farrell."

Collin motioned towards the door. "Go tell my uncle he can come in."

Jeff stood, left, returned with Rudy. The man's face glowed. "How are you doing, Superwoman?"

Collin felt heat rise in her cheeks. "No Superwoman. Thank you for bringing me in like you did."

Rudy shrugged. "Part of my bucket list. Rush a woman in labor to a hospital."

Collin held out her hand to him. "Thank you just the same. I honestly had no idea I could be close to having these babies." Rudy took the chair beside the bed. Collin's face broke into a wide smile. "There's three of them, Rudy. Triplets. A houseful, all in one fell swoop."

"Should I say congratulations, or you have my condolences?"

"Congratulations works." Collin pursed her lips. "I'm sorry we dragged you away from the house. And the work."

"You didn't drag me anywhere." Rudy's eyes narrowed slightly. "I'd had the funniest feeling all evening I should leave. I don't know why. But I couldn't ignore it. When your water broke, the feeling hit stronger than ever, and I grabbed the keys."

Rudy stood and paced around the room. "I had no idea why I felt I should leave. But the compulsion was so strong, I knew I had to obey it." He stopped pacing and looked at Collin. "Does your god deal in compulsions?"

Collin eyed Rudy. She kept her tone even. "Sometimes. Sometimes it's His way of getting our attention or warning us about something. We can ignore it, of course. But it's usually a mistake if we do, and we don't see it until later. If we obey the feeling, we may never know why we got it. We trust God He knows what He's doing and go on."

Rudy frowned at Collin. "So your explanation of my feeling would be your god trying to warn me about something? Even though I don't believe in him?"

Collin held Rudy's eyes. "You love your daughter. If you saw danger ahead of her, would you wait until she acknowledges you're her father before you warned her? Or would you just warn her because you love her?"

Rudy's frown deepened. His voice grew soft. "Mason called me. Told me there had been a DEA raid on the lake house late last night. Wouldn't say who they were looking for."

Collin swallowed all the gloats wanting to invade her face. "That's interesting."

Rudy looked at Collin, his eyes narrowed. "Your god protected me and probably everyone else at the meeting. You say it's because he loves me. I ask why, you say because he made me, and he loves everyone he created. Just like that, huh?"

She chose her words prayerfully. "God loves everyone. He created everyone. He wants a personal relationship with everyone. But on His terms, not our own. We come to Him as we are, but we can't stay that way. Jesus lived and died and rose again to make it possible. We have to acknowledge He's the Only Way we can come to God."

"Your brother tried to tell me it was simple."

"It is. And it's also the hardest thing you'll ever do. It means letting Him change you from the inside out. Change you into His image. Make you more like Christ."

"And I find all those instructions in one book. Is that how it is?"

"That's how it's done. Like that compulsion, He tells us how to live the way He wants us to. And He gives us the ability to change. We decide how much we obey." She snorted, but only a little. "Life's a whole lot easier when we do."

Rudy nodded his head. Slowly. "I can see where it would be."

He stood. "I should let your husband back in here. I'll go hang out where no one expects me to be." He paused. "If I knew of a place."

Collin hesitated. Felt the nudge. "I know a place. There is absolutely nothing that will connect any of us to it and to you. It's a homeless shelter over on Fifth Avenue. Sanctuary House. Caitlin Winger hung out there when she needed a place to go. They're good people. And no one will expect you to be anywhere like that."

"Homeless shelter. Sounds about right."

"Rudy…" He faced her. "Thank you."

He half waved at her and walked out.

Collin lay back in the bed. *Lord, whatever You're doing in him, keep him safe. Bring him all the way to Yourself. Save him, Father. In Jesus's Name, amen.*

MONDAY

Reckoning day. While Collin and the triplets rested comfortably and well cared-for, Erin's team had worked hard through the week to get everything together and in one place. Now, together they would rise or crash and burn. Adrian, Peters, their assistants. Erin's tech team and their assistants, Ken and his assistant, Mason (who didn't have an assistant), Vy, and Erin all met at Ren Farrell's office across the street from the Federal Building.

Erin picked up his phone and examined it. "Looks like a phone."

Eli, one of the two tech wizzes, grinned. "That's the idea. Turn it off, lay it on the table, it takes a 360^0 scan of the room. It can sense noises one range above or below human hearing. Records them, too."

Erin gazed over at Psi, the other tech wiz. "And?"

"And shifts the recordings to this receiver here. Which boosts the signal to reach Adrian's live feed to the network. Where Peters gets his feed and broadcasts it to his YouTube channels."

Eli threw in, smiling, "And you can still call home to mama. Unless they put it under some ultra-high sensitivity microscope, they'll never know it's there."

"Great work. And Ken's phone—"

"Has all the same capabilities. You two are recording everything you see, hear, and say from the moment you leave this building. If they tell you to shut them off, you tell them you'll shut your phones off. Which activates the secondary systems."

"Good." Erin could feel the moths in his gut trying to break out. *Thought I'd lost you years ago. Robert Winger prepared me for confrontations like this from the time I was sixteen. Did this for ten years. What's different now?*

Erin withdrew into himself. What was different?

An electrical shock went through his frame, dropping Erin to his knees. Ken and Vy rushed forward. Ken didn't move him but encouraged, "Hang in there, Erin. Hang in there."

Erin waited. Waited. Waited.

The pain left in increments. Erin came back to himself, hearing the noise and hubbub and concern and near-panic of the voices around him. He reached to Ken, who grabbed him by the arm and pulled him to his feet, then to a chair. Erin drew in a deep breath, let it out. "I'm fine, people. Okay? Just a few pre-trial jitters. Go back to work."

All but two faces disappeared. Ken, and most noticeably, Vy. The fire in her eyes said all she needed to say. Erin frowned. "Okay, not jitters. Spasms. Yes, they've been happening more often. No, I haven't called anyone since I got back. Yes, it's stupid. Yes, I'll call when we're done." He raised his eyes, and the concerned looks hadn't changed.

The nudge tapped him. Erin closed his eyes and lay his head in his hands. He covered his eyes and groaned. Head down, he said, "I've felt nervous about this all morning. Couldn't figure why. What's different than the hundreds of other times I've done this?"

He lifted his head. "I always did it in my own strength. Being in a wheelchair, I had to fight harder. And I did."

Erin looked around at Vy. "But today, finally on my own feet, I thought I had this handled. God led me all the way to this point, and but because I'm standing, I think I can negotiate without Him? I'm an idiot. And He just reminded me of that." He shook his head at himself. "I'm sorry. Ken, if you want to take this on alone, I'll understand."

Ken gripped Erin's shoulder. "No way. I'm not going in there without you, and you're not quitting." He snapped his fingers for an assistant, who ran to his side. "Medical supply store, four blocks from here. Go get a wheelchair. Make it a good one. Doesn't need bells and whistles. Go." The assistant disappeared.

Vy lay a hand on Erin's shoulder. She sat beside him. "In a chair or out of one, you're not an idiot. Wheels don't make or unmake the man. It's Who's in the man that counts. And I know Who's got your heart, Erin Winger. You can do this. Consider all the negotiating you did before as training for this moment." She smiled at him, and her eyes were gentle. "Go in the strength He gives you, and you can't lose."

Her eyes twinkled. "We still haven't had that talk about Jesus and other things." She winked at him, rose and walked back to her station.

Ken's eyes laughed, even if his face didn't. He drawled, "Well, if that don't energize you for the fight, I don't know much that will."

Erin chuckled. "I'm not dead yet."

The assistant returned with a wheelchair. With Ken's help, Erin transferred into it, rolled around, backed up, rolled the opposite direction, parked. "It'll do. Won't be my personal choice, but it'll work for now." He lifted his chin. "Let's do this."

Ken yelled, "Everyone, we're going."

General cheers followed them out the door of the conference room. Ren Farrell waited for them at the door. He shook Ken's hand, batted Erin's away. "Get out of here, slacker. Go do some real work."

Erin smiled. "I'm about to."

"Fight 'em hard. Mom and Dad are leading the prayer warriors."

Erin held up his fist. Ren bumped it.

They gave their names at the DEA reception desk and waited. A black-suited administrative assistant approached them. "Mr. Paxton?"

Ken added, "And Mr. Winger." Erin raised a finger to indicate he, too, belonged in the summons.

The man coughed. "Of course. Mr. Winger. Follow me."

Through several corridors, up an elevator to an unmarked floor... Around a corner, through two sets of double doors... Finally, into an office with its door open but no signage. Erin wanted to chuckle. *A man so valuable they hide him so no one can find him. Is that any way to do business?*

Director Smith stood as Ken and Erin came in. He extended his hand to Erin first, then to Ken. "Gentlemen. Welcome to the inner sanctum. Pleasure to have you here."

He motioned for Ken to sit then sat himself. From his research, Erin knew him to be sixty-two. Three years from full retirement. He'd come over from Logistics when the last Ops director passed of a heart attack five years ago. Word was he'd been good for the department's reputation.

Erin took the lead. "Director Smith, I'll get to the point. We want to place DEA agents as volunteers in our rec centers, so the youth can learn your people are not the enemy. 'Officer Friendly' or some such designation back in the old days. But we need to know your agents can be trusted to operate with integrity. Break a young person's trust, and you never get it back again."

Director Smith nodded. "Absolutely. I would never put an agent in the field if I didn't know I could trust them implicitly."

Ken leaned forward. "The same goes for your agency, sir. I'm afraid 'word on the street' doesn't judge you as favorably as you might want."

Director Smith drew in a long breath. "I can understand. There have been unfortunate breaches of trust in the past. I want to assure you both, we will do everything to maintain the highest level of trust."

Erin pushed a file folder across the desk to Smith. "I doubt that. Not with these kinds of dealings."

Smith began skimming through the folder. His eyes darted back and forth across the pages, lifting now and again to stare at Ken or Erin, then returned to the folder.

Ken detailed, "Fifteen years ago, this office inserted an agent we'll call Rudy into a South American drug cartel. Rudy spent three years working his way to the top of the organization, where the big boys play. His instructions were to communicate with a regional contact, who would send the information upline to the next man, and so forth. But as Rudy got higher in the cartel, his reports bypassed the middle operatives and went up the supervisory echelon. Finally, he reported directly to the top regional liaison."

Smith's mouth opened. Ken waved him off. "Let me finish, then we can answer questions." Smith went back to reviewing the folder's contents.

Erin picked up the narrative. "Rudy noticed his organization in the cartel seemed to bring in the most cash and have the fewest problems with federals of either nation. He dug. The deeper he dug, the dirtier it got. And at the bottom was—"

Smith's eyes were dark pools of anger. "The special ops director."

Erin smiled a grim smile. "And the country's military leader. And the U.S. Ambassador. They had a cozy train of intel rolling along. Rudy learned the Special Ops director collected drug movement reports from the field and sold them to the highest cartel bidder. The President General of the South American country figured out the pattern and demanded a piece of the action. Which the Ops director was obliged to do. The Ambassador found out. Which won him a slice of the pie, too."

Ken added, "Rudy's only alive today because he also sent his reports to a friend in Intel. That friend watched Rudy's information come in and wondered where it disappeared to. He wasn't high enough on the food chain to make a difference while things were happening, but he could protect Rudy by getting him out of the field."

Erin's voice darkened. "Rudy wanted to bust the whole ring wide open. People up the pipeline promised him there would be an investigation. The ambassador would be arrested, as would the special ops manager."

Erin rolled away from the desk, turned a half-circle. "Rudy need only stand by and watch. Oh, and be willing to testify when they needed him."

Ken's turn again. "But these cases take time, you understand. A year, maybe two. Three tops. The wheels of justice and all that. Keep your head down, stay around 'til we need you, and we'll let you know."

Now Ken began to pace. "Two years go by, and Rudy sees nothing happen. Oh, the Ambassador got moved to another assignment, then retired when the new administration got voted in. The Special Ops director? Moved up the ladder. The President General? Who knows. I think he's living on a deserted beach somewhere. The point is, no one ever got charged with anything. And Rudy was still living out of dirty hotel rooms and keeping his head down. So he did what any frustrated civil servant does: he threatened to go to the press."

Erin couldn't keep the venom out of his voice. "Before Rudy can, though, his daughter, a sixteen-year-old kid, has a run-in with the police. Terrible thing. Bunch of kids out on the town. They get approached by a dealer. Words are exchanged, the dealer calls over some buddies. Someone starts shooting. One of the dealers dies. And guess who is holding the gun?"

Smith's eyes narrowed to slits, laser-sharp. He continued reading the files while Ken and Erin continued the story. Ken said, "Poor Rudy's daughter. She's terrified, swears she doesn't remember firing the gun. But there's forensics to say she held the gun at least. Enough to have her booked for murder. Out of the goodness of the DEA director's heart, the charges will be suspended if Rudy disappears. For good. Permanently. If anyone suspects him of being alive or finds out he is, the charges get re-instated, and his kid goes to prison."

Ken flipped a second file folder and handed it to Director Smith. "Because Rudy's friend is now higher up the ladder, he can at least do something to help him. He knows of a perfect place where no one will find Rudy, ever. And Rudy will be able to live out the rest of his days in semi-peace. Problem is, it's a hole in the ground."

Erin said, "Not a dark, nasty hole. Seems back in the Cold War, when bomb shelters were all the rage for government officials but not for the common people, the worthies of Indiana decided to dig a compound under a patch of ground owned by Jeremiah Winger. My great grandfather. Grandfather was in the process of giving away his fortune and sold it to the great state of Indiana for $1.00. They didn't want the whole property, just the little patch under which they would hide their underground bunker. They dug the bomb shelter, built the compound, set up the air and water and power. But no one occupied it.

"The property reverted back to the Winger Estate, without my grandmother's knowledge of the underground facility. She married Fenton Mudd, who inherited the property from her. Fenton, a lawyer, discovered the provision in the land contract stating the forests could never be cut and developed. He investigated, thought the idea of an underground hideaway sounded inviting, and continued to maintain it."

Erin stretched in his chair. "And that is how it came to be Rudy started living under the woods in Eastern Indiana. And has lived there for the past ten years."

Smith raised his eyebrows. "And now he wants out?"

Ken asked, his voice sharp, "Wouldn't you?"

Smith harrumphed. "I'd want out the day I went in." He looked at the file folders. "Mr.….Rudy doesn't just want out, though, does he?"

Ken nodded. "No, he doesn't."

"What exactly does he want?"

Erin enumerated. "One. He wants the Ambassador and the Special Ops manager arrested, tried, convicted, and serving prison time. Two. He wants the President General extradited, standing trial along with the Ambassador and the Ops manager. And also doing prison time. Three. He wants all the agents involved in setting his daughter up on the phony murder charge brought to trial. Four. He wants one million dollars in back pay and his benefits restored. And five. He wants his daughter's name cleared."

Director Smith glanced from Ken to Erin and back again. "Does he honestly believe I can arrange all of that?"

Erin shrugged. "You asked what he wanted. That's what he wants. He will settle for the Ambassador, the Ops manager, and all the agents involved being arrested, charges brought, and the courts decide their fates. But no cutting deals that don't include significant prison time. He wants his benefits restored, and he wants his daughter cleared. Those are the non-negotiables."

Director Smith sucked in his bottom lip. "And if I can't—or the department won't—then what?"

Ken smiled without mirth. "We have a press release just waiting to go out. Full news coverage. Names, dates, witnesses, supporters, all ready to put on a show to correct a terrible injustice to this man and the people of this nation."

Ken put a knuckled fist on Smith's desk. "We'll make it as big and as loud and as memorable as we can."

Smith scribbled something on the back cover of the file. He thought a moment, wrote again. He looked in his desk drawer for a card, checked it, noted something more on the file. Looked in his phone, wrote an additional bit of information down. Erin wanted to grab the folder, but proper decorum dictated he wait. *Just once…just once, I'd like to kick decorum in the shins and let my base nature have its way.*

Silence.

I know, I know. I won't. I'll honor You. I will. And be happy about it.

Smith wrote furiously, closed the folder and slid it back to Erin. "I'm sorry, I can't help you. Policy and procedure won't allow me to involve the agency in a personal matter." He stood. "If there's anything else I can do for you, please don't hesitate to contact me."

He extended his hand to Erin, then to Ken. "Oh, and tell whoever put those files together to stop by my office sometime. I have some other cases I'd like them to look into for me."

Erin took the folders off the desk. "Thank you for being honest with us. I appreciate the time." He smiled. "I'll pass along your message."

Ken repeated Erin's thanks. They turned and walked out of the office. An aide escorted them down the elevator and back onto the street. Erin resisted the urge to peek at what Smith had written until they reached the safety and shelter of Ren's office. Only once they were inside did he open the folder.

Erin's crowed. "Hallelujah! Yes!"

He slid the folder across to Ken. Erin shouted, "We got two Senators and a Federal Judge. Private numbers, personal assistants. We got some muscle on our side. This thing is a go."

Amid the cheers and celebration, Vy slipped to his side. Erin took her hand. "Let's go find a quiet place."

Vy gave him a sideways stare but followed. Erin led the way to Ren's outer office away from the revelers. He brought her to a place where she could sit with him eye-to-eye.

Vy held him in her gaze. "What's going on, Erin?"

Erin tapped his hand on the arm of the chair. He stared at the floor "Um… Director Smith said he wanted whoever put the files together to come to his office. He has some…um…other cases he'd like looked at." He lifted his eyes to meet Vy's. "I think God wants you to stay here. With the DEA anyhow."

Vy's smiled gently. "And you disapprove?"

Erin ducked his head. "I…uh…I'm not sure."

Liar.

He corrected his statement. "Okay, I'm sure I don't want you to stay with the DEA. Because I'm selfish, and I want you to be around so I can get to know you better and have a real relationship with you."

"And you think if I'm in the DEA I can't do that?"

Erin held her gaze. "I'm afraid they'll send you all over the country doing undercover kinds of things, putting you in danger, and I wouldn't know where you were. Or if you were coming back." He pouted. "Or if you met some handsome guy who knows the Lord better than I do and can dance with you and do all the things I may not be able to do for you." Erin lifted his chin. "Because you deserve that kind of man."

Vy hung her head. "Erin Winger, what am I going to do with you?"

"What?" Confusion laced his voice.

"I deserve nothing. I accept whatever comes from the Lord's hand." She touched the side of his cheek. "And I'd consider myself fortunate if He graces me with someone like you. Someone who loves the Lord, doesn't have it all figured out yet, but is trying. Someone with a heart that wants to help others, even after they've tried to kill you. Who doesn't back down from a fight but knows the battle belongs to the Lord."

Vy interlaced her fingers with his. "I would believe the Lord had been exceedingly generous to me if He sent me that kind of man."

Erin stared into her eyes. "Even if he can't walk?"

She smiled. "Even then." Vy reached in, turned her head, and they kissed.

They broke. Vy's eyes twinkled. "Do you always blush when you kiss a woman?"

Erin lowered his eyes. "I don't know. I haven't kissed a lot of women. Especially in front of a mirror." He turned his head, gazed off to the side. "Collin might know. But you'll have to ask her yourself."

Vy stood. "Very well, Mr. Winger. I will ask her that question. I have a feeling she and I have a great many areas to discuss."

Erin smiled. "She'll look forward to that. She always wanted a sister. Got stuck with me. I never could get the hang of dolls." He stopped. "She never did, cither. But do not challenge her on the basketball court." He caught her eyes and held them. "The thing with my lack of color and your abundance…we will work through it. I know my people won't have a problem. And if they do, they're not my people."

Vy held his eyes. "Let's say most of my people won't have a problem. There may be an aunt or uncle somewhere. We can cross those bridges one at a time."

She extended her hand to him. Together they went back to the conference room.

* * *

It took ten more days—and half a dozen meetings at the lake house—before everything came together. State Senator Danforth, U.S. Senator Giles, and Federal Judge Fred Percy met with the "squad" twice. They set a date for the news conference, alerted the networks, and groomed Rudy (not an easy task, that one). Jim Russo came through with finding Rudy's daughter, Deidra. She had been searching for her father and couldn't be happier to meet him, finally. And introduce him to his grandchildren at last.

The only thing that could have made the day a total triumph would have been if Collin had been able to be there. Erin felt his sister's absence as a hole in the proceedings, a shadow on an otherwise perfect day. He'd been to see her every day he could, usually once a day anyhow. She'd been moved to Children's Hospital as it had the best NICU in the state. She'd been at risk when they thought there were only two babies. With three, no one wanted to take any chances.

The good news: the babies were gaining weight. The bad news: Collin continued to go into labor on a semi-regular basis that would require medication to end it. Best reckoning, the babies were about thirty-one weeks. If they could make it to thirty-six, the doctor would be thrilled. If they could make it even one more week, Erin would be happy.

He'd gone to see her the night before. Her face was drawn, her eyes dull, her energy gone. He kissed her on top of the head. "That bad?"

She hugged him around the middle. "I'm so tired, A-One. I can't sleep. They're pumping me full of liquids which makes me not want to eat, but they keep bringing me these meals I can't stomach." Collin reached out to take his hand. "I don't want to complain. Tell me what's going on."

Erin sat beside her bed. "Russo found Deidra. She's beyond excited to be with her dad." Erin sniffed. "I think it's given Rudy a will to fight. After the interviews and speeches are over, I'm going to take him to the Kettering Cancer Center and see what we can do to give him a better prognosis."

"What's Mason been doing?"

"He turned in his retirement papers. Said he'd had enough. I think Director Smith wants him to head a street-level DEA squad to visit the rec centers. Like Jeff used to do for the fire department over on the west side until he got uppity and married some Southside chick."

Collin slapped at him. "I'm not a chick." Erin saw color returning to her face.

"No, but you did steal my most promising forever student of chess. Everything that man knows about chess, I taught him. Including knowing the fact that he'll never be a chess master."

Collin laughed. "Poor Jeff. He's a fireman. He'll always be a fireman."

"I know. I can see it in his business dealings. 'We'll wait and see how the wind blows.' Never, 'Let's make the wind blow the way we want it to.' I give up on him."

He smiled. "Love you, Cane." He reached over and kissed her cheek. "Don't give up. You and me, we never gave up before, and we're not going to start now. Got it?"

The light returned to her eyes. "I got it, A-One. I'll keep fighting."

"Don't. Don't fight. I said, don't give up. Big difference." He linked his hand in hers. "Give it to Him. Let Him carry it. You're still here trying to control everything."

Collin's eyes softened. A tear dribbled down her cheek. "They're so little, Erin. They need more time."

"Time the Lord will give them. As He sees fit." He hung his head. "All I know about faith, I learned from you and Jeff. Now it's my turn to give back. Let the Lord have them, Cane. He'll carry them."

Collin closed her eyes, buried her head in his hand. Tears filled his palm. She sniffed. Erin jerked his hand away. "Gross! What's wrong with you?" He wiped his hand across the back of his jeans. "Yuk!"

Collin laughed. "Get out of here. I love you, A-One. I'll see you tomorrow."

"Yes, you will. Watch us on TV at noon. Hopefully, we'll be the headline news."

* * *

And now here he was, standing on the steps of the Federal Court House, watching a bank of reporters shoving microphones into a tangled spider web. Each vyed for the perfect spot to hear from Judge Fred Percy, U.S. Senator Giles, and State Senator Danforth as they launched an investigation into the DEA's handling of a drug case from ten years ago. A drug case that held the fate of one Simon Eastern, aka Rudy the Red. Horrible affair. Travesty of justice. Correction long overdue. This man suffered for years under the oppressive weight of bureaucracy and corruption. Justice must be served.

Erin sat in his wheelchair and watched from across the street with the assembled crowd of supporters. Vy stood on his left, Jeff on his right. Mason had been stationed forward as a witness, to be interviewed by reporters after the initial announcement. Members of the 'team,' with families and friends, came to lend their support and weight in numbers. A respectable showing. Not quite the 'throng of thousands' Erin had imagined in his head, but still, it served its purpose.

Finally, the pleasantries and interviews and statements were all made, and the crowd told to go home. The inner circle, the 'squad' from the compound, retired to the dayroom in Children's Hospital. Jeff brought Collin. Erin could see color had returned to her face, and her eyes shone with delight as she listened to the replay of the announcement on the steps.

Harmon and Lacey assembled with the group, making it a true family affair. As the excitement wound down, conversation turned to the next most pressing matter of business: what to name the babies. Some were helpful, some were ridiculous, and none stuck.

Vy touched Collin's hand. "Are you going to try for a second girl so she's not outnumbered all the time?"

Jeff held up his hand. "No. When they start out in multiples, we're not taking any more chances. I'll make sure of that."

Harmon chuckled. "Just don't ask your Uncle Rich to help you with it."

Jeff's head snapped around. "What do you mean?"

Erin glanced at Collin, then at Lacey. "Huh?"

Lacey laughed. "We never have told you that story, have we?"

Erin saw Jeff's eyes narrow. Even Collin leaned forward to hear better. "What story?"

Harmon smiled. "Your mother had a terrible time with Leesa's pregnancy. Developed eclampsia. Seizures and high, high blood pressure. We thought we might lose her."

Lacey lay a hand on her husband's arm. "But you didn't, did you?"

He gazed on her with such love, Erin blushed. Vy shoved his chair with her hip. He giggled. Silently.

Harmon continued his story. "Well, in the days after Leesa's birth, Rich came to me and told me if your mother ever had another pregnancy, it would kill her. Not maybe. Not might. One hundred percent would kill her. And if I loved her, I would never let that happen. Me being the impetuous man I am—"

Erin guffawed, Jeff laughed, and Collin tittered.

Harmon raised his head in defiance of the response. "I made the choice to have surgery. That Rich performed. I'd say 'under the table,' but that would be…wrong. Let's say he used his medical training and licensure in an unauthorized manner."

Lacey snorted. A lady-like snort. "And his knowledge and ability. Three years later, and lookie here! I'm pregnant again." She smiled at Jeff. "And I could never be happier." She straightened. "But you were the absolute last."

Jeff looked at Harmon, his mouth hanging open. Erin glanced from Jeff to Collin to Harmon. And asked what needed to be asked. "So, what did you think about Mom Lacey being pregnant after Rich had supposedly done your surgery?"

Harmon squeezed Lacey's hand. "What should I think? My wife was pregnant. There could be only one conclusion."

Erin led him. "And…"

"That Rich should stick to neurology, and God had circumvented my will for His own." Harmon held Lacey's eyes. "What else could I think?"

Lacey's drawled. "That I'd had an affair."

Harmon bowed his head. "Well, it crossed my mind."

"When Rich insisted it could be the only answer, right?" Lacey nailed Harmon with a look.

"Yes, dear."

"And I denied it."

"Yes, yes you did."

"And I asked you who were you going to believe? Me, or Rich?"

Harmon lifted his head. "When she put it that way, I had no problem. I went, punched your uncle in the nose, and that settled that." He grinned. "And we're still friends after all these years. And why I made him your godfather. So he'd never forget it."

Jeff and Collin exchanged glances. Erin watched Jeff lean in and give Collin a full-on, lasting kiss that made even Vy blush. Erin turned away. After a moment, he cleared his throat, "Um, you two…there are children in this room."

Collin turned her face to the sky, her eyes closed, a smile of pure peace on her features. Erin closed his eyes as well. *Thank You, Lord. Thank You.*

EPILOGUE

Mason stood beside the casket, one hand on its side. "Back underground, old friend. Last time." He rubbed the top of the cold metal. "I'm gonna miss you, you old crank. Say 'hi' to the guys."

Mason turned away. He looked at the silent assembly giving him his time alone. Jeff, Erin with his arm crutches, Vy with her arm linked in Erin's, Deidra, her husband, and children. Collin stood by the van, waiting to release the krackens when signaled.

He walked to the group. "Thanks." He tried to think of something else to say, something to put some closure on the moment, but couldn't. So he repeated, "Thanks."

Mason raised his arm in the air and circled it. Collin acknowledged by opening the van door. Three small figures tumbled out and came running towards him. "Uncka Mason! Uncka Mason!" Collin followed at a more dignified pace.

He kneeled and caught the trio in a group hug, letting the giggles and grins and laughter wash over his soul. The medicine he needed.

After a moment, he stood, a triplet wrapped around each leg and his hand on the head of the little girl.

* * *

Deidra had a large bag with her. She handed it to Collin. "He wanted you to have it."

Collin peered inside. "His chess set? Deidra, I can't…it should be yours."

Deidra shook her head. "He was very adamant about you having it. I'm not going to disappoint him."

Collin took the set out, running her hand along the smooth surface of the box. Tears welled in her eyes. She bit her lower lip. "Thank you."

Deidra and her family walked away to their car. Mason helped load the trio in the van, kissed each head, hugged Collin, shook Jeff's hand, walked off to his own car. Erin and Vy stood by the van for the final good-byes.

Erin touched the case. "I never did get to play him. Always wanted to."

Collin opened the box. A piece of paper lay inside. She picked it up.

Rudy's handwriting. Collin lifted her head against the flood that wanted to wash away her composure.

Count the stars, Rudy.

Have you been outside and looked up yet? Have you counted them?

Why create a god in your own image? A god that can only know what you know and do what you can do?

But God, the God of the Universe, He sees. He knows. He loves.

Have you talked to Him, Rudy?

Collin let Jeff read the last of it out loud.

"Yes, I have. And I own Him as Savior and Lord. I'll meet you in glory. Love, Rudy."

THE END

If you enjoyed *Accusations*, sign up for Colleen Snyder's Newsletter to stay up with new books and new projects. It will also give you a place to talk to the author directly!

Emails will NOT be sold, shared, or used for any other purpose. Promise!

Go to: colleensnyderauthor.com and leave your email to sign up.

Did you miss the first book in the Collin Walker series? Verdict at the River's Edge

What terrifies you?
In the dark recess of your soul, what is it that you've managed to avoid, to hide, to bury deep, never to be faced? And what if the Lord asked you to face that fear for no other reason than, "Because I'm asking?" What would you do?
Welcome to Collin Walker's world.
Collin Walker, a social worker from the innercity of Oakton, Ohio comes to Camp Grace for what is billed as "an extreme sports camp." Her single purpose: to show her ward, Rob Sider, that there is more to life than the streets "...show you can be strong and still love, win without cheating, and succeed in life without all the bells and whistles..." Collin has no way of knowing that God has other plans for her week: facing a lifelong terror of rushing rivers, and perhaps her greatest fear of all, the possibility of real love.
Available now on Amazon: Verdict at the River's Edge
Also available, Book Two in the Collin Walker Series: Inheritance
Three hundred MILLION dollars. *Your inheritance. Buy anything you want, go anywhere you want, do anything you want. All yours. Except...*
You're a social worker. How do you maintain "street cred" with the kids you've devoted your life to?
How will that kind of money affect the man you love?
And then there's your birth family. The ones that abandoned you to die at fourteen. The ones you suspect even now are trying to have you killed over the money. How do you share with them? Or do you?
What would Jesus do? What would He want you to do? Would you do it?

Welcome back to Collin Walker's world

Collin's life has been both turned upside down and inside out. With her grandfather's passing, Collin has been forced into a position she never wanted. Her inheritance of millions comes with baggage. Her father and his brothers have been fighting for it since before she was born. It is the very heart of the reason she's been estranged from her family the past twelve years.

But now, with the will coming into effect, Collin must revisit all the old relationships and all the old traumas. She thought she had made peace with her past through the Lord. But when the past becomes the present, will she still forgive? Even if it's her family that wants her dead?

Join her and find out.

And coming in late fall…

Book Four in the Collin Series:

Erin stared at the computer screen. The family tree, traced by DNA, branched and flowered and twisted. He knew the branches, the assortments of aunts, uncles, cousins. He'd become familiar with the offshoots of grand-uncles and great-great-greats. All on his father's side. But his mother's side…

There had only been the name. Pulled from the marriage license found buried deep in a pile of papers hidden in a box of legal tax records that had yet to be filed. Felicity Meadows. Daughter of Catherine Pond and David Meadows. People Erin had no memories of. His mother passed when he and his sister Collin—Caitlin, at the time—were five.

But the leaf…

The leaf that indicated a DNA match on the maternal side. Erin had clicked on the leaf out of curiosity, thinking it might lead to some cousins or remaining aunts or uncles on his mother's side.

But there it was. A sibling. Three siblings. A half-sister. Two half-brothers on the maternal side. And the first birth date…seven years after he and Collin were born. *After?? How is that even possible?*

It had to be a mistake. Had to be. His mom was dead. He didn't remember a funeral. Five years old? Who remembers something like that? Who takes a five-year-old to a mother's funeral?

But the leaf… The names…

Erin stared at the screen. Did he want to know? Did he really? Was he ready to find out how much more of his life had been built on a lie? How much more had been stolen from him and Collin? *Our mother? Mom? We have a mom?*

Two questions rattled in his brain, *Where?* And most important, *Why?*

* * *

Erin drove to the Farrell house and let himself in the back door. Quietly. In case the triplets were asleep.

Fat chance of that. One might be. Two at most. But all three together? No. Never happen.

And he was right. Collin sat in her rocking chair, Talitha draped across his sister's shoulder. Caleb and Joshua, the twins, lay on a blanket on the floor, asleep. Collin was rocking and humming and trying to put the littlest Farrell back to sleep. Or to sleep. Didn't matter.

Erin slipped in and picked the infant up. He kept his voice low. "Give her to me. I have the touch."

Collin leaned into her brother's arm. "That you do."

Erin snuggled the little girl close to his chest and danced slowly around the room, crooning. The two-month-old (by "brought-home" date, not "birth-date." The two months in NICU didn't count as "real" days) yawned and cooed and closed her eyes. Erin transferred her quietly and successfully to the playpen. He rubbed her tummy to make sure she settled, then stood up and smiled at Collin. He held his hands out wide. "It's all in the moves, Cane. All in the moves."

She shook her head at him. Erin walked over and kissed the top of her head. "You look terrible."

"Thank you for the vote of confidence, A-One. This motherhood gig is exhausting."

"I believe it. Jeff asleep?"

"Yeah. He was up with them during the night so I could sleep." She leaned back in her chair. "You think the Lord will ever let us get them on a schedule we can all live with?"

"Probably. In about five years."

"Thanks a lot. You're a bundle of good news this morning."

Erin walked into the kitchen. "You want coffee?"

"Pleeeeeeeeease."

Erin chuckled and made a fresh pot. He guessed the last one had been made by Jeff during the night. No filter. That's Jeffrey.

While he waited for the pot to finish, he straightened up the countertops, put the dirty dishes in the dishwasher, folded a load of baby t-shirts sitting on the table, and generally made himself useful. As soon as the amber brew was ready, he filled two cups and carried them into the family room. He handed one to Collin and sat down across from her.

Collin sipped the coffee, let out a satisfied but quiet aww of satisfaction. "No grounds. Thank you."

"Maybe you should rethink that prohibition on single-serve makers. At least until they're out of diapers."

"If I have to chew through too many more cups of coffee, I might." She leaned back in her chair. "Okay, baby brother, you're not here to rescue me from my children. What's going on?"

Erin stared into the coffee cup. "I got a hit on Mom's side of the family."

Collin's eyes lit up. "Really? This soon? I thought it would take longer, somehow."

"Yeah, like never?" Erin considered his words. "It's…it's a ninety-nine percent match."

"Wow. That's good. Grandfather?"

"No." Erin held Collin's eyes. "Half-siblings."

Collin stared at him. Her eyes widened, narrowed, widened, dropped, finally looked up at him. "You're sure?"

"I'm sure that's what the site is telling me. Two brothers and a sister. The oldest boy was born about seven years after we were. He'd be about twenty-two. Maybe twenty-three."

Collin stared at her babies. "You know what that means?"

"I know a whole lot of things it means. Which one are you thinking of?"

"Let's start with our mother is alive."

"Right. That's the easy one."

"Then comes how and when and where and why and what do we do about it?"

"That's pretty much what I came up with, yeah."

Collin took a long drink from her coffee. "Wow."

"Yeah."

They were both silent, listening to the triplets breathe.

Collin rocked. "The babies could have grandparents. Not ones in prison, real grandparents."

"And aunts and uncles that don't hate them for being yours and mine."

Collin cocked her head and looked at him. "Yours?"

"My blood. Not mine, mine. But related to me. You knew what I meant."

Collin smiled. "I know. I wanted to lighten the moment."

"Did it, too."

Collin's smile disappeared. "What do you want to do about it?"

"I want to contact them. I want to know all the answers to all the questions. I'm half afraid of what we'll find, but after what we've already learned about our past, what more can there be?"

Collin shook her head. "Finding out your father and uncles murdered their father before we were born. And that Grandmother was the one who put them up to it."

"And hid the evidence so you would find it when you inherited everything…"

Collin held up her hand. "Stop. We're not going to rehash the litany of wrongs the Winger side of the family has done to either of us. We've moved on."

"Right. But then this opens up. And we're back to square one."

"Did it give you an address? Like what state, maybe?"

"They're here. In Ohio. I got that much from the site."

Collin's mouth dropped. "Here?" She closed her mouth, sat back, and rocked. After a moment, she whispered, "You think she knew us?"

"I don't know, Cane. But I'm going to find out."

"Find out what?" Jeff stumbled into the room, but quietly. "I smelled coffee. And it wasn't mine."

Erin chuckled. "Sit. I'll get it."

Jeff leaned over and kissed Collin. "Morning, milady."

"Morning, sir."

Erin carried the coffee in for Jeff. "Here you go. No grounds."

"Thank you. You need to move in here, bro, and help us keep this place going."

"Hard to impress a woman with a job title of 'Manny.'"

Collin's mouth crinkled. "I thought you were well beyond trying to impress Vy. She loves you as you are."

"Yeah, but I still have all those aunts and uncles to win over. That's a work in progress."

Jeff chuckled. "That's why it was easy marrying you, my love. No family approval to get. Except Erin, and he already liked me."

"Truth." Erin looked at Collin and raised his eyebrows. She nodded. "We…uh…think we've found some relatives on the maternal side of our DNA."

"Really? That's good, right?"

"Could be. Except it's from our mom."

Jeff looked at Erin sideways. "That's what maternal DNA is, bro. From your mom's side."

Erin shook his head. "No, I mean, it's our mom's DNA. She's alive. And has three children from another marriage. We've got two brothers and a sister we didn't know existed. Maybe."

Jeff's eyes moved from Erin to Collin to the babies back to Erin. "Wow."

"Your wife's words exactly. Except she said it backward."

Two sets of eyes rolled. Erin shrugged and smiled. "A little levity now and then."

Jeff sneered at him. "Very little." He addressed Collin. "Is this something you want to look into?"

Collin rocked in her chair. "I don't know. I haven't had time to consider it." She pointed to Erin. "What about you?"

"I'm torn. Part of me wants to meet the siblings. Part of me is afraid of the answers I'll get to my questions if we meet our mother. Part of me is afraid she won't want to meet us."

Collin smiled, and it was gentle. "Any other parts of you have opinions?"

Erin stared at the ceiling, squinted. "Probably. But not right this moment."

Caleb wiggled on the floor, put his fist in his mouth, and began sucking on it. Jeff picked up the still-sleeping infant and placed him on his shoulder. "Shhh, little one. Don't wake up the others. It's not time yet." Jeff eyed Erin over the head of the baby. "What are you going to do?"

"I'll make first contact and see if they want to answer. That's how the game is played."

Collin nodded. "And keep me posted of what and who you find. I may not be ready to meet our mother, but yeah, more aunts and uncles for the babies would be fun."

"Except I'll have to invite them to the wedding. We were trying to keep this a small affair, under a thousand, you know?"

Collin laughed. "Yeah, I know. There's always someone you forgot to include that needs a last-minute invite."

Erin sighed. "I know. Vy keeps saying we should elope. I'd do it, but I'm afraid of her mom and dad. Especially her mom. She nails me with that look and asks, 'Are you taking care of my daughter the way she deserves?' To which the answer is no, but that's because Vy deserves the world and everything in it. I might be able to make a small downpayment on it, but it will never be nearly enough."

"You know she loves you. And you treat her with absolute respect."

"At least that part her dad agrees on. I wouldn't dare not respect her. All those sisters? Yikes!"

He checked his watch. "I need to go. I've got pre-marriage counseling in an hour, and I don't want to be late."

Also by Colleen Snyder…

Finding Freedom **a novella, part of the** A Hero's Heart **Kindle Set:**

The stakes couldn't be higher.

Thirty-six years of marriage. Two children. Two granddaughters, the lights of her life.

Her home. Her friends. Her church. Her God?

Will she throw it all away for freedom? Freedom from abuse? From neglect? Subjection?

And what if he comes after her?

For Sheridan (Dash) Warren, the options have never been more clear. Stay, keep the status quo and watch her life descend further and further into the soul-stealing denial of all that is Dash Warren, all that is life and light and joy and peace…

Or abandon it all in a desperate flight to save what little of her true self she has left. If God is for her, who can be against her? But is God for her? Is He leading her out, or is it her own voice she's listening to?

And what will her husband, Roy, do if she does run? He's been violent before. Will he come after her? What if he catches her? What will her future look like? Will she even have a future?

Dash must make the decision of her life. Can she make the right one?

Finding Freedom **available in paperback and Kindle**

The Knights of the Octagon: Benefactor: **a Kindle Vella series!**

They are the Knights of the Octagon (because no one had a round table.) Four modern young men, the "brightest and best" – fighting for their dreams and for each other.

Until life—a teen pregnancy, an abusive parent, and a single mother with health issues—derailed their hopes and plans. Now they are high school drop-outs, fighting the daily grind just to make a living.

When "one final camping trip" goes wrong, Micah, Tav, Luke, and Jeremiah face a life-or-death struggle. Lost in hostile terrain, they are chased by a crazed militia leader who wants to execute them for treason. Will the four men fight for each other—or against each other? Can the Knights rise one last time?

Join their quest and see.

ABOUT THE AUTHOR

Colleen K. Snyder has always had a passion for writing. She authored two previously published books: *Journey to Amanah: The Beginning* and *Return to Tebel-Ayr: The Journey Continues* (B&H Publishing). She lives on a "ranchette" in California and is the juniorest ranch hand. She serves on her church prayer team, writes the weekly prayer letter, facilitates a women's Bible Study and exercises a ministry of intercessory prayer. She has worked as a factory line worker, pharmacy technician, USAF missile systems analyst, janitor, nanny, teacher, accounting manager and anything else the Lord required. Her son, Bear and his wife Krystal, their two daughters, Mara and Kaylynn, and her daughter Katie all live in Ohio.

Colleen's story is for His glory, always.

Connect with her on Facebook at Colleen K. Snyder, Author and on her website colleensnyderauthor.com.